ALSO BY ROXIE NOIR

One last Time

USA TODAY BESTSELLING AUTHOR
ROXIE NOIR

ONE

DELILAH

The seamstress pats my butt again. It's a very firm, professional pat.

A moment later, she follows it up with a pinprick.

"Sorry," she says, though it sounds more like *thowwy* because of the pins clenched between her teeth. "Please hold still."

That comes out as *peesh hole shtiwu*, but the fact that I can understand her perfectly is a testament to how much time I've spent a bridesmaid dress while a well-meaning but stern woman frowns at my backside.

Usually that woman is a seamstress. On occasion it's been my stepmom or the bride, because a bridesmaid dress that looks pretty and proper on the rest of the bridal party inevitably makes me look like I'm heading out to work the pole.

"She was standing on a chair on top of an end table?" asks my stepmother, Vera, from her seat at the massive dining room table. "With a shotgun?"

"Apparently she'd had it up to here with the squirrels in the attic," I say, still holding perfectly still.

"She's lucky she didn't break her neck. Or a hip. At her age, that's nearly as bad."

"Does she have something against ladders?" asks my sister Winona, sitting off to my right on a huge leather couch. She's carefully putting custom snow globes into small, decorative boxes.

"Her ladder broke last year when she tried to patch the roof during a thunderstorm," I say. "She hadn't gotten around to replacing it yet."

"Well, bless her for being spry enough to fix a roof in her eighties," Vera says. "I certainly couldn't manage that."

I'm not sure Vera's ever been on a ladder in her life. Vera doesn't go on ladders. Vera hires people to go on ladders.

Next to her, my sister Ava sighs.

"Well, what should we do with Beauford's seat?" she asks.

"Just leave him out," I say, shrugging.

Behind me, the seamstress huffs.

"Sorry," I tell her.

"Then we'd have an odd number of people at the head table, and it'll look strange," Ava says, looking slightly worried. "I mean, another table, *maybe*, but people will be paying attention to that table."

"May I see that?" Vera asks Ava, who slides a sheet of paper over.

Vera contemplates it. Intently. Ava takes another sheet of paper on floral letterhead and consults it. Winona keeps putting snow globes into boxes.

I keep my doubts about whether anyone will be examining our table to myself. No one looks at bridesmaids. No one cares how many people are at their table. There's no way this matters.

On the other hand, my youngest sister didn't become president of Kappa Gamma Alpha by glossing over details.

"You know, it would be a shame for that meal to go to waste," Vera finally says, sitting back in her chair, legs crossed, and looking at me. "It's already paid for, you know, with the wedding two days away."

"I'll bring Lainey," I offer. "She'd have a great time."

"You can't bring a girl friend to a wedding," Vera says, looking back at the seating chart. "Wait, she's just a girl friend, isn't she? Not a *girlfriend?*"

"If she were my *girlfriend,* could she be my date?"

"Norman and Wes are coming," Ava pipes up, still looking at the list. "You wouldn't be the only gay couple!"

I wish I were surprised that, of three hundred and sixty-something guests, there's one gay couple, but I'm not. My family isn't explicitly regressive, but they do run in some very traditional circles.

Vera ignores my hypothetical question.

"This could be a good opportunity for you," she says. "You need a date, isn't there someone you'd like to ask?"

"Not really," I say, as the seamstress moves around to my front, still frowning. "Can't I go alone and spend time with my family?"

Vera doesn't take the *family time* bait.

"What about the man who owns that bakery next to your shop?" she asks. "Everett?"

"Evan Hill," I tell her. "He's married. I think his wife is pregnant. Or maybe they just got a dog."

"One or the other," Winona deadpans, loud enough that only I can hear.

"I don't know, he's been going on a lot about responsibility lately," I mutter back. "I kind of glossed over the details."

"George Thompson," Vera calls out, running a highlighter over a sheet of paper. "His quarry business is going quite well—"

"No," I call back, because George Thompson is both insanely boring and currently trying to legalize mountaintop removal mining so he can make more money, which makes him evil.

"William Obach."

"Married."

"Jonathan Haynes."

"Married. With four or five kids, I think."

"Or dogs," Winona says, too quietly for Vera to hear.

"Brian Sutton. Jethro Long. Timothy Newhall?"

"Married, no, and married," I call back.

Vera sighs. She caps the highlighter, then looks over at me, the look on her face mostly thoughtful but slightly annoyed. The seamstress pats my butt softly.

"It's the small-town south," I point out to my stepmother. "Everyone my age has been married for seven years, and they've already got three kids and a minivan."

"And you're *sure* Beauford can't just pop back by for a few hours?" she asks.

"*Mom*," Ava admonishes. "His grandmother's in the hospital. In Tennessee."

Vera sighs.

"I know, I know, I'm sorry," she says. "What about Tucker Yates? I heard his divorce from Cathy was finalized at last."

"Tucker's divorced because he's a lunatic who thinks the earth is flat and the President of the United States is a lizard in disguise," I say.

"And because he cheated on Cathy with an eighteen-year-old," says a new voice as Olivia, my middle sister, walks through the door. "Have y'all seen — oh, there they are. Why are we talking about that sorry excuse for a man?"

"Delilah's date canceled last minute and she's refusing to go with anyone else," Vera sighs.

"Beau's grandmother is in the hospital," I explain.

"Because of squirrels," Ava adds.

Olivia just raises her eyebrows.

"Aren't you still doing your nun thing?" she asks me.

I shoot her a good, hard glare.

"What?" she says, blinking her wide blue eyes, oblivious.

"Delilah hates it when you mention the detox in front of Mom," Winona explains.

"You can't still be doing that," Vera says, politely astonished. "It's been nearly two years."

"Two years Tuesday, actually," I say. "Some families would give me a certificate in recognition of my accomplishment."

"Then this is the perfect time to re-start dating," she says, ignoring my *certificate* comment. "You've had plenty of time to sow your wild oats" —she waves one genteel hand in the air— "take your stripper class, do your meditation, all those things you've been up to."

"Two years is the goal," I say, as patiently as I can. "I won't make it if I go on a date Saturday night, will I?"

"Isn't it close enough?" Vera asks, in a tone of voice that means *I think you're being ridiculous.*

I take a deep breath. Vera and I have had this argument before. We know one another's positions on my single-and-celibate-by-choice state, and I know I'm not going to change her mind this time, either.

Vera thinks that being thirty and *choosing* not to date is crazy as a shithouse rat, though she'd never use that phrase. She's excruciatingly old-fashioned in some ways, from a time and place where a woman's worth stemmed from the man she was with.

For Vera, it's unimaginable that I actually like being single, so I think she assumes I'm lying about it and must be longing for a man to come in and sweep me off my feet.

I am not.

"I'd like to go alone," I say.

Simple, direct, firm, yet polite. My therapist would break into applause if she heard. I hold my breath, hoping that it was polite enough and not *too* direct.

I've heard rumors of families where people can just tell others what they want and their wishes are respected instead of debated. Sounds nice, but I believe it about as much as I believe in unicorns.

Vera and Ava look at each other.

They frown, both brows gently wrinkling in an almost-identical pattern.

Then Ava sighs and grabs her iPad, and I wonder what those other families are like.

"Okay," she says after a moment, flicking her finger along the screen to scroll. "Donald Craw. Jeffrey Preen."

"Ava," I say, closing my eyes and willing myself patience.

"Andrew Haulier — oh no, wait, apparently *it's complicated* with him."

My eyes snap back open.

"Are you going through my high school graduating class on Facebook?" I ask, staring at my little sister.

"Cory McGarvey," she says, ignoring me and tilting her head, still looking at the screen. "He's kinda cute?"

I take a deep breath and glance around the room, trying to give myself a moment. Off to one side of me, in front of a plush leather armchair, is a triple mirror featuring a tall pink column topped with curly orange hair.

Of course Ava's bridal seamstress makes house calls. For the amount Vera and my dad are paying for this wedding, you can't expect the bridal party to go somewhere and slightly inconvenience themselves, for goodness' sake.

I glare at the hottie in the mirror. She glares back.

I whisper a serenity prayer to myself, though admittedly I start it with *for fuck's sake, please.*

This is *exactly* why I asked Beau to attend my little sister's wedding with me. We're friends, so I'm happy to spend several hours at an open bar with him. He's single, so no one would going to get mad. And he's gay, so it wouldn't get awkward.

It was perfect.

Damn those squirrels.

"Norward Yapp," Ava goes on. "You went to school with someone named *Norward*?"

"I think he went by his middle—"

"Oh!"

Vera and I look over at her in unison. I don't like that *Oh!*.

"Did you know Seth Loveless is single?" Ava asks us.

My heart thumps clumsily in my chest. My stomach tap dances. I think all the blood in my body rushes to my head, and I'm pretty sure time has slowed down and I can now hear oxygen molecules bonking together.

Yes, I know Seth Loveless is single.

Seth Loveless is always single, because he'd much rather sleep with every girl in a fifty-mile radius than be tied to just one. Nice of him not to cheat, I guess.

"Is he?" I say, forcing myself to sound more casual than flip-flops at a Jimmy Buffett concert.

"That's perfect," Vera says.

Does she... know? That Seth is the town bicycle and everyone's taken a ride?

"No," I say without thinking.

Vera stands up and walks toward me. Even though I think she got up at five this morning, she's immaculate in well-fitted khaki pants, a white button-down shirt, and a black cardigan, not to mention that her hair is *done* and her face is *on*.

"I don't think it's a good idea," I say, like my heart rate didn't just double. "We dated in high school, you know."

Ava shoots me a withering *no duh* look as Vera lifts an elbow-length faux-fur cape from a hanger on a clothes rack, inspects it, then walks toward me.

"You know, I ran into him at the market a few weeks ago and we chatted a bit," she says, holding it out to me. "He's a very nice young man. Handsome, too. He asked me to say hello to you for him."

She doesn't know. There's no way that Vera's aware of Seth's *reputation*.

"Thanks," I say.

Sometimes, despite a lifetime of etiquette training, I still don't know what response a situation requires of me. For example, *going to a wedding with Seth is literally the worst idea either of you have ever had in your lives* isn't on the table.

"If you see him again, tell him I also say hi?" I hazard.

"Do you mind trying this on again? I know you already did, but it'll give me peace of mind," she says, holding out the half-cape.

"Have you even seen Seth since you broke up?" Ava asks, still looking at her iPad.

Then her eyebrows go up.

"Oh, wow, Mom. You weren't kidding. Does he look like this in real life?" she goes on.

Somehow, more blood rushes to my head. My face in the mirrors goes pink. Redhead problem #4501: blushing *way* too easily.

"He's very good looking," Vera says.

"I haven't really seen him, no," I lie, swooping the cape around my shoulders and hoping we can stop talking about how hot Seth is. "Just around town and stuff. Here and there. Nothing major."

I'm over-explaining, but only because I think telling Vera the truth might cause me to spontaneously combust, so I'm lying my face off.

I also blush more. How? How is that even possible?

"You two could catch up," Vera says, closing the clasp at my neck for me, then smoothing her hands down my arms. "I always thought you were a sweet couple."

"We were teenagers," I object.

"So? Plenty of people marry their high school sweethearts," Vera points out.

"I did," says the seamstress, gently straightening the cape behind me. "When Mack and I started dating, I was fourteen and he was sixteen."

"See?" Vera says, stepping back.

"Michael and I were high school sweethearts," Olivia says from somewhere behind me.

"Delilah, go with Seth!" Ava gushes. "It would be so sweet."

There's a feeling in my chest like my heart's in a tin can and someone just dropped it. *Clonkthump. Squish.* I take a deep breath.

"I'd rather celebrate your special day with friends and family instead of awkwardly catching up with some guy I haven't seen in, what, eight years?" I say.

That's right, I pulled out the big guns: *special day*.

Ava makes a face and keeps scrolling the iPad.

"Please?" I ask.

"I wish you'd give this some consideration," Vera says.

"I'd hate for you to be the only one there with no date and no one to dance with all night."

"I'll dance with Wyatt," I say, naming my favorite cousin, who is attending this wedding with his sister and therefore cannot be my date. "I'm sure there will be single men there. I'll dance with one of them. I'll dance with *all* of them if you want."

Vera sighs.

"And you don't want some random weirdo at your table during dinner, right?" I cajole. "What if it turns out that he's deep in some pyramid scheme and he spends the entire time trying to sell us essential-oil-infused leggings?"

"All right, all right," Vera says, holding her hands up. "If you're really that committed, fine. Shrug your shoulders?"

I shrug my shoulders. Inside, I'm pumping one fist because hallelujah, *hallelujah*, I get to attend this wedding solo.

It's a mid-January miracle.

"Now relax," Vera says. I do, and her eyes flick from elbow to elbow, searching for the barest hint of blue or black or red peeking out from the bottom of the cape.

I stand there, statue-still, heart racing. Not because of the cape. At the last fitting, where it was decreed that bridesmaids would be wearing (faux) fur capes, I was measured and fitted and re-measured and re-fitted, so there's no doubt in my mind that my half-sleeve tattoos are adequately covered.

But what if I did take him?

It's not even a real question. I can't take him, and I won't, and I shan't.

Seth and I have a pact, and attending a wedding together would *definitely* violate its terms.

"Ava, does this look all right to you?" Vera asks,

standing off to my left side. "I can still see a few lines that the cape isn't covering, but I'll leave it up to you whether we re-hem or not."

Ava puts the iPad down and stands, swishing her long blond hair over her shoulders. My youngest sister still moves like the cheerleader she used to be, her steps five percent bouncier than average.

"Where?" she asks, standing next to Vera.

"Here," Vera says, tracing one finger right above the crease of my elbow. "It's not much, but — Delilah, shrug and relax again."

I do it, having long ago accepted that my role as brides-maid is essentially decorative, like a throw pillow.

"It's barely visible under the lace," Ava says. "And we're standing so close, I think from any further away you won't be able to see it at all."

I turn my head. The two of them could be twins, born thirty years apart. They have the same willowy figures, the same blonde hair, the same blue eyes and high cheekbones.

I stick my tongue out and cross my eyes at them.

"Hold still, we're almost done," Vera says. "If you hadn't gone and done *that* to your beautiful skin we'd be done already, you know."

She doesn't like my tattoos. It's not a secret. She didn't like the bird I got on my hip right after my divorce, she didn't like it when I got two half-sleeves and an upper back piece, and she certainly didn't like it when I decided to become a tattoo artist.

Admittedly, I'm successful enough now that she's come around on that last part. I even heard her bragging about her small-business-owning stepdaughter once.

If she knew about my chest piece, currently hidden under a thick layer of coverup, she wouldn't like that one either.

11

I put my hands up to my head and make moose antlers, still sticking out my tongue and crossing my eyes.

"Now we can *really* see them," Ava deadpans as Vera just sighs.

"I'm gonna stand exactly like this for your entire wedding ceremony," I say.

"*Moooooom*," Ava says, laughing. "Make Delilah be normal."

"Delilah, don't pretend to be some sort of... deformed moose monster... on your sister's wedding day," Vera says.

"Fine," I say, and resume a normal stance.

We discuss the clasp on my cape. We discuss what we're going to do with my hair. The seamstress — whose name is Louise, I think — chimes in with some updates on my *derriere*.

Then, at last, I'm done.

The rest of the afternoon passes in pleasant chaos, as I put personalized Hershey's Kisses into the small fancy boxes with the snow globes, call the florist, help with seating charts, and do a hundred other minor pre-wedding tasks.

I wonder, privately, if the days before my own wedding were this chaotic. Were our place cards embossed? Did each of our guests get chocolate with our names on it?

All I really remember is a sense of uncertainty that got worse every day.

I'm putting on my coat and scarf, about to go home, when Vera stops me.

"Delilah," she says, crossing the high-ceilinged foyer, walking between the two staircases. "You're sure?"

I free my hair from the scarf and settle it around my neck.

"About Beau?"

"About not taking a date to the wedding," she says, her

voice quieter as she steps up to me, one hand on my shoulder, her touch light through my thick wool coat.

"Yes," I say, instantly. "I'm really sure."

"It's no trouble at all," she goes on. "I know how awkward it can be to go to something like this alone, when everyone else is paired off, and how lonely it can feel."

Her hand squeezes my shoulder lightly, and I look into her face, filled with nothing but motherly concern.

Vera's not wrong. When I was Ava's age, I didn't think I'd be single at thirty. I figured that I'd still have a husband and some number of adorable children. I thought we'd be that family who sent an irritating Christmas newsletter every year about how wonderful and great and perfect their lives are.

Clearly, that didn't happen, but I've never been able to convince Vera that I'm happier for it.

"Vera, it's fine," I say. "Promise."

"I worry," she says, softly.

"I promise the answer isn't Seth Loveless," I say, matching her tone.

"Oh, I didn't mean him specifically," Vera says. "I just want you to be happy, and if I can help, so much the better."

"I'm happy alone," I tell her. "Really."

"Okay," she says, and gives my shoulder one more squeeze. "Love you. Drive safe. Watch out for cops at that curve right before you cross the creek, they've been hiding in a blind spot lately and I know how you like to speed."

"Thanks," I say as she stands on her toes and presses a quick kiss to my temple.

"Don't be late tomorrow!" Vera calls after me as I open the heavy front door of her house, then let it fall shut behind me.

I exhale, my breath fogging in front of me like I'm a

dragon with its light extinguished, and I head down the front stairs of my parents' mansion and onto the curved, paved driveway, the fountain in the center shut off for the winter and oddly quiet.

Everything is quiet, stark, dead. It's not even five o'clock yet, but the sun is a faded memory in the western sky, the moon and stars hard and bright above. The trees that line the long driveway to the house are bare, branches stabbing at the sky like skeletal hands.

Virginia is far enough north that it gets cold but too far south to get much snow, so for four months every year the world is dead and brown and gray. The little we do get sends everyone into a panic for forty-eight hours before melting into dirty scraps at the side of the road, so it's not much help.

I head for my car. I breathe the cold air deep, then exhale hard. It's cold and gray and shitty, the time of year when it feels like spring will never come, and I had to think about Seth again today.

I don't want to think about Seth. I don't want to think about our shared past, and I particularly don't want to think about it this close to Ava's wedding, but here I am.

As I'm driving down the tree-lined lane, away from my parents' house, I wonder how much longer it's going to take to get over him.

· · * * * ★ ★ ★ * * · ·

I TAP my pen against the paper as Vera slows to a careful stop. In the back seat there's the swish of drycleaning in garment bags swinging together.

"Is there anything else we need on the *absolutely do not play* list?" I ask, trying to think.

"You've got 'Lay Lady Lay' on there?"

"There's a zero percent chance that the band is going to play a weird Dylan song at Ava's wedding," I point out as she eases the car forward.

"There's a zero percent chance if you put it on the *no* list," she says.

I write "Lay Lady Lay" on the list, just to humor her.

"'Every Rose Has Its Thorn,'" she goes on. "'Pour Some Sugar On Me.' They're stripper songs."

"Sure, that's why," I tease, writing them both down.

"They *are*."

"You're just afraid that you won't be able to hold back your true inner self if they come on," I say. "I've seen pictures of you from the eighties."

"Delilah, are you calling my true inner self a stripper?"

"I'm calling your true inner self an Axl Rose fangirl who might not be able to resist an air guitar solo," I say, grinning. "Nonna told me all about your bedroom walls in high school."

There's a secret, sneaky smile on Vera's face, and she glances at me quickly while she drives.

"I've still got some of the pictures," she says, raising an eyebrow like she's being really bad. "Don't tell your father."

I make a lip-zipping motion, then throw away a pretend key.

"And 'Don't Stop Believing,'" she says. "You young people have ruined that song for me."

I sigh and write it down, even though I kind of like it.

It's Friday, the day before Ava's wedding, and I've been out with Vera since nine this morning running wedding-related errands. In the back, we've got bridesmaids' dresses, cummerbunds, the flower girls' and ring bearers' outfits, plus all the outfit-related odds and ends anyone could possibly want. There's a roll of duct tape back there, next to a small sewing kit. I don't know what it's for. I'm afraid to ask.

Officially, she wanted me to come along because she also dropped in to see how the flowers and cake were coming, and I've got an "artist's eye," but really, I think having someone along on these errands soothes her anxious, micromanaging psyche.

If Vera were acting this way about a Saturday afternoon barbecue, I'd push back. But it's Ava's wedding, which is a very big deal. I'm pretty sure she'll be back to normal sometime next week. At least, that was the case with the other three weddings she's planned — mine, Winona's, and Olivia's — so I just need to smile and nod until it all blows over.

"Any other beloved anthems you want to make sure people don't hear?" I tease, looking down the list of songs that includes all of the above, as well as "The Chicken Dance," "YMCA," and "Friends in Low Places."

That last one was Ava's addition. She *hates* that song.

"'Paradise by the Dashboard Lights.'"

"I'm not writing that down, there's absolutely no way that—"

I glance out the front window as I'm talking and realize we're not in town anymore, nor are we on the road back to my parents' house.

"—Where are we going?"

"Oh, I have to run one more quick errand," she says. "It'll just take a few minutes."

I glance down at the dashboard clock.

"I promise I'll be in and out," she says, and because it's Vera, I do not make a *that's what he said* joke.

"My hair's not gonna tame itself," I say, pointing at my high, messy bun, tendrils already popping out all over the place. "And I told Winona I'd help her with makeup and she's got that hideous mole—"

"She does not," Vera says. "Be nice to your sister. It'll be five minutes, I just need to swing by the brewery and order some more beer, because more of your father's golfing buddies are going to be there than I originally accounted for."

Then it clicks. This is the road to Loveless Brewing, which is a little ways out of town and, yes, it's owned by *that* Loveless.

My heart starts knocking against my ribcage as if it would like to be let out, and I'm immediately suspicious. Vera was being *real* cagey about where we were going, not to mention our delightful discussion of Seth yesterday, a topic I thought was closed.

"We can't just call?" I ask, stating the obvious.

"I'll feel better if we go in person," she says. "The telephone is just so impersonal, don't you think?"

"We're adding to a beer order, not asking someone to prom," I say.

We go around a curve and the brewery comes into view: a large, low-slung building styled after farm outbuildings.

"Yes, I know," she says. "But since this is a last-minute request, I think a little face-to-face contact is nice."

Something is up, and I suspect that we're not so much working on *Project: Ava's Wedding* as we are *Project: Find Delilah A Man*, a project that I have repeatedly and firmly denounced.

She flicks on the turn signal with one manicured hand. This time, I say nothing. What's the point? She already knows my opinion on this, and furthermore, if I accuse her of dragging me specifically to the brewery, she'll scoff and tell me that she just needs to order more beer.

17

They're going to have Loveless beer at the wedding, so of course that's the one and only reason we're going to the brewery, and do I always have to read devious motives into something so simple?

According to my therapist, that's called gaslighting. Also according to my therapist, there's little we can do to change the people we love, we can only change our reactions to them, particularly when they're your stepmom and have been set in their ways for longer than you've been alive.

"The rehearsal dinner starts at five and you said you wanted to be there by four," I remind her, closing the binder on my lap. My fingers slide a little along the smooth plastic, my palms already sweaty, my heart thumping just a little too much.

It's no big deal, I remind myself. *You probably won't even see him, and even if you do, it's fine. You're adults.*

You've made small talk before, for fuck's sake.

Vera pulls carefully into a space and turns the car off.

My stomach whirls. Still. Even after all this time, seeing him makes my insides twist and knot like a tree growing from a cliff's edge, buffeted for years by the wind.

"Come on," Vera says, getting out of the car. "Ten minutes, I swear."

TWO

SETH

The big metal refrigerator door closes behind us with a *whomp*, and I put one hand on it, just to make sure it seals.

"I'm just saying that technically, it's child labor," I say.

"She also sells Girl Scout cookies," Daniel points out. "Is that child labor?"

"That's a volunteer position for a nonprofit organization."

Or at least, I assume it is. Surely the Girl Scouts of America are tax-exempt.

"Well, she gets fifty bucks per half-bushel," he goes on as we walk back toward our offices, past the huge silver cylinders. Each of them has a nozzle and a dial, and out of sheer habit, Daniel gives each one a quick look as we pass it by.

"Fifty? Are *we* a charity?"

"Those things are tiny," he says, sounding a tad defensive. "Do you have any idea how long it takes to pick half a bushel of juniper berries? Besides, it's skilled work, you've got to find the right tree and get a ladder——"

"All of which her uncle does for her," I point out.

"If you want to renegotiate her rates, you're welcome to try," he says, a small smile on his face. "Eli made some kind of pact with her about cake a few years ago and she *still* gets payment. Ruthless, I tell you."

He's right. At nine years old, his daughter Rusty has all four of her uncles wrapped around her little finger.

"Did you have her fill out a W-9?" I ask. "Or is she also dodging her taxes?"

He stops, leans toward one dial, then looks up at the tank. It all looks fine to me, but then again, this part isn't really my specialty. I can run it just fine if Daniel's not around, but he's the brewmaster.

I'm the spreadsheet master. It sounds less sexy, but trust me, it's just as important.

"You gonna call the IRS on her?" he asks, looking at me and grinning. "Maybe you could also mention the time she set up a lemonade stand and didn't collect sales tax."

"That's more of a county matter," I deadpan.

"Look, Rusty likes hanging out with her uncle Levi and collecting juniper berries," Daniel says. "It's a good bonding experience for the two of them."

"SETH!" a voice hollers behind us, and we both turn.

Catherine, our operations manager, is standing at the far end of the row of steel tanks, waving both arms in the air.

I wave back.

"Someone here to see you," she calls out, walking toward us.

"Who?" I call back.

"Am I your secretary?" she says as we meet in the middle of the room, under the steel tanks.

"Do you have any information at all about this mystery

person?" I tease. "Or am I walking blind into some kind of ambush?"

"It's a fancy-looking blonde, so you tell me," Catherine says, raising both her eyebrows. "Hopefully she just wants beer. You know what I told you about hanky-pank during work hours."

"Was it that as the owner, I can hanky whatever pank I want?" I shoot back, but I'm just razzing her. I know my reputation. I'm the one who earned it.

Behind me, Daniel sighs.

"You want me to take this one?" he asks, folding his arms over his chest. I'm ninety percent sure he's giving me a hard time, but my annoyance flickers anyway.

"No, I'd like to make sure that this beer order is properly logged, accounted for, and doesn't fuck up the rest of this month's numbers," I say, a little testy.

"I did that *once*," he says. "Three years ago."

"Yeah, and Nancy still calls me every month to make sure that the Dixie Pub is getting the right kegs delivered on the right day," I say.

"She calls you because she's got a crush and because you always remember her grandchildren's names," he says, a sly smile starting to take over his face. "Do you know I once overheard her talking about the things she'd do to you if she were twenty years younger?"

FWEEEEEEP! sounds a sudden, ear-splitting whistle, and Daniel and I both step back.

"Boys!" Catherine says, sternly.

"Does she know we could fire her?" I mutter to Daniel.

"Good luck with that," Catherine laughs. "She's in the big room, are you gonna go—"

"Yes, I'll go see the fancy blonde," I say, and start walking. "What is this, a Hitchcock movie? If she wants me to help her kill her husband, I am *out*."

The big room is just what we call the brewery's main public space. It's got a bar along one wall, dartboards along another, windows along a third. The side without the dartboards has three long wooden tables running the length of the room, all made by Daniel's wife Charlie.

All in all, it's pleasant, slightly stylish, a little cozy, and a very nice place to hang out with friends on a Saturday afternoon.

I head toward it between the colonnades of big steel tanks, past our offices, running through a list in my head. I've still got a few invoices to pay, including the one that Cloverdale Organics *finally* corrected, I've got to figure out why Iris's direct deposit didn't go through yesterday, and then my other brother Eli will be here because tonight is the soft opening —

The moment I get to the doorway, I stop. It's only for an instant, but my mind empties out and all I can hear is the single *thud* of my heart, the slow surge of blood through my veins, the whisper of adrenaline as it pricks over the back of my neck.

Delilah's standing there.

She's in the center of the big room, all red hair and freckles. She's wearing a long black wool coat, her hands in her pockets. She's talking to her stepmother, Vera, laughing.

I'm derailed, all thoughts of direct deposit and my brother Eli gone, like Delilah's the copper penny on the tracks and I'm the train unfortunate enough to run it over, the one-in-a-million that crashes because of such a simple, lovely thing.

I take my right foot off the floor, remind myself of each individual movement of my legs that comprise the action *walking*, and I move forward.

"Hi there," I call out. "I heard you were in need of beer assistance?"

I cross the room toward them, a smile on my face. As if there's nothing at all interesting about this.

"Seth," says Vera, who is both fancy and blonde. "Thank you so much for taking time out of your day to help me out."

And then I'm standing there, facing them. I clasp my hands in front of myself and look from one to the other and think *charming, helpful, friendly*, and I keep smiling.

"It's no trouble at all," I tell Vera, running one palm over the other. "What exactly is it I'm helping with? I should probably find that out before I make any promises."

"I know it's very last-minute," Vera says. "But we had more RSVPs than we expected for Ava's wedding tomorrow, so I'm hoping that I can add another ten or so cases of beer to our order."

I don't look at Delilah, but I can see her anyway: watching Vera, face giving nothing away, still lighting up the place like she's the sun.

"Well, I don't know," I deadpan. "We're only a brewery, I'm not sure where we'll get all those beers."

Vera laughs, reaches out and puts one hand on my shoulder.

"This is what I have to put up with for Ava," she says to Delilah. "Seth Loveless sassing me."

"She's probably worth it," Delilah says, the corners of her eyes crinkling. "Though we could also just go back to Kroger and grab a couple cases of Coors Light. Coors Light never sassed anyone."

"That's true," I say. "It just hasn't got the personality. But if you'd like sassy beer, then of course I can help. What do you need?"

"I have to admit that I don't remember exactly what

we've already ordered and I didn't bring my food and beverage notes with me today," Vera starts. "But we planned on three hundred and fifty people at the wedding, but more were able to attend than I thought…"

Delilah glances from Vera to me, then back, but I feel as if someone opened the oven door in a freezing house. Everything about her is warm: red hair, the color of an ember about to catch in kindling. Copper-toned brown eyes. Freckles that pepper her skin like autumn leaves on the last sunny day.

"…but since most of the unexpected RSVPs are from Harold's golfing friends and Thad's lacrosse team, I'd say we'll take about ten percent more than what we originally ordered," Vera finishes. "Is that all right?"

"Absolutely," I say. "I'd be pretty bad at my job if I couldn't get you eight more cases of beer. You want them in the same proportion as the rest of the order?"

I never say numbers aloud to customers if I don't have written proof of them in front of me, but I've got everything memorized anyway. I don't mean to. It just happens.

Vera ordered eighty cases of beer, split into thirty cases of Loveless Lager, twenty cases of Southern Lights IPA, ten cases of Solstice Stout, and ten cases of Boondocks Brown. At twelve bottles in a case, that's nine hundred and sixty beers.

In other words, if Vera wanted me to stand on my head right now, I'd at least try.

"That would be perfect," Vera says. "Thank you *so* much."

"It's no problem at all. We'll get them loaded up tonight and delivered tomorrow," I say, sliding my palms over each other in the opposite direction. Oven door, cold house. "How's the wedding prep going?"

Vera sighs.

"Everything is completely insane and there are a million things to do," she says. "You know how it is."

I don't. I've never planned a wedding or been married. I'm the only one in this room right now who hasn't, and despite myself, I glance at Delilah.

She glances away, and I wonder why the fuck I did that.

"Completely," I say. "I've never done it myself, but Daniel ran me ragged for the week before his wedding. So did Eli, even though that was just a glorified courthouse ceremony."

"I didn't realize Eli had gotten married," Vera says. "Congratulations!"

"I'll pass it on," I say.

"Who's his wife?"

"Her name's Violet Tulane," I say, easing into the small talk. "She went to high school with us."

"I know that name," Vera says, a small, delicate frown ghosting across her brow. "Why do I know that name?"

"Did she wrangle the fireworks permits at Winona's wedding?" Delilah suddenly says. "When the fire marshal didn't want to let us set them off, but she negotiated to have a fire engine standing by, just in case?"

"Sounds like Violet," I agree. "She used to work at Bramblebush Farms."

"Yes!" exclaims Vera. "Yes, that's exactly right. I quite liked working with her, she really got things done. Poor thing must have been disappointed to have a small wedding."

I almost laugh.

"I don't think so," I tell Vera.

"There are plenty of people who don't want half the eastern seaboard at their weddings," Delilah points out.

"I refuse to believe such nonsense." Vera laughs, adjusting an expensive-looking purse on her shoulder.

"Anyway, we should get moving. The rehearsal dinner is tonight and Delilah claims that her hair takes hours to style."

"Only if you don't like the frizzy bun look," Delilah tells her, one hand going to her head, orange curls tied up and twisted on top. "If you're into that, by all means, keep quizzing Seth about weddings."

Vera adjusts her purse again, then looks from Delilah to me like she's thinking.

"Actually," she says, that familiar, genteel smile on her face again. "Could I trouble you to use the ladies' room before we go?"

"Of course," I say, and point the way. "Can't miss it."

Vera thanks me, smiles again, walks away.

Suddenly it's just us, Delilah and I, alone together in this room.

It's the first time we've been alone in two years. Two years, three months, and sixteen days, but who's counting?

"How's it going?" I ask, as good a question as any.

"It's all right," she says, hands in her coat pockets. "You?"

"About the same," I say, as nonchalantly as I can muster. "Nice day, huh?"

It's a lie. Every single piece of what I just said is a lie. Delilah's in the same room as me and I feel a thousand different ways, not one of which is just *all right* or *nonchalant*.

But two years and three months ago, we made an agreement, by God I'm sticking to it.

"It's kind of cloudy," she says, glancing at the windows. "Hopefully tomorrow is nicer. Ava's itinerary has us doing pictures outside."

"You're a bridesmaid?" I ask.

"Yup," she says. "Third time's the charm, I guess."

There are so many things I want to say to her. I want to

ask *how are you, really?* I want to say *these weddings are insane, right?* I want to tell her *I know you're worried for your little sister.*

"Vera driving you crazy yet?" is what I settle on.

Even that's probably too familiar, but I have to say something and we already talked about the weather.

"I've seen her worse," she says. "I guess she's getting the hang of wedding planning after three."

"Four," I say.

The silence from Delilah is expansive. Total.

"Unless she didn't—"

"No, you're right," Delilah says, her voice suddenly brittle. "Four."

"Just giving the woman her due," I say, standing up a little straighter. Like I'm bracing for a fight.

Delilah just gives me a simmering look, then takes a deep breath.

"Sure," she says, and looks away. "How's your family?"

Just like that, we're back on safe ground.

"They're well," I say. "Eli got married. Levi's getting married this summer. Daniel had another kid, and Caleb is…"

I trail off, because right now Caleb is heartbrokenly building bookshelves in my living room. He's a math professor and an idiot who had an affair with a student that didn't end well, and of course, I'm picking up the pieces.

Actually, his girlfriend called me yesterday, and I'm supposed to let her into my place so she can see him in an hour. Hopefully they don't break any of my stuff, either by fighting with it or having sex on it.

But none of that qualifies as *small talk*, so I just say, "Caleb's doing well. Yours?"

"The usual," she says. "Winona's already strategizing on how to get Bree and Callum into Harvard, Olivia's pretty much running the Junior League —"

We both hear the door shut, and Delilah's looks over her shoulder. I make myself relax my arms, take a deep breath, and I can see her shoulders move as she does the same.

Just like that, another casual encounter is over. We didn't kill each other. We didn't burn anything down. I'll feel hollow for the next week, but that's all.

"All right, Delilah," Vera calls. "You've still got plenty of time to do your hair."

· · · · · ★ ★ ★ · · · ·

THIRTY MINUTES LATER, my phone rings. I ignore the first two rings, still staring at the wall like I'm trying to burn a hole in it. There are a thousand things that I still need to do today, and I haven't started any of them.

I've replayed our conversation over and over again, even though there was almost nothing to it, and that's what kills me. I hate that we talk about the weather like we're strangers, that there's so much silence between us. That I never get to make her laugh, see her smile.

Sometimes, I think this is worse than fighting.

The phone rings again. I grab the receiver and close my eyes.

"Loveless Brewing, this is Seth," I say, hoping it's a telemarketer or a wrong number or something I don't actually need to deal with.

"Oh, thank goodness," Vera answers.

My eyes pop open in alarm.

"I was beginning to think perhaps you'd already left for the day, and I don't think I have your personal phone number," she goes on.

"Don't tell me you've changed your mind about the wedding order again," I say, and even though I'm trying to

28

sound lighthearted, my voice sounds like dead weight to my own ears.

"No, no, nothing like that," she says. "I'm actually calling to ask a personal favor."

I swear the hairs on the back of my neck stand up.

"And what would that be, Mrs. Radcliffe?" I say, making myself smile at the wall of my office so she can hear it in my voice.

"Well, seeing you today gave me an idea," she says, the hint of genteel drawl to her voice suddenly a little more pronounced. "You see, Delilah's date to Ava's wedding had to cancel on her at the last minute, so now the poor thing is planning on going alone, and I just feel so awful about it."

I hold my breath, and I have the sensation that I've just stepped into quicksand and I'm slowly going down.

She had a date.

"I know this is terribly last-minute and probably quite a surprise, but is there any chance you would be Delilah's date tomorrow?"

I get deja vu so hard I have to close my eyes, because I know this sensation. Not from Vera, but I've been here, done this, been on the other end of the phone when Delilah suddenly needs male companionship. It feels familiar, like being punched where I'm already bruised.

I still have to bite the inside of my lip so I don't say *yes*.

"Tomorrow?" I echo.

"I know this is so sudden, but the man she intended to go with was called away on family business," Vera confirms. "Their ceremony is at five o'clock at Pinehall Manor, reception to follow, of course."

She had a date.

It shouldn't feel like anything, but it feels like betrayal.

I have to fight the urge to say yes. I want to show up,

just to see Delilah's face, get into a fight with her because it feels better than nothing.

And then I have the opposite urge. I want to show up and sweep her off her feet and steal her from whoever the fuck she's dating, even if only for one night.

My heart beats into the empty space on the phone line.

"Seth?"

"Sorry, I'm still here," I say.

I clear my throat.

"I'm afraid I have a prior commitment," I say.

Vera sighs across the line.

"Well, darn it," she says. "That's too bad, I'm sure Delilah would have loved catching up with you."

"Another time," I tell Vera.

"Well, it was lovely to talk to you anyway," she says. "And Seth, could you do me one small favor?"

"Is this one going to be about beer?"

Please, God, let this one be about beer.

"Not at all," she says, laughing. "But would you mind not mentioning this to Delilah? If she knew I'd tried to find her a date, I think she might be angry with me."

"Not a problem," I say, and remember my manners at last. "And I'm sorry I can't help you out, but I do appreciate the invitation, Mrs. Radcliffe."

We exchange a few more polite statements, and then finally hang up. I'm sweaty despite the season, my palms clammy like I've just escaped danger, heart thumping so loudly I was afraid she could hear it.

"What invitation?" says a voice from the door of my office, and I jump.

"Are you kidding me right now?" I say, pushing a hand through my hair. "What the hell are you doing? Do you listen in on all my shit?"

"Only if it sounds interesting," says Eli, who looks

30

much too comfortable in the doorway to my office, leaning against the frame as if he owns it.

"It was nothing," I tell him, grabbing some papers on my desk and pulling them in front of myself, then pretending to examine them like they're the Rosetta Stone and I've recently come upon a Pharaoh's tomb.

Unsurprisingly, he does not take the hint.

"Did you need something?" I ask, still not looking up at him.

"No," he says, and doesn't leave.

I tap a pencil on my desk, rest my head on a hand, and consider my options.

I have four brothers. Eli is the second-oldest. I'm the second-youngest. Daniel's in the middle; the oldest is Levi, who loves trees and camping, and the youngest is Caleb, who loves math and also camping.

Actually, we all like camping, though I admit I like it the least. I don't mind sleeping in a tent on the ground, but what's wrong with a bed?

Anyway, the four of them are the nosiest assholes who've ever lived. Maybe some families understand the concept of keeping information to oneself; mine doesn't seem to.

Regarding the invitation, that gives me two options where Eli's concerned: tell him and get him out of my hair for now, surely setting up some further questioning in the future, or refuse him and never get him out of my office.

"Vera Radcliffe invited me to her daughter Ava's wedding," I say. "I didn't think going was a good idea, so I declined."

Eli is silent. He's silent for too long, and I don't like it.

"I'll get to the bottom of this later," he finally says. "Where are your circuit breakers?"

I squeeze my eyes shut for a moment.

"Why?" I ask.

"Because I tripped a circuit breaker," he says, as though explaining it to a four-year-old. In retrospect, I guess it was a dumb question.

"Doing *what*?"

"Don't worry about it."

"Please don't burn my brewery down," I tell him, standing. "Come on. What did you do? Do we have enough fire extinguishers for tonight?"

"We're fine," he says, soothingly. "I don't even start worrying until the flames are three feet high."

As I walk past him, through the door, I shoot him a *not today* glare.

He just grins at me.

THREE

DELILAH

The doorman opens the door, and I thank him as I step across the threshold and into the cold winter night.

"Please?" Ava says, still behind me. "Come on, Delilah. It'll be fun. Come on. Come on!"

"Ava, I—"

"Come on."

"I don't want—"

"Come onnnnnnnnnnnnn. Delilah. Come on. Come on!"

I stop in the middle of the brick walkway, keys in my hand, my car already pulled into the circular driveway of the Blue Ridge Country Club, where Ava's rehearsal dinner has just concluded.

"It'll be *fun*," my little sister says, stopping in front of me and looking up, hair swept back from her bright blue eyes. "You do remember fun, right? It's the thing you do when you're having fun?"

I didn't count how many glasses of wine she had at the dinner, but it was several.

"I like fun," I say, a little defensively. "But I have to get up early tomorrow because *someone* is getting married and decided that I have to get my hair done first in case it takes, and I quote, 'ten hours to wrestle into shape.'"

She blinks up at me like she can't believe her ears.

"Delilah," she says. "It's *nine-thirty*."

"I also want to call Lainey and see how her match went," I say, grabbing my keys from my purse, then shrugging it back onto my shoulder. "They were playing the Blacksburg Brawlers tonight, and you know those college girls are all twenty years old and completely fearless."

That's all true, but I also just want to talk to Lainey because I feel like I almost got into it with Seth today and I don't even know why. I just know I've got that distant, trampled feeling I get after we fight, like I'm a patch of grass in front of an elementary school.

Ava rolls her eyes, tosses her hair, and plunges her hand into her own purse, coming out with her phone and typing furiously. Behind her, the door opens again, and our cousins Wyatt and Georgia walk out.

"Seth won't be there," she says, half-distracted, her face glowing with the reflected light. "He's the owner, not the bartender."

I feel like my heart slips a gear. *Kerthunk.*

"What? I don't care if Seth is there," I tell her. "That's not why I don't want to go, I don't want to go because—"

"You get weird every time I mention his name," she says, still looking at her phone.

Well, we can barely see each other without either fucking or fighting, I think.

"No, I don't."

"You're weird now," she says, glancing up at me and raising one eyebrow.

"I'm not weird, I'm tired and slightly annoyed and *you're* being a total Bridezilla," I say.

"Ooh, throw a shoe," says a voice off to the side.

"No one is throwing a shoe," I say, calmly, as Georgia and Wyatt join us on the walkway.

"I could throw a shoe," Ava says, tilting her head to one side. "And I'd get away with it. I'm the bride."

"Probably," Wyatt agrees.

"See?" Ava says brightly, and then her phone dings. "Ah! Cool, Lainey's gonna meet us there."

"What?"

"Lainey," Ava says, loudly and slowly. "Is going to meet us" —she circles her forefinger overhead, indicating the four people standing there— "at the brewery."

"You're a monster," I tell her.

"A Bridezilla." She grins. "Come *on*. Lainey's expecting you and it'll be a fun, exciting family time! And your hot ex won't even be there."

Thank God it's dark, because I can feel my face warming up.

"I already told you, I don't care—"

"Being weird!"

"Your ex is coming?" asks Georgia. "Wait, is your hot ex *Nolan*?"

She sounds confused, and I can't blame her. *Hot* isn't the first word most people associate with my ex-husband.

"She's talking about a guy I dated in high school," I explain.

"Sethhhhhhhh," Ava says, sounding like a drunk, lisping snake. "And he's not going to be there, which is the whole point. When I bring him up, Delilah gets weird."

"I do *not*—"

"Seth. Seth. Seth. SETH. SEE—"

"Okay!" I hiss at my increasingly-loud little sister. "Fine. I'll go for half an hour, but I am *thirty years old* and I can't get wasted until three in the morning and get up at seven and be fine anymore."

"My God, thirty," says Georgia. "Positively ancient. How are you standing there without blowing away into dust?"

Georgia is twenty-nine.

"Must be a miracle," I tell her, as Ava steps closer to me.

Then she sandwiches my face in her hands, points my head toward her, and stares deep into my eyes.

"Delilah," she whispers. "You are not old. You are a wonderful, beautiful unicorn. You are a tiger. You are a fierce, strong, unicorn tigress and I believe in you."

I put my hands over hers and force myself not to laugh at my little sister, because even if she's pretty drunk and a little bit bratty, I think Ava has the purest heart of anyone I've ever met.

"Thank you," I say. "Let's get going before I turn into a pumpkin."

· · · · ★ ★ ★ · · · ·

AVA RUNS the last five steps to the brewery, grabs the door, then pulls it open triumphantly and gestures to the big room inside.

"Ta-da!" she shouts, holding both arms up and spinning in a circle. "See? No Seth!"

I have never wanted to muzzle my little sister more than I do right now.

"Okay," I say, like she's an insane person, which she kind of is.

"I told you!" she chirps. "It's totally fine and safe and free and you don't have to be all—"

She's cut off by the sound of many voices squealing in

unison. We all turn to see a cadre of young women descend on my little sister.

"It's my girls!" she shouts, and then she's giggling and hugging at least five of them at once, jumping up and down, a white sash settling over her shoulders as they bear her away.

Georgia, Wyatt, and I look at each other.

"Is that a sorority?" Georgia whispers.

"I think it's the Borg," whispers back Wyatt. "Except, you know, blonde?"

"Dork."

"It seems kind of nice," I say, still watching the giggling mass that enveloped Ava. "I mean, they're happy for her, right?"

"That's how they get you," Georgia says very, very seriously.

As we're contemplating beers at the bar, my sister Winona floats over. It takes me precisely one look at her to realize that she's *also* had a lot of wine.

"Guess who's got two thumbs and opened a tab with Mom and Dad's card?" she asks, grinning and jerking her thumbs at herself.

With that, my normally-very-proper sister spins and drifts away, leaving Wyatt, Georgia and I to look at each other.

"That was an invitation, not just a brag, right?" Wyatt asks, one eyebrow raised.

"It was now," I tell him, gesturing expansively at the chalkboard beer list over the bar. "Go hog wild. Get you the fanciest beer on tap."

Beers in hand, we find spots at the end of a long wooden table. A few minutes later, I wave over Lainey when she comes in.

"Harold Radcliffe's tab," I tell her. "And you know Wyatt and Georgia, right?"

"Yeah, we met at Vera's July Fourth shindig," she says, still standing, shaking hands with the two of them, her shoulder-length locs falling over her shoulders as she leans in. "You're the guy who thought it was okay to put cream cheese in guacamole."

Wyatt grins.

"I stand by that," he says. "It's delicious. You can't argue with delicious."

"It's an abomination," says Lainey, though she's also grinning.

"Two sentences and I'm already under attack," Wyatt says, taking a sip of his beer and looking at Georgia and me. "You're seeing this, right? She's out to get me."

"This isn't an attack, this is a conversation," Lainey says. "Hold on, I need a beer."

She walks off toward the bar, and Wyatt's eyes follow her.

Lainey comes back a few minutes later, and we all drink beers while she tells us about her roller derby match, complete with a track diagram on a napkin. Her team—the Blue Ridge Bruisers—lost, but only by a few points.

"Their track was too slippery," she says, taking a sip from her half-full beer. "We kept falling down."

"I'm sure that was it," Wyatt deadpans, but Lainey just laughs.

From there, we move on to whether rollerblading is still cool, then skateboarding. Wyatt says he can do a couple tricks, but no one believes him, and that leads to Georgia telling us a story about the time that my dad apparently pushed theirs into a pool and nearly drowned him, or so he claims.

After a bit, Wyatt and Georgia get up to grab more

beers.

The moment they're out of earshot, Lainey glances around skeptically, then turns to me.

"Not to question a free beer, but what exactly am I doing here?" she asks.

"Are you not enjoying the after-party to my little sister's rehearsal dinner?" I say, gesturing vaguely at the rest of the brewery. "Is this not your preferred way of spending a Friday night?"

"Ava's never contacted me before in her life, and suddenly it sounds like if I don't meet you at a bar some-one's gonna die?"

"She's drunk," I say. "She's been drunk since about five-thirty, I think."

"Please tell me she doesn't have a hostage."

"We're all hostages to the bride."

Lainey snorts.

"Sorry about her," I say. "I don't even know where she got your — what am I saying, I'm sure she got it from my phone during dinner when I went to pee or something, because Ava doesn't know what the word *boundary* means."

"You *have* to passcode that thing," she says.

"They're trying to sabotage my dick detox," I sigh. "Vera's being *Vera* about it, and I'm sure Ava thinks she's helping somehow. I don't even know why she dragged you into it. You might be bait to get me to come here. I'm sorry."

She takes another drink and looks around, frowning slightly.

"Wyatt's your cousin, how are they sabotaging — oh, shit," she says, as it finally dawns on her.

"He's not here," I say. "Remember, it's a drunk twenty-two-year-old's plan."

"And she doesn't know."

"Fuck no, she doesn't know," I say. "She thinks we were high school sweethearts and that's it, not…"

I trail off, because there's not a word for what Seth and I are. At least, there isn't in English. German probably has a word for *people who were together a long time ago and have repeatedly and unwisely hooked up in the years since, even though their brief couplings inevitably lead to anger and heartbreak.*

"Fuckbuddies?" Lainey offers.

"We're not really buddies."

"Fuck… compatriots?"

I contemplate this for a moment. I also contemplate telling her about our non-fight this afternoon, but I don't really feeling like doing it in his bar, while I look over my shoulder every ten seconds to see if one of my sisters is listening in.

"It's technically accurate," I finally say.

"Just one of the many services I offer," she says, and clinks her glass against mine, then glances up. "Quit talking about Wyatt's weird chin, he's coming back."

"Now I know you're just fucking with me," Wyatt says, sitting and grinning at Lainey, who's clearly enjoying herself. "My chin is *perfect.*"

He rubs his face like he's in a shaving commercial, and Lainey laughs. Georgia, once more seated next to Wyatt, rolls her eyes at her younger brother.

"Chin jealousy," he says. "Totally normal. I get it. I'd be jealous of my chin. It's great chin."

"Sure, that's it," laughs Lainey. "You know, this sort of over-the-top self-aggrandizing behavior can often be defensive—"

"LAINEY! HIIIIIIIIII!"

Ava's back, and she sits with a whirl of blond hair and the feeling that the energy at our table just went from six to eleven.

"Hi," Lainey says, grinning at my adorable and drunk little sister. "Congratulations on your wedding! You nervous?"

"Oh, my *gosh* yes," Ava says, wide-eyed, both her hands around a half-empty glass. "When we did the rehearsal a few days ago, one of the bridesmaids tripped on some flower petals, and the ring bearer got distracted by something on one of the chairs, and I'm really worried that the band might miss our entrance cues or play the wrong song! I saw it happen at one of my sorority sister's weddings a few months ago and it was *awful*."

Lainey's smiling politely, trying not to laugh.

"I'm sure you'll have a wonderful time even if something does go wrong," she says, soothingly. "It'll give you something to laugh about later."

"Everyone keeps *saying* that," Ava huffs, brushing her blonde hair out of her face. "But I don't want something to laugh about, I want something — *oh!*"

She squeals the last word, then points so emphatically that we all grab our beers and turn our heads, expecting a loose bear or at least a squirrel.

It's not an animal. It's a person, and he's looking directly at us.

For a split second, my insides feel like they're falling through the floor.

"DELILAH!" Ava whispers so loudly she's probably audible in Richmond, arm still outstretched toward the bar, finger extended. "IT'S SETH!"

"That's Eli," I say, grabbing her hand, putting it on the table, and turning my head away from where he's standing behind the bar.

Ava frowns dramatically.

"Are you sure?" she says, still several decibels too loud. "I think that one's Seth."

She's trying to point again. I hold on to her wrist so she can't.

"Yes, I'm sure, and for the love of God *stop pointing*," I hiss. "Were you raised by wolves?"

"It looks like Seth," she says, dubiously.

"Well, they're related."

"Is Seth also kinda hot?" asks Georgia, who's sipping her beer and casually observing Eli, like she's in a box seat at the opera.

"Please quit gawping like he's a tiger in the zoo."

"They're all kinda hot," Lainey offers. "That's their whole thing."

"I'd like you to elaborate on *all*, if you don't mind," Georgia says, eyebrow raised.

She does not quit gawping, though at least she's doing it somewhat politely.

"There are five Loveless brothers," I explain, carefully releasing Ava's wrist. She doesn't point again, but I keep an eye on her. "Two of them own this brewery, one of whom I dated when we were in high school."

"But they're mostly married," Lainey offers, then looks at me and jerks her thumb at Eli. "Is that one married?"

"That's also pointing," I hiss.

"He looks like he's got a ring," Georgia says.

"He's kinda far away to tell," Ava adds.

"He's married," I interrupt, already imagining Eli telling Seth that Delilah was at the brewery and her little sister was acting like she was on safari and he was the world's last rhinoceros. "That one's married, the middle one is married, and the oldest one's engaged."

Now everyone is looking at me, but at least no one is pointing at Eli anymore.

"Any further questions?" I ask, sarcastically.

"So you're an expert," Wyatt drawls, clearly enjoying this.

"Knowing that someone is married is not insider knowledge," I say.

That's technically true, but do I also sometimes have a drink or two and then stalk Seth, and by extension his brothers, on the internet?

Of course I do. Show me a person who's never nosy about their ex, and I'll show you a damn liar.

Levi, the eldest, has no social media of his own, but occasionally appears in posts from the Forest Service. A few months ago he did a short video about identifying poison ivy that got almost five hundred thousand views, some *very* thirsty comments, and wound up on several Buzzfeed lists. I don't think it was because of his practical wilderness tips.

Eli, the second-oldest, has all his stuff set to private, but occasionally turns up in foodie articles and whatnot around southern Virginia, including some food blog's "Five Sexiest Chefs."

Neither Daniel or Seth ever seems to post anything of their own, but Loveless Brewing has reasonably active social media accounts, which have supplied me with plenty of updates and pictures of the owners, even if they're completely impersonal and designed to sell beer.

And finally, Caleb, the youngest, is a math professor at Virginia Southern University. He's easy to find on the internet, but boring unless you're really interested in academic papers or symposium sessions.

Georgia sighs.

"The good ones are always gay or taken," she says, finally looking back at us instead of staring at Eli.

"Hey, I'm right here," Wyatt says.

"You're my *brother*."

"But I'm single, straight, and great."

"Well, hold on," says Lainey.

I risk another glance Eli's way, just in time to see him disappear into the back of the brewery.

I finally exhale.

"I don't see why a simple statement of self-assurance means you both have to jump down my throat," Wyatt says, but he's grinning. "A modern gentleman can't be self-confident?"

"What's this *gentleman* thing?" Lainey teases.

"Lord," Georgia mutters into her beer glass.

Ava flits off somewhere else, probably back into the arms of her sorority sisters. Thad — her fiancé — has shown up with a gaggle of matching fraternity bros, and the two pools seem to be mixing.

Georgia and Lainey keep harassing Wyatt, who not only takes it in good cheer but eggs them on. Secretly, I think he likes the attention from Lainey, but I know better than to say that out loud to either of them.

He's literally just pulled up his sleeve and is flexing his bicep, presumably to prove that he's a catch, when I hear my name *yelped*.

"Delilah!"

It's Ava, and before I can even react she's next to me, a whirlwind of blonde hair, her arm shooting straight past my face.

"*That* one is Seth," she says, smacking her other hand on the table for emphasis. "Right?"

I grab her arm and haul it to the table.

"I'm gonna cut you off if you don't stop —"

Well, fuck. Ava's right this time.

That one *is* Seth, and he's standing behind the bar with one hand on his hip and the other in his hair, the same gesture he's always made when he was trying to get a handle on a situation.

And then, he looks at me, probably because my little sister is being a total lunatic.

I feel like the air's been squeezed from my lungs. It takes everything I've got not to duck under the table, but I don't. I just go silent and stare back, mouth open, holding my sister's hand on the table like I'm trying to keep a toddler out of my drink.

Finally, I just shut my eyes.

"—Pointing at people, and yes, that's Seth, congratulations on getting it right this time."

"They really do look alike," muses Georgia.

"Right?" says Ava. "Can I have my hand back?"

"Are you going to point at him like he's a dancing bear?"

"I just wanted to make sure you saw him," she pouts.

"Thank you," I say, diplomatically. "I saw him. That is indeed Seth. Were there any further questions?"

She leans in toward us, her blond hair dragging across the table, and stage-whispers again.

"Sometimes he's here at night," she says. "I lied earlier! Bye!"

Just like that, she's gone, back to her giggling friends. I feel a little bit like someone just shone a very bright light in my eyes and demanded that I perform long division, but despite that, I don't look over at where Seth was again.

I'm over here, and he's over there, and I'm going to drink the remaining third of my beer very quickly and then leave and everything will be totally fine.

"So," Lainey says brightly, her spine straightening. "You guys watching any good TV right now?"

Bless her.

．．．．．★ ★ ★ ★ ．．．．

I WAIT TEN MINUTES, and then I force myself to wait one more, just to prove that I'm a mature, adult woman who doesn't leave a room just because Seth is across it, pouring drinks behind the bar.

After eleven minutes, my beer is empty, so I yawn, make some excuses, pull on my coat, and leave.

When the door shuts behind me, I finally relax. I take a deep, cold breath, and I blow it out into the night air where it blurs the stars, already half-obscured by the orange light flooding the brewery's parking lot.

It's fine, I tell myself.

It's getting better.

But God, I feel shitty. Between Vera and Ava and my cousins and the madness of the rehearsal dinner and the whirlwind of getting talked into the brewery, this is the first time I've been alone with my feelings all day.

And, honestly? They suck. Seeing Seth and talking about the damn weather feels unique awful, like opening a cookie jar to find out that it's filled with sawdust.

"Delilah!"

Fuck.

Every single muscle in my body tenses. I hold my breath, grit my teeth, keep walking like I didn't hear him.

Maybe I can pretend I'm wearing earbuds or something and get to my car before —

"Hey. Delilah."

I turn, despite myself, like I'm on a string held by some invisible puppeteer.

"I didn't think you'd be here," I call out.

He's one row of cars away from me, walking between a dark sedan and a medium-colored SUV, both shades of gray in the bleak color of the floodlights. His hands are stuffed into his pockets and he's moving just quickly enough to fire up my defenses.

"I kn—"

"You don't have to chase me down in the parking lot, I'm not coming back," I cut him off, the words snapping across the pavement between us, whisked by a cold breeze. "It wasn't my idea. Ava talked me into coming tonight and she pulled the whole *I'm getting married tomorrow* thing and she swore up and down that you wouldn't be here, so—"

He's stopped in the middle of the blacktop, hands still in his pockets, wearing nothing but a shirt and jeans in the cold night.

I keep talking like a ball of yarn unraveling.

"—And I figured you're the owner, not the bartender, so why would you be here on Friday night? But apparently Eli has some food thing going now with you guys—"

"Delilah," he says, and it's just one word but I feel it in my bones.

I stop talking, exhale, swallow. My hands are fists in my coat pocket, my body ready to fight for the sake of my stupid, defenseless heart.

"What?" I say, softer now, the word floating up to the parking lot lights, the stars above.

"I didn't chase you out here to fight. I came to apologize."

It takes me several seconds to compute that statement.

Then I'm stunned and I stare, open-mouthed, at Seth.

He rubs his hands together in front of himself, bigger and rougher than the hands of someone who mostly does payroll and invoices should be. I can see the hairs standing in goose bumps along his arms, because it's gotta be in the low forties out here.

"I'm sorry I was kind of shitty earlier," he says, still rubbing his hands. He looks away from me, over the shining cars parked outside the brewery. "I should have just…"

He closes his eyes, tilts his head back, hands still working in front of him and I do my best not to notice the cords in his neck, the muscles flexing in his forearms.

"Fuck," he sighs.

It's the best and only apology I've ever gotten from Seth, and to be honest, I sort of wonder if I'm hallucinating.

"You're right," I say, after a moment. "It was four weddings."

He folds his arms in front of himself, looks at me, half-smiles. I take a step forward, away from the massive truck I'm standing next to, into the empty space of the parking lot aisle.

"I didn't have to point it out," he says, shrugging.

I uncross my arms and I take another tiny step forward, examine Seth's face just in case it's actually Eli or some other imposter.

It's not. I knew it wasn't. I think I'd know Seth blindfolded and underwater from fifty feet away.

"Sometimes I forget to count mine because I've spent the last week trapped in some sort of matrimony-worshipping cult, where the bride is king and the D-word is verboten," I tell him. "Slowly but surely, they're brainwashing me."

He raises one eyebrow.

"*Divorce.*" I laugh. "Though I'd also die before saying *dick* in front of Vera, to be honest."

"I can only imagine what her wedding night advice is like," he says.

"No," I say, and squeeze my eyes shut. "Please, no."

"I imagine it's to be one thing in the streets and something else entirely in the sheets," Seth says, voice low and quiet and laughing.

"Okay, now I wish you'd come out here to start a fight,"

I tell him, opening one eye to look at him.

He's just grinning. It's a real, true smile, like he's just about to laugh, and it makes my stupid heart skip another beat.

"Well, if the cult needs a virgin sacrifice, at least you're safe," he says, and winks.

I ignore the wink, tilt my head at him.

"I'd be a terrible sacrifice anyway," I say. "They're supposed to go peacefully, but you know I'd be kicking and screaming all the way to the altar."

"I see you as more of the priestess type anyway," he teases.

"Oh, so I'm the one holding the knife over some innocent maiden?" I ask, but I'm laughing.

"Well, you're not the innocent maiden," he says. "And if you said you were a conduit to some ancient god, I'd buy it."

"Thanks, I think," I say. "But maidens have nothing to fear from me. At least where ritual sacrifice is concerned."

"I think a vanishingly small number are worried about that, truth be told," he says.

The thought flits across my mind — *does he know many virgins? Are they still?* — but I push it away.

"It's been a while since I knew what virgins worried about," I admit, and Seth laughs again, his breath escaping in puffs.

"Right?" he agrees.

We're both quiet a moment, alone, in the cold and the dark, and it's nice. It feels a little like dancing on a blade, on the edge of a cliff, but for right now we're twirling and upright and if I let myself, I might believe it could always be this way.

"You should go inside, it's freezing out here," I finally say.

"Back to the agreement?" he asks, and his voice is suddenly intimate, quiet, and I start nodding before I can even think about it.

"Yeah," I say. "It's been working, hasn't it?"

"Mostly," Seth says, and glances over his shoulder at the building, then back at me. "You're right, I should get back."

Something flashes on him, and I tilt my head.

"There's something on your neck," I say.

He rubs at it with one hand.

"Other side," I say.

He tries again, misses, something pink and shiny winking at me in the dark.

"Right here," I say, pointing at my own neck, covered by a scarf, and he frowns, drags his finger over the cords there, still doesn't get it.

"Anything?" he asks, still pawing.

"Here."

I step forward, close the distance, reach up and take a pink sticker off of the spot where his neck meets his shoulder, his skin hot beneath my fingertips. Even though I'm wearing layers of clothing, I think every hair on my body stands on end until I step back, hold up one finger.

On it is a shiny, skateboarding shark, and I hold it up for Seth to see.

"Rusty was here earlier," he says. "She must've gotten me."

"Apparently," I say. "You want it back?"

"Sure."

He makes no move to take it. After a moment I lean in, press the sticker to his chest.

"Thanks," he says, and I look up at him, and I remind myself to breathe.

Somehow, even in the washed-out dark, his eyes are blue as anything, a shade I could never quite pick out no matter how hard I tried. Not quite cobalt, not quite ultra-marine, not indigo or cerulean or lapis or anything else I've ever put on a canvas.

Clear blue eyes, dark tousled hair, the hint of stubble at the end of a long day, shadow of a smile on his lips.

I want to kiss him. I want to press myself against him, wind my fingers through his hair, crush his lips against mine. I want to do it so badly that for a moment I don't trust myself to move so I just stand there, silent, stuck.

Then he raises one hand and touches the sticker himself and thank God, it breaks the spell.

"Go inside before you freeze," I tell him.

"So you *do* care," he teases, and I roll my eyes.

"Bye, Seth," I say, taking a step backward.

"Bye, Delilah," he says, and we both turn away, walk in opposite directions.

I shake my head, pull my keys from my pocket, focus on finding my car and unlocking it and getting in and starting the engine so I don't think about going after him. I drive away so I'm not tempted to go back, turn him around, kiss him against the side of the building.

It's always like this with us, the push and pull, the feeling that Seth and I are rubber banded together and the more we try to escape, the harder we snap back together. Usually we at least fuck before we fight, but apparently this time we skipped the fun part.

Maybe that means it's getting better.

I stop at the end of the brewery's driveway and glance in my rearview mirror, but there's nothing behind me except a few people walking to their cars. I don't know what I thought I'd see — Seth, forlorn, waving a white handkerchief at my departure?

I turn my music up, blast the heat, and turn onto the main road.

FOUR

SETH

I head back to the brewery, feet scuffing over pavement and then crunching over the brown grass that's been dead for a few months now, thin cold stalks still sticking out of the ground.

Apologizing. It was just that easy. I was a dick, and I apologized, and now — it seems — we're back to the plan. Back to exchanging small talk at coffee shops and meaningless chatter about our families and our jobs and sometimes running into each other at the grocery store and discussing strawberries, that sort of thing.

It's all right. It's good enough. It's at least better than fighting with her for no reason, then spending hours feeling as if someone's cinched an anvil to my chest and I've got to drag it around.

Outside the back door to the brewery, I stop at the edge of the floodlight. Behind the building, the thick forest is black, the sky above it the deepest blue, the grassy field surrounding the building charcoal gray.

This is January in Virginia: leached of color, cold but not a deep cold, dark but not a deep dark. Cold enough that I'm freezing in nothing but a T-shirt and jeans, not so cold that I can't spend a moment gathering myself.

She touched me, twice. They feel like brands on my skin, like she's imprinted the ridges and swirls of her finger-prints on me, even through my shirt. I rub my hand over them — neck, chest — my own fingers cold, but it doesn't help. They're still there.

Back to the plan, then. I take a deep, cold breath, look up at the sky.

I know it's not there right now. During the winter it doesn't come into the sky until it's almost morning and then the rising sun obliterates the faint stars, but it doesn't matter because I've always got it on me, haven't I? Even if it's faded to blue, the dots and lines slightly blurred, it's still there.

"Grounds inspection go okay?" Eli asks the moment I cross the threshold.

The heat of his makeshift kitchen prickles across my skin, and the door closes behind me.

"Did you know there're *plants* out there?" I ask, jerking my thumb at the door. "Just plants and plants, as far as the eye can see. Trees and grass and all kind of shit."

Eli stops monitoring the grill for long enough to give me a half-concerned, half-what-the-fuck *look*.

"I suspected," he says.

"Someone ought to do something," I say, already walking away, toward the swinging doors that lead to the big room, heart booming even though I know for a fact that Delilah's not there anymore.

She's not out there and we're *back to the agreement*.

My hands are still cold, and I rub them together, walking past the cabinet behind the bar where we keep the kegs. Another wave of goose bumps rises on my skin, now that the relative heat of the building has worn off, but I ignore it.

I walk. Away from the bar, away from Eli in the kitchen, cooking and noticing things. Away from the light and the noise and from anyone who could talk sense into me right now.

Back to the agreement.

Into the back of the brewery and between the massive metal tanks, the bready, sweet smell intensifying. I keep the lights off, because I know this path by heart. The only light I flick on is the one in my office, and only so I can see the display on my office phone.

It's been two years, three months, and sixteen days since the last time she touched me on purpose. I don't want to know that number but I can't seem to help it, as if there's a calendar in my head slowly ticking upward. I touch my hand to my lips, still cold, rub the back of my hand across my mouth and tell myself that this is a bad idea.

I punch the down arrow on the office phone until I find the phone number I'm looking for.

The receiver's in my hand and in one motion I hit the call button, hold it to my ear, step back, turn off the light as if darkness will make what I'm about to do any better. I hold my breath as the other end of the line rings once, twice —

"Hello?" Vera's voice says, and I finally exhale.

FIVE

SETH

I flip on the lights in the storeroom, look around, and silently curse whoever's been organizing our kegs, because they're doing it the same way that my computer's hard drive stores data: cramming random shit wherever it fits.

But while I can de-frag my computer by clicking something, defragging our storerooms involve a lot more physical labor. Usually, it's my physical labor, because I'm the one with a specific filing system in mind. Sometimes Daniel helps, but he's got Rusty to deal with so I let him off the hook.

Love the kid, but last week she asked me if I thought it was fair that Grandpa was dead but lots of criminals are still alive.

Lifting kegs onto high shelves for hours is easier than trying to explore the concept of an inherently chaotic universe with a six-year-old, particularly when I was expecting to discuss her pitch for a *My Little Pony* spinoff called *My Little Wombat*.

I push a hand through my hair and start looking. At least the kegs are labeled and color-coded, so I don't have to actually wade through all of them looking for more Bonfire Stout.

"Seth?" a voice calls, and I duck out of the storeroom to see Caleb, my youngest brother, heading through the warehouse toward me.

"What's wrong?" I call back, one hand automatically going to check my phone. There's nothing new.

"Wrong?" he asks. "Nothing! I just wanted to come see if you needed some help."

"They're not out of anything else up front?"

"Beth didn't say she needed anything."

Caleb walks up to me, his hands in his pockets, his long hair pulled back in a man-bun, and he smiles at me.

I can't put my finger on it, but there's something weird going on. I've known Caleb for twenty-six years now, and the man is up to... something.

"I'm trying to find more stout," I say, popping back into the room. "If you see a keg, take it to the front. We're going through it faster than I thought we would."

"Gotcha," he says.

Then he looks around, puzzled.

"Is there a system in here?"

I just sigh.

"The system is that we need to have an all-staff meeting in which we hammer home the importance of organization," I say.

For a long moment, we both just look. Finally, Caleb points.

"Is that it with the yellow tape?" he asks. "I don't have my glasses on."

"Sure is," I tell him, making my way over to the keg. "Weren't you gonna get contacts?"

"They bother my eyes," he says. "I think there's another one right next to it."

We each grab one, then carry them out, through the warehouse and between the huge silver vats. Today is the brewery's Fall Fest, and it's going even better than last year's.

The front room is jam-packed with people buying beer. The patio — which is at least twice the size of the front room — is hopping. This year a couple of food trucks set up in the overflow parking lot, we rented a pumpkin-shaped bouncy house, and later tonight we'll be lighting the bonfires.

There's a part of me that can't believe all this is really happening, but I also know exactly how much blood, sweat, and tears went into it. I've got the spreadsheets.

"Thanks," I tell Caleb as we put the kegs down. "I'll hook this one up, then I'll be out—"

"You don't think we need more of the... blond?" he says.

"Are we out?"

"Seems like you should be sure. Also, the cider. People have been talking about it a lot, you should probably grab some more of that one too."

I'm crouching by the empty keg, disconnecting the tap, but I stop what I'm doing and look up at him.

"What's going on?" I ask.

"Nothing," he says much, much too quickly.

"Caleb," I say, slowly. "You're as jumpy as a long-tailed cat—"

"There you are!" says a female voice, and I turn.

It's Daniel and his fiancée, Charlie, both coming toward me.

"Hi," I tell them, more suspicious by the second. "Everything all right?"

"Completely fine," Charlie says. "But do you remember that time you asked if I could make custom tables for the big room? What size were you thinking?"

I unhook the old keg, move it out of the way, tap the new one and slide it into place without answering. All three of them are just standing there, watching me, while I work.

"What *happened*?" I finally ask, standing and brushing my hands together.

They look at each other.

"Nothing," Daniel says.

"Did someone pop the bouncy house and you're trying to fix it before I see it so you don't have to listen to me bitch about insurance?" I ask. "Is there some..."

I trail off. I'm so confused that I don't even have a suspicion about what's going on. I'm just certain that something is, indeed, going on.

"You've lost your marbles," Daniel declares. "We just came to say hi."

"So it's cool if I go outside and make sure the bouncy house is still up to code," I say, pointing at the door.

"I do think we should talk about the tables——"

Charlie gives up on that as I walk past her, toward the door that leads outside.

"Seth!" Daniel shouts. "It's so nice in here!"

"Shit," I hear Caleb say as I step through, the door closing behind me.

It's fucking *beautiful* today. This is the reason people move to the Virginia mountains: it's clear and crisp and cool, the forest behind the brewery mottled orange and red and gold, the mountains unfolding into the distance the same bright hues of autumn.

It smells good. It feels good, and all the better for knowing that autumn never lasts nearly long enough.

That said, nothing seems to be on fire behind the brewery, so I head around the side, an unpleasant twist in the pit of my stomach at what I might find. Really, they should have just left me alone. I'd probably still be in there, double-checking that we had enough of each kind of beer.

As I walk, I can't find anything wrong. The bouncy house is fine, if bouncy. The tower of hay bales isn't on fire. Everyone seems to be having a perfectly good time out here, so maybe my brothers were just being —

Then I see the hair.

I know *instantly* why they didn't want me out here.

She's here, standing fifty feet away. Her back is to me but I still see that shock of red curls in my dreams. I'd know it anywhere.

I'm still walking. I don't think I could stop if I wanted to.

I had no idea she was in town. I haven't seen her — haven't *heard* from her — in two years, not since I called her at midnight after my buddy's wedding, a little drunk and filled with the kind of loneliness that a stranger with a nice ass can't fix.

"Seth!"

It's Caleb again, and now he's power walking across the patio, barreling toward me.

I just cross my arms over my chest.

"You gotta go back in there," he says, closing the distance. "There's, uh, everything exploded. All the tanks. Stuff is on fire? Your computer is an arc reactor now? It's mayhem."

"I'm sure Daniel can fix it," I say, and start walking again. Behind him, I can see Levi, his secret girlfriend June, and his best friend Silas watching us. I'm tempted to wave, since apparently I'm a spectator sport now.

"Godzilla showed up," he says. "And there's a hostage situation."

"I'm just going to say hello," I tell him. "That's all. I swear, Caleb."

"*Shit*," I can hear him say as I step around him.

A breeze blows. I swear all noises hush. I walk up, reach out, tap her on the shoulder.

Delilah turns, and for a moment, she just looks at me.

Then she smiles, and I feel like the sun just turned on.

"Hey," she says. "I thought you might be here."

"You thought right," I say. "How have you been?"

SIX

DELILAH

Still Two Years and Three Months Ago

"Go ahead, I want to say goodbye to someone," I call across the dark patio to Lainey.

"You want us to wait?"

"Nah, I'm good," I say.

"I'll text you tomorrow about hiking," Beau shouts as they head off, past the glow of the bonfires.

There's a part of my brain that knows what's good for me. It's the logical part. The rational part. The part that identifies patterns and understands cause and effect.

That part of my brain is politely suggesting that perhaps I could also leave right now.

But the rest of me — not just my brain, of my entire being — isn't interested in leaving. The rest of me doesn't give a shit about pattern identification, or about cause and effect, or about knowing what's in my best interest.

It cares that Seth Loveless is back there, and that three hours ago he gave me a hug that I've been replaying on an endless loop ever since.

That's all. A hug. It wasn't an embrace. He didn't wrap me in his arms. He certainly didn't hold me close. Nothing but a friend-I-haven't-seen-in-a-while hug, and here I am still thinking about the way his body ever-so-briefly felt against mine.

I try to look casual as I head back to the bonfires, as if I've got my eye out for someone but it doesn't really matter if I find him or not. I walk as though I'd *prefer* to find this person and say a proper goodbye, but if I don't, it's no big deal.

Truth is, I think my hands are shaking. The truth is that before today I haven't seen him in two years, not since he called me at midnight, his voice like silk and sandpaper, to ask if we could meet somewhere halfway between us.

I haven't seen him since I said yes and grabbed my keys while he named a town. I called Joshua, my then-boyfriend, from the road and told him I didn't think we should see each other anymore. When I got to the Old Dixie Inn, I'd been single for about two hours.

Two days later, I left at four in the morning while he was still asleep. I didn't say goodbye. I didn't say anything, just put on the clothes I'd worn on the drive up and left.

Until today, we haven't talked since. We still haven't really *talked*, because the polite chatter of *hi, how are you, what are you up to these days, oh you moved back to town?* can't be counted as *talking*.

Just like that hug can't be counted as a hug. Here I am, though, wandering through the half-dark with my hands shaking and an entire nest of bats fluttering through my chest cavity, feeling like they might burst out into the night.

Maybe he's seeing someone now. Maybe if he's not seeing someone — and Seth is never really *seeing* someone — he's already got some other girl tonight.

Maybe I'm going to go up to him only to realize that

he's got his arm around her, and I'm going to feel like an idiot. Maybe last time was really the last time, like we always swear it is.

Finally, I spot him. My heart leaps.

My stupid heart always leaps.

He's standing there, holding a beer, talking to someone. A man. It's hard to tell in the firelight, but it looks like his older brother's best friend whose name I don't remember right now, but who used to be around the Loveless house sometimes.

Steve? Simon? Skip?

And then Seth looks over at me, and in the dark his face is exactly like I remember it.

I stop wondering if he's with someone else.

"Delilah," Seth says as I walk up. "You remember Silas? Levi's friend."

"Hi," I say, and we shake hands. "You look familiar."

"Likewise," he says, smiling at me.

It's a nice smile. I vaguely remember a *lot* of girls talking about this smile when we were in high school.

"Delilah just moved back to open a tattoo shop," Seth tells him.

Something touches my jacket, moves it against my back. Presses in right against the base of my spine.

Seth's hand. I breathe, focus on the inhale, the exhale.

"Where from?" Silas asks. If he sees what Seth's doing, he says nothing.

"Leesburg, up north," I say. "I just got back a few weeks ago."

"Weeks?" Seth says, a frown in his voice.

"Well, welcome home," Silas says. "I, for one, am glad you're here because the only place to get inked up now is Deadbeat Tattoos over in Grotonsville, and from what I hear you're better off with a ballpoint pen and a needle."

Seth glances at me, an odd look in his eyes. He presses his palm against my back and even through a jacket and my shirt, heat flares.

Silas seems nice and all, but we *have* to wrap this conversation up.

"Well, if you ever need anything, look me up," I tell Silas. "Southern Star Tattoos. Grand opening in a few more weeks. Tell all your friends!"

"Tempting," he says. "I've been considering getting the text of the Fifth Amendment somewhere so I can quit repeating myself to rich idiots who don't know the law. On my ass, maybe."

I laugh, starting to remember Silas a little better.

Seth's thumb strokes my spine. I stand a little straighter, concentrate a little harder.

"That's a good place for text, actually," I say. "Plenty of space, and since they don't tend to be exposed to much sunlight, the art is less likely to fade and blur."

"Huh," he says, thoughtfully. "Interesting."

I glance at Seth again. His eyes meet mine, indigo in the dark. On my back his hand lifts briefly, then slides under my jacket. Skin on skin.

My hands have stopped shaking.

"I actually just came by to say goodnight," I tell the two of them, a lifetime of politeness training taking over. "It was good seeing you today."

"Likewise," says Silas, waving his beer in the air.

Seth's still looking at me, that expression on his face, and it feels like the firelight is his gaze: rushing, flickering, heated, relentless.

"I'll walk you to your car," he says after a moment, one side of his mouth lifting into a small smile. His thumb strokes my back again, dips into the valley of my spine.

"Thanks," I say, softly. "You never know what'll happen between here and the parking lot."

"No, but you can make an educated guess," he says.

His thumb strokes my back one more time. It's not a gentle stroke. It's firm, like he's trying to find the notches in my spine. Like he's testing me.

I don't budge.

"I'll see you later," he says to Silas, turning his head.

"Later," Silas says, holding up his beer, and we walk into the dark.

SEVEN

SETH

STILL TWO YEARS AND THREE MONTHS AGO

The three hundred feet between the bonfire and the parking lot is the longest walk I've ever taken. It's long because the whole way, I can feel my brothers watching from where they're standing by the bonfires, and I know what they're thinking. After all, they did their best to keep me away from her earlier.

It's long because there are still people here, at Fall Fest, waving and saying hello.

But mostly it's long because she came over to say goodnight. It's long because she didn't move away from my hand on her back, because she sank into me. It's long because when I touched her she gave me a look that made me feel like I could throw lightning bolts and make it rain.

In my less lucid moments, I sometimes wonder if she's a sorceress. A witch, maybe. Some sort of enchanting demon, because what besides black magic could explain her hold over me?

"You do this every year?" she finally asks.

"By *this*, you mean Fall Fest? Yes," I say.

"You guys make good beer."

"You mean Daniel makes good beer," I tell her. "I make good business decisions."

That gets a smile out of her, a quick laugh.

"Of course you do," she says, teasing. "I'm sure you've got a complicated flow chart for every decision."

"Who says they're complicated?"

"So there *are* flow charts," she says, laughing.

Her laugh makes me feel like silly putty, like she can mold me however she wants. It always has.

"I can't make staffing and overhead decisions based on a whim and a prayer, can I?"

"You *could*," she points out.

She looks at me, her eyes dancing, her smile in the fine creases around them. I'm light as a feather, needy as a black hole. Her car is on the other end of the parking lot, and it feels like miles away.

"Can I show you something?"

"What?"

I reach into her pocket and take her hand. It's warm as the bonfire we just left, and her fingers wrap around mine just like I remember.

"A surprise," I say, and steer toward the shadow behind the brewery, a spot where the lights from the parking lot don't reach.

The surprise is that when we reach the dark I turn, pull her in, push her up against the wall. The surprise is that she's already pulling me toward her as I do, head back, lips slightly parted.

The surprise is that when I unzip her jacket, her nipples are already hard.

"This the goodnight you were looking for?"

"Something like it."

I push myself against her, already rock-hard. She makes a noise. I do it again.

"Good, I was afraid I might misinterpret," I say. "Usually when you summon me, you're a little more direct."

"Silas was there," she says, releasing the zipper on my jacket, her hands sliding over my shirt. "Half your family was ten feet away, I couldn't just walk up and say *hey Seth, wanna fuck.*"

I grab one leg, hike it over my hip. She gasps, one hand clenching my shirt, cool knuckles against my warm skin.

"You could say it now," I tell her, stroking my thumb along the gusset of her jeans.

"Hey Seth," she whispers, her lips so close they're brushing mine. "Wanna fuck?"

At last, I crush my mouth against hers.

· · * * ★ *★* ★ * * · ·

SOMEHOW, we make it to her car with our clothes on. She drives, and I don't ask where we're going. I just watch her, face lit by the dashboard lights. Lips dark, skin pale, chest still heaving.

She turns off the main road onto a gravel one that disappears into the forest, turns right. Before she shuts the headlights off I see the NO TRESPASSING sign, and then it's dark as a tomb and I pull her onto me.

The first time is always rough, haphazard, frantic. We fuck like we're time bombs. Usually it's on the floor, sometimes a table. This time we spill into the back seat of her car, half-shedding our clothes as we go like we're in high school again.

The only thing she says is *are you still good?* And I answer *as long as you are* and then I'm inside her, up against the back seat, and she's bracing herself with one leg against the driver's seat, the Jesus handle in one hand, her shirt and bra shoved up over her breasts as I wrap a seat belt around my fist and use it for leverage.

It doesn't take long. The first round never does. When we both finish we're a tangle of limbs and clothing and car parts, and I rest my forehead against hers and for a few moments, the world stops spinning and we float.

Then I clear my throat and ask if she keeps napkins in her car.

· · · · ★ ★ ★ ★ · · · · ·

DELILAH IS STAYING IN HER PARENTS' guest house, so I offer to take her back to my place. There's no point pretending that we're done, so I don't.

Instead, she drives us to the Hillside Motor Hotel, right outside the national forest. She doesn't say why she doesn't want to go to my place, and I don't bother asking. I'd rather fuck again than fight.

We take the second round slower, though not by much. Being with Delilah is otherworldly, elating and terrifying, addictive. I feel like some other version of myself, one unweighted by the outside world, pure and primal and on a plane beyond this one. I feel like the wrong parts of me are gone and whatever's left is what's right.

We're still in bed when the sun comes up, pink rays nudging their way through the closed curtains. She half on top of me, fingers pushed through my chest hair, big toe wiggling slowly against my leg.

I know that like a drug, this is the high and the comedown will be here soon. I know it, but I tell myself that this time will be different. This time, when we're done with each other, we'll part on mutually friendly terms and go back to our lives.

I've told myself that for years now.

Finally, we fall asleep.

EIGHT

DELILAH

STILL TWO YEARS AND THREE MONTHS AGO

I toss the phone book onto the bed, then flop myself down in front of it. It's late afternoon on Saturday, the sun trickling in between the curtains.

"Does anyone deliver out here?" I ask. "I think most places have a five-mile delivery radius, or something like that."

On the other side of the bed, a very naked Seth shifts slightly, reaching one arm over his head.

"I don't even know where we are," he says. "Are we five miles from town?"

"We're off Route 238."

"That's a long route."

"Just past where it crosses Bitterroot Creek."

"That's the opposite direction from town," he says, like he's mildly surprised.

I flip a page, pretty sure he's not expecting an answer.

"I didn't think this part through when I drove here last night," I admit. I don't make eye contact. Instead, I read an

71

ad for the Golden Dynasty Pan-Asian Buffet like I've never heard of mediocre Chinese food before.

"But you were thinking enough that you didn't want to go to my house?" he says, still lazy. I can feel his glance, though, and I read about the buffet's hours for the fifth time.

"I like this place," I say. "It's cute. It's rustic. No neighbors."

"My townhouse has very thick walls and a pantry," he says.

"Of course it does."

The instant it's out of my mouth, I squeeze my eyes shut and wish I hadn't said it. I know better than to passive-aggressively snipe at someone, but old habits die hard.

"You say that like I built the place myself," he says, pushing himself to sitting.

"I say that like it was on your list of must-haves in a home," I tell him, and finally meet his eyes.

We hold the gaze for a long, long moment, and I'm the first one to look away. I manage not to say anything else bitchy, like *I'm sure your neighbors are glad to be spared the sound of you humping an endless parade of women.*

Even so, now is when I start to hate myself. Now is when I start to come down from the high, when I start to remember the reasons that we don't do this all the time.

The reasons have names, like Mindy and Danica and Laura and probably dozens more. The last time I saw him I was dumb enough to ask how many and who, and Seth told me in that brutally honest way he has.

And then I fucked him one more time, even after he told me, as if I thought a few more orgasms would make me forget that I knew. They didn't.

I take a deep breath, look at the phone book again. It's

been years since I used one of these, but both of our phones are dead since we didn't exactly plan this outing.

"I can go grab takeout," I offer. "What are you in the mood for?"

.   "There's a Thai place in town now," he says. "And I'll always eat pasta. Or…"

I look at him, raise one eyebrow.

"The Woodhouse has happy hour from five to seven."

"You can't get booze with takeout," I point out.

"We could go," he says, resting his hands on his head.

Duh. The combination of more sex than sleep and no food since yesterday means I'm not quite on top of my game, and for a long moment, I just watch him, two fingers tapping the open phone book.

I don't want to. Sprucevale is a tiny town, and even on a Sunday night, I'm practically guaranteed to run into someone I know, or worse, someone Vera knows. By this time tomorrow, everyone will know that Delilah Radcliffe and Seth Loveless were having drinks together, and from there it's half a step to bitchy comments about how little self-respect I have if I'm riding the town bicycle.

I know I'm far from the only notch on his bedpost. Doesn't mean I like it.

"Why leave?" I say, and manage to smile at him. "It's pretty nice here."

"It's nice there, too," he says.

"I've only got what I was wearing yesterday."

"No one will know."

I sit up, lean on one hand, give him what I hope is a coquettish, flirty look.

"What's wrong with staying in and eating takeout in bed?" I ask, tilting my head to one side.

It doesn't work. I didn't really think it would.

"What's wrong with appearing together in public?" he asks, quietly.

I don't answer, because he knows the answer. We just look at each other for a long time, and I think: *we don't usually get to the fight this fast.*

"Right, someone might see us," he says, finally looking away. "People might *talk.*"

"Forgive me for wanting to preserve my remaining shreds of dignity," I say, sarcastically, as I stand from the bed.

"Dignity? Is that what you wanted when you fucked me in your car last night?"

I snort.

"I just wanted an itch scratched," I say, starting to pace at the foot of the bed. "Not a referendum on why I shouldn't mind being the hundredth name on your list."

"A hundred, huh? That your guess?"

Suddenly, I feel nauseous.

It's because you haven't eaten, I tell myself.

"I'm not guessing," I say. "I don't care who you fuck or how many of them there are—"

"You're not *that* far off."

The nausea rises, and I swallow it down.

"I'm not asking and I don't care," I say.

Now Seth stands from the bed, walks to the window. He glances behind the curtain, casually, like he's checking the parking lot.

"You sure seem like you don't care."

"You're free to fuck whoever you want. I'm not getting in the way. God forbid."

Seth laughs. It's a single, hard bark of a laugh, just one *ha!* That makes goose bumps rise on my skin.

Then he's across the small room, standing in front of

me, looking down. He's got my chin in his hand, tilting my head up.

"You got *married*," he growls.

"Don't touch me."

His hand drops.

"You stood on that sidewalk outside the Whiskey Barrel and said you'd never loved me to begin with, and now you're angry that I fucked someone else?" he says, venomous and angry. "As if you didn't fuck someone else and more?"

His blue eyes are cold, hard, flat, his dark hair wild, stuck to his forehead on one side.

The guilt stabs me like it always does, and I think: *at least he stabs me from the front, while he's looking into my eyes. At least I know when I'm being stabbed.*

"And you couldn't even do that right," he muses.

I'm vibrating with anger, its hot spikes pricking at my throat, behind my eyes. I hold my breath so it doesn't spill over into furious tears.

I hate that I cry when I'm angry.

"Maybe I should have fucked our entire graduating class and their cousins instead," I say. Seth blurs in my vision. "I've always wanted my name to be another word for *slut*."

"You like it well enough to keep me in your phone, just in case you get lonely."

I snort, trying to sound derisive. A tear spills out of one eye, and I turn away from Seth, march to where my pants are spread on the floor.

"You haven't turned me down yet," I bite back. "Every time I think, surely he'll have found someone new by now, but you never have."

He strides to the other bed in the room, pulls his shirt from where it landed on a pillow.

"That door swings both ways."

I button my jeans, biting my lip so hard I draw blood, but it doesn't work. Another tear tracks down my cheek.

"Does it feel pathetic to wait around for someone who doesn't love you back?" I say, my voice shaking.

"Love me back?" he says, incredulous, his shirt on, his jeans in one hand.

I feel like an idiot.

"I haven't loved you in *years*," he goes on. "These days you're just a good fuck."

I find my shirt and grab it, bra nowhere to be seen. I don't care.

"Good," I snarl, pulling it over my head. "I never loved you at all."

I grab my jacket from the back of the chair where it's lying, slam the door open, and walk out. The moment my bare feet hit cold concrete, I realize I forgot my shoes, but I can't go back. Fuck going back.

Behind me, Seth is laughing. It's an ugly, harsh laugh.

"Call me when your next boyfriend figures out who you really are," he shouts. "I'm happy to fuck you without liking you."

The door shuts. I stomp off the concrete walkway and onto the pavement of the parking lot, still cold beneath my feet, teeth gritted together, breathing ragged, eyes leaking.

At least I make it to my car before I start sobbing, the steering wheel in a two-hand death grip, nose running, mouth open. I think I'm drooling, and I don't give a shit.

I don't know how long I stay there. Five minutes? Five hours? I feel like an empty sack, crumpled on the floor. Like a hollow tree that's finally fallen over. I'm just praying that Seth can't see me through the window.

Finally, I get a hold of myself. Sort of. I get enough of a hold to sit up straight, buckle my seatbelt, fix the rearview mirror. I'm still crying, but not so much I can't see through the windshield, so I start the car and turn the heat up and peel out of the motel parking lot with no shoes, bra, or underwear on.

And I drive and drive, and over and over again I think: *why do I do this to myself?*

NINE

SETH

When the door shuts behind her, it feels like the air shakes, like the whole room rattles, but it's just me, so angry I'm practically vibrating.

She came to *me*. She's the one who showed up at my event, at my brewery. She's the one who walked over to me last night, batting her eyelashes and practically rubbing herself on me like a cat in heat. She's the one who pulled off the road into an abandoned driveway so we could fuck in the back seat of her car.

All that and she won't have drinks with me, as if I owed her my celibacy while she married someone else. Fuck that. Fuck her.

Most of all, fuck me for letting this happen in the first place.

I take a shower after she leaves, because despite everything I'm tempted to look out the window and see if she's still there. I'm tempted to go after her, because I thought of ten more things to say that will hurt her and I want her to hear all of them.

It's not until I'm out of the shower and leaving the motel room that I remember my car isn't there. It's still at the brewery, where my horny idiot self left it last night.

"Fuck," I whisper to myself.

It feels good.

"FUCK!" I whisper louder.

Then I take a deep breath, suck in the fall air. It smells like rain and leaves and the hard promise of darkness and cold coming all too soon.

There are people I could call for a ride. Even though my phone's dead, I've got numbers memorized and the room has a landline.

I walk back to the brewery instead. I don't know how many miles it is, but it's full dark by the time I get there, half moon, plenty of stars. Almost by accident, I find the scorpion's tail as I walk along the highway, peeking above the black forest.

"Fuck you," I mutter, but my mouth is dry, my feet hurt, and I'm tired. Now, it just feels hollow.

* * * * * ★ ★ ★ * * * * *

"C'MON," I mutter, leaning forward. "Come on, just — don't fucking—"

Red splashes across my screen and I sigh, dropping my head. This is the fifth time in a row I've tried this stupid mission, and I swear, it's gonna be the death of me.

"Okay," I say. I crack the knuckles on my left hand, switch the controller, crack the ones on my right. "Just the stairwell and you're done."

I blink hard, because my eyes feel like sandpaper, and then go talk to the security guard again.

Just as I've hit *Accept Mission*, there's a knock.

At first, I think it's in the game, because after all I'm in some mafia-controlled apartment building, but then I hit *pause* and hear it again.

Then I start worrying, because it's nine-thirty at night. If it were a good knock I'd have gotten a text first, so as I shout "Coming!" and walk to my front door, I'm inventing scenarios.

My mom got into a car accident. One of my brothers got into a car accident, or something happened with Rusty, or Levi's fallen off a cliff, or —

I glance through the peephole first.

It's Delilah. Standing on my front steps, something in her hands, as she looks off to the side, like she's watching something in the dark.

I almost don't open the door. It's been three weeks since she drove off and left me at the motel, and I don't ever want to see her again. Even if she showed up on her knees in nothing but a sexy French Maid outfit, I wouldn't want to see her again.

"Seth?" she calls through the door.

Maybe with the French Maid outfit I would.

"Can we talk?" she asks.

I take a deep breath and open the door.

It's a fruit basket. The thing she's holding is a fruit basket with a pineapple on one side, a bunch of bananas on the other, and some exotic-looking stuff in the middle.

"Hi," she says.

"What the fuck is that?"

"It's a fruit basket."

I don't say anything, just watch her until she speaks again.

"Is now a good time?"

I fold my arms over my chest.

"Are you asking if I'm alone?"

"No, I'm asking if it's a good time."

In that moment, I wish I weren't alone. I wish I'd found some random hookup and brought her home just so I could see Delilah's face when she walked out. I wish I'd brought home two.

"It's fine," I tell her.

She looks down at the basket, then up at me.

"Can I..." she gestures at the door.

I lean against the frame. No, she can't come in. She can stand there.

"What do you want?" I ask.

"I came to offer terms," she says, her voice soft, perfectly steady. Like she's practiced this.

"Terms for what?"

"Our continued existence in the same town."

If I were still angry, I'd tell her that I don't want terms, that I've always lived here and she can fuck off. If I were angry, I'd laugh in her face and shut the door.

I don't.

"Go on," I tell her.

"I think it would be best if we pretend to barely know each other," she says, unblinking. "We're going to run into each other, obviously, and I think we should have a plan."

"Which is?"

"If you can be polite to me, I can be polite to you."

It sounds perfectly reasonable. Perfectly normal.

All the same, her words feel like tree roots, growing into my cracks, slowly pulling me apart. Delilah takes a deep breath.

"No purposeful contact," she goes on, her gaze hard on mine. "No calling, no texting, no going to your brewery or coming by my shop."

"You want us to be strangers."

"I want us to be acquaintances."

I take a long moment just to study her, the way she looks right now under my porch light. She's holding the fruit basket, her leather jacket open over a brightly colored shirt, something just barely peeking up through the neck. It looks like tape. Maybe gauze.

She sees me looking and frowns down.

"Oh, oops," she says, and pulls the neck of her shirt up a fraction of an inch.

"What happened?"

"It's nothing."

Another pause. I wonder what's on her chest. I wonder what it is I want from her, exactly. I wonder why the fuck she brought a fruit basket.

"Seriously, it's nothing," she says again.

"Okay."

"Okay…?"

"Okay, we're acquaintances."

She holds my eyes for another pause in this conversation full of them, then takes a deep breath and looks down.

"Thanks," she says, then holds out the fruit basket. "Um, here. I brought you this."

I don't want it, but I take it.

"It's fruit," she says. "You know, never go to someone's house empty-handed and all. Impolite."

I don't tell her that it's impolite to fuck someone and then tell them they're unfit to stand next to you in public. I don't tell her that it's impolite to strand someone at a motel in the middle of nowhere.

"Thanks," I say simply, to the point. "Anything else?"

"That was it," she says, jamming her hands into her jacket pockets. "I guess I'll see you around."

"I guess," I say.

Then I turn away and shut the door while she's still on

my porch, and it feels *good*. I put the fruit basket on my kitchen counter, collapse back onto the sofa, and start killing rival mafia members before I can start thinking.

The fruit basket stays there, slowly rotting, until one of my brothers throws the whole thing away weeks later.

TEN

DELILAH

PRESENT DAY

I glance along the hallway at Monica, Ava's wedding coordinator, but she seems busy, so I crouch and hold the end of my bouquet to the floor as requested.

"There's a big tree," says a two-inch-long blue plastic plesiosaur.

"I think we should eat it," answers a green stegosaurus.

"Please don't eat me," I say, wiggling the bouquet slightly. "I've got a wedding to attend!"

Bree, my three-year-old niece, starts giggling. The dinosaurs advance.

"Nooooooo," my bouquet says. "Not my flowers!"

The giggling intensifies, and she looks up at me, pure mischief in her blue eyes.

"CHOMP!" she giggle-shouts, as the plesiosaur somehow launches itself, face-first, into a lily. "Chomp chomp chomp!"

"Auuugh!"

"CHOMP."

That's the stegosaurus getting in on the action.

"My beautiful tree!" I bemoan.

"This one's tasty," one of the dinosaurs advises, though I can't tell which one. "Mmmm."

"Flower girl?" Monica calls, and my head snaps up. "We need the flower girl, please."

"That's you, kiddo," I tell Bree.

"Chomp chomp," she says, looking back at the bouquet.

"Places, please," Monica says, striding toward us. She's holding a clipboard *and* she has a Bluetooth receiver in her ear, so you know she means business.

"C'mon, you gotta throw flowers so your aunt Ava can get married," I coax. "She can't walk down a naked aisle, can she?"

Bree giggles again.

"The aisle is naked?" she asks, and I immediately regret my choice of words.

"Only if you don't put flowers on it," I say, and hold out one hand. "Here, I'll keep the dinos safe, okay?"

"Bree, honey," her mom Winona calls.

She deposits the plastic figurines into my hand, looking very serious. I nod, and then she's off, running full-toddler-tilt to the front of the line.

"No running," I hear her mom say as I stand, smooth my skirt, and put the dinos into my pocket.

Pockets: it's the one saving grace this dress has. Not that there's anything really wrong with this bridesmaid dress, but there's nothing really right with it either. It's long and dusky pink and lacy and isn't at all what I'd pick out for myself.

Besides the pockets. Everyone loves pockets.

"All right, everyone," Monica calls, holding up one hand to get our attention.

She's standing in front of a massive double door, facing the neatly-lined-up wedding parties

"Are we ready to release the groomsmen?" she asks. "Let me know when it's time to give the signal for the signal."

All eyes turn to Thad, and for a quick second, he looks terrified.

Then he remembers to smile and overcompensates by smiling too much and giving the crowd a big double thumbs-up.

"Ready and willing!" he says, and there's polite laughter.

No one asks Ava, because she's in the bridal suite. She doesn't want Thad to see her until she's walking down the aisle, and even though I've told myself over and over again that she wants it that way for tradition's sake, I can't shake the quiet suspicion that it's also so she can't back out.

I look down at my bouquet of dusky pink roses and white lilies, at my bare fingers, and ignore my unease.

Thad isn't Nolan. Ava isn't me. My worries have nothing to do with them and everything to do with me.

The beginning strains of *Canon in D* float through the doors. I hold my breath, steeling myself for my least favorite part of every wedding.

The doors swing open.

Fuck me sideways, that's a lot of people and they're *all* looking in my direction.

I take the arm of Thad's older brother Chad, my companion. I stand up straight. I hold my bouquet properly at about boob height, as instructed, and when it's our turn, I fuckin' *promenade*.

Nothing exciting happens. Thank *God*.

I smile nicely, don't trip, find my spot in the front, and I'm done. That's my entire job. This is almost certainly the last time I'll be walking down an aisle at a wedding of this magnitude, and I'm not even a little bit sad about it.

After that, it's a wedding. It's lovely and meaningful and heartfelt, but I also admit that I spend much of the ceremony studying the ceiling, wondering if the decorations are original to the manor or re-created.

They exchange vows and rings. Thad kisses the bride, and everyone cheers, including me. We all walk back down the aisle and just as I'm thinking about how glad I am that I'll never have to do this again, I swear to God I see Seth.

Or, at least, I see a brief glance of a quarter of his head. Really, it's just some dark hair at approximately the right height, but the part of my brain that's always on the lookout starts shouting and poking me, but he's already disappeared behind the crowd.

I snap my head forward and complete my journey.

Not Seth, I tell myself. *Other people have hair, and also, someone would have told you if he were coming.*

Right? Right.

Before I can get any further down that particular mental path, a pink streak clomps up to me.

"Delilah!" Bree gasps, and I bend down to her height. "I saved you these!"

She throws a fistful of rose petals into my face and laughs.

· · * * ★ ★ ★ * * · ·

"I need the bridesmaid on the end to step in a little," the photographer calls, waving her hand in the universal *scootch* motion.

Behind her, I can see the wedding guests through the big arched windows, mingling and drinking and eating finger foods. They look warm.

Did they end up getting the mini crab cakes? I wonder, watching a woman in a long blue dress take something from a tray. *Those were good, but I know Ava was worried about*
—

"Delilah," Vera says from her place next to the photographer, and I jolt to attention.

Right. I'm the bridesmaid on the end.

I scooch, careful not to put a foot wrong on the cobblestones, and Chad scootches with me. We resume our delicate-hold-from-behind-without-really-touching prom-esque pose. The camera clicks.

"Smile!" Vera calls, and I resist the urge to shout *I'm already smiling, dammit.*

More pictures. More adjusting. I'm freezing my tits off out here despite my faux-fur capelet, and I silently hope that one of the waiters with a tray of champagne will take mercy on us and swing by the photoshoot. I only managed to grab one glass before being herded outside, and it was not enough.

I elbow Chad by accident during another adjustment and apologize; he's very gracious about it. I smile and glance through the windows again, because that definitely wasn't Seth, right? I'm just being a little crazy, right?

"*Delilah,*" Vera says. It's clearly not the first time she's said my name.

"Sorry," I say, and glance around to find the groomsmen gone.

"Bridesmaid picture!" Ava chirps. "Oh, I want to do one of those ones where everyone is jumping in the air!"

Please, God, no. I'm wearing heels and a strapless bra. This is not a jumping outfit.

"Let me get the formal one first," the photographer says. "Good, good—"

"Those jumping photos never turn out," I say, still smiling.

"I've seen them," Ava says.

"Those are models," I point out, adjusting my bouquet slightly. "They're jumping photo professionals. It never works with regular people."

"Now look at the bride," the photographer instructs.

Ava smiles. She's radiant, filled with pure light and joy.

I wonder what it feels like.

"Now act natural!" the photographer calls, and I have no idea how to do *that* so I just move around some.

"Delilah, it'll be fine," Ava tells me, laughing. "I believe in you."

"Jumping photo is next," calls the photog. "The key to getting a good one is for everyone to jump at the *exact* same time, and remember to smile! We'll need a few takes, so get ready."

The things I do for my little sister.

The photographer counts down from three. I jump — in heels, on cobblestones, wearing a strapless bra contraption — and I don't die.

Then we do it again. And again. I remember to smile. We're advised to really throw our hands up and kick our feet out, and by God, I *try*. I'm pretty sure that I look completely insane and probably like a baby camel on a trampoline, but I try.

It takes two jumps for my undergarments to start shifting. I try to discreetly adjust them under my cape, but it doesn't work.

After three jumps, I'm in trouble.

After four, I feel the unmistakable sensation of lace on my left nipple. That can mean only one thing: my nipple has been freed.

After six, my right nipple joins its partner. Thank God for this cape.

After eight jumps, we get to stop. The other bridesmaids are all laughing with each other, still looking perfectly put together, as though they frequently do jumping jacks in strapless bras and simply don't see the issue.

"All right, can I have the groomsmen over here?" the photographer calls, and I'm free.

Just like my nipples.

I hold my cape tightly closed and make my way to the edge of the group, subtly trying to pull everything back into place, but it's not really working. I swear this bra has somehow turned itself inside out and upside down.

After a moment, my sister Winona sidles over to me.

"You need some help?" she asks.

I make a face and wriggle. She laughs.

"My boobs made a run for it," I mutter. "I have time to go to the bathroom, right?"

Winona grimaces and glances over at the photographer. Sunset is minutes away, and according to the Official Photography Plan, we're doing the big group shots then.

"Here," she says, and nods at the side of the manor house. "Come on. Callum just peed in a bush over here, you'll be hidden."

I let her guide me and don't point out that Callum is a toddler, I'm a full-grown woman, and we have different expectations of privacy.

Pinehall Manor was built in the 1890s as a mountain getaway for some Yankee industrialist with a serious hard-on for the antebellum South. It's huge and white, brick walkways extending from every side like it's the center of a compass rose, a wraparound porch on each of two stories.

Winona leads me onto the lower porch, around a

corner, our shoes louder on the wooden surface than on the brick. I glance into one gauzily-curtained window, but the guests' cocktail hour is on the second floor, not the first, so there's no one inside.

"Okay," she says. "Lift up your cape and use it like you're at the beach changing into your swimsuit. I'm gonna undo you back here."

There's a brief rush of cold air as she lifts the back of my cape and gets to work. For reasons I'll never understand, this dress has a long series of tiny buttons that start at the waist and go all the way to the nape of the neck.

To be honest, there's a lot about this dress I wouldn't have chosen. It's pink, which I don't love. It's got a plunging, low-backed strapless bodice with a long-sleeved lace overlay, which made finding a bra feel like the quest for the Holy Grail.

When I finally found The One, I was *this* close to just duct-taping my boobs and hoping it worked. Now, I kind of wish I had.

The skirt is long, flowy, A-line, and has pockets, making it the best part of my entire outfit. Well, the skirt and the cape, which does make me feel a little like a Russian empress.

"There," Winona says, and I start wriggling out of the top of the dress, cape still over my shoulders. "You fix yourself, I'll stand guard."

"Thanks," I say, already heaving at the bra, which isn't just any bra. It's more like a bra-and-corset combo that goes down to my sternum in the front but, through some miracle of engineering, still holds both boobs in place while also fastening low enough in the back that it's invisible.

There's lots of padding, elastic, and wires, and God knows what else. Truly, a wonder garment.

I straighten, adjust, and wriggle. I glance around and

then bend over, tugging at the thing with both hands, letting gravity do some of the work. When I'm upright again, Winona grabs the back and together we tug while I hop, both of us grunting slightly.

At last, it's back in place. I shimmy slightly, double-checking my boob security, but all seems well as long as I don't have to leap in the air again.

"Ready," I say, pulling the cape up.

"Gotcha," she says, and begins buttoning.

After a few, she sighs.

"Can you take the cape off for a sec?" she asks. "These buttons are an absolute bear to do up and I can't see. I don't know *why* Ava picked this dress."

"She liked the delicate details," I offer, and Winona just sighs.

"When she and Thad have kids, I'm taking my revenge by giving her really cute baby pajamas with a thousand snaps," she says. "See how she likes—"

Behind us, a child *wails*.

"Shit," Winona hisses, and before I can even turn around, she's gone, my dress still half-buttoned.

"Winona?" I call, twisting around.

The wail turns into a screech. Another wail joins the first, and I grimace. I know that it's probably nothing worse than a sibling-induced scrape, but it's one hell of a sound.

I wait for a few minutes. The wail fades into a cry, then disappears. I wait another minute or so, watching the shadows get even longer, willing Winona to come back and finish me.

She doesn't. It's like Winona never even existed.

In the meantime, I gently toss my cape into a bush and try to button myself.

It doesn't work. It doesn't even *almost* work.

"Winona!" I shout.

Nothing.

"*Winona!*"

I sneak to the corner of the building and peek around, hoping that maybe I can flag down some female relative.

I see no one. Not a single soul. I don't even know how that's possible, given that there are at least four hundred people around right now, but none of them are here.

Shit.

"WINONA!" I holler. "HELP!"

Silence drifts back to me, as if the rest of humanity has disappeared from the earth.

Now I have a dilemma. Do I stay here and wait? Do I try to dislocate a shoulder in the hopes that I can button this dress myself?

Do I walk back, dress agape, to the group that contains all three of my brothers-in-law and also my dad?

Even though I know it's just my back and a bra clasp, I really don't like that last option. The thought of Winona's or Olivia's husbands seeing even part of my undergarments just... feels wrong.

Okay, so that's the last resort, I decide, and walk back to the side of the building. I take a deep breath. I stretch a little, then square my shoulders.

You got this, I tell myself. *Finally put all that yoga to use.*

It's slow. It's unnatural. Twisting my shoulders that way kind of hurts, but at last, I get one.

Then I get two.

I've got the third tiny, silky, slippery button almost through the fabric loop when there are footsteps behind me.

"Oh, thank God," I say. "I think I tore my rotator cuff on this last one."

Winona doesn't say anything, which is weird, but whatever. I let the button go and hold the dress together at the top, bending my head forward.

"I don't know why they didn't also put a zipper on this thing," I say, still bitching about the dress. "It'd still have the *delicate details*, but we wouldn't need a lady's maid to get decent."

More silence, and this time my skin prickles because I'm starting to suspect it's not Winona behind me but from my position, the only thing I've got a view of is my armpit.

"Winona," I say, turning my head further as they tug on the next button.

I still can't see, so I straighten, start to lower my arms.

"Are you—"

"Hold *still*," says Seth. "These things are impossible."

ELEVEN

SETH

Delilah whirls, jerking away from me so fast that a button comes off between my fingers.

"Seth?" she blurts.

Then: "What the *fuck*?"

"I heard a damsel in distress, so I came running," I say, as if it's something I do all the time.

"From *where*?" she asks. "You're… hold on."

She's not angry. Not yet. Right now she's just astonished, lips parted, brow furrowed as she looks me over, processes the fact that I'm standing here wearing my best suit.

Behind me, the sun is settling in the sky, and the fading rays catch her in their light. Delilah glows golden, even as she closes her eyes and shakes her head like I'm an etch-a-sketch she can erase.

"Specifically, I heard you in distress," I offer, closing my fist around the tiny pink button.

"As if you wouldn't answer any damsel's distress call," she says without moving, eyes still closed.

I squeeze the button a little tighter, breathe, bite back the first three answers that spring to my lips.

"I sure didn't come out here to fight about it," I say, after a moment.

"Right," she breathes, scrunches her face, shakes her head again. Opens her eyes. Clears her throat. "Sorry, that was unfair."

"Thanks," I say, and just like that, the fight we nearly had drifts away in the breeze like so much dust.

Then we look at each other. Just look. It's a strange, unanchored moment, and I can't help but smile.

"Did we just display surprising maturity?" I ask.

She laughs.

"Surprising for you, maybe," she says.

"Excuse me, I'm a paragon of maturity."

"I'm surprised you're not blowing raspberries and calling me a stupidface," she teases.

I grin, then stick my tongue out. She laughs again, and I feel like I'm jumping on marshmallows.

Don't tell me it could have been this easy all along.

"I'd like to reiterate my question, though," she says, leaning over and grabbing her fur cape off a bench. "Which was: what the fuck?"

"I told you, I heard—"

"I know you know what I mean, Seth."

I do, because I'm not an idiot, but I don't want to tell her. This is nice. This is *fun*. This is just the two of us, unweighted for once, and telling her that I went behind her back and made a deal with Vera will surely ruin that.

"I'm sure I don't," I tell her.

Delilah narrows her eyes, then glances around. Over her shoulder. Through the window to the still-empty first floor, her hair catching fire in the low sun as she takes a step toward me.

"Are you crashing?" she asks, voice low, one eyebrow raised.

"Crashing?" I echo, as if astonished. Solemnly, I put a hand over my heart. "I would never."

"I bet you would."

"I might crash another wedding, but I'm not brave enough to crash a Vera Radcliffe affair," I tell her. "That's God's honest truth, and you know it."

Delilah just laughs, hands buried in the cape as her eyes crinkle at the corners, shoulders shaking.

"Okay, I believe that," she says. "There was some issue with the beer and Vera made you wear a suit to come fix it?"

"Nope," I say. "I was invited."

"No, you weren't."

"Hand to God."

"Seth, I saw the guest list yesterday and you weren't on it," she says, as if she's catching a child out in a lie.

"You must've missed my name."

"I don't think so."

"There are five hundred people here," I point out. "Easy to gloss over a single entry in a list."

"There are three hundred and sixty-something people here, and if you were supposed to be one of them, I'd know," she says, simply.

It's an admission, and I feel it down deep like a string tugging on my spine, tied into a notch she carved long ago. I grab it, hold on.

"Someone invited me at the last minute," I say, and at least it's the truth.

Delilah looks down, unfurls the cape in her hands, spins it around herself, settles it over her shoulders, all without looking at me.

"Does this *someone* know you're out here, rescuing damsels in distress?" she asks, fastening the clasp.

She thinks I'm on a date. Her voice is light but brittle, like a glass bubble that might explode into shards at any moment.

"What damsel?" I ask.

"Your wording, not mine," she points out, smoothing her cape, still not looking at me.

"I'm thinking of walking it back."

"Even though I'm so *very* helpless in heels and a corset?" she says, that sharpness still in her voice. "I can't even button my own clothing, for fuck's sake."

Corset?

I'm intensely, fervently glad for the cape that mostly covers her.

"There's no way you're a damsel with a mouth like that," I say.

"You should hear me in my natural state," she says.

"Come to think of it, I have," I say, unable to help myself. "And you can be *incredibly* unladylike."

It works, pink flaring up her cheeks from below. She's always blushed this easily, this obviously, and I've always liked making it happen.

All it takes is a quick whisper. A suggestion. Sometimes, a look.

"You should probably go back to your date, I'm sure she's looking for you," she says, pretending I haven't made her blush. "I mean, if you actually have one and you didn't just sneak in for the free snacks and whiskey."

There it is again. My date. Delilah is *jealous*, and God help me, I don't hate it.

I put one hand to my chest, as if hurt.

"What kind of lowlife do you take me for?"

"Should I really answer that?" she asks, but there's a hint of a smile underneath the words.

"Maybe after more free whiskey," I say, then pause. "I can finish buttoning your dress, if you want."

"Are you going to rip them all off?"

Don't tempt me with a good time.

"That one was your fault," I point out. "I'd almost gotten it and you pulled away."

"You sneaked up on me in a state of undress," she says, and now she's keeping her voice low, like she doesn't want to be overheard.

"I've seen it before," I say, matching her tone.

It could be my imagination, but I think I'm rewarded with the faint glow of pink.

"That doesn't mean now is appropriate."

"I didn't know you'd be in disarray," I tell her, my voice lower still. "Imagine my surprise. I never even asked why you were getting dressed on the veranda."

"I'll tell you after some more free champagne," she says, laughing.

I've taken another step closer, or she has, and now there's isn't much distance between us at all, the sun still lowering, the breeze drifting around the corner of the house.

In a flare, I feel the spots where she touched me last night. Neck and chest, one finger, pulsing with every beat of my heart.

If she gets closer, I might do something I promised I wouldn't.

"What did Winona *do* to you?" I ask, now close to a whisper.

"It wasn't her," she says, looking at me through impossibly long, thick eyelashes. "She's also a victim, she just fared better than I did."

"If you need revenge exacted, just say the word," I murmur.

She just laughs.

"It was Ava," she says, and I raise one eyebrow. "And I told you, more champagne first."

"If you insist."

Delilah undoes the clasp on her fur cape, tosses it back onto the bench, turns her back to me.

"Thanks," she says. "In return, I promise not to tell your date about this."

Her back looks exactly like I remember, only half-covered with delicate pink lace. The moon, the sun, an eight-pointed star, descending her spine. The lines are thick, exacting, the colors bold, like a stained-glass window rendered by Sailor Jerry. From one shoulder, two red tentacles of a squid curl in; from the other, two bold-but-delicate leafy vines.

I don't touch her. The backs of my finger brush against her skin, ever so lightly, as I carefully do up the rest of her buttons, but I don't *touch* her even though I want to.

She says nothing, and I match it. I think of a hundred things I could say, but don't let any cross my lips.

"There you go," I finally say, stepping back. "Sorry about the broken one."

"It's all right," she says, one hand coming over her shoulder, fingers drifting over the buttons, checking them. "Nobody looks at bridesmaids anyway."

I clench my jaw so I don't tell her how incredibly, wildly untrue that is. I don't tell her that I spent the whole wedding ceremony staring at her without hearing a word anyone said, or that the only reason I heard her shouting for her sister is because I was looking for her.

I couldn't tell you what the bride's wearing. I think it's white. But I know the lace of Delilah's sleeves just barely covers the hull of a sailing ship, that her skirt ends half an inch from the floor, that her pearl earrings swing and bump her neck when she turns her head.

This was a mistake, I think, and then I hear someone step onto the porch.

"Sorry!" calls Winona. "Callum got a hold of one of Bree's—"

Delilah's younger sister stops so short that her dress flows in front of her, carried by the momentum.

"Seth?" she says, clearly baffled. I guess Vera's kept this close to the vest.

"Good to see you again, Winona," I say, because I know my manners.

"Likewise," she says. "I'm sorry, I just came back to help Delilah, I'm not…"

"He heard me shouting and appeared," Delilah says, grabbing her cape again.

"Ah," says Winona, who clearly has more questions.

"Picture time?" asks Delilah, whirling the cape around herself again, then clasping it.

"Yup," says Winona. "Right now Ava and Thad are just giggling and making out for the camera but surely that will get old soon and they'll want you for group shots."

"Can't believe I missed that," Delilah deadpans, walking back down the veranda, toward her sister.

"It's been a joy," Winona says dryly.

"Thanks for the hand, Seth," Delilah says, just before she disappears around a corner. "I can't wait to meet your date!"

"Any time," I call, and then she's gone, their bright voices quickly fading.

I watch the spot where she disappears. The late afternoon chill is sinking through my suit jacket, but I've already had a whiskey, so it's easy enough to ignore.

I know I should tell her that she's the date she keeps bringing up. I know it, but there's a petty, wounded part of me that's enjoying her jealousy. Every time she says *your date* another black bloom unfurls, and it doesn't matter that my satisfaction is poisonous. It's still a flower.

I think again of the tattoos on her back, of how I've licked the sweat off them before, slid my hand along them on the way to bury my fingers in her hair —

I shake myself out of it. I walk for the doors, pull one open, and head straight for the bar.

Tonight calls for more whiskey.

TWELVE

DELILAH

As soon as we turn the corner of the building, Winona glances over her shoulder.

"Is he friends with Thad?" she asks.

My spine tingles all the way to my hairline, and I think I can feel every individual button beneath the cape including the spot where one's broken.

Why is he here? Is he with someone? Why wasn't he on the guest list? How come no one —

"Delilah?" she asks, concern edging into her voice.

I quickly rewind the last ten seconds.

"I don't know," I finally answer. "He said he was invited last minute, so maybe someone else's date canceled."

She's still looking at me, and her look is a question, but I ignore it.

"Is something up?" Winona asks after a moment.

"What? No," I say, stepping carefully on the cobblestones. "Why would something be up? Nothing's up."

"I did just find you with your ex doing up your buttons."

I don't point out that she abandoned me in the first place.

"He's not my ex, we just dated in high school," I say.

"You're sure nothing happened?" she asks. Graciously, she ignores all the problems with my last statement.

"I'm fine," I tell her. "I just didn't know he was coming. I was surprised is all, really."

I might be lying. Did something happen? Was it *something* when he brushed stray hairs off the back of my neck, or when he reminded me that he's seen me naked, or when he didn't let me pick a fight?

Was it something when he wouldn't tell me who he's here with?

I flex my hands under my cape and ignore the feeling that my organs are trading places with each other.

"Okay," Winona says, shrugging. "I was just making sure. You seemed a little off and I wanted to check in. I know today might be a little fraught for you."

She reaches under my cape and takes my arm in her hand, hugging us together as we walk.

Technically, Winona is my younger sister, but practically speaking, our roles have always been reversed. When I came to live with them after my mom died I was fifteen and she was twelve, a decade into being the eldest. I was in no shape to do anything but let her baby me. I'm obviously still older, but even now she's the one with a stable, happy marriage, two kids, a five-year plan, and an effectively managed household.

My household is managed fine, thanks, but it also consists of me, a few house plants, and a Roomba.

"I'm just hungry," I tell her.

Winona sighs.

"Amen," she mutters. "A fruit platter? Seriously? And *one* tray of champagne?"

"I'm telling Vera you complained," I tease.

"Don't you dare," my sister says.

· · · · ★ ★ ★ ★ · · · ·

MIRACULOUSLY, when I get back to the family photo area, there's a new tray of champagne sitting there, as if there really is a God and he just watched me interact with Seth Loveless. I down a glass before family photos, and then another after, just for good measure.

After photos, it's time for *our entrance.* While we were all outside, smiling and leaping and freezing and falling out of bras, the guests got herded back into the ballroom, which is now a banquet hall.

Which we have to enter. In pairs. To music. As our names are announced. I don't really understand why this is necessary or desirable, but one night last week I went down an internet rabbit hole and spent an hour watching videos of wedding parties forced to enter the reception while doing a synchronized dance.

It could be way worse, is my point.

When I walk in on Chad's arm, the lights are dimmed except for a spotlight on me as a man on a stage says *Mister Chad Middlebrook and Miss Delilah Radcliffe!* very loudly, so I couldn't see Seth even if I were trying to, which I am not. I also don't manage to spot him once we're in our places on the dance floor, again, not that I'm looking for him or that I'm particularly interested in who he's with.

That's me: uninterested in Seth, his movements, or his companion.

"And now," the announcer on stage booms. "Can everyone please welcome to the reception! For the *very first time*! Mr. and Mrs. Thad and Ava Middlebrook!"

The doors open again, and they walk in, hand in hand.

I don't think I've ever seen Ava smile bigger or look happier, and still, *still* the voice in the back of my head whispers that I should worry.

They wave. They grin. Halfway to the dance floor, Thad picks her up, whirls her around, sets her down, kisses her.

The crowd goes wild. I still don't see Seth, who I'm not looking for. Thad and Ava promenade to the dance floor, where she whirls into his arms to the opening strains of a slow country song I don't know, and they dance. She looks happy, and he looks like he's concentrating very hard.

At the end, during the final, drawn-out bars of the song, Thad suddenly leans her backward, spilling her into a low dip and holding her there as everyone cheers.

I close my eyes, even though I'm applauding, and I try not to remember a different wedding where I very, very distinctly said *please don't dip me during our first dance.*

Then she's upright again and they're kissing. The announcer invites all married couples to join them on the dance floor, so I nod goodbye to Chad, slip away, and head off the dance floor, slipping between elaborately decorated tables and toward the bar.

I have to admit that it's beautiful in here, not to mention unlike any other wedding I've ever been to. The room is high-ceilinged and old, the plasterwork around the two chandeliers intricate and detailed, the crown molding in the same pattern.

The wall is dotted with lights in sconces between the wainscoting panels, giving the room a romantic, pre-electricity feel, and the tall windows are hung with dreamy, gauzy curtains edged in fairy lights.

The really wild thing, though, is the decorations that Vera and Ava dreamed up. The centerpieces of each table are easily five feet tall, elegant towers of evergreen boughs and white flowers that make it feel like I'm walking through a wintertime forest.

But, like, a really fancy forest. Not a regular forest. This forest probably has lots of cozy little cottages and peaceful babbling brooks in it, not abandoned hunting shacks, old fridges, and rusted-out cars.

I don't necessarily think that dropping half a million dollars on a wedding is a good thing — how many kids could you send to college for that much? Start a scholarship instead, seriously — but since I'm already here, I may as well enjoy it.

A few minutes of aimless wandering later, I find myself in front of the place card table, half-empty glass of champagne in hand. Or rather, in front of the tables, plural, because three hundred and sixty-whatever names don't fit on one table.

I grab my own place card, even though I don't really need to. They're simple and classy, thick paper folded into a tent shape. The front is calligraphed *Delilah Radcliffe*, and the back says *Table Two*.

I stick it into my pocket and take another sip of champagne, feeling slightly aimless during the first unstructured moment I've had since six this morning.

The champagne gives me an idea, and I oh-so-casually walk to the middle name table. I casually take the last sip from the glass, and I casually stand there, perusing the names on the neatly laid out cards.

Hanson, Hemsfield, nope. *Johnson*. Closer. *Klein*.

I step sideways, eyes running down the neat column.

Lee, Lewis, Long—

"You're not dancing?" he says suddenly behind me.

This time when I turn, I don't break anything.

"You do know it's impolite to sneak up on someone, don't you?" I ask, even though my heart thuds.

"I said your name twice," Seth says, leaning over and grabbing his table place card from the column, quickly glancing at the table number on the back. "Maybe trumpets and a town crier next time?"

He's got a whiskey glass in his hand, and now he raises it to his lips, watching me with that cool, slightly sarcastic expression that he always seems to have.

"It's the married people dance," I explain, tilting my head in the general direction of the dance floor. "You didn't come over here to pick a fight this time, did you?"

Seth glances over in the direction of the dance floor, through a forest of evergreen and white and even in that easy, casual gesture is something that makes me ache. Maybe it's just the way he's standing, tall and confident, looking for all the world like not only is he exactly where he's supposed to be, he's in charge.

Maybe it's the suit. Seth would look good wearing a burlap sack — even cargo shorts — but Seth Loveless in a suit is *devastating*.

The last time I saw him in a suit, it was after one of his brothers' weddings — Daniel, I think, though I wouldn't swear to it — and I was doing some light internet research. He looked good in the photo.

He looks better in person, because photos don't ever capture the way he moves, or the way he looks at you, or the sheer force of magnetism that is Seth Elwood Loveless.

"I didn't," he says, and now he's looking back at me, and I wish this glass were full again. "I just came over to see if you wanted to dance."

"Your date won't mind?" I ask too quickly.

The smallest, slyest smile tugs at his lips.

"Should she?" he asks.

"I can't speak for her," I say. "I have no idea what other women tolerate from you."

"Would you mind?"

"Would I mind dancing with you?"

"If you were my date, would you mind me dancing with you?"

I tilt my head to one side, cock my hip, and examine Seth through narrowed eyes. I don't think I'm usually this sassy with my body language, but I also haven't usually just downed half a bottle of champagne all by my lonesome.

"Am I me in this hypothetical scenario, or am I your date?" I ask.

"Yes," Seth says, and takes another sip of his whiskey. It's getting pretty low.

"You can't answer an either-or question with—"

"If you," he says, pointing at me, "Were my date, would it upset you if I danced with you?"

"You can say it as loudly and slowly as you want, it still doesn't make sense," I tell him. "Am I me as in me, or have I transmogrified into your date and am, from afar, judging whether or not you" —I point at him somewhat obnoxiously, like he did to me— "should be dancing with me, Delilah."

I point at myself from overhead, pointer finger waving a big circle in the air. Seth takes another sip from his drink, and he's obviously trying not to laugh.

"Let's say transmogrified," he says. "If you were some other girl—"

"Excuse me, do you mind if we—"

"Sorry," I say, and move away from the table as a middle-aged woman starts looking for her table card. The song is still playing, couples still swaying on the dance floor, and I glance over at Seth and start strolling toward the bar.

"If I were some other girl, I'd probably light you on fire if I saw you look at someone else," I tell him. "But then again, if I were your date to a wedding, I'd probably be the kind of girl who's chill enough that nothing bothers her. Or maybe I'd just be dumb, I don't know."

Seth gives a low whistle at this revelation, and I've barely stopped talking before I regret that whole *light you on fire* thing I just said.

"And what if you were you and you were my date?" he asks, right as we step into the short line at the bar.

"Then we're in a parallel universe where something's already gone horribly wrong," I deadpan.

"Ouch," he says, into his whiskey.

Oops.

"You know what I mean."

"That bad, huh?"

The line moves forward, and I give Seth a *look* because I have no desire to bring up yesterday's dumb fight, but also, how is not remembering that slightly more than twenty-four hours ago, we got into it over sand?

I will always have hurt him, and he will always have hurt me, and it sure feels like those wounds are a chasm that we can't bridge.

"Really?" I finally ask, and I think he gets the message because he glances away.

"You still haven't answered my question," he says, and I sigh.

"Are you going to let this go?"

"Probably not."

"Any chance your date is going to come whisk you away and rescue me?"

"It's not looking good for that either. Come on, Delilah. If you were my date, would you be mad if I danced with you?"

"Well—"

"But a different you. Not *you* you."

"My evil twin?"

"Sure."

I tilt the empty champagne glass into my mouth and get the last remaining drops out, just to give myself that much more fortitude and buy that much more time.

"You sure are dead set on this answer."

"I sure am."

I watch the guy behind the bar shake something in a silver cocktail shaker, take the top off, pour through a strainer and into a glass.

I don't know why Seth is being like this, all of a sudden, two years after he claimed he never wanted to see me again. I don't know why he's picking fights and then apologizing for them, showing up at my sister's wedding, haranguing me with dumb questions.

But I know I don't hate it. I know that there's a mean, ugly part of me gloating over the fact that he's got a date somewhere, but he's here, asking me to dance. I don't like that I feel that way, but I do.

"I'd hate it," I finally say, still watching the bartender. "If you were here with me and dancing with another me? I'd *hate* it."

There's a long, long pause. The line moves forward again, we're almost next, and I have no idea why I didn't just lie.

It would be fine. Why the hell didn't I just say that?

"Would you light me on fire for it, or..."

"You'll never find out, will you?" I tease, even though the champagne glass has gone slippery in my hand and my heart is beating too loudly. "I'm not your date, and I don't have an evil twin. I think."

"It might explain a lot if you did," Seth muses, and the couple in front of us takes a beer and a glass of champagne and finally, *finally*, we're at the front. Seth gets more whiskey. I get more champagne. The married people dance finally ends, the strains of music fading gently away to a smattering of applause, probably because Ava and Thad are doing something cute and romantic.

My stomach squirms for reasons that have nothing to do with them.

"Which table are you at?" I ask Seth. We're strolling slowly, aimlessly, and I'm not even sure that we're walking *together* but it also feels like I should say something.

"Good question," he says, and digs in his pocket, pulls out the tented piece of paper, turns it over.

Then he pauses.

"I think it says two," he says, frowning at the hand-calligraphed script on the back.

"You're not at table two," I tell him, glancing over at the card. "That's the bridal party…"

I trail off. It's right there, in black ink. Table two.

I stare up at him, the pieces suddenly falling into place as he smiles, a little sheepish, and shrugs.

"You're fucking kidding me," I say. "What — did she —"

"There you two are!" Vera says, suddenly emerging from the crowd, resplendent in royal blue and done up to the nines. "Good, you found each other."

I swallow hard and try to breathe. That's not enough, so I do it again, but I can already feel the heat rising into my face and my throat closing with embarrassment and surprise and bright, sharp anger.

"You set us up?" I ask, my voice brittle enough to snap in two. "And *you* played along?"

Vera reaches out and cups my face in one hand. To my credit, I take a step back instead of smacking it away.

"Delilah, you know how you are," she says. "I should have told you, but I just *knew* you'd be so happy to see him again, and I knew you didn't want to be the only one alone at the wedding just for the sake of your detox. You deserve a little happiness, sweetheart."

I can't speak. I can't even move. All the blood in my body has rushed to my skin and I'm boiling over, a droplet of sweat already trickling down the back of my neck, my throat constricting.

"Have a wonderful time," she says, then kisses me on the cheek. "Now, I've got to go see about a cake! Try the mini quiche!"

Just like that, she's gone, swirling away into the crowd. No big deal, she just casually mentions that she went against my explicit wishes, decided she knew best, and set me up with the one person in the entire world I shouldn't be at a wedding with.

"You okay?" Seth asks.

I swallow, breathe, breathe again.

"I'm going to kill her, and then I'm going to kill you," I whisper.

THIRTEEN

SETH

Delilah doesn't move. She's just staring at the spot where Vera blended back into the crowd, her jaw flexing, her face bright red.

"I'm that bad?" I tease.

It's the wrong thing to say, because her head snaps around and now the full force of her fury is concentrated on me, as if I've opened a blast furnace.

"You didn't think to tell me?" she hisses. "I saw you *twice* yesterday and you still opted to let me look like an idiot at Ava's wedding?"

I push a hand through my hair, forgetting that it's supposed to be neat today.

"She asked me not to tell you," I say. "It was supposed to be a surprise."

"I can't fucking believe her," Delilah whispers, tears wobbling in her eyes. "And I can't fucking believe you, because *you* are complicit and *you* are *not my date.* Excuse me."

Delilah strides off without another word, then disappears through a door in a swirl of dusky pink and fury.

Fuck. *Fuck*. That's not how I thought this would go. I didn't think she'd like it, but I didn't think that she'd react with this kind of pure, iridescent rage. I thought maybe she wouldn't hate the idea of spending a few hours with me.

I thought maybe we were ready for something new, after two years of pretending we don't know one another. Friendship, maybe.

But clearly not. Clearly she hates the sight of me, hates the thought of me so much that she stormed out of the reception at the mere suggestion that I might be sitting next to her at dinner.

I down the rest of my whiskey in two gulps, which is a shameful way to drink whiskey this expensive, but the Radcliffes can bear the expense. I put the glass on a table with other empty glasses, and I wipe my thumb along my lip to collect the stray whiskey drops.

Then, something strange happens: I feel bad. Maybe she has a point. Maybe I should have told her.

Maybe this was a total dick move after all.

I shake my head, straighten my tie, and go find the guy with the crab cakes.

· · · · ★ ★ ★ ★ · · · ·

I FINALLY FIND HER UPSTAIRS, in the rooms where the cocktail hour was held. The overhead lights are all off, the only illumination from the fake candles in fancy brackets on the wall, and it's very, very quiet.

She's sitting in a deep windowsill, turned sideways, back against one side of the nook, feet flat against the wall on the other, and she's looking out.

I clear my throat as I enter the room, because I think I've surprised her enough today. Delilah doesn't move.

"I wasn't kidding," she says, still looking at the window.

"Dates require consent. You have to *ask* someone to be their date, and if they say no, even if you still attend the same event, you're not doing it as dates. You're just doing it as people who happen to be in the same room."

Her voice sounds funny, and she still doesn't look at me. I swallow hard, grit my teeth, then relax my jaw. Delilah has always felt like a lit match near gasoline, and it's hard not to catch on fire.

"I brought a peace offering," I say, holding up a plate of crabcakes and brie puffs and a glass of water.

"Did she make you?" Delilah asks, bitter and sarcastic. "Can't have Delilah getting mad and ruining the wedding. People might *talk*."

"I thought of it by myself, thanks," I tell her, then pause. "Well, sort of. Daniel once told me that when Rusty's in a bad mood, he always gives her a snack and a drink before trying to reason with her."

"Don't you dare try to reason with me," she says, but she finally turns her head. "And I don't know how I feel about being compared to a... five-year-old?"

"Nine," I correct.

Her face is blotchy, her eyes puffy under those eyelashes, her lips a deep pink as she rests her head against the wall, drapes her elbows on her knees, the skirt of her dress falling from her shins.

"You're kidding," she says. "That kid's nine?"

"Going on nineteen," I say, and offer the plate.

Delilah sits up straight, swinging her feet to the floor, her heels making a quiet *thunk* as she stands.

"What did she offer you?" she asks, grabbing a crab cake and popping it into her mouth. "Riches? A horse? Some kind of business deal?"

"I could've gotten a horse?"

"So she blackmailed you," she says. "Which is presumably also why you didn't tell me yesterday. You feared Vera's retribution."

She's holding her left arm around her ribcage, clamping it down with her right elbow as she eats the brie puff, watching me. There's a hard edge to her voice, but it's not bayonet-sharp anymore.

"Actually, I only agreed after I chased you down in the parking lot," I admit.

Delilah frowns in alarm.

"I left the brewery at like... eleven-thirty last night," she says. "Did you talk to her this morning?"

I grab a crab cake and pop it into my mouth.

"No," I say. "She actually asked after the first time you were at the brewery, and I said no. But then I called her back later."

"At midnight."

"It wasn't technically midnight yet."

She chews for a minute, both arms folded over her midsection.

"Good," she says, after a moment. "I hope you woke her up from a really amazing dream, and I hope she never properly got back to sleep. I hope she woke up every thirty minutes *all night long*."

"She was very courteous about it," I say.

"Of course she was," says Delilah. "Vera knows her manners, unless you're her actual family, in which case she pulls shit like this behind your back because she thinks that —"

Her fists clench and she draws in a long, deep breath, clamping her lips together with her teeth.

"Imma kill her," she says again, under her breath. "Imma kill you too, but I'm *really* gonna kill her."

"I also brought water," I say, holding up the glass.

"In case I'm actually the Wicked Witch of the West?"

she asks with a snort, eyes still closed.

"In case you're thirsty."

She breathes again, then exhales.

"Thanks," she says. "It's too bad, I'd love to have some flying monkeys under my command right now. And a broom that could shoot fireballs. You know, I always felt she was treated unfairly."

I take a sip of the water myself.

"Yesterday it was virgin sacrifices, and today you're an apologist for the Wicked Witch?" I say. "Are you trying to tell me something?"

Delilah laughs, her head tilting back, her earrings swinging from her ears.

"Double, double, toil and trouble," she chants, waving her fingers in the air. "Cauldron burn, and fire... wait, no."

I glance down at myself.

"Not a toad," I say, and Delilah just sighs.

"I tried," she says. "Can we sit? These shoes are stupid."

Delilah turns, leads me back to the window nook, hops up. I sit on the other side, the appetizer plate and the glass of water between us.

"I can't believe she did this to me," she says, leaning her temple against the wall, her neck long. Underneath the lace of her sleeve, I can see snow-capped mountains, a lake, clouds, a sun.

"I brought you snacks, I can't be as bad as all that," I say.

Delilah laughs. It's a short, quick, rough *ha*, but it's a laugh and I'll take it.

"Well, you are, but I mean *this*," she says, waving her arm in the air to indicate the whole building. "I mean that even though I made my wishes perfectly crystal fucking clear, she decided that I'm not allowed to be single."

Another deep breath, her skirt twisting between her fingers.

"She's always been this way," she says, and now there's an unsteady edge to her voice. "She thinks that because I'm single and thirty I'm some pathetic, sad spinster who must be crying herself to sleep every night because, as we all know, the only true path to happiness is through dick. She thinks I'm some object of pity that she has to fix."

Her eyes are bright again, her jaw clenching as she stares straight ahead into the dim room. I turn so I'm facing her, one leg folded under me, the other foot flat on the floor, knee in the air. I doubt I'm supposed to sit like this in a suit, but James Bond sprints in tuxedos all the time and he looks fine.

"You're not," I tell her.

"And, of all people, she had to tell *you* that I'm lonely and desperate for a date," she says. "And you had to agree to this shit show for some godforsaken reason."

I pull the blue handkerchief from the pocket of my suit jacket and hold it out.

"Here," I say.

Delilah takes it, holds it for a minute like it's a rare bird, then tries to hand it back.

"This is silk," she says.

"Okay," I tell her, not taking it back.

"I can't actually use it, I'll fuck it up. I've got about fifteen layers of makeup on."

I just shrug.

"It matches your tie and everything."

"Just use the damn thing," I say, leaning my head back against the wood paneling of the nook.

Delilah laughs, and it's welcome but unsteady, as if she's walking along a balance beam and could fall off to either side.

"Thanks," she says, then takes a deep breath and dabs very, very carefully underneath her eyes. "I still cry when I'm angry. As you can tell."

For a long moment, I just watch her in the low light. Delilah drinks the water, takes several deep breaths and tilts her face toward the ceiling with her eyes closed, neck long, chest rising and falling.

"I didn't agree to be your date because I think you're pathetic," I finally tell her.

"Not my date," she says without moving.

"I agreed to *co-attend this event with you* because it sounded nice."

Now she looks at me, her face less red, her lips less puffy.

"Nice?" she says, sounding genuinely surprised.

"What if we were friends?" I ask. "It's been a long time. We haven't even done what we normally do."

Delilah pushes herself so she's facing me, one leg hanging off the edge of the nook, the other tucked underneath her, pink dress pooled around her.

"You mean fuck and then fight," she says, looking at me, absent-mindedly wrapping the silk handkerchief around one finger, then another.

It's not for lack of wanting. Even right now, as I tell her it's been a long time, even as I imply that I'm finally over her, I'm not. I want to lean across this windowsill and kiss her swollen lips, slide my hand under her skirt, undo all those buttons I fastened before.

But I also know that some old hurts fester instead of heal, and giving into temptation with her is like tearing off a bandage and rubbing salt into a wound.

"Exactly."

"We did fight," she points out, sounding dubious.

"That's only half the equation."

"Can I be honest?"

"Don't tell me you're just starting now."

Delilah rolls her eyes, half-smiles.

"I've got no idea how to be friends with you," she says, her free leg swinging. "We've never been *friends*, Seth."

"It's all right so far," I point out.

"Yes, a fantastic five minutes," she deadpans.

"It could have gone differently."

She just looks at me, her eyes drifting over my face like she needs to memorize me for a quiz later.

"True," she finally says, then sweeps her leg off the nook and lands on her feet, shakes out her skirt, stands tall, breathes deep.

"We should get back before someone comes looking for us," she says, and then she holds out one hand. "C'mon."

I don't need her hand to help me down, but I take it anyway, hold it for an extra moment once I'm on my feet.

"Wait," she says, before we walk out. "Be honest, do I look like Courtney Love on a bad day right now? Is my eyeliner *everywhere*?"

I turn to her. Step closer. She tilts her head up slightly, watching me, and despite myself, despite every single thing I just said to her, I put my hand under her chin.

Delilah's eyes flutter closed, her impossible lashes brushing her cheeks.

I hold my breath. I'm afraid of this moment, of what she does to me, but mostly I'm afraid of myself. I don't like the Seth who's been angry and hurt for eight years. I don't like the Seth who's still heartbroken over something she did when she was twenty-two.

I don't like him, but I know he's there, just waiting to surface the moment I slip up.

"I think you're fine," I say, still taking in the feel of her skin under my fingertips, the wash of freckles all over her, darker where the sun hits and paler in her shadows.

"My eyelashes aren't falling off?"

I pause, confused. After a moment, her eyes slide open.

"They're fake," she says.

"Oh," I say, and take my hand off her chin.

Delilah laughs.

"My real eyelashes aren't practically an inch long," she says, and slides her hand around my elbow.

"I know," I lie, and she laughs.

FOURTEEN

DELILAH

A single, lonely *clink* sounds across the vast space of the ballroom, like the tolling of the bell on a ship lost at sea.

I pick up my wine and pretend I didn't hear it, even though the sound makes my shoulders tense a fraction of an inch.

"That's a common misconception, actually," my brother-in-law Michael is saying as he wipes his fingers on a napkin, then leans back in his chair. "You can find video of people on any kind of vehicle hitting a ball around a field and calling it polo, but *real* polo is only played on horses."

Next to him, my sister Olivia is nodding, her wine untouched. I have suspicions about the untouched wine, but now is neither the time nor the place.

"What about water polo?" asks Chris, my other brother-in-law, Winona's husband. "That's polo, isn't it?"

The background clinking has intensified from a single, forlorn sound in the wilderness to... many sounds, I guess. It's getting louder, is what I'm saying.

"That's completely different," Michael says, waving his

hand and speaking a little louder. "I'm talking about proper polo, where you've got to maneuver" —he holds his hands up in front of himself, like he's grasping reins— "a form of conveyance that's not yourself, WHILE ALSO MANIPU-LATING THE BALL."

He shouts the end of the sentence, because now the clinking is a cacophony, as hundreds of people hit their silverware against their glasses. We all pause, turn toward the small table at the front of the room where Ava and Thad are sitting together.

They kiss. A cheer goes up. I clap, a little half-heartedly, because this has to be the fourth time in ten minutes that this has happened, and it's starting to get old.

That, or I'm just a jerk who hates romance. One of those two things.

"Where do you practice?" Seth asks, his own wine glass in his hand.

I swear, every woman at the table leans toward him, like they're flowers and he's the sun. It's microscopic, sure, but impossible not to notice.

"My buddy Edward has some land up by Blythe, so we go up there every so often and shoot some goals on his back forty," he says, waving his hand in the air. "Though truth be told, we don't get in as much practice as we should."

Some land is several hundred acres of beautiful, hilly property that includes several ponds, barns, a mansion, and at least one horse stable. It's not *some land*, it's an estate, but of course Michael thinks of it as just his friend's back yard, because all his friends are loaded.

Everyone knows rich people only hang out with other rich people. How else would you concentrate wealth in the hands of the few?

"Do you have to take the horses to the practice grounds every time you—"

Seth is cut short by a loud *thump, thump* coming through the speakers.

"Sorry," says the voice that follows. "This thing on? Haha."

Vera sighs. At least, I'm pretty sure it's Vera. I haven't dared look at the section of our table that contains her, because I'm a little bit afraid I'll suddenly develop laser-sight superpowers and set her on fire.

Mark my words, Vera and I are going to have a reckoning. It just won't be tonight, because I'm not going to ruin my little sister's wedding.

"Yeah, that's why we don't practice that often," Michael tells Seth, *sotto voce*. "Really takes the whole day."

"Hey, y'all," the man at the microphone says, unfurling a few sheets of paper from his pocket. "In case you don't know me, either in person or by reputation, I'm Brad, this guy's Best Man."

There's another smattering of polite laughter. I smile and take another sip of my wine, which is still full, thanks to the wine fairies who keep coming around and topping me off without even asking.

"Anyway, when he first asked me to do the honors, I tried to talk him out of it. I really did. I told him that I'm completely unfit for the job, obviously, but for some reason he really had his heart set on me standing up here…"

There's a tap on my shoulder, and I turn my head to see Seth leaning toward me, crooking one finger. Wine glass in hand, I cross my legs and lean toward him, hoping that I don't overestimate my current leaning capabilities and wind up sprawled in his lap.

Or maybe I do hope that. As a location, Seth's lap has been pretty damn good to me.

"What do they know?" he asks, his voice low, rich, quiet.

I just look at him and raise one eyebrow, then lean back in.

"Your family. About us."

"…like that time he thought he could outrun a State Trooper in our dad's Z3…"

I settle back against my chair, head still turned toward Seth.

"Nothing," I tell him.

"Clearly, they know *something*."

"We're not really a *talk about your problems* kind of family," I say, huddling closer, lowering my voice.

Seth settles back, watches Brad for a moment. He's telling some anecdote about how Thad got out of a speeding ticket, and he's telling it like it's surprising and funny that a rich white kid got away with something.

"Leaving aside that you just classified me as a *problem*—"

"Sorry."

"—Thanks. Where exactly does their knowledge end?"

I take another sip of wine, both hands around the glass, and contemplate Brad for a moment.

I'm not close with my family in *that* way. I've shared relationship woes with Winona a couple of times, since we're the closest in age, but in general my closest confidants have always been friends, not them.

Like Lainey. Poor Lainey could probably quote fights that Seth and I have had almost verbatim.

"Seth," I say, turning my head.

He's looking at me. Has he just been looking at me this whole time?

"You should hold on to your butt," I murmur. He glances away, a smile creeping onto his lips.

"Is that considered proper etiquette for a black-tie event?"

"They think we haven't seen each other since our mutual and amicable breakup your senior year of college," I say in a rush.

Seth stares at me. He blinks once.

I take a sip of my wine and stare back, because I've finally done it. I've stunned Seth Loveless. After a moment he glances at the rest of the table, turns back to me.

"Mutual?" he murmurs, totally incredulous.

I pin my lips together with my teeth and nod.

"*Amicable?*" he goes on, his eyebrows raised, one corner of his mouth twitching like he's going to break into laughter at any moment.

I give him what I hope is an apologetic, charming smile and shrug dramatically. Seth shakes his head. He grabs his own wine glass, takes a drink, leans back in his chair again.

Then, he slides his arm along the back of my chair, the fabric of his shirt sliding over the lace that covers my upper back, pulling at the tiny buttons.

Every hair along my spine stands up.

"So I take it they don't know about the Whiskey Barrel either," he says.

"Not that I can tell."

"I thought every soul in Sprucevale knew about that."

I let myself lean back a fraction of an inch until his arm is touching his shirt is touching my dress is touching my back, and I can feel the faintest whisper of his warmth.

"You're not quite as notorious as you imagine," I murmur. "Besides, do you really think any of them—" I nod at the table, filled with people quietly listening to Brad, " —have friends who frequent that establishment?"

"I like the Whiskey Barrel," he says. "Or, I did."

"My point exactly."

"…so if Thad's got to tie himself down, I can't think of

127

a better ball and chain than Ava," Brad tells an entire room full of people.

By the way, this is why I drink at weddings.

"All right," Seth goes on, leaning in farther, his lips closer to my ear. "I'm guessing you also didn't mention the Mariott in Harrisonburg?"

He's not even close to touching me, but I can't stop imagining it: his lips moving against the shell of my ear, his voice like roughed-up silk vibrating through me.

I turn my head toward him, and he's *right there*.

"No," I say, barely audible to myself. "I didn't mention to my very proper, old-school family that I booty-called you the moment I'd properly filed for divorce."

As soon as I say that, I want to walk it back. I want to grab those words out of the air and replace them with *after I got divorced*, but that's not how talking works, is it?

Seth is just watching me, not even pretending to care about Brad's speech, like he's trying to read the right response in my freckles.

"What?" I finally say.

"Nothing," he says, but there's a smile on his lips so faint I almost miss it.

"Obviously I haven't told them anything else," I say quickly, under my breath. "Which is probably why you're still the perfect, courteous, dashing, handsome golden boy in their eyes."

We're both facing forward now, pretending to be utterly absorbed by whatever Brad is saying.

"You say that like you think I'm not," he teases.

"I think of you as considerably more human," I say, just as Brad picks up a champagne glass and holds it aloft.

"Please join me in raising this toast to my little brother and his beautiful bride!" he says. "To Thad and Ava!"

"Woo!" I say. The table clinks glasses with each other.

We murmur *to Thad and Ava*, and then we drink, and then Olivia rises from her seat and heads up to the microphone.

Since she's my sister, I actually shut up during her speech.

· · · · ★ ★ ★ · · · ·

SETH TWIRLS the stem of his wine glass between his fingers. He's sitting back in his chair, his jacket off, his shirt sleeves rolled up to his elbow, one arm slung over the back.

"How big are we talking?" he asks, still twirling.

"Big," I say, holding my hands about a foot apart. "Way bigger than real life. I think it took twenty hours, plus some for touchup."

"But *why?*" he says, still clearly baffled. "Did he lose a bet? Did an eccentric uncle die and leave him millions of dollars, but in order to collect he had to get *that* tattoo?"

"I still don't know," I say, leaning my head on my hand again. I'm half-turned in my chair, facing Seth, elbow on the table. Dinner and speeches are finally over, people are mingling, and I think there'll be dancing any moment now. "I kept trying to be subtle about asking, but I never got a good answer."

"Did you try *why are you getting a huge tattoo of a Snickers bar?*"

"I didn't think I could ask without sounding judgey," I admit. "I mean, we had twenty hours alone together, and I kept trying to start conversations about it, like, *so I guess you like Snickers?* But he never cracked, and after the first session, I figured my window had passed. Now I'll never know."

"I can't believe you didn't ask," he says, shaking his head.

"Delilah!" someone calls, and I turn.

It's Wyatt, weaving his way between two tables and

ducking under some greenery, which isn't quite tall enough for my cousin.

"Sooner or later I'm gonna take one of these things down by accident and ruin the whole shindig," he says, glancing backward at the lovely evergreen arch.

"How's the weather up there?" I ask him, still leaning on my fist.

"Hilarious," he deadpans. "And original. How do you come up with these? Hi, I'm Wyatt. You're the beer guy."

He holds out his hand to Seth as he says that last part, and they shake.

"Seth," Seth says.

"Yup," confirms Wyatt. "Well, I'm sure your presence here is fine and not at all weird for Delilah."

"Wyatt," I say.

"Seems like she definitely knew you'd be here," he goes on, Seth's hand still clasped in his.

"Are you here for a reason?" I ask him.

"Oh, just checking in on my honorary little sister," he says to me, then faces Seth. "That's her, by the way."

"I'm three years older than you," I point out.

"She's my favorite cousin," he tells Seth.

"I'm sure the feeling is mutual," Seth says.

"Right now I'm really leaning toward his sister, actually," I say. "Wyatt. Can I help you?"

Clearly, Wyatt's also had a few drinks. Not that I can blame him.

"Yeah," he says, and finally lets Seth's hand go.

For his part, Seth looks more entertained than anything.

"We're putting cans and shit on the getaway car if you want to come help," he says, jerking one thumb over his shoulder. "Georgia brought a fuckton of streamers. I think her goal is to get them pulled over before they hit the county line."

I swivel and look at the rest of the table.

It's empty. Oops. I was so absorbed in telling Seth about weird tattoos I've given people that I didn't notice we were alone.

"Right, yes," I say, rising.

To my credit, I only wobble slightly. See? The wine fairy would never overdo it. All hail the wine fairy.

"I should go do my bridesmaidly duty," I tell Seth. "How will everyone on the road know they got married if I don't?"

"Have fun," he says, grinning.

"Behave yourself," I say.

Then I point two finger guns at him. Finger guns. I blame the wine.

"Must I?" he asks, and fingerguns back at me.

It feels like a splinter of something works its way between my ribs, because there's always a reminder. Always.

"Guess not!" I say, fifty percent too brightly, and then I turn and my dress swirls and I don't look back as I take Wyatt's arm and we walk away.

He ducks under the greenery again, then looks down at me.

"You know you don't *always* have to say what everyone's thinking, right?" I ask.

"I don't *have* to, I *choose* to," he says. "Someone oughta."

"You could leave me out of it."

Wyatt's quiet for a moment as we wind between a few more tables, then emerge into the open space before the door.

"Everything is good, right?" he finally asks.

Fuck, I don't know. *Good* seems like far too banal of a

word for whatever's going on right now, but it's not exactly bad either, right?

"Delilah?"

We stop. I sigh.

"I'm going to murder Vera dead," I tell him, matter-of-factly. "But I can wait until tomorrow so I don't ruin Ava's big day."

Wyatt just raises one eyebrow, and I wave my hand dramatically.

"All shall be revealed in time," I say, because I don't have the emotional reserves to rehash it right now.

"Well, it's very grown-up to kill her later," he says, and we start walking again.

"I strive for maturity in all scenarios," I tell him.

Wyatt just snorts as he opens the door for me.

FIFTEEN

SETH

Bernadette rolls her eyes, the wine glass in her hand sloshing side-to-side as she shifts her stance.

"It's all isopods all the time right now," she says. "I swear, those blind nightmare shrimp are gonna be the death of me."

"They are," the man she's with says, nodding. "One day last week I swear she woke up screaming, *isopods!*"

Bernadette just laughs.

"Are there too many, or too few?" I ask.

"Yes. Both," she says. "See, I can't even answer that question. Did you know that each cave in the region has a slightly different subspecies? Sometimes they're two hundred feet apart. Different subspecies. Nightmare."

"I had no idea," I say, which is certainly true.

Bernadette is a biologist for the Forest Service, and we used to date.

Okay, we didn't date. We just fucked. We had a thing that lasted a few months. Purely physical, just two people scratching an itch. It ended about two-and-a-half years ago when she met someone she was serious about — this guy, maybe. Our split, if you can even call it that, was perfectly amicable.

I've slept around. It's not a secret.

But let me say this: I'm not a dick about it. I state my intentions upfront. I don't lie, cheat, or promise something I'm unwilling to give.

I like the game of it. I like the moment of clarity when I realize that a woman's interested. I like the rush of seeing someone new naked for the first time. I like the ego boost. I like how easy it to get what you want, as long as you don't want too much.

Or at least, I liked all that once upon a time.

"…whether it even matters if some subspecies go extinct," she's saying. "I mean, of course it matters because of biodiversity and on some level, every critter is precious, but does it *really* matter?"

"She gets like this when she's drunk," the man jokes. "Starts talking about wiping them all out."

Bernadette laughs, then shakes her head.

"I would never," she says, just as a hand slides through my elbow. "But keeping track does get exhausting."

"There you are," I say, looking down at Delilah. I say it casually, as if she takes my elbow all the time. As if her hand on the other side of my shirt and jacket isn't suddenly all I can think about.

"Sorry, Georgia got very specific about the streamers," she says, smiling and rolling her eyes. "And then poor Olivia managed to spell *married* wrong, and we had to wash it off and start over, you know how these things go. Hi, I'm Delilah."

Her hand on my arm tightens as she holds the other out, fingers pointed and bladelike.

"Bernadette," the other woman answers, smiling. "This is my fiancé, Gary."

"Bernadette works with Levi for the Forest Service," I explain while they shake hands. "She was just telling me about all the problems with forest shrimp."

Technically, I'm not lying. Everything I just said is completely true, but the lie-by-omission still feels bad as it settles in the pit of my stomach.

"Is the first problem that there are shrimp in the forest?" Delilah asks, hand still on my arm, laughing politely.

"Shockingly, no," Bernadette says, and before I know it, Delilah and Bernadette are talking about blind freshwater crustaceans who live in caves and how there are both too many and not enough, why it's important to have a dozen different subspecies, or why they might not be important at all.

When we say goodbye and head in opposite directions, Delilah keeps her hand on my arm.

"Drink?" she asks. "My first few are wearing off and there's still *so* much wedding to get through."

I glance over, through the pseudo-trees and across the ballroom to the stage and the crowd dancing in front of it.

"There is?"

"They haven't even played the shoe game yet," she says.

I just look down at her, because I have no idea what she's talking about.

"Eli didn't play the shoe game at his courthouse wedding?" she asks, dryly.

"I'm not even sure if this is a euphemism or not," I tell her.

"Sadly, no," she says. "The bride and groom interrupt the fun party to sit in chairs, back-to-back, hold each other's shoes, and then someone asks cute questions like *who snores louder?* and they hold up that person's shoe."

We pause at the bar. Delilah orders something called a

Dark and Snowy that comes with part of a tree stuck in the glass. I just get more whiskey.

"How do you score points?" I ask as we keep walking.

"It's not that kind of game."

"So how does one person win?"

"Oh, everyone loses."

We come to a stop in front of one of the tall windows, the old glass wavy, sheer curtains floating gauzily at either side.

"I feel like I'm missing something," I admit, and Delilah finally laughs. "They answer questions by holding up shoes and no one gets points and no one wins?"

"You got it," she says merrily, taking a sip of her cocktail. "That's it. That's the whole thing."

I glance out the window to the dark garden, pools and squares of light beyond it, a few lit paths leading away from the manor house.

Don't ask, I tell myself. *Don't ask, don't ask.*

I take another sip of whiskey.

"Did you play it?" I hear myself say.

Delilah goes perfectly still, one hand holding her drink, one hand on the windowsill. She watches me warily, like she thinks I might suddenly transform into some toothsome beast.

"No," she says, after a long moment, her voice polite, neutral. "Vera pushed for it, but I stood my ground for once."

I want to ask her a hundred more things. I want to ask if her wedding was like this. I want to ask if she glowed when she walked down the aisle, like Ava did; if they kissed every time someone clinked a glass; if her sisters decorated their getaway car.

I want to ask why *him*. Why then. What the hell he had that I didn't.

Instead, I drink more whiskey.

"I wouldn't want to touch someone else's dirty shoe either," I admit.

"It's a good thing we didn't. We'd have lost pretty badly," she says.

"I thought everyone lost."

Delilah laughs again.

"True," she says. "But it's really bad when the shoe game makes it obvious that the two people who just got married barely know each other."

I wonder, for a split second, how we'd have done at the shoe game, but I chase the thought away with another sip of whiskey. We promised not to fight, and asking Delilah about her wedding feels like standing next to a pool of lava and debating whether to step in.

"I can imagine," I finally say.

She looks away. She takes a long drink from her cocktail, head turned to one side, pearl earrings bobbing at her neck.

I watch her, unabashedly. Openly. I start at her elbow and follow the colors and shapes upward, onto her shoulders, hard to see through the pink lace but I know most of it by heart anyway.

The tattoos are new, though they aren't really. They're new since we broke up, and every time I've seen her over the past eight years, during our very intermittent couplings, she's had a new one. It's part of the rush, part of the discovery, seeing how she's changed.

Now I'm looking at her left arm: an ocean, a sailing ship, a tentacle wrapped around it. Another ship, a similar fate; a third being pulled upward by a flock of birds, and at the top, a purple-red Kraken, tentacles trailing across her shoulder blade, curling onto her chest.

Though today, the tentacle seems to end just past her

shoulder in a blurry line, and I'm still studying it as she speaks.

"Bernadette," she says, still looking away. I follow her gaze to where the other woman is standing across the room, talking to an older couple I don't recognize. "Since we're asking questions. Did you?"

She turns back, looks me square in the eyes.

"Yes," I tell her, and make myself stop.

Delilah looks over at her, then back at me.

"Two-and-a-half years ago," I say. "Just a summer thing. It was nothing."

"Don't say it was nothing," she tells me, softly, her glass up to her lips.

I push a hand through my hair, glance out the window into the darkness. I fight the urge to confess everything to Delilah, as if she'll absolve me of my sins even though she's made it clear she's not interested in doing so.

"It was casual," I amend myself. "That's all."

"She seems nice," Delilah says.

"She is."

I don't say: she was almost last. I want to tell Delilah that it was Bernadette that summer and into autumn, then a one-night-stand with a woman named Susan, and then it was Fall Fest and the backseat of Delilah's car and then it was nothing and no one.

Two years, three months, and seventeen days of no one.

"You got shorter while you were gone," I say, changing the subject.

"Oh, I stopped by my chateau on the way to doing the car and changed into flats," she says, sticking one foot out from under the dress that now falls all the way to the floor. "I think I've already got blisters, though."

I glance over at her, frowning down.

"Your chateau?"

Delilah laughs, though she still doesn't look at me.

"It's a cabin," she says. "But because this place costs a fortune, they insist on calling the rental cabins *chateaus* because if you name something a French word, they're suddenly worth a thousand dollars a night."

I just make a noise. It's unintentional, but holy shit.

"I know," she says, finally looking up at me. "And yes, I've suggested that they could probably end hunger in the state and *still* give Ava a very nice wedding, but my thoughts were not taken into consideration."

"Please tell me that liquid gold comes out of the faucet," I say.

"I wish."

"Precious gems sewn into the sheets?"

"Just fabric."

"Trained monkeys to fan you and feed you ripe fruit."

"There's a fireplace, a flat-screen TV, and jacuzzi jets in the tub," she says. "I imagine the closet has some nice robes. I didn't check, though."

Outside the window is dark, the moon behind the manor house, paths through the garden picked out in low yellow light. I can see two rows of small buildings that must be the chateaus, and beyond that, a deep darkness that can only be forest.

"But no, it's not really worth nearly a thousand dollars a night," she goes on. "Particularly when you live in the area and could easily get a ride back to your house and sleep there, but since I'm not the one paying for it, I choose not to look a gift room in the... door."

"Look a gift room in the door?"

"In the fireplace?" she tries again, laughing, her nose wrinkling.

"What's *in* that?" I ask, pointing at her drink. "Besides a tree."

She takes the very small branch between two fingers and stirs the drink with it.

"This, Seth, is Ava and Thad's signature drink, a Dark and Snowy," she says. "And the tree is a *rosemary garnish*, thank you."

"Looks like a tree," I deadpan.

"For someone who makes a living from booze, you sure are shockingly unsophisticated," she teases.

I grin and drink the last mouthful of whiskey in my glass.

"Shockingly?" I say, putting my glass down. I hold out my empty hand. "Can I try?"

She takes another sip, then holds it out to me.

"It's rum, ginger beer, cider, and… I forget, something else," she says.

I take a drink of it, the garnish grazing my face, faint lipstick smudges visible on the rim of the glass.

"Cranberry," I say when I finish, handing it back to her.

"Not bad, right?"

I take a step closer to her and there it is again: the urge to touch her, brush a stray curl from her temple, take her hand. I do exactly what I should do and ignore it.

"Finish it and come dance with me," I tell her.

Her eyebrows go up and her lips twist slightly as she keeps herself from laughing, an expression I learned long ago.

"I think what you mean is, *I'd be ever so thrilled if you would honor me with this dance, Delilah*," she says, her voice breathy as she fakes her worst *Gone With the Wind* accent.

"What I mean is *come dance with me*," I say. "You still owe me one from before."

"I owe you no such thing."

140

"Well, you said you'd light me on fire if I danced with anyone else," I say. "Here's your chance to avoid arson."

"Is that a threat, Seth Loveless?"

"No," I say, and now I'm grinning as she tries not to laugh. "It's an opportunity."

"I don't think I exactly said I'd light you on fire," she points out. "I'm pretty sure it was much more confusing than that."

I take a step closer. How long ago was it that I touched her chin? An hour, ninety minutes? Too long. I feel like we're in a bell jar, the outside world hushed and blurry, just the two of us here.

I feel like I should kiss her, even though I know that's not true.

"Delilah," I say, quieter, lower. "Come fucking dance with me."

"That was even less polite," she whispers, eyes alight.

"If I asked nicely, you'd chew me up and spit me out."

"No, I wouldn't," she says, and she actually looks puzzled.

"Well, I'm not going to risk finding out," I say.

"Would it be so bad?"

"Letting you chew me up and spit me out again?" I say. It's too honest.

I manage to stop my tongue before I say *I don't mind, so long as you leave teeth marks*, which she has. She's left them more than once. I think she's left teeth marks on my heart.

"You're really overestimating my powers, Seth," she says softly.

I'm not overestimating a damn thing. I'm half convinced Delilah's a sorceress for the power she has over me.

I lean down until our bodies are just barely touching, put my lips an inch from her ear.

"Please?" I ask, and I swear I try to sound as polite as I can but it comes out all dirt and gravel, the word ripped from somewhere deep in my chest.

Her hand is on my shoulder, and it feels more dangerous than staring at a pack of hungry wolves.

"Only because you asked nicely," she murmurs, and she takes my arm, and we head to the dance floor.

SIXTEEN

DELILAH

I'd forgotten how Seth can dance.

It's not that he's an amazing dancer from a technical standpoint. He knows the same handful of moves as anyone else, knows how to stay on the beat, can move his body in the same rhythms.

It's that none of those things account for the experience of dancing with Seth, the way that he throws himself into it wholeheartedly, as if being on the dance floor with this wedding cover band is the crowning experience of his life.

He's mesmerizing, magnetic, perfectly careless in the most breathtaking way, and before I know it I've forgotten about my family, about the crowd, about everyone else on the dance floor and it's just the two of us, touching and swirling, pulling closer and pushing farther as the band works through a long medley of golden oldies.

We dance without speaking for three songs, or maybe five, or maybe ten. I have no idea, because there's nothing but the moment, nothing but Seth's hands around my waist, nothing but the swish of my long dress as I twirl and he pulls me back, nothing but his hands on my hips as I lean back against him, my head on his shoulder, his lungs filling against my spine in a brief, still moment before we're moving again.

Everyone's watching us. I can feel it, that strange, heady rush of being the center of attention, or at least in its reflected glow. I'd forgotten what it was like to be the girl with Seth, the girl who's got the guy no one can ignore.

Of course he's fucked his way through Sprucevale. How could I have ever imagined differently?

The singer belts out one last note and the trumpets flare and Seth is watching me, smiling, his jacket off and his sleeves rolled up, my hand in his. There's sweat trickling down my spine and between my breasts. I'm breathing hard, I'm suspicious of my bra again, and I can only pray that my makeup is still in place.

But it doesn't matter because my hand is in his as the song ends and he pulls me in hard, catching me, breathless and still a little unsteady on my feet.

"You're a better dancer than I remember," he says, fitting one hand around my waist and the other into my own, my arm over his, my forehead briefly against his heated shoulder.

"I'm afraid to ask what you remember," I say, even as I try to ignore how easily we fit together like this. Being with Seth is instinct and muscle memory: arm here, hand here, head turns like this and hips move like this and then, and then, and then...

"Senior prom?" I guess.

"Was that really the last time?"

I take my head from his shoulder, right myself from where I fell into him, stand up straighter. Not too straight. Not so straight that we aren't still touching.

"It must have been," I say. "I didn't join the kind of

sorority that did formals, and I don't recall your Econ department having a spring gala or anything."

"Thank God for that." He laughs. "Can you imagine those nerds trying to dance?"

"So says the Nerd King."

Seth just laughs. His fingers tighten on my back. Just slightly. Just enough.

"Well, this is better than being eighteen," he says. "For one thing, whiskey sure makes me a better dancer."

"For two, I'm not wearing a poofy princess dress that looks like my bottom half is made of purple cotton candy," I say.

"It did come in handy later," Seth says.

"I was hoping you'd forgotten that."

"Not a chance, Bird."

The old nickname flutters onto me so lightly that it takes me a moment to realize what he said. I'd almost forgotten it.

"I'm afraid that covering myself with purple taffeta while explaining to Officer Capaldi that we were just looking for your contact lens is forever burned into my memory," he goes on.

I start laughing. I can't help it. This memory should probably be awkward, given that we were literally mid-coitus in the back seat of my car when there was a knock on the window, but somehow it's just... funny.

"He didn't believe you," I point out.

"Yeah, no shit," Seth says dryly. "I'm pretty sure the only reason we didn't get arrested is because he knew my dad."

"Did I ever tell you about the lecture I got when I got home that night?"

"From who, Vera?"

"Of course. Apparently I was somewhat disheveled

when I showed up, and she was still awake so I got to hear all about how good girls don't," I say.

"Can't say I ever got that one," Seth says.

"Clara had her hands full," I point out.

"Though I do have a very clear memory of the time that she stomped out onto the porch as I was getting into the car to go somewhere, shouted *and don't knock anyone up!* then walked back inside like nothing had happened."

I start laughing, and Seth grins at me. On my back, his fingers are wandering up and down, over the bump where my bra-corset-device clasps. I wonder if he knows he's doing it or if that's muscle memory, too.

"You never told me about that."

"I never knew what to make of it."

"Seems like a pretty simple instruction," I point out.

"I followed it to the letter, did I not?"

"True."

I almost say *is it still true?* but I don't. If Seth knocked someone up the whole town would know.

We dance in silence for a moment. I lean my head against his shoulder again, his jacket left behind somewhere, his shirt sleeves rolled up, forearms exposed. A bead of sweat trickles down his neck, from his sideburn to his collar, and despite myself I want to lick it off him.

I lied earlier.

When I told Seth that I don't want to know anything, I was lying through my teeth. I want to know everything.

I want to know the name of every woman he's fucked. I want to know dates, times, frequency. I want to know what position they did it in and where they were and how kinky she was and if she was better in bed than me. I want to know which ones he loved and which ones he didn't even like.

I want it all. I want every last dirty detail, but I'm also

finally wise enough to know that what I want isn't always what's good for me.

So I'm not going to ask, even though I know he'd tell me. I've made that mistake before. It took a long time to get over.

It's none of my business, and it doesn't matter, and it doesn't matter, and it's none of my business. We're just friends who happen to be at this wedding together, dancing and reminiscing about how we used to be in love.

"Don't look now, but I think there's some kind of meeting going on," he says after a while.

"What kind of meeting?"

"Your sisters, your stepmom, and the other bridesmaid," he says.

"Evelyn."

"Sure. Evelyn's shaking her head, your one sister is sort of making a motion like she's clutching pearls, but I don't think she's wearing any—"

"Turn me."

The slow song begins trickling to its end, something faster rising in its place. The crowd on the dance floor shifts, re-finds its footing. We spin slightly, Seth's back now to my family.

"Am I hiding you from them, or were you tired of my play-by-play?" he asks, grinning, as we pull apart slightly.

"Both," I tease as he lets my hand go and pulls at his tie.

"My play-by-play was great," he says.

"You didn't even know which sister it was."

He grins, shrugs, tugs.

"Stop it," I say, and grab his tie myself, pull one end gently from the knot. The backs of my knuckles brush against his skin and I tug gently, re-center his tie, pause. I don't let go.

And then, before I quite know what I'm doing, I'm unbuttoning the top button on his shirt, drawing closer, the material stiff and the button small in my drunk fingers.

Seth flattens his palm against my back, his thumb on the bump of my bra closure again. I unbutton another button. Pull back, my hands on his chest. Look up at him.

"Undressing me in public?" he murmurs, so low I can barely hear him over the band.

"This is the highly exclusive society event of the year," I say. "I'd hardly call it public."

"Still, we're in front of all these people."

"Am I embarrassing you, Seth?"

He answers just as the band crescendos, the new song picking up volume and tempo, drowning out his response.

"I didn't—"

He pulls me to him, leans in, and then his forehead is resting on mine and our noses are touching and his hand is flat against my back, the other covering mine on his chest, and I think my heart has stopped.

"Not in the least, Bird," he says again.

My eyes are closed. Did I close them?

The music swirls around us, rising. We're swaying back and forth slightly, like seaweed underwater, people around us dancing and laughing and talking, and I know some of them are watching us and some of those people are thinking *there's that Loveless boy and his latest bridesmaid conquest. How cliché.*

I wish I didn't care what people thought, but I do. We sway together with our faces touching and our lips an inch apart and I think: *I was here first.*

As if that makes me somehow special. As if it makes me different from every other woman he's fucked.

"You have to stop calling me that," I finally murmur.

"Sorry," he says, a smile in his voice. "Old habit."

Deep breath in, eyes still closed. Still swaying.

"It's been years," I say softly. "Don't habits die?"

"Doesn't feel like it."

Before I can answer he pulls his face away from mine, keeps his arms on me.

"Incoming," he says, and I open my eyes to see my sister Olivia striding across the dance floor toward us, couples parting around her like she's Maid of Honor Moses.

Moses of Honor?

"Delilah," she calls, all business.

"Hi," I answer, the best I can come up with.

She stops a few feet away, raises her eyebrows, and gives us a long, speculative look. You wouldn't know that she's had her hair and makeup done since eight this morning, or that she's been at a wedding for the past several hours, because she somehow still looks picture-perfect.

It's a skill I have yet to master.

"So you *did* end your detox," she says. "An hour ago you were swearing up and down that—"

"Do you need something?" I interrupt.

"Do you have the knife?"

I blink.

"Why would I have a knife?" I ask, turning slightly away from Seth, though he keeps his hand on my back. "*Where* would I have a knife?"

"The cake knife," she says, as if it's obvious.

"Where would I be keeping the cake knife?"

"*No,*" she says, exasperated, waving one hand. "Do you know where it is?"

"That's not what you asked."

"Do you? You were the last one with it."

I stare blankly at my second-youngest sister, and

wonder if the pregnancy she hasn't told us about yet is affecting her brain.

"Bree was putting dinosaurs on it and then you were using it as a boat or something, back in the bridal suite," she says. "No one's seen it since then, and they want to cut the cake soon."

I stare at a dancing couple for several seconds. It was a space elevator, actually, and Bree was sending her dinosaurs on a mission to find aliens, but then we had to go line up for the wedding and I have no idea what happened to the cake knife.

"It's there somewhere," I finally say.

"*So* helpful."

"Can't they just use a regular knife?" I ask, even though I already know the answer.

"This one's *monogrammed*."

I close my eyes, take a deep breath, rub my knuckles to my forehead.

"It might be on that window ledge," I finally say, the last place I remember seeing it. "If not, try one of those shelves."

"Thanks," she says, and turns away. Then she turns back. "Oh, and they want you and your date to line up over there for the shoe game."

"He's not my date," I say, just as his thumb skips over my bra clasp again, then stops.

"Then *you* go line up over there," she says, half-shouting over the music. "They want us in the background of all the shots."

Now she turns away and does her Moses thing back through the dance floor. I turn to find Seth looking at me, still undone as his hand slides off my back.

"What? You're not," I say, briefly closing my eyes. "I gotta go do this thing."

"Of course," he says, perfectly polite if also cool, distant.

I step away, walk across the dance floor. Whatever power Olivia has I don't seem to possess, because I'm weaving and dodging all the way back to where the rest of the bridal party is standing.

When I get there, Vera looks around.

"No Seth?" she asks.

Just like that, I feel shitty. Not about Vera. Vera can still go fuck herself, but telling Seth he's not my date and just walking off was kind of a dick move, wasn't it?

Crap.

"No," I tell her without further explanation, and her brow furrows slightly, then relaxes.

"Well, I guess the sides will just have to be uneven," she sighs. "All right. You're all going to stand behind Ava and be her backdrop, and the groomsmen will do the same for Thad."

"Cool, sounds great," I lie, and Vera pats my shoulder, then walks off.

My sisters are chatting with each other, laughing about something. As I move into their circle, I glance over at the dance floor, but I don't see Seth. Not even dancing with someone else. Bernadette maybe.

I was definitely a dick.

SEVENTEEN

SETH

I lean against the huge stone column and take another cold, deep breath. Behind me I can still hear the noise of the wedding, even though I'm out on the manor's wraparound porch, staring out over the barely-lit garden, the chateaus vague beacons of light at the other end.

A thousand dollars a night. Holy *shit*. I know Delilah's family is loaded — I've been to their mansion, I've seen their horse stables — but every so often I get a solid, stark reminder that money means something completely different to them.

One night in that chateau is almost a mortgage payment on my townhouse. Who the hell pays that for *one night?*

It's easy to feel inadequate at events like this. Even though I'm far from the only person wearing a suit instead of a tuxedo, I feel underdressed. I've never played polo in my life. I don't golf. I don't fly first class.

Sure, I own a successful business, own a home, and even paid the last of my student loans off last year, but right now it feels like those things pale in comparison to inheriting my parents' ridiculous wealth. Work hard and achieve goals? Cool, but have you ever thought about spending a month in Europe and never looking at how much anything costs?

I don't think I could ever buy something without knowing the price. Hell, right now I could tell you the price of gas at every station within a ten-mile radius of my house.

The breeze outside shifts, works its way down my collar, and I finally shiver. It's cold as hell out here, but after the heat of the dance floor inside it felt good, like the next best thing to a cold shower.

And after the one-two punch of Delilah unbuttoning my shirt and telling Olivia I'm not her date, I could sure use a cold shower.

I stand up straight. I shake my head, run one hand through my hair, the roots slightly damp with sweat. I remind myself that she's right, that I'm not her date, that I blindsided her on Vera's request, and right now we're just friends at the same wedding together.

And then I walk back inside and tell myself that I was just taking a quick breather and Delilah holds no power over me. Maybe if I keep telling myself that, it'll become true someday.

The door shuts behind me. The atrium is empty, warm, and mostly quiet though I can hear the music through the doors to the ballroom, the horns in the band kicking up once more.

Or did they ever stop? I've had far too much whiskey to know how long I've been gone, and I don't have any idea whether they're about to play the shoe game or whether it's over and done with and everyone's back to dancing.

The furthest door opens. In the low light a pink dress swirls out, the door stops. An arm holding a champagne bottle emerges, and that's all I need to know it's her. She whirls around the door, dodges, watches it close, holding something in her other hand as well.

Then she sees me. She pauses, takes a tentative step, starts walking.

"That's you, right?" Delilah calls.

"Who else would I be?"

I watch her as she walks carefully toward me, balancing something in one hand. I watch the rigid, careful line of her shoulders, the side-to-side sway of her hips, the way each leg is briefly outlined in dusky pink as she moves.

Fucking witchcraft, I tell you.

"There's like a bajillion people here, you could be anyone," she says, her voice quieter as she walks up to me, then holds up her hands: a bottle of champagne in one, two plates of wedding cake in the other. "Pick your poison."

I take the champagne. It's still corked, so I pull at the foil around the top until it tears.

"Should I even ask how you got the whole bottle?" I say, unwinding the wire cage.

"It's classified information," she says, raising one eyebrow. "Let's just say that it was a... sticky situation."

I crumple the foil together with the wire cage, put it on a mirror-top side table, and give her a questioning look.

She laughs.

"I just told the bartender the bride asked for it," she says. "It's late, I'm a bridesmaid, they assume I want it for official wedding reasons."

"What possible official wedding reason would your sister have for wanting an unopened bottle of champagne?" I ask, turning the bottle in my hands.

"She had monogrammed plates made for the two of them, so they could eat their first meal as husband and wife

154

on something *special*," she says. "At this point, no one questions her."

I glance along the atrium: slim side tables against the wall, flower vases on top, windows, lighting sconces with electric candles.

"Think I could put a light out?" I ask, gesturing at one with the champagne bottle.

"If I say no, will that just make you more determined to try?"

"There's one way to find out."

"Seth, if you break something I was *never* here," she says, but she's laughing, still holding two plates of wedding cake. "I swear I'll leave you here to deal with Vera all on your own, may God have mercy on your soul."

I grin at her, then take the cork in one hand and twist.

"You're no fun," I tell her as it pops off into my palm.

"I'm just trying to be a good big sister and not ruin Ava's wedding," she says as I tilt the bottle to my mouth and drink. "God knows I've probably come close."

It's good, cold and fizzy and stiff. I wipe my mouth with the back of my hand when I lower the bottle, then look over at her.

"What did you do?"

Delilah holds out one of the plates of wedding cake, so I put the champagne bottle on the side table and take it.

"I haven't had my blowout fight with Vera yet, if that's what you mean," she says, picking up her own fork.

"Of course not," I tell her. "You're here, not shoveling the horse stables back at the estate."

Delilah snorts.

"She's a regular stepmother, not an evil fairy tale stepmother," she says. "I'm not exactly Cinderella. This dress wasn't made by mice and birds."

"Good. I'm not exactly Prince Charming," I say, which

is an odd thing to say to your friend because didn't Cinderella and Prince Charming fall in love? Didn't they kiss at midnight and live happily ever after?

Delilah clears her throat.

"Sorry about the date thing," she says.

I lift a piece of wedding cake into my mouth and try to really, really focus on it though the whiskey and champagne are making it hard.

It tastes like... cake?

"You're right," I say, scooping another forkful. "I'm not your date. I'm just some guy who happens to be seated next to you at this wedding."

"I was so right that you came out here and missed the whole shoe game?" she says. "Not to mention the cake cutting. The server spatula thing was *monogrammed*. Made the whole ceremony feel super romantic."

"I needed some air," I say, and eat another bite.

Delilah takes a step back until she's against the wall, then sighs, leans back, looks at the ceiling.

"Seth," she says after a moment. "Would you like to be my date to my little sister's wedding?"

I eat another forkful and pretend to think.

"When is it?"

She just looks over at me.

"I think I'm busy that day," I tell her.

"You're impossible." She laughs. "Come on, there'll be good whiskey and you can drink champagne straight from the bottle."

"Can I drink the whiskey straight from the bottle?"

"What were you, raised by wolves?"

"I'm not the one who brought champagne and no glasses," I point out.

Delilah steps closer, reaches around me, puts her empty

cake plate on the side table. I stack mine on hers as she takes the bottle.

"I only have two hands, and I figured you'd prefer cake to manners," she says, taking a long drink.

Maybe it's the whiskey, or the dancing, or the way she's lit or maybe it's everything, but there's something fierce and defiant and beautiful in the way she moves, drinking champagne straight from the bottle.

When she finishes she wipes the corner of her mouth with the pad of one finger, the movement delicate, precise, oddly graceful for the moment.

"Here," I say, and swipe at my own lower lip. "You've got icing."

She runs a finger along the outer edge, raises her eyebrows at me.

"Almost. Closer to the corner."

Delilah tries again, misses. I shake my head, and she tries again.

It's nothing. It's the barest pink streak of icing, almost unnoticeable, certain to come off of its own accord in the next few minutes. I should just tell her it's gone and move on, but I don't.

I reach my hand toward her, stop an inch before her chin.

"Can I?" I ask.

"Thanks," she whispers.

I flick one finger along the edge of her mouth. She's soft and warm and I'm teetering on the edge, standing on a cliff, staring down into a pool I promised I wouldn't dive into.

But I could. I could dive right now, ignore the rocks at the bottom, let the cold water submerge me and knock the air from my lungs just one more time.

Without thinking, I stick my finger in my mouth, lick it off. I take the bottle from her hand, drink again.

She's staring, and her gaze feels like molten steel sliding down my body. Good. Delilah can stare at me all she wants, especially when I've had this much whiskey.

"Think you can still dance?" I ask, handing the bottle back.

"I think champagne only ever makes me a better dancer," she says, drinking.

She turns her head to the side. I watch her from a foot away, unashamedly, unabashedly, too drunk to care if she notices and too cognizant of the past to worry about her reaction.

I've spent *far* too much time with my face between her thighs to care that she knows I think she's pretty.

Behind the lace over her chest, in her slight cleavage, there's an odd, hard shadow. She pulls the bottle from her mouth, wipes her lip with one finger.

"You got a new tattoo," I say, pointing at my own chest.

"Shit," she says, and looks down, pulling at the lace. "You can see it?"

"Only a little."

She hands the bottle back, lifts the lace away from her chest, looks into her dress.

"Where?"

"Farther down."

She pokes gently at her chest, like she's afraid to touch it.

"Farther," I prompt, and she glances up at me.

"Don't watch," she says, though she's half-laughing. "This is unladylike."

"I've never seen that before."

"C'mon."

Ever the gentleman, I turn my back, take another drink of champagne.

"What is it?" I ask the flowers on the side table.

There's a pause.

"Nothing," she says.

"Something you don't want polite society to see," I say. "Just how raunchy is this tattoo, Delilah?"

"It's a huge, photorealistic dick," she says, and I turn back before I can stop myself.

Delilah bursts into laughter when she sees my face.

"Veins and ball hairs and *everything*," she says, still laughing, poking at her chest through the neck of her shirt. "It's just, like, the dick-est dick that ever did dick."

I don't have a comeback for that, so I just watch her as she smooths the lace back over her chest, looking down.

"Better?" she asks, grinning.

I take a good, long moment to stare at her.

"Better," I confirm and hand the bottle back. "You gonna tell me what it really is and why you don't want anyone to see it?"

"I don't want *Vera* to see it," she says, drinking.

"I've never been more curious in my life."

She takes one more drink.

"It's a clockwork heart," she says. "Vera still doesn't know because it's a giant tattoo right on my chest, and I think it might give her a stroke."

A memory taps at me, floats into my brain: Delilah, holding a fruit basket at my front door, pulling her shirt to cover gauze.

"Seems like she's about to know if I figured it out," I say, taking the bottle back.

"She's got better things to do right now," Delilah says, shrugging.

I take a drink.

"Than stare at your tits?" I ask. "Like what?"

Right here, right now, I cannot think of a better pastime to save my life.

"I thought we were friends, Seth."

"It's a friendly stare," I say, but I lift my eyes to her face. "Friends can't look at tattoos?"

Suddenly the lights in the hall dip low, until they're almost out, then slowly brighten. When they stop, they're dimmer than they were before.

"How long have you had it?" I ask.

It's so quiet in this hallway that I think I can hear the old house settling, each individual wooden slat shifting a millimeter down.

"Two years and change," she says quietly, her eyes meeting mine.

My hand drifts to her waist, and she moves into me. A tiny, almost imperceptible movement, amplified until her warmth under my hand is all I can feel.

I can feel her breathing under my fingers. I can feel her heartbeat, thumping away, and I force myself not to read into the timeline or into the tattoo.

Instead, I lean into her, again. My face against hers, again, the feeling that my bones are dissolving at her nearness, the feeling that I've forgotten how to breathe.

"Do you have anything new?" she asks, her voice nearly a whisper.

"No tattoos," I say, and I keep tracing the flowers on the lace with my fingertips, pressing into her soft flesh, and she puts her hand on my chest, her thumb sliding between the buttons on my shirt. I don't know if it's an accident or not, but either way, she doesn't move it back.

"I did something stupid and got a new scar. It's on my shoulder, I'll show you if you want."

Delilah gasps, the tiniest, slightest gasp.

"Right now?" she murmurs.

"Unless you'd rather see it later."

Now her hand is on the tie that she loosened earlier, the lightest pressure pulling against the back of my neck.

"What else?" she asks.

"That's all."

"Two years and nothing else has changed?"

I haven't been with anyone else. I haven't even kissed anyone else, not since the last time we were together, not since she moved back to town.

Before, when she was hundreds of miles away, I could push her from my mind. I could forget about her for hours at a time.

Now, that's impossible.

"Two years, three months, and seventeen days," I say, my voice rough and raw with the truth, and there's a pull at the back of my neck as she pulls at my tie and finally, finally, I kiss her.

I feel like a stadium when the lights go out. Like a concert hall when the orchestra stops tuning and suddenly plays the first note of a symphony. The background noise stops and the note swells, shifts, breaks into harmony.

This is all there is.

Delilah is all softness, but never pliant. Nothing about her yields even as I feel like I'm sinking into her, lips already parting under mine. She makes the softest noise and it explodes across me like a shock of hot water as she pulls me in harder and I bend to her.

I snake my hand up her neck, her pulse hot under my fingertips, find her cheekbone with my thumb as she pulls back slightly, my lower lip between her teeth before she comes in again, her softness defiant, pushing, needy.

I push back. I press myself against her. There's a rumble coming from somewhere deep in my chest that I can't locate and can't control, but now her hand is on my neck, her fingers twisting in my hair and I skim my other palm past her breasts, her stomach, along the outside of her thigh as she makes another noise and stands on tiptoe and pushes her hips against me.

I'm hard as a rock. She knows. Our tongues curl together and she rises against me and I close my hand around her thigh, trying to pull her into me, and she knows where this is going and I know where it's going.

I don't want to wait to go somewhere private. I want to kneel right here, duck under her long skirt, and make her come in this hallway outside her sister's wedding. I want to push her against the wall and fuck her without caring who finds us.

I feel like a time bomb with the counter started: tick, tock. I feel like Delilah reroutes the wiring in my brain, like she bypasses the synapses for reason and logic and self-control and connects lust to impulse to sheer madness.

I grab her a little harder, growl a little louder, catch her lip between my teeth and curl my fingers in her hair. She rewards me with a breath that hitches in her throat.

Delilah pulls back, just so our lips are almost touching, clenches my hair in her fist, a cascade of sparks shooting down my spine. She's breathing hard and I think she's laughing, so I find her ass and squeeze it as hard and I can, pressing her body against mine.

The door to the ballroom opens.

Delilah yelps into my mouth and jolts backward, but my fingers tangle and catch in her hair, her hand going to my wrist.

"Shit," she hisses as the open door hesitates, its blankness facing us. "Fuck, that's my hair. Ow. *Ow.*"

"Hold still," I whisper, flexing my fingers, relaxing them, pulling back slowly and steadily, her curls sticky with heat and sweat and whatever women put in their hair at weddings.

Fifty feet away, the door wavers, and then finally, my fingers come out and Delilah exhales.

"Yeah," a male voice says, calling back into the ball-room. "One sec."

He steps out, sees us, hesitates a moment.

"Delilah?" he calls.

EIGHTEEN

DELILAH

"Yes?" I call back, and to my relief my voice comes out steady strong and *normal*.

I stand up straight, shoulders back, hands clasped in front of me. Like I'm getting ready to sing in the church choir or something, because even though I'm pretty sure it's either Wyatt or his father, my uncle Doug, it's hard to tell from that single word this far away.

At least it's not Vera. Or, God forbid, my dad.

He takes a step further, though he doesn't let the door close and the light and music spills out of the ballroom behind him.

"Hey," he calls again, sounding tentative. "Is that Seth?"

"Hello again," Seth says.

He's got his arm around me, his palm right where my lower back becomes my ass.

"Huh," Wyatt says, and leans one arm against the edge of the door, above his head, as though taking his time to consider the two of us.

"Do you have a message, or were you just dispatched to make sure I'm behaving myself?" I ask, my voice pointed.

Wyatt laughs.

"Lucky for you, the first one," he says, drawing out the words, clearly enjoying himself. "Ava's gearing up to throw her bouquet, and Aunt Vera has requested the honor of your presence."

Seth's hand moves a fraction of an inch lower. I stand a little straighter.

"You mean she's demanded I stand there and let Ava hurl flowers at my face?"

"That wasn't her phrasing," Wyatt says, politely.

"That was her meaning."

"I'm sure I can't speak to that."

Seth's hand moves another fraction of an inch downward, his warmth soaking through the thin fabric of my dress, drowning out every other thought I'm trying to have. I slide my hand behind myself, put it in his.

"Tell her I'll be there in a sec," I tell Wyatt. "I need to…"

My mind goes blank.

"Yes, go on," Wyatt deadpans.

"Prepare myself for more bullshit?"

That gets a grin from Wyatt.

"I'll pass along that you're using the powder room first," he says. "Get that game face on."

He turns back and before the door even shuts, I've stepped around Seth and grabbed the champagne bottle.

"Preparing?" he asks as I drink, swallow after swallow.

When I finally pull the bottle away I wipe my finger along my bottom lip, short of breath.

"I thought I was done after the shoe game," I tell him.

He's just standing there, in the low light, sleeves rolled to the elbow, tie loose, collar unbuttoned, and I can barely keep my feet planted on the floor. If Seth is hot in a burlap sack and devastating in a suit, then like this, undone and slightly rumpled, he might be the most fuckable thing I've ever seen.

"But no," I say, tearing my eyes away. "I forgot the bouquet toss, so if you'll excuse me, I have to go be the desperate and unwanted divorcee who serves as a warning to any woman who thinks—"

Seth kisses me with the words still on my lips. It's rushed, impulsive. His hand slides around my waist and I step back to catch my balance, find the side table with the flowers behind myself.

"Unwanted?" he says, voice rough, lips barely leaving mine before he kisses me again, and this time it's deeper, harder, his other hand curling around the back of my neck. "Desperate?"

"I wasn't fishing for compliments," I say, one hand holding the bottle, the other on his chest.

"I'm not giving you compliments, I'm stating facts," he says, blunt as ever.

We kiss, kiss again.

"Fact: if Ava thinks you're the worst-case scenario, her entire worldview is *fucked*."

I'm grabbing his tie again, pulling his mouth down to mine. Behind me the side table quivers with the movement of our hips, his hard length against my lower belly, desire and lust and pure, unabated *need* roiling up inside me.

Does my sweet, angelic little sister really think all those things of me? I don't know, but after a year of hearing about this wedding constantly and a week of doing almost nothing but helping her prepare, it sure feels like the world revolves around getting that ring and it sure feels like I'm being pitied because I couldn't keep mine.

Suddenly, someone clears his throat *very* loudly. I jerk

away from Seth, who turns around casually, drifts one hand down my back.

Wyatt's standing at the door.

"In my defense, I don't love this either," he says. "But, uh…"

I step forward and smooth my hands over my skirt as if it can erase Wyatt's memory.

"I'll wait," Seth's voice says in my ear, and I look over at him.

Then I look back at Wyatt, at the light leaking out of the ballroom behind him, and I imagine walking in and Vera steering me to just the right spot and Ava looking over her shoulder to sight me before she throws. I imagine everyone looking at me, each of them thinking, *didn't she have her chance already?*

I imagine the forest of hands reaching for the bouquet while it's still in the air, each of them eager for the mantle of *next to get married*, a mantle I'm not even interested in wearing.

"You're gonna want to head that-a-way," Wyatt says, pointing.

"Fuck it," I say.

Wyatt pauses.

"*It* being the bouquet toss, right?"

"Right. Fuck the bouquet toss," I say, glancing from Wyatt back to Seth. "Fuck catching some flowers so Vera can feel better about my life choices."

"Can I just quote you verbatim?" Wyatt says, sounding exasperated. "'Hey, Aunt Vera, Delilah says fuck the bouquet toss. Ow, why are you killing me with your mind?!'"

"You'll live," I say, and I step closer to Seth.

I take his tie in both hands, adjust it slightly, look up at him through my massive fake eyelashes.

"Want to get out of here?" I ask, too quiet for Wyatt to hear.

Despite all manner of history and evidence, adrenaline spikes through my veins. I'm afraid he'll say no. Afraid he's moved on, that this is some fucked up game he's playing to get back at me.

"Fuck yes I do," he says, lips curving into a smile.

"Remember me? Still over here, looking at you with my human eyes," Wyatt calls from the doorway.

I take Seth's hands in mine. At the foot of the staircase is a dark hallway, leading into some other part of the manor house, and I walk backward, pulling him toward it.

"Wrong way," Wyatt says, sounding defeated.

"Make up an excuse for me!" I shout.

"What? No," he calls, but I'm already half-gone.

"Thanks!"

"Delilah! *Delilah.* Come *on.*"

"You're my favorite!" I shout, and then we slip into darkness.

Not complete darkness. This hall runs along the side of the manor, overlooking yet another lawn with yet more perfectly-managed decorative elements, all blue-white in the moonlight that doesn't come through the windows.

Seth locks his hands around my hips, walks me backward, his thumbs right on the points of my hipbones. He's disheveled, undone, a look on his face like he might either kiss me or laugh at any moment.

"I bet this place is haunted," he murmurs after a moment.

It's not what I was expecting.

"Haunted?"

"You know, with ghosts."

"Oh!" I say, and roll my eyes. "I thought you meant the other kind of haunting, with kangaroos."

"Kangaroos?" he asks, voice low, still walking me backward. "That's just—"

Seth grabs my ass with one hand, squeezes.

I squeak with surprise.

"—shit, that's a frisky ghost," he says, grinning. "I didn't think somewhere this fancy would have ghosts who would be that inapprop—"

This time he grabs my ass with both hands, and I start laughing.

"I think he's trying to tell us something," Seth whispers.

"How do you know it's a male ghost?" I whisper back.

He's still walking me backward, ass firmly in both hands, his fingers sliding a little with the dress at every step.

"Maybe it's a lesbian," I go on. "I'm very popular with Lainey's derby — *oof.*"

I didn't know there was a wall behind me until Seth backs me into it, takes his hands off my ass, slides them over my hips, along my torso.

"Can't imagine why," he says, and kisses me. It's a short, teasing kiss, and I stand on my tiptoes. "You're just some feisty, tattooed redhead with an incredible rack and a gold medal ass."

I'm still laughing as we kiss again and I take his lower lip between my teeth, just hard enough to let him know I can.

"Thanks for the compliment, but I've never even qualified for the ass-Olympics," I say.

"I could arrange some tryouts," Seth says, his voice low and gravelly and teasing.

I slip two fingers under the waistband of his trousers, nothing between the hard warmth of his hip except the tail of his white dress shirt.

"That's the worst pickup line I've ever heard," I murmur into his mouth.

I pull him closer, on my tiptoes. He's hard as a rock already and I shift my hips against his erection, his tongue in my mouth, my heart pounding. It's all I can do not to pull down his zipper, wrap my legs around him, and let him fuck me against this wall.

"It doesn't have to be good," he says, as my other hand strays to his open collar, finds the next button. "It just has to work. Quit it."

"You let me before," I say, fingers still fumbling.

Seth grabs my wrist, pulls it away from his shirt.

"You can't just undress me here, you know."

"It's just one button."

"There are only so many on a shirt," he says, not relinquishing my wrist. "Keep undoing them and the whole thing comes off."

"Is *that* how that works?" I tease, faux-astonished. "What about pants? Same thing?"

"You can't take those off me here, either," he says, and lets my wrist go.

I kiss him again, my back arching. His shirt rides up under my fingers and the feeling of skin on skin sends a jolt up my spine.

My hand's on his chest, and I find the button again.

"Just one," I bargain, teasing.

"Absolutely not," he says. "You know one thing leads to another and then your entire family is going to round that corner only to find me on my knees with my head up your skirt, and then Vera will never invite me to another event, ever."

I'm silent for a moment, thighs squeezed together, grappling with the thought of Seth under my skirt, the heat inside intensifying to a slippery ache.

I haven't had sex for two years, and now I've had plenty of champagne and the man whose business cards should say *good with his tongue* is talking about eating me out practically in public.

I'm somewhat aroused, is what I'm saying.

"I don't think she'd invite me either," I finally say. "She was mad enough about the tattoos."

"And she doesn't even know about all of them."

"She knows about enough to hate them," I say, playfully tugging at the button.

"But not the new one."

"Nope."

His nose brushes mine and we kiss, open-mouthed, as I tug him toward me by his clothes.

"She know about the garters?"

"Please."

"How about the butterfly?"

As he asks, he puts his palm right over the spot where it used to be, the crease where my hip meets my thigh, and he squeezes. Silk slides over my skin, my dress moving slightly askew, every tiny hair on my body standing at the sensation.

I prop one foot against the wall, knee against the outside of his leg.

"What butterfly?" I ask, all innocence and eyelashes.

"The one you like licked," he growls, his thumb moving over the spot again. "Don't tell me you got rid of it."

"It was a terrible tattoo."

Now his thumb's circling that spot, catching on the edge of my panties, and with every stroke, my hips move like he's winding them up.

"I liked it," he says. "The garters? Don't tell me the garters are gone."

The button on his shirt finally pops open beneath my finger as his thumb moves and my hips respond, my other hand fisted around his belt, my knuckles against warm flesh.

"Those old things?" I tease.

"I liked those old things," he says, and his hand moves away from my hip and down my thigh. "You can't just get rid of all your old tattoos."

"I *could.*"

His hand closes around my thigh, exactly where I've got a tattooed lace garter.

"You didn't," he says, his voice lowering. "C'mon."

"Find out," I tell him, bringing his mouth back down to mine.

Instantly, there's cool air on my leg and I make a *hmmm?* noise into Seth's mouth. It takes half a second for me to realize that in one flourish he's grabbed my skirt, pulled it up, and now he's hiking my knee against his hip and steadying me with his other arm and then pulling away from our kiss to look down.

"I meant later," I say, a little breathless. "I was trying to be *coy*—"

"Didn't work," he says, looking down at the tattoo, then up at me, grinning. "Coy? For fuck's sake, Delilah."

"A girl can try."

He runs his fingers over the inked lace, circles them to the back of my thigh where I've got a bright red bow tattooed, a matching one on my other leg.

After I got divorced, I went through kind of a wild phase. I wore a lot of short skirts, tried burlesque, smoked, drank too much, had my first and only one-night stand, and got lingerie permanently tattooed on my body. The phase didn't last the year, but tattoos are more or less forever.

Besides, I got rid of all the short skirts. No one ever sees the garter tattoos.

"Being coy doesn't exactly play to your strengths," he says.

His fingertips push underneath the gathered pink silk on my thigh. I look down, watch his fingers disappear underneath the fabric: knuckles, hand, wrist, and then he finds the edge of my panties from under my skirt, toys with them.

My heartbeat feels like it's pounding through my whole body, my skin one big delicious ache. I have to remind myself to breathe, my corset-bra tight over my ribcage.

"Seems like it's working now," I point out, sliding my hand around the back of his neck.

"That's because your attempt wasn't very coy, was it?" he asks.

Lightly, almost casually, he flicks the tip of his thumb across my clit.

My entire body jerks, and I gasp.

I swear to God Seth's pupils dilate, as if he's a predator who's spotted his prey. The wickedest smile spreads across his face.

"Want me to try again?" I whisper.

"To be coy?"

He moves his thumb again, this time sliding it over my clit through my panties. This time I'm ready and the only part that moves is my hips, rolling toward him, seeking a rhythm.

I just nod to answer his question, and his hand keeps moving: slide, slide, his movements becoming tempo, even if it's slower than I'd like.

"Go ahead," he says, that hungry, delighted grin still on his face. "Tell me something coy while I play with your clit right outside your sister's wedding."

He moves the tiniest bit faster, and my eyes stutter closed. My head goes back against the wall, and I take a deep breath, bite my lips together with my teeth.

"*Fuck*," I hiss.

"I don't think that's it."

I force my eyes open and look at him.

"This isn't…"

A wave of pleasure knocks me backward. My train of thought dissolves. My eyes are closed again and the back of his neck is cool beneath my fingers.

"Go on," he says after a moment.

He's laughing. I can tell. I'd like to kill him but then he'd stop.

I haven't had sex in the two years and few months since the last time I fucked Seth. In all that time it's been me and a few different vibrators, and while I'm strongly in favor of some self-love, it's not the same.

A vibrator doesn't slowly tease your clit the tiniest bit slower than you want. A vibrator doesn't move a little faster when you make a noise. It doesn't bite your earlobe when you turn your head to one side, cool plaster under your cheek, wainscoting gripped in your other hand.

And I've never once heard myself whisper, "I'm gonna come," to a vibrator, nor has a vibrator ever whispered back, "Please."

Somehow, when that wave crests and slams through me, I don't make a noise. I don't moan or shout Seth's name or even whimper, I just gasp for breath and press myself against the wall and feel my face flushing and my legs tremble.

Seth pulls his hand away. My skirt hasn't even hit the floor when he kisses me again, his hand going to my face and his fingers locking into my impossible hair, pinned back and sticky with hairspray and a dozen other things.

He pushes me against the wall like he can push me through it, kisses me like we're fucking. His shirt's come untucked and I slide my hand under it, his happy trail tickling through my fingers.

"The fuck are you doing?" he growls into my mouth. "I already told you not to undress me here."

I don't answer. I just slide the palm of my hand down until it finds his cock, thick and hard as fuck below the zipper of his pants.

"I don't need to undress you," I tell him. "Just unzip."

He pushes me even harder, his hips driving his erection against the flat of my palm as he groans softly into my ear.

"Cabin," he says. "Now."

"It's a chateau," I tease as I stroke him again, tip to root.

"I don't care what it's called, we need to go there before someone catches us fucking against this wall."

"Is that a prom—"

He puts the pad of one thumb over my mouth.

"You know goddamn well it's a promise," he says.

I open my mouth. Lick his thumb. He pushes it between my lips and I close them, suck on it gently.

His cock twitches against my palm, and I lick his thumb one more time, let him pull his hand away.

"It's the last one in the row," I say. "Number twelve. Here."

I pull the key from my pocket, and Seth takes it, those ferocious eyes alight.

"You're not coming?"

"I better be."

The key's in his pocket, both hands on my ass. He squeezes in response.

"You're not accompanying me?"

"I'll be there in five minutes. Ten, max."

"That long?"

His fingers find the notch between my ass and my thigh, slide inward, and I want to climb him again.

"At least let me pretend I'm not the bad sister."

"Oh, you're the *very* good sister."

"Ten minutes," I say, and tug on his waistband again, pulling him in for another long, slow, deep kiss.

"If you're not there in ten minutes, I'm finding you and throwing you over my shoulder," he promises. "And I've had more than enough whiskey to make good on that promise."

"Go," I whisper.

One last kiss, and he does. I watch Seth as he walks from the dark hallway into the brightly lit foyer. He nods at someone I can't see, and I take a deep breath, lean my head against the wall. I think my legs are still shaking.

Seth doesn't bother getting his jacket from the ballroom. He just heads for the outside door, looking casual as you please, shirt half undone, tie loose, sleeves rolled up, hair looking like someone's been grabbing it.

He gives me one last look as he exits, eyes filled with smolder and promise, and then he's gone.

NINETEEN

SETH

I don't understand why this place is a thousand dollars a night. Don't get me wrong, it's nice. It's nice as hell — stone fireplace, two leather couches, separate bedroom with an enormous four-poster bed, marble-covered bathroom complete with jacuzzi — but a thousand dollars?

I'm just saying, I'd spend it differently.

While I wait for Delilah, I flip every switch in the place. I turn the lights on, then off, then dim them halfway. I check the blinds. I start the fireplace, find another in the bedroom, start that one too. I even plug my phone into the provided charging dock, and she still hasn't shown up, so I sprawl on one of the couches, both arms along the top, and wait.

I think about the way she gasped when she came, up against the wall. I think about my thumb in her mouth, about her saying *just unzip*, about the garter tattoos that she still has, and I'm so hard it hurts.

She's still not here. It's been nine minutes. She gets two more — one because she said ten, and an extra one because I'm fucking polite — and then I'm going in there after her.

Just as I'm about to get up, the doorknob turns and the door opens and there she is, that pink dress swirling around her, the fur cape around her shoulders, cheeks and nose pink from the walk.

"I see you didn't get lost," she says, unclipping the cape and hanging it neatly on a hook.

"I assume this key only works on one door," I say. "C'mere."

Delilah bends down, takes her shoes off. She leaves them in a pile by the door and walks over to me, the drapes of her dress shining dully in the low light, the sway of her hips mesmerizing.

I think I could watch Delilah walk for *hours*.

"You said ten minutes," I tease as she crosses the room.

"What's it been, eleven?"

When she reaches me she pulls her skirt up, over her knees, and then she's straddling me, her heat and her weight right against my aching cock.

"Closer to twelve, now," I manage to say, pushing her skirt higher over her thighs, her flesh cool from the cold walk.

Delilah leans in, puts her forehead against mine. She rolls her hips and slides a hand under my shirt and I almost groan out loud, half from sheer desire and half from the pleasure of knowing she wants this just as bad as I do.

Someday, I know, she won't. Someday she'll move on without me, but not today.

"You had two whole extra minutes and you've still got your clothes on?"

My hands are all the way up her skirt, gripping her bare ass, my fingers sinking in, her skin cold but quickly warming.

"I like it better when you do it," I tell her as she rolls her hips again and we both hold our breaths for half a second, that whisper of friction utterly delicious.

"Even though you stopped me twice?"

"That was all about context," I say. "Your fancy chateau is a far cry from the hallway where anyone could walk in."

Friction. I grab her tighter, pull her against me, and I can't tell if I imagine the sound she makes or not.

"Door's locked," she says. "Is that enough, or should I go jam a chair under the knob?"

"That depends," I say, and now my hips are just barely rising to meet hers, both her hands on my skin. "Are you gonna be so loud someone calls the fire department?"

Delilah pulls my tie through my collar and tosses it across the couch, finishes off the last few buttons of my shirt, pulls me forward and I tug it off, follow it with my undershirt.

"Me, loud?" she asks, and her mouth is on mine, her heat grinding into my erection like she can fuck me through our clothes. "I didn't make a peep before."

I'm back against the couch as her fingers trace down my chest and the kiss deepens, my tongue in her mouth as I taste her, explore her. Rediscover her.

She undoes my belt, unbuttons me. She sits back with her weight on my knees, lips flushed pink, unzips me.

My hips are off the couch the moment her fingers wrap around my cock, still boxer-clad. She grabs the cushion behind my head to steady herself. Squeezes. Nuzzles her face against mine and grazes her teeth along my earlobe and strokes me again, tip to root and back, until I groan.

"Jesus, I want you," I whisper. I thrust again and she squeezes even harder, the friction of the thin fabric torture and pleasure all at once.

Then she pushes herself upright. Stands. Regains her balance. I replace her hand with mine, stroking, watching as she pulls her skirt up with a teasing smile on her flushed face, hooks her thumbs under her thong, wiggles as she pulls it down.

Delilah leans in again, her long skirt falling over her as if nothing happened, but before she can straddle me again I grab her, push her onto her knees on the couch, and then I'm standing behind her. I sway, regain my balance as she does the same.

Laughing, earrings swaying as she steadies herself. I find her spine beneath her dress and run a hand up it, slow and steady, and she arches into me as I do until my fingers are at the nape of her neck and the underside of my still-boxer-clad cock is pressed against her slit, pink silk separating us.

This time she moans, and it's not my imagination. She moans softly and pushes back against me, and before I know what I'm doing I'm taking her by the shoulder and pulling her into me, my other hand in the notch where her hip meets her thigh.

Delilah reaches back, grabs her skirt again. Pulls it up and over her hips yet again, like a pink curtain revealing the canvas of her thighs: the red bows on the backs of the garters, a shooting star, roots of a tree. One ass cheek has a tiny, delicate crescent moon on it, a tattoo she told me she got as a joke from a fellow tattoo artist.

And she's wet. God, she's wet, so wet that it soaks through my boxers instantly as I press the tip of my cock against her opening before sliding myself down, teasing her clit. She arches, pushes back again, draws a circle with her hips.

I unbutton one tiny pink button, then another. A third. Delilah stops, looks over her shoulder.

"Just rip them," she says.

I undo another, another.

"I don't want to ruin the craftsmanship," I tell her.

"It's a bridesmaid dress," she says, her voice husky, like she's forgotten how to talk. "I'm never going to wear it again."

"Still, I hate to ruin it," I murmur, just to tease her, still unbuttoning.

The truth is that these tiny buttons are the purest form of torture, a test of self-control. If I can get to the end of them without tearing one off I can do anything in the world, and when the last one comes undone I pull her up and push the lace over her colorful shoulders, and then Delilah is standing and shoving the dress off but she's still wearing some kind of bra that covers most of her torso as she leans back against me, head against my shoulder.

"Are you fucking kidding me with this?" I growl, and she laughs as I take her breasts in both hands, let her soft skin push through my fingers. She wiggles against my cock, and I find the edge of the bra, pull down.

"Better," I say, and pinch both her nipples at once.

Delilah gasps, arches, her hands fluttering to cover mine, alighting there like hummingbirds. I pinch harder and that gets a moan, another rock back against my aching erection. She leans her head back, stands on her toes.

I capture her mouth with mine, lips and tongues and teeth at this angle as she reaches behind herself, does something, and then all at once the bra is gone and it's just Delilah in her full glory.

"Really?" she says, turning. "Bras are what gets you?"

I push her onto the couch and she sprawls, one arm over her head, legs askew, gazing up at me from under those eyelashes practically made for fuck-me looks.

"That wasn't a bra," I say, planting a knee between her legs. "That was a defense system."

She drapes one arm over my shoulder as I kneel on the couch.

"Clearly, it was no such thing," she says.

I reach for her, run one thumb under her lips as she watches me, cocks her head slightly. I skim my hand down her jaw, along the jugular vein beating double time, over her naked, freckled collarbone, to where the blankness ends and the tattoos curl in from each shoulder. Over her chest they disappear into a cloud of flat tan, the makeup she still has over her newest tattoo, but lower down they wander onto her breasts.

A tentacle spirals around one nipple, a vine around the other, and before I know it I'm tracing them with my fingers, brushing them over the hard points. Delilah stiffens, inhales. Below her breasts, over her sternum is a stained-glass raven with its wings spread, a million shades of gray and blue and purple and black, almost but not quite at odds with her pale skin.

They're *her*, living and breathing and just as much *her* as her freckles or her lips or the birthmark on the back of her knee.

I bend my head, suck one nipple into my mouth, and Delilah gasps and moans and pushes her hand through my hair. She's hiked against my thigh and I hike her harder. I bite, hear the way her breath hisses between her teeth. I suck until her breathing is ragged and her nipple is puffy in my mouth, and then I do the same to the other one.

Somehow, we shift on the couch until she's under me. Somehow, my hand found its way between her legs again and I'm stroking her wetness, dragging my fingertips between her slippery, swollen lips before plunging inside her up to my knuckles.

Delilah groans. I find her clit with my thumb, stroke it as I crook my fingers inside her against the spot that makes her hips rise off the couch. She squeezes me back, pussy like a vise around my fingers, the sound coming from her like it's being ripped from her chest.

Dear God, this is what I have wet dreams about.

"You gonna make me come again before you fuck me?" she gasps.

I crook my fingers again, thumb firm on her clit.

"You tell me," I say. "Fingers or cock, Bird?"

I push my fingers deeper and move them again and whatever answer she might have given me gets lost in a desperate gasp, both her arms over her head as she grabs the arm of the couch, eyes closed.

"Cock," she finally whispers.

I pull my fingers from her though I keep my thumb on her clit for another moment and she bucks her hips against me as I pull away.

At last, I take my pants off. Delilah sits up, tugs at my boxers, wraps her hand around my shaft the moment it's freed, strokes me as one leg curls around my hip, drawing me in.

"You still good?" I ask, voice rough as anything.

"Still good," she says, strokes me again. "You?"

I bite my lip, brace one hand on the couch arm, next to her head.

"Good," I manage to get out, and then I'm bare at her entrance, slippery and tight and warm and she's half sitting up with her elbows beneath her and one leg wrapped around my hips, breath coming in gasps, tattoos and breasts moving with every inhale.

I sink into her with one hard, deep stroke, all the way to the hilt. We both make an animal noise, both clench the leather of the couch tighter in fists. Every muscle in my body tenses and Delilah does the same, arching under me, rocking slightly.

I pause, just for a moment, so I can bookmark this, come back to it later. I pause because I know it's impossible to go slow with Delilah, not when she's always felt like her pussy fits me like a glove, not when she moans while she takes every inch of me on the first stroke, not when her nails rake down my back and her legs wrap around me and I'm completely, utterly under her spell.

"Jesus, you feel even better than I remember," I whisper.

I slide my hands up her torso and let her breasts fill my hands, nipples between my fingers and she lifts her leg, drapes her knee over my shoulder and I'm fucking her again. Harder this time, millimeters deeper, and this time she moans louder, braces one arm against the couch, arches into me.

"Hard," she murmurs. "Please?"

As if I could deny her. As if I could do anything but drive into her again and again, each stroke better than the last as she gasps, whimpers, moans. We fuck hard and fast, tangled together, impossible to tell where I end and she begins.

Delilah comes hard. She comes shouting *oh fuck yes*, one leg still over my shoulder and the other locked around me. She shudders and she shakes and I follow her by milliseconds, the world filled with white light and heat and nothing else as I come inside her.

The comedown is slow. I keep rocking against her long after I'm finished, my head in the crook of her neck, both of us slick with sweat. Her fingers are in my hair again, this time gentler as I lift my head and kiss her, both of us panting for breath.

I kiss her lips, still inside her. I kiss her jaw, her neck.

Delilah is intoxicating. Enchanting. Being with her feels like standing in full sunlight: I know how easy it is to get burned, but the way the warmth feels on my skin is worth it.

My lips find the Kraken on one shoulder, red and purple and orange, tentacles intricate and delicate and I find myself following them, powerless to stop.

When my mouth reaches a nipple again, she gasps. I flatten my hand against the raven on her sternum, damp with our sweat, flick my tongue over her nipple again.

"Seth," she murmurs.

"Hmm?" I ask, nipple between my teeth as I look up at her.

She inhales again, the sound sharp and delicate.

"Nothing," she says. "I just wanted you to look at me."

I slide my hand downward, away from the raven. I slide it across the blank softness of her belly, over the hill and valley of her hips, over the velvet of her inner thigh. Finding Delilah's clit is second nature and she sighs as I slide two fingers around it, one on either side, pinching it gently.

She groans softly, shifts her hips.

"Again?" she says, her voice slightly rough.

"You're not tired, are you?" I ask.

I'm already on my knees on the floor, lips pressed to one inner thigh.

"Not yet," she says, her fingers winding through my hair again.

"Good," I say, and suck her clit into my mouth.

Her whole body jerks. Her hand in my hair tightens and she pulls me against her, hips bucking against my face as she makes a noise somewhere between a groan and a grunt.

I stroke my tongue across her, feel the vibration that

runs through her. I push her thighs apart, let her grab my hair as roughly as she wants. Delilah fills my senses: the scent of her arousal, mingled with sweat and my own scent. Her taste. The sounds she makes, breathy and gasping. The feel of her thighs on my hands, her fingers in my hair. The sight of her from this angle, nothing but plush curves with her head thrown back.

She comes fast, without saying a word, only noises. Her hips buck against me, but I don't relent. I lick her harder, faster, slide my fingers into her and stroke her from the inside, even wetter than before, her juices and mine mingling, dripping out onto my hand and the couch.

This time she gasps my name just before it slams into her, one quick breath — *Seth* — and then she's trembling, both legs shaking, and when she finishes, I rest my forehead against the inside of one thigh, my hand on the other.

I'm still drunk, sex-addled, half-exhausted, and I think: *what if I didn't have to give this up?*

TWENTY

DELILAH

Between my legs, Seth takes a deep breath, his forehead still pressed into my thigh, just above the tattooed lace garter. He's got one hand on my calf, the other, stickier hand draped over my thigh, half on my hip.

Before I can ask if he's all right, he pulls back and practically drapes himself on the floor, one arm curled over his head, the other by his side on the smooth hardwood.

"You okay?" I ask, half rolling over, propping myself on one elbow.

He gives me a thumbs-up from the floor, looking over at me, blue eyes half-closed. I flop over onto my belly, half off the couch, and reach a hand toward him.

Then I lift my head and actually look around for a moment.

"Wasn't the couch over there?" I ask, nodding at an area rug that's at least three feet away.

Seth glances from the rug to the couch, then at me.

"Yeah," he says, a grin sneaking onto his face. "It also used to have more cushions."

I look over my shoulder, and he's right: throw pillows

187

and cushions are liberally scattered at the other end of the couch.

"Oops," I say, and absolutely don't mean it.

"You're an animal," he tells me, closing his eyes, grin intact.

"I'm not the one on the floor."

"You pushed me off the couch."

"I did no such thing."

He doesn't answer right away, so I just lie there and let myself look at him in the half-light and the flickering of the fire. It's a luxury, looking at him like this: stark naked and half-asleep. Relaxed. Defenseless and oddly sweet.

And beautiful. Just so fucking *beautiful*.

You're not alone in that opinion, I think.

How many other women have laid like this, thinking the exact same —

I half-roll, half-stand from the couch before I can finish that thought, manage to get my feet under myself before I fall over completely, even though I feel like my bones are made of rubber. Seth just casts me a skeptical glance from the floor.

"Be right back," I say, and head for the bathroom.

· · * * ★ ★ ★ * * · ·

TWENTY MINUTES LATER, I'm carefully removing my eyelashes when he knocks on the bathroom door.

"Come in, I'm just — ow."

I accidentally yank on my own eyelash. How do people wear these all the time? They're hell.

"Just making sure you hadn't fallen in," he says, stepping through the door. He's wearing a very fluffy, very white robe, a second one dangling from his hands.

"Still undoing my face," I say, leaning on the counter.

I'm still fully naked, and in the mirror, I can see the slow path his eyes take down my body, not that he makes any effort to hide it. "You're not supposed to see this part."

"Which?" he asks, blatantly not making eye contact.

I'm still watching him look at me in the mirror.

"The part where I either put on or remove makeup," I say. "Really, if I were any good at being ladylike, you'd never see me without my face on."

"You can't possibly be worried about whether or not I think you're ladylike," he teases, finally looking at my face again.

"Don't tell me what I can't worry about," I tease back, finally pulling the final eyelash from my right eye and flicking it onto the counter, then blinking a dozen times in a row.

"Brought you one in case you were cold," he says, holding up the fluffy, white robe.

I take it from him, pull it on, knot the belt, reach into my hair and start searching out bobby pins.

"I'll be out in a few," I tell him, pulling one out. "I'm sure there are several issues of *Fancy Horses* or *Overpriced Trinkets* or *Spend All Your Money* magazine out there."

"I've already got too many fancy horses," he says, stepping into the bathroom until he's right behind me, looking at me over my head in the mirror.

Then, lightly, gently, he runs his fingers over my hair and deftly pulls out a bobby pin, puts it on the counter. He pulls out another, and I let my eyes close.

God, *everything* he does feels good.

"You worried about Ava?" he asks, after a moment.

I sigh, fingertips rooted on the cold countertop.

"Of course," I admit. "She's my baby sister. She's known this man, what, a year? It's—"

I stop myself before I can say *even less time than I knew*

Nolan, because we're not fighting tonight. By God, not tonight.

"— Not long enough," I say.

He pulls another pin out, gently probes my hair with his fingers, searching for the next one.

"No," he says, quietly.

Pull, probe. My head nods with the gentle rhythm.

"Speaking of idiot younger siblings, Caleb just gave up his academic career over a twenty-two-year-old," he says, and my eyes fly open.

"What?" I ask, cautious. I know what it sounds like, but I can't possibly be right.

"He got caught fucking his student," he says. "Took all the blame, and now he doesn't have a job and probably can't ever teach again."

My mouth falls open.

"They're sleeping on my sofa bed right now," he says dryly. Probe, pull. "Hopefully they're sleeping. It's not the sturdiest bed."

"Caleb *fucked* his *student?*" I say, still very stuck on that part of the statement.

"He did," Seth says, pulling out another bobby pin. "I gotta say, it's nice not being the worst brother for a while."

"Why are you the worst?" I ask without thinking.

Seth just meets my eyes briefly in the mirror, then goes back to my hair.

"You know," he says.

Right.

"I think I got 'em all," he says. My hair's come out of the low knot that the bobby pins held it in, though it's still full of mousse and hairspray and several other kinds of goop. I push my fingers into it, shake the rest free as best I can. Scrunching. Combing.

It is… not my best look.

"Thanks," I tell him, but he's already halfway across the bathroom, pulling a washcloth from a towel rack, running it under the water.

"Here," he says, and rubs it over my chest.

I'd totally forgotten my heart tattoo is still covered up, and for a moment, I'm tempted to leave it that way. Let it stay secret. Let him wonder what it really looks like, because I'm afraid that he'll take one look at it and my entire soul will be laid bare: the heartbreak and the crying and the slow getting over him, the lacing myself back together with yoga and painting and karaoke with friends and reading late into the night.

I don't want him to know all that. I want him to think that we fuck and then we fight and I stop thinking about it. I want to be the heartless witch he thinks I am, but I might have ruined that by getting a prominent tattoo of a literal heart.

After a moment, Seth frowns, then looks down at the washcloth, which has done almost nothing to budge the concealer.

"That's gonna need the big guns," I tell him.

He raises his eyebrows, looks from my tattoo to my face and back.

"I don't know what that means," he finally says.

He already knows about the tattoo. What's the point of hiding it, really?

"Here," I say, and grab a package of makeup removal wipes, then hand it to him.

"These are the big guns?" he asks, pulling one out. It's decidedly smaller and flimsier than the washcloth, and I can't blame him for being skeptical.

"It'll work," I say, and he shrugs.

I lean back against the bathroom counter, hands against the edge, and he works in slow circles, taking the thick, sticky concealer off. It takes five wipes and several minutes, and if he thinks anything about the tattoo he's revealing, he doesn't say it.

The bathrobe opens as he works, and when the whole thing is revealed, so are the edges of both nipples.

For once, that's not what he's looking at. He's looking at the tattoo, the heart with gears and levers, the heart that's riveted together and indestructible.

Neither of us says a word. We both know when I got this, and if he doesn't know exactly why, he's certainly smart enough to guess.

After a long moment, he reaches out and touches it. He doesn't ask permission, but we both know he doesn't need to: alone like this in hotel rooms, amidst our bad decisions, my *yes* is automatic and understood.

"I like it," he finally says. "It fits."

"Thanks," I say, and his hand trails down my sternum, over the raven, falls away from me.

On a whim, I take his hand. I pull him a little closer, until our feet are nearly touching, and then I reach out and push his robe over his right shoulder.

It doesn't take me a moment to find the scar he told me about, still slightly pink and raised, starting under his collarbone and slicing over his shoulder, ending just above his armpit.

"You volunteer to clean your mom's gutters again?" I ask.

Once, when we were nineteen, he cut his forearm open on the edge of a rain gutter. He's still got the scar if you know where to look.

Seth smiles, oddly sheepish, runs a hand through his hair.

"Not exactly," he says. "Can you keep a secret?"

"I kept you one, didn't I?"

"Dirt bike accident."

It takes me by surprise, my fingers still tracing the scar.
"A *what?*"

He shrugs, that same smile still on his face.

"A buddy of mine races 'em, so he let me take a spin around the track. I got too cocky on a turn, there was a rock…"

"And you didn't get stitches?"

From the looks of it, he probably should have at least seen a doctor and had the cut taped together. It's not a huge scar, but it could be smaller.

"That seemed like it might result in my mom knowing I'd gotten on a dirt bike," he admits.

I just give him a look.

"I didn't want her to worry?"

"You're a grown man who doesn't want his mother to chastise him," I tease.

"Whereas you would never hide something like that," he teases right back.

Point taken.

"At least see a professional next time you fuck yourself up," I say, running my fingers over it one last time. "And keep it bandaged until it's completely healed over. It'll take longer but scar less."

"Anything else, Dr. Radcliffe?"

"Be a smartass all you want, I know a lot about avoiding scars," I say, pulling his robe back over his shoulder. "Hell, just call me next time. I'm not a doctor but I can do better than that."

Without asking, I push down the other side of his robe, expose his left shoulder, pull it gently toward myself.

The tattoo is still there: black dots connected by black lines. If you know how to look at it, you'll see a scorpion.

"You know you could get that removed," I say.

"I could."

"Or covered," I go on. "This would be a cinch."

"You really want it gone, huh?"

I don't know what I want. I know that every time I see him, I look for it, and I know that when I find it, relief and guilt back me into a corner with a one-two punch. I don't know whether to be glad that he doesn't want it gone, or to be sad that he doesn't think about it enough to do something about it.

"It'd be pretty easy to make it into another constellation," I say, pretending I didn't hear his last statement. "You could still match the others."

All five of them have constellation tattoos, gotten right after the youngest turned eighteen. Their mom is an astronomer.

I'm a Scorpio.

"I could do a lot of things, Bird," he says, and I take my hand off the tattoo, let him pull his robe back over his shoulder.

He pulls me off the bathroom counter, turns me around, drapes an arm over my shoulder, holding me against him. I rest my head where the scar is, turn my face away from the mirror.

"You shouldn't call me that," I say.

"Why?"

"Because it's an old nickname."

"So?"

I swallow, take a deep breath, feel the ever-familiar push and pull of wanting to believe that he means it and knowing that all the hurt and anger and resentment is still there, like lava just below the surface. I know because I can feel it there, bubbling, heating.

All those other women.

"It's too old," I say. "It doesn't apply now. To this."

"You sure?"

"Yes."

He doesn't say anything, just puts his chin on top of my head, keeps looking at us in the alternate world that the mirror shows, where we're just two people sharing this moment of intimacy. Two people who've never hurt each other, simple and sweet and straightforward.

"This isn't real life, Seth," I finally go on. "This is *drunk at a wedding* life. We both know what's going to happen next, so let's just agree that tonight is tonight, and when the time comes you're going to leave before we fight about how I got married and you fucked everyone we know and then starting tomorrow, we go back to what was working."

I've got my eyes closed while I speak, but I can feel his body shifting even before I'm done: from relaxed to tense, defensive, ready to strike back.

"You mean back to pretending I don't know you?" he says, and his voice is tense, tight. It feels like a band around my ribcage.

"That worked, didn't it? For two years?"

Seth doesn't answer. Instead he drops his arm until it's around my waist, brings his other hand up to the heart tattoo.

Slowly, intensely, he traces a path through it, as if he's following the gears from chamber to chamber, coming in one side and out the other. As he does my robe opens more until I'm fully exposed and he's still covered, the reverse of before.

"Come back to bed," he says, his voice suddenly soft and warm. He drifts his hand to one breast, strokes his thumb across my nipple. It puckers instantly, like it's sitting up and asking for him.

"We haven't been to bed yet," I point. "We've only been to the couch."

"Then it's high time," he says.

Just like that, we're back to the language we know: the language of bodies and muscle and touch, of mouths and tongues and skin on skin. The language of desire so over-whelming it overrides everything else.

The bedroom is dark, lit by one lamp in the corner and the flickering glow of the fire. It gives Seth shadows where he had none before, makes him seem translucent, like he's there but already sliding away from me.

And beautiful. He's beautiful, of course. But that's half the problem, isn't it?

This time I'm on top. This time we go slow, as slow as I can stand, and as I come I grab his hand, press his palm to my face and I don't know why.

We don't speak when we're finished. What else is there to say?

Instead, we fall asleep in the huge bed, covered by expensive sheets and firelight, and as I drift off I take his hand in mine.

TWENTY-ONE

SETH

SIX AND A HALF YEARS AGO
(FOUR YEARS BEFORE THE PREVIOUS FLASHBACK.)

We're sitting at my mom's kitchen table. It's the same one that's been here my whole life: scarred but sturdy, worn and refinished, slightly ugly. It's the kind of heavy furniture from a bygone era that looks as if it could be repurposed as a battering ram if need be.

"We don't even have a place to store it," Daniel is saying. He's looking down at a mess of papers in front of us, my laptop off to one side. "It's an IPA. They don't even store well. There's a reason you never see *barrel-aged IPA*, because no one wants them."

If I didn't know my older brother so well, I'd think that maybe he was starting to panic.

"You said it can stay in the holding tank a little longer, right?" I ask, glancing at a calendar on the laptop.

Daniel nods.

I rub my hands over my eyes, wishing I'd gotten a degree in marketing and not economics. Right now I know what has to happen for this possibly-insane venture to work, but I have no idea *how* to make it happen.

"We should give it away," I tell him, a bolt of inspiration from the blue.

"We can't afford that," he says, pulling a paper toward himself. "I thought we figured that—"

From the living room there's a crash of blocks, followed by hysterical giggles.

"I crashed the tower!" toddler Rusty shouts between peals of laughter. "I crashed it!"

"Oh *no*!" responds my mom in faux-alarm. "What will we do now?"

We look at each other again, then down at the papers.

"—Figured that we'd have to sell almost everything we made in order to stay in the black," he says.

"Well, right now we haven't sold it, don't have a place to store it, and no one knows if it's any good or not," I point out. "We've got a couple more months before we go belly-up, so if we can solve two out of those three problems—"

My phone clangs from where I set it on the table, and we both jump.

"You *have* to change that ringtone," Daniel grumps. "I swear it sounds like you're in an old-fashioned fire station."

"It gets my attention," I say, and grab my phone to turn it off.

When I glance at the phone, I freeze.

THE WITCH

I clear my throat, still looking at my phone, thumb hovering over the *decline call* button.

"Butt dial?" Daniel asks, his voice grim as he looks up at me.

"No idea," I say, evenly.

"Seth—"

"I'll be back," I say, and stand so fast I nearly knock the chair over.

At the screen door to the back porch, I clear my throat, then answer.

"This is Seth," I say, as if I'm expecting a business call.

As if I deleted her number from my phone and don't know exactly who this is. Caleb wanted to, but I wouldn't let him, so he just changed her name to THE WITCH.

"Hi," she says, after a pause. I can hear background noise, but I can't put together what it is. "It's Delilah."

I think about hanging up on her, just to let her know I'm still angry. I think about demanding to know who the fuck she thinks she is, calling me. I think about telling her that she must have the wrong number, I've never heard of a Delilah in my life.

But there's a tiny, flickering glimmer deep in my heart that just came back to life, and it doesn't allow for any of those responses.

"Can I help you with something?" I ask, casual, neutral, politely curious without betraying the agonizing clench behind my breastbone.

"Do you remember what you said to me at the Whiskey Barrel?" she asks, her voice so quiet I have to strain to hear it.

"At the Whiskey Barrel?" I repeat. I need to know that I heard right.

"Yes."

Of course I remember. We got kicked out of the bar. We screamed at each other in the parking lot. I'd have punched her fiancé if Levi and Caleb hadn't been there.

"I remember," I say.

I can hear her inhale on the other end, street noise behind her. A car going past. Voices.

"Nolan and I are getting divorced," she finally says, the words rushed. "It's, um — it's over, I guess? I moved out, I filed, we're separated, he texted me that he got served his papers at the office and how it was just like me to embarrass him like that, as if I put any fucking forethought into how he got his papers. Sorry."

She says it all in one breath, and at the end, she exhales like she's coming up for air.

Delilah's not married anymore. She's not married anymore and she's calling me to tell me that she's not married anymore —

"And you're calling me?" I ask, staring out at my mom's back yard, the sun going down behind the trees. It's early August and the past week has been brutal. Real scorchers, my dad would've said.

"Do you want to come get a drink or something?" she asks, and she sounds nervous, terrified, or maybe it's just the connection. "I know we didn't really end things on good terms, but I wanted to just... talk it out, maybe?"

Yes. My heart thumps, pounds in one syllable: *yes, yes, yes*, with a fervor that surprises even me because I thought maybe I was getting over her.

If nothing else, I've definitely moved on.

"Tonight?" I ask.

"It doesn't have to be," she says. "I mean, I don't really have plans—"

"I can make tonight."

"Then yeah, tonight."

I'll have to cancel on someone else, but it doesn't matter. I don't think Abby will care, and if she does, so what? She's not my girlfriend, just a way to pass the time.

"Where? Are you still in Leesburg?"

"Don't come here," she says quickly. "It's not a good

idea, someone might see us and it's not a good look and Nolan might drag things out."

"Where?"

"The Marriott in downtown Harrisonburg," she says. "There's a bar in the lobby, Harrisonburg is about halfway between us, it looks like it's pretty nice."

I go silent for a long moment. The pit of my stomach swirls, ebbs. That deep-down glimmer grows and burns.

"You want to meet in a hotel?" I ask.

"In the bar. In the lobby."

"A hotel bar, in a hotel lobby."

Delilah says nothing. I fantasize about saying *no* and keeping the plans I've already got because Abby's a nice girl. Eager to please. Likes it when I talk dirty. Doesn't mind that I don't spend the night, says she doesn't care that I see other people.

It's just a fantasy, though.

"Downtown Marriott," I say. "Harrisonburg. I'll look for you in the bar."

"Thank you," Delilah says before I hang up, then put both elbows on the wooden railing around the porch and cover my face with my hands.

A moment later, I straighten, slide my phone into my pocket, go back inside.

"Something came up," I tell Daniel. "I gotta go. Talk about this tomorrow?"

"No," he says. "Seth. Are you kidding? Don't fucking—"

He glances at the living room, lowers his voice.

"Whatever she told you, don't do it," he goes on, *sotto voce*. "Be rational."

"It's nothing," I assure him. "Just an old friend. Bye, Mom. Bye, Rusty."

"Wait!" Rusty shouts. It's the most dramatic *wait* I've ever heard. "Wait, *wait!*"

Then she powers over on her short legs and runs straight into my leg, both arms going around it, and I can't help but laugh.

"Bye Seth," she says into my upper thigh.

"Bye, kiddo," I tell her, and lean down to plant a kiss on the top of her head. "Keep your dad on his toes, all right?"

She looks up and just bares her teeth at me, making a *grrr* sound.

"Just like that," I tell her, and then she runs back to her blocks.

I leave my mom's house, get in my car, and drive to Harrisonburg without stopping.

TWENTY-TWO

DELILAH

STILL SIX AND A HALF YEARS AGO

I get to the hotel before he does, and I have a drink. Then another. Both whiskey sours, both stronger than you'd think in a hotel bar.

Then I get a room and pay in cash. Not two days ago, my lawyer suggested that any *unseemly* behavior could be used against me in court if Nolan felt like making this more difficult or dragging this out.

Not that it really matters. We've agreed in writing to split the house down the middle, and after that, he keeps what's his, and I keep what's mine. It's all in a trust, anyway. We don't have kids or other shared property, so according to my lawyer, after the mandatory six-month separation I'm free and clear.

Right now I'm subletting, using my dad's money to live, figuring out what to do next. I know it's a luxury that I don't need to have a plan yet.

Another whiskey sour. I try to make friends with the

bartender, but she's not really interested. I google *go to college for art* on my phone.

When Seth walks in, it feels like the whole bar turns sideways, then rights itself. He looks around for a moment, sees me sitting on a stool, walks over. Hops up himself.

Orders a whiskey and puts his hand on my knee below the bar, on bare skin. I turn toward him.

"Thanks for coming," I say. "And on such short notice."

Seth just gives me a long, slow look. I'm wearing a tank top and shorts, and I wish I were wearing either more or less. More, if I wanted him to take me seriously.

Less, if I were being honest about what I want.

"Want to go sit in a booth?" I ask, nodding toward the back. His hand has already crept a couple inches up my thigh, and there's a corresponding ache in my core. "Easier to talk."

"Sure," he says, that sandpaper-on-velvet voice low.

We pretend to talk for another five minutes, but we don't really say anything. Already his hand is up my shorts and I'm practically in his lap, his erection thick steel under my thigh, when we finally kiss.

I moan when we do, because I'm drunk and a little desperate and a lot horny, because I'm twenty-three and just got divorced and I want someone to fuck me without hoping he'll knock me up.

In response, Seth bites my lip and shoves his hand under my panties, stroking one thumb over my slick folds right there in the hotel bar.

The booth's not dark enough. People are starting to look over at us but before anything can say anything, we throw back the rest of our drinks and I pull Seth to the elevator, the fifth floor, into the room I haven't even seen yet.

I'm out of my clothes in seconds, then him. We haven't

even gotten to the light switch and I'm on my knees, his cock in my mouth and then my throat and his hand in my hair, and I moan again with pure relief that this is happening, that my long mistake is finally over.

Relief that I'm wanted, not tolerated.

Too soon Seth pulls my head back, drags his thumb over my lips.

"Bed," he says, quiet in the dark. "Now."

He pushes me in front of him, sprawls me back onto the white expanse. Spreads my thighs and slides three fingers into me and strokes himself with the other hand and oh God I can't stop moaning, whimpering, making desperate little noises like I'm starved for attention.

"Condom?" he asks, crooking his fingers inside me so hard my hips rise off the bed in pleasure.

"It's okay," I whisper.

For the first time since he walked into the bar, Seth pauses.

"Birth control," I say again, pushing my hips against his hand. "It's fine."

Technically it's an IUD. Technically those three little letters are the lynchpin of my divorce, but none of that's important right now.

The only important part is how much I want Seth to fuck me bare.

He pulls his fingers out, licks them clean as I stare up at him. It's something he's never done before but holy shit it's hot, watching him casually taste me as he strokes his huge, thick cock.

I'm alight with anticipation.

"Hands and knees," he says, and I obey, arching my back, offering myself as he climbs onto the bed behind me.

Hands on my thighs, my hips. One rough thumb brushing past my clit and I move my hips backward with a gasp, practically begging. I know what he must think, but I don't care.

Then he's at my entrance and his fingers sink into my hips and my fists clench in anticipation and I hold my breath, waiting, waiting.

He bottoms out with one hard stroke, and I *groan*. My toes curl and my face is somehow buried in the hotel bed comforter, hands fisted around the ugly floral pattern. Seth uses my hips as leverage and on the next hard, fast stroke I swear he sinks even deeper and then even deeper and I'm rocking back against him, moaning and whimpering and God, I missed him.

It doesn't last long. I come at near-lightning speed, still shouting into the comforter, and he's right behind me, burying himself deep and growling *so fucking good goddamn* while he comes inside me.

He rolls off. We clean up. We don't get dressed, but we do turn on the lights.

Twenty minutes later, we do it again.

· · * * ★ ★ ★ * * · ·

FOR NEARLY FORTY-EIGHT HOURS, we don't leave the room. I put on the robe to accept room service a few times, but it's the most clothing I wear the whole weekend.

If think about this too much, I know I'll feel guilty, so I try not to think. I know what people would say if they knew that practically the second I filed for divorce, I was in bed with my ex. I've got a feeling that if Nolan, my almost-ex-husband found out, he'd use it as grounds to drag this out a little longer.

Six months, my lawyer said. We were only married for twenty. We should've been married for zero.

"I should head back tonight," Seth says from the other

side of the bed, propped on three different pillows. "I've got work tomorrow and they might have reported me as a missing person already."

"They?" I ask, lazily, lying flat on no pillows, staring up at the ceiling.

"My brothers," he says, pushing himself to sitting. "I left somewhat abruptly, and my phone ran outta juice last night."

"My charger's on the desk," I say, pointing. "You can unplug mine."

"Thanks."

He stands, walks to the desk, plugs in his phone. He's completely and utterly naked, moving as if he's never heard the word *modesty* in his life, running a hand through his messy hair, tossing his phone onto the desk, scratching his chest while it boots back up.

I just watch, because Seth is beautiful. He looks pretty much the same as the last time I saw him naked — tall, wide shoulders, tapered waist, hint of a six-pack, muscled thighs, huge dick — though maybe a little bigger in the arms and shoulders, like he's been working out.

The tattoo is still there, the only one he's got: the constellation Scorpio on his left arm. I'm surprised. I know he and his brothers all got star tattoos at the same time, I just thought he'd have covered up my astrological sign with something else.

"All right," he finally says, lazily. "Be right back."

He pads to the bathroom, closes the door. I wonder when I should go join him. If I should go join him. Sitting for two hours on the car ride back home, to the apartment I got two weeks ago in downtown Leesburg, is already going to be an adventure in discomfort.

But then again, I do remember saying *fuck me so hard I walk funny*, so whose fault is that?

I'm still debating a nice shower fuck when Seth's phone buzzes on the desk. I look down at it, past my toes, vaguely wondering if it's important and if I should at least see what it says, and then it buzzes again.

And again. And again.

Damn, Seth's phone is blowing *up*. Maybe his family really did report him missing.

I take a deep breath and lever myself to sitting. I yawn. Tentatively, I pat my hands over my hair, then decide not to find out yet. Semen leaks out of me as I stand and walk over to the desk, grab my own phone, and glance down at Seth's.

Daniel wants to know where he is. His mom wants to know where he is. Levi wants to know where he is. Caleb's texting that everyone is worried, what's going on? Eli says he just woke up to a hundred texts and would someone *please* tell him what's going on.

In the bathroom, the shower goes on, and I lean against the desk, still naked. I tap one fingernail against the wood-veneer surface, run my tongue over my front teeth as I think.

Then, despite knowing better, I reach out and scroll down Seth's notifications with one finger.

It's just his lock screen. These all came up, completely of their own accord, while I was here and he wasn't, right? I just *happened* to see them while I was grabbing my own phone, and besides these are publicly available, it's not like I'm breaking into his phone or someth —

There's a picture. It's tiny on the lock screen so it's hard to see, but it's from someone named Stacey and I've already tapped it, gone into his texts, and now it's taking up the entire screen and Stacey is nearly naked.

I stand there, naked myself, frozen. My fingertips go

cold and after a long, blank pause, my brain starts shouting a thousand things at once.

It's a selfie. She's a brunette. She's wearing a thong, nothing else, striking a pose with one leg up on the bathroom sink. There are toothpaste spots on the mirror. She's got a blue shower curtain behind her, a nice enough bathroom, triangle-shaped pale patches on both breasts, a belly button ring, the thong is black, holy fucking shit that's Stacey Hepp.

Stacey Hepp is sending sexy pictures to Seth and I want to know what the *fuck* that whore is thinking, sending my ex-boyfriend shit like this. I haven't talked to her much in a couple of years, but we were friends in high school — we had a bunch of the same classes, we used to hang out sometimes. Not best friends, but friends.

Absolutely friends enough that she knows Seth is my ex.

I close the picture, and now my entire body is flushed, hot. I glance in the mirror over the desk and I'm bright pink from my face almost to my nipples, and I look back at the phone, at the text thread I've now opened because I guess Seth's phone isn't passcode-protected.

Then I stop again, because a few messages earlier is a picture of Seth's hard dick, his hand gripped around the base.

Tears stab at the backs of my eyeballs. I'm holding my breath and I feel like I'll pop, but I can't seem to find the muscles that let me exhale.

Earlier texts. Another half-naked selfie of Stacey.

I'm so hard for you.

Show me.

They're from Wednesday. Two days before I called.

He was sexting with my former friend *last week*, and I feel like I might throw up. Stacey? What the fuck is he doing with *Stacey*?

My thumb is shaking as I go back to see all his texts. I'm now fully snooping in Seth's phone but I don't care, and holy shit I'm right not to care because there are a bunch from his brothers and a few from friends, but once I scroll down, it's all women's names.

I start opening them and feel like I've swallowed a black hole.

Still on for this weekend?

Hey, you up?

I had a really good time last night.

Touched myself and wished it was you.

There are naked pictures, going both ways, though Seth never shows his face. There are logistical time-and-date confirmation texts and there are sexy texts and there are logistical texts that turn sexy and sexy texts that turn logistical.

This isn't real, I think to myself. *There's some other explanation, like his number got mixed up with someone else's and he felt bad so he just went along with it, or —*

I barely even notice when the bathroom door opens.

"Shower's free if you need one," he says, coming back into the room. His towel is knotted so low on his waist that I can nearly see his dick, and I hate myself for noticing that right now.

"Why are Stacey Hepp's tits on your phone?" I hear myself ask, my voice higher-pitched than usual and shaky.

Seth stops. He looks from me to the phone in my hand, then back at me, his face going hard.

"You went through my phone?" he snaps, half growl, half disbelief.

"Are you fucking her?"

"Give me that."

He swipes for the phone, but I step back, clutch it to my chest.

"Answer me."

"You just snooped through my goddamn phone, I'm not answering anything."

I step backward again, the charger pulling out of Seth's phone with a light *snap*.

"What about Amber Stremp?" I spit, even as tears well in my eyes. "How about her? She sent an ass picture. You seemed to like it, you sent your cock back."

Seth says nothing. He just glares at me, jaw clenching, his beautiful blue eyes furious.

"How about Jenna?" I go on. "Is that Jenna Cowles from the grade below us? I always thought she was sweet, but apparently she had a real good time with *you*."

Liquid spills from one eye, and then the other.

"You really went through my goddamn phone?" he asks, voice low with controlled rage.

"You left it out!" I yelp. I'm suddenly loud and there's a hysterical edge to my voice, and I try to take a deep breath, hold it back. "You left it out and got texts and one was from that goddamn slut Stacey—"

"That doesn't mean you can go through it!" he says, his pitch rising to match mine. "You offered to let me charge it, I didn't know that you were going to *go through it*."

"It's not even locked!"

"I thought the people in my life were trustworthy, not backhanded sneaks," he says, and steps forward again, hand out, the veins in his forearm practically jumping.

I whisk the phone behind my back.

"Did you fuck Stacey?" I ask.

More tears. My voice is shaking. I bite my lips together, trying to win back some kind of control, but it's pointless.

"Yes," he growls. "Give me my *goddamn* phone."

The word feels like a punch, right below my sternum. Seth knocks the wind from me without so much as a touch.

"When?" I whisper.

Seth shrugs, the movement cruel in its carelessness, his hand still out for the phone.

"A few weeks ago, maybe? I don't remember."

"She sent you her tits today!"

"Then maybe I'm gonna fuck her again tonight."

Behind my back, I try to snap his phone in half with my bare hands. It doesn't work.

"What about Jenna?" I demand, naming another girl from the texts. "You fuck her?"

"Yes."

I'm silent a moment. I thought he'd say no. For some idiot reason, I thought he'd say no.

"Amber Stremp?"

"Yes."

"Lindsay Colber?"

"Yes."

"Alexis Minton?"

"Yes."

That's five. Five other women and I barely scrolled down, five women in a matter of what — weeks, months?

"Are you kidding me right now?" I ask.

Before I can react, Seth steps in, reaches around me, snatches his phone back.

"Hey!" I shout. "Don't touch me, don't you dare fucking touch—"

"Don't look through my phone!" he shouts, turning away, crossing the hotel room.

Suddenly I *feel* naked, more naked than I've ever felt in my entire life. I grab a pillow and hug it in front of myself, so at least he can't look at my tits while I scream at him.

"Tiffany Finley?" I say, still half-shouting, still out of control.

Seth is facing away, doing something on his phone, doesn't answer.

"*Seth!*"

"Yes!"

I squeeze the pillow a little tighter, knuckles white.

"Who else?"

"It's none of your goddamn business," he says, turning sideways to me, still looking at his phone.

"Who *haven't* you fucked, then?" I snap, nasty and vicious.

Finally, he tosses the phone onto his bed, turns to me, paces forward.

"Your friend Lainey," he says, bending to grab his boxers from the floor. "Your sisters. Most of our high school teachers. Anyone currently married, though I'm more than happy to fuck a divorcee. Obviously."

He pulls on his boxers, grabs his jeans, pulls them on.

"You think you're the first woman coming out of a bad marriage in desperate need of a good hard fuck?" he asks.

I watch him pull on his clothes in stunned silence, teeth clenched against the big, ugly, angry sobs threatening to break free.

"What the fuck?" I finally ask, my voice a frantic, high-pitched whisper. "How could you?"

Seth stops, his shirt in his hands. He looks at me in disbelief. Turns. Takes three steps forward so full of menace that I nearly fall back.

"You got *married*," he says.

His voice is pure vitriol, so toxic that I close my eyes.

"So you fucked everyone I kn—"

"*You* broke up with *me*," he says, voice rising, louder but less venomous. "Out of nowhere, you broke up with me in the most careless, brutal breakup and then not eight months later you were *engaged*."

I say nothing, because there's nothing to say.

"You said you loved me and then less than a year later you let someone else put a ring on your finger and you *married him* and now you're mad that I fucked someone else?"

"Everyone else, apparently," I say, quietly.

"I'll fuck whoever I want. You made it pretty clear I'm no concern of yours."

Seth turns away, his shirt balled in his hands, shakes it out, pulls it over his head. I shift my stance and wipe my eyes on the pillow I'm still holding, and then the stickiness between my thighs reminds me of something.

A new spike of horror drives itself through me.

"We just barebacked all fucking weekend," I say, and my voice is shaking again. "Seth. You goddamn *asshole*, you've been fucking anything that moves and you thought it was okay to just go ahead and—"

"I used condoms with everyone else," he says.

"That's not foolproof!" I say, pitch rising again. "You can't just go fucking people and not say a *single goddamn thing* before I let you fuck me bare. Jesus, I'm going to have chlamydia and the clap and syphilis—"

"It was your idea!" he shouts. "You're the one who was all *Seth, fuck me ba*—"

"I didn't know everyone in town had taken a ride on your dick!" I shout.

I throw the pillow back on the bed. I'm crying again, still fighting sobs as the hot ugly tears run down my face and I don't bother getting them off.

"I wrapped it up!"

"I've practically had sex with Stacey now!" I shout, snatching my underwear from the floor.

There's a brief, tense silence. I find my pants.

"She did *beg* for it raw," Seth finally says.

I look up. He's in the entryway, leaning against the wall, face hard and cruel.

I turn away, button my jeans.

"Always wanted me to spank her while we fucked," he muses.

"Stop."

"Tried calling me Daddy once, but I shut that down."

"Don't tell me this," I snap, searching out my bra.

"Amber likes getting tittyfucked," he says, his voice hard, lethal.

I pull the bra on, reach behind myself to close it and look him in the eye as I do.

"I'm so glad I didn't marry you," I say.

It works. He looks away, jaw working, something flickering across his face for a split second.

"Why, so you could get divorced and come crawling back?"

"It's better than finding out what a whore you are after we said our vows," I tell him.

I'm still looking him dead in the eyes from across the room. Still crying. Still fighting sobs, but all I want right now is to hurt him so deeply that he never hurts me again.

Seth just snorts.

"Whores get paid," he says, standing up straight. "I'm free. Bye, Delilah."

With that, he turns and walks out of the hotel room and leaves me there, half-dressed. To my credit, I don't open the door and scream at him down the hallway, I just get back into the bed and turn on the TV.

A few days later, I get my first tattoo: the silhouette of a flying bird on one hip.

TWENTY-THREE

SETH

Present Day

I wake up unmoored, like I'm floating in time. It could be midnight. It could be five in the morning. All I know is that it's dark and silent, the room too warm from the fire, light leaking in from the other room.

Delilah's still next to me, sprawled on her stomach, her face toward me, her hair frizzed around her like an electrical storm. The blankets are kicked down to her waist, and when I sit up, my head spins, and I spend a long time looking at her.

The arm nearest me is the ocean, done Sailor-Jerry-meets-stained-glass style, the same as the rest of her tattoos. The easily visible ones, at least; I know her well enough to have seen the ugly, sketchy, self-made ones on her thighs, the faded butterfly on one hip, the lace garters with the bows on the back.

The ships and the waves flicker in the firelight, almost as if they're moving. Almost as if the doomed boat could escape the tentacle closing around it, as if the Kraken might change its mind at any moment and sink back into the depths.

But it doesn't. It stretches over her shoulder and onto her chest and back, red and orange and purple. It's breathtaking, the way the tentacles look alive on her skin, the way that one wraps around one of the stars along her spine.

She's got freckles there, too. She's got freckles everywhere, if you know how to look for them: they're obvious on her face, her shoulders, her arms, the places where the sun hits easily, and they fade slowly into almost nothing on the rest of her body where the light never sees. Delilah is a gradient, a map, her islands ever-moving, everchanging.

The only sound is her breathing, the only movement the rise and fall of her back. It's perfect, and peaceful, and even though my head is pounding and I feel like hell, I want to stay.

I can't.

I know that. Even though I'm hungover as fuck, I know I can't stay. She said last night that this isn't real, and she's right: this is drunk wedding sex. It's a fantasy, a bubble, a brief glimpse into some other universe before ours comes crashing back around us.

The past is permanent, locked in, carved into stone. It will always be there, always be true, and the best we can do is ignore it for a few minutes here and there while we have some fun.

It's unfixable. I'm unfixable. I'm broken in some deep and vital way, and no matter what, I'm always going to be angry at her.

Finally, I get up. I find my clothes, pull them on. I splash my face with cold water in the bathroom, fighting a wave of nausea so strong I nearly vomit. I fantasize about getting back in bed, putting my arms around her, waking up with her a few hours from now but she made herself clear last night.

Leave before we fight.

Before I do, go back into the bedroom, watch her for another moment. She's facing the other way now, still asleep, and this time I take in the mountain vista and lake and delicate-but-bold swirling vines that rise up, over her shoulder, wrap around a different star from the other side of her body.

I don't leave a note, just put the key on the table where she'll find it. Anything I've got to say she knows already, so it seems pointless.

The cold air is instant, biting. I left my coat and jacket in the ballroom last night so I walk to my car wearing nothing but half a suit, the sky in the east turning the blue-gray of a winter sunrise.

It feels like punishment and victory all at once. It feels like penance and triumph, like I'm paying the price for something I shouldn't have done, but also like I'm celebrating the tiniest of steps forward because we didn't fight. We could have. The fight was there, waiting, wanting to come out, but we kept it at bay.

And now, back to the rules, I think as I reach my car, get in, crank the heat up. I sit in the driver's seat for a long time, head against the headrest, letting the warm air soak in until I can really feel it.

Virtual strangers. Polite acquaintances. Hello and how are you and nothing more.

I close my eyes against the sunrise. If this is victory, it feels hollow.

· · · ★ ★ ★ ★ ★ · · ·

CALEB'S CAR is in the parking spot next to mine when I pull into my complex's lot, and that's when I remember: he and his twenty-two-year-old girlfriend are sleeping on the pull-out sofa in my office.

"Fuck," I say softly to myself, rubbing my temples. "*Fuck.*"

I don't want to deal with a happy couple today. Even though Caleb just tanked his entire academic career for this girl — this *student* — ever since they reunited two days ago he's been disgustingly, blindingly happy, and I can't handle that right now.

Worse, Caleb doesn't like Delilah. I can't even blame him, because every time I've gone to her again only to be left shipwrecked, he's the one who's found me and put me back on my feet. If someone did that to him, I'd hate her, too.

I unlock my front door as quietly as I can, praying that I don't wake them up. I just want to get into my bedroom and into a shower before I have to deal with another person.

It's quiet as I close the door. It's quiet as I walk into the kitchen, hit the button on the coffee maker that Caleb set up last night. It's quiet as I climb the stairs toward my bedroom and the sweet salvation of a shower.

I'm two steps away when my office door opens.

Fuck.

"Did you just get home?" Caleb whispers.

"I went out for a run," I say, voice hushed.

"In jeans?" he asks, not fooled for a second.

I turn, look my little brother full in the face. His hair is flat on one side and sticking out on the other, voice groggy, wearing nothing but boxers. The door's shut behind him.

They're trousers, not jeans, but that point seems unimportant.

"What?" I ask, looking him dead in the eye.

"Don't do this," he says, and I fold my arms over my chest.

"Do what?"

Caleb swallows, stands up straighter. He crosses his own arms, mimicking my stance.

"Don't go back to her again," he says. "Do you remember the last time? You *swore*—"

"I was lying," I say, voice flat.

I don't say, *I'm always lying when I say I won't go back.*

If I ever say it again, I'll be lying then, too.

"Please?" Caleb says, a soft, pleading note in his voice.

My eyes are adjusted, and now I can see him better: green eyes and light brown hair that favors our mother, his face a vague echo of my own.

"I'm fine," I tell him, even if I don't know that it's true.

"Are you?" he says.

He may be an idiot, but my little brother is too smart for my bullshit.

I turn away again, walk to my bedroom door.

"Of course I am," I say. "I'm totally fucking fine, just like always. I'm gonna take a shower, see you in a few."

With that I walk into my bedroom, close the door, and don't look back at my brother standing there in the hallway.

He's right. I know he's right. It just doesn't matter.

I stand under the hot shower for a long, long time.

TWENTY-FOUR

DELILAH

When I wake up, I'm hungover and Seth is gone. Neither fact is a surprise, but I hate them both. My mouth feels like someone's glued it shut, my brain feels like it's been replaced with razor wire, and the other side of the bed is cold and empty. He's been gone for a while. I don't know how long.

There's not even a note. No, *Thanks for a good time, Seth.* No, *That was pretty fun, Seth.* There's nothing. No clue that he was ever even here aside from the stickiness between my legs and a slow, dull emptiness that I try to ignore.

I told him to leave, I think, lying in the huge bed, staring at the ceiling. We left the fireplace on overnight, and now the room is too warm, the air pressing in on me from all sides.

I said you should leave before we fight, and he did, and now I'm upset about it.

What did you expect?

I know what I expected — this, exactly this — but I don't know what I wanted. To wake up with him next to me so we could get into a fight? For him to accompany me to the brunch with my family that's in — oh, shit — seventy minutes, still wearing his suit from last night?

I get up. I shower Seth off of me and tell myself I should be happy that he's gone, because at least we didn't fight. That's the pattern half-broken, right? Fucking without fighting?

And now we go back to how things were before, where I see him around town and pretend we used to know each other and I act like it doesn't bother me that I'm probably not even the only woman within hearing distance who he's fucked.

I get out of the shower, dry off. A layer of lotion, then a layer of sunscreen, everywhere that has even a chance of seeing sunlight, because UV light and I are *not* friends. I find my brunch dress, ensure it's wrinkle-free enough, dry my hair and then fight it until I'm presentable.

I drink a glass of water, then sit on the edge of the tub for a full five minutes until the nausea passes.

Just as I'm looking in the mirror to make sure I've got no visible ink, there's a knock on the door and for a second, my heart leaps.

He came back.

He didn't, of course, and I know that before I even open the door to find my cousin Wyatt, standing on my porch and trying not to make a face.

"It's safe," I tell him. "Just me, and I'm decent. You get sent to collect me?"

"I was asked to make sure that you're all right," he says, breath fogging in the air, hands in his coat pockets. "You look nice."

"I feel like shit."

He grins, because he's an asshole.

"Shut up," I mutter, turning back and motioning for him to come in with me.

"Here," he says, holding out something in one hand.

I take it: a small packet of Gatorade powder. The flavor is *Pure Energy Championship*, which is not a flavor.

"I thought I should come prepared," he says, and he's clearly very proud of himself. "I may have forgotten underwear for today—"

"Didn't want to know that."

"—But I did come prepared for a hangover."

"Thanks," I say. "You can stay my favorite cousin."

"Thank God," he deadpans. "I tremble to think what you put lesser cousins through."

· · · · · ★ ★ ★ · · · · ·

"DELILAH!" Ava squeals, practically the moment I enter the breakfast room.

"There's the married lady!" I say, trying to match her enthusiasm.

I fail — hangover! — but I swear I try.

Ava, bless her, doesn't notice. She just gives me a giant hug and then pulls away, positively glowing with inner happiness.

"Are you feeling better?" she stage-whispers, blue eyes wide with concern.

"Yes," I stage-whisper back, though I'm not quite sure what I'm feeling better than.

"Oh, good," she says, looking relieved. "I really hope that it wasn't food poisoning or something, I know that Mom was really worried about those shrimp appetizers, and — oh, there she is."

Ava smiles radiantly, then waves across the room to where Vera's standing, drinking a mimosa and looking utterly put together, just like always.

"I think it was champagne poisoning," I tell Ava, just as Vera catches my eye.

Then she waves me over.

Crap.

"Champagne poisoning?" Ava asks, frowning. "You think the champagne was — oh."

Then she laughs. I can't help but laugh along with her.

"Gotcha," she says, and winks a truly outrageous wink at me. "I hope you're recovering from *champagne poisoning.*"

"Wyatt poured Gatorade down my throat," I say. "I gotta go see what your mom wants. Congrats, kid."

"Thanks!" she says, and I cross the room to where Vera's standing. Behind her is the mimosa bar, where a man in a vest is custom-making mimosas and various other breakfast cocktails. Wyatt's currently ordering something pink and horrifying-looking.

I have to look away when he pours champagne. I'm not sure I can ever look at champagne again. Seems like a bad idea.

"You're feeling better?" Vera asks, breaking off from a conversation with another woman who looks vaguely familiar.

"Yes, much," I say, demure and polite as you please. "Champagne really gets to me sometimes."

She just nods. It's a little judgy, as nods go, but I'll live.

"Well, I'm glad to hear it. And Wyatt told us that Seth was *very* sweet and concerned and offered to help you back to your room."

Behind her, Wyatt turns, as if he heard a cue.

He takes one look at my face, glances at Vera, and then shoots me finger guns.

"Yes, it was so kind of him," I say, and blush.

I blush so hard I think I start sweating, and Wyatt's shit-eating grin isn't helping matters.

"Well, if you see him again, I believe he left his coat and jacket in the ballroom," Vera says, voice completely cool and neutral and oh my God she knows and now I want to die.

I clear my throat. I blush harder. I think I'm sweating champagne.

"I'll let him know," I say. "Thanks."

"Of course," she says. "I'm so glad you two had a nice time."

"Such a nice time," I echo, and Vera smiles.

* * * * * ★ ★ ★ * * * *

BLESSEDLY, the brunch is a less formal affair than the wedding itself. There's no seating chart, no speeches, and the food is all buffet-style, which means that I get two cups of coffee and one piece of toast, then sit at a table in the corner and pretend that no one can see me.

I've gotten through one and a half cups of coffee and two-thirds of the toast when a plate of bacon appears in front of me.

That's it. Just bacon. A *pile* of bacon.

"Toast won't help you," Wyatt says, pulling out the chair next to me and sitting.

"Nothing can help me," I say. It's a tad dramatic, but I'm feeling a tad dramatic.

"Bacon can," he says, raising his eyebrows and pointing at the plate. "Name me a problem bacon can't solve."

I look at the bacon. Despite the current state of my appetite — nonexistent — it looks pretty good, all greasy and crunchy and... bacony.

"Vera knows what I did last night," I tell him. "I don't need bacon, I need one of those flashy things from *Men in Black*."

225

"Oof," he says, and casually takes a slice off my plate. "Well, I tried to tell her that he was just taking care of your dumb drunk ass."

After Seth went to my chateau last night, I went back into the wedding to grab my cape and also tell Winona that I wasn't feeling well and was going to bed. I didn't even think to grab Seth's coat and jacket.

"Thanks," I say, and pick up a slice myself. "Doing the Lord's work out here."

"Am I?" he asks, taking a bite of bacon reflectively. "Is lying to Aunt Vera about you hooking up with some rando the Lord's work, Delilah?"

I look at the bacon in my hand without eating it.

"One, yes, it is," I say. "Two, not a rando. We dated in high school. And have... seen each other a few times since."

Wyatt chews his bacon and watches my face, clearly running this information through the Polite Family Translator and coming to a conclusion.

"Does Aunt Vera know that?"

"She knows we used to date."

"But not the other part."

I just give Wyatt a *how much do you tell your parents about your sex life?* look.

"Delilah," he says, very seriously. "I think you won the wedding."

"Is that why I'm drinking a bucket of coffee and solving problems with bacon?" I ask, waving my slice at him. I still haven't taken a bite.

"You somehow got Aunt Vera to hand-deliver you a booty-call to the swank society event of the year," he says. "That's amazing. That's next-level."

I want to say *yes, but now the booty-call is gone and Vera knows what happened and also everyone at the wedding last night*

226

knows I'm Seth Loveless's latest fling in a long-ass line of flings, and I kind of want to crawl into a hole in the ground, but I don't say that.

"Thanks," I say.

"Teach me?"

"No."

"Is it witchcraft? I'd learn witchcraft," he says.

"You could always just ask Vera to set you up with someone," I say innocently, tilting my head.

Mistake. MISTAKE. I carefully point my head upright.

Wyatt just narrows his eyes, chewing another piece of bacon.

"I'm not sure society girls are my thing," he says, slowly. "I mean, I'm sure plenty of them are nice, but I've never like... had a super-stimulating conversation with any of her friends' kids, you know?"

"I don't think the interesting ones come to her events," I agree. "I think the interesting ones are off doing interesting things."

"Exactly," he says. "I need me an interesting woman to be my booty-call wedding date."

I finally take a bite of the bacon, chew it very slowly, then swallow. Everything seems to go well.

"I'm not sure I recommend it," I say. "I think I might wake up in the back of a truck, heading for some sort of charm school boot camp."

Wyatt just grins, then pats me on the shoulder.

"Won't happen," he says, standing. "We all know you're way past help. I'm getting another Bellini, you want anything?"

I just put my face in my hands and groan.

TWENTY-FIVE

SETH

The second I pull into my mom's driveway, I contemplate leaving. I've showered and eaten and drunk my weight in Gatorade and then coffee, so I'm at least passable, but I'm far from *good*.

I'm also not excited about facing my brothers. After this morning's run-in with Caleb, he and Thalia hung around my house for a bit before heading out to brunch in town, because they're a couple who does cute couple shit.

I still don't like their origin story. No matter what, I'm always going to think it was a fucked up thing for Caleb to do.

But I also have to admit that I can't help but like Thalia. For a twenty-two-year-old, she seems to have her shit fairly together, and you know what? She loves my brother.

Hard to fault that. I love the idiot too.

Before I can get out of the car, the screen door slams open and a puff of hot pink takes off like a rocket across the porch, down the stairs, and across the driveway.

I take a deep breath, get out of the car, and hope my

nine-year-old niece can't tell that Uncle Seth is feeling a little rough right now.

"*There* you are!" she says, skidding to a stop by the trunk of my car. "Guess what!"

"Chicken butt?"

Rusty gives me a look like I've just suggested she roll in sewage.

Note to self: *chicken butt* is no longer funny.

"No," she says, that look still on her face. "We went to the hardware store yesterday! Uncle Levi is gonna help me do the construction but he said you and Uncle Caleb would be better for helping with the plans. Come on."

Every Sunday, my mom hosts dinner at the house where we all grew up. All five of us are expected to attend Sunday Dinner if we're able, and over the years that's grown to include anyone else we'd like to invite — girl-friends, wives, best friends, you name it.

"Is your uncle Caleb here yet?" I ask, opening my trunk and grabbing a basket covered with a tea towel, wedged between a first aid kit, emergency blanket, extra jacket, and pair of old-but-usable hiking boots, because you never know what you'll need.

"No," she says, walking backward while waving her arms around in circles. "Violet and June made name tags."

"Name tags?" I echo, shutting the trunk.

I probably should have had *one* more cup of coffee. Maybe it won't be too suspicious if I make some inside.

"So Thalia knows who everyone is," she says, then pulls her jacket open.

HELLO
My name is
RUSTY
• Daniel and Charlie's daughter

229

• Knows skateboarding tricks

"Do you?" I ask, and she looks down, then back up at me.

"Of course," she says. "Come *on*. I got a ruler and a calculator and big paper and everything!"

Rusty turns, waving one puffy pink-jacketed arm for me to follow her. I lean into my car, grab the basket of scones, then remind myself that there are much worse things to be doing while hungover than helping a nine-year-old draw up plans for a trebuchet.

Right now she's into unicorns, sparkles, and medieval siege craft. Aren't all third graders?

"Seth!" she shouts, already back on the front porch while I'm still standing by the trunk of my car. "Are you—"

"Hold your horses, kid, I'm coming," I call back.

"I don't *have* any horses."

"It's a figure of speech."

"I know, I was making a joke," Rusty says as I clomp up the porch steps. "It was funny. What's that?"

"Scones," I say, flipping aside the tea towel I've got wrapped around them to show her. "There's blueberry-lemon, cardamom-vanilla, and—"

She's already taken one and bitten into it.

"—Double chocolate chunk," I finish.

"Mmmm," she says, her mouth full, tiny crumbs flying out. "It's good!"

"Thanks," I say, dryly. "Save some for everyone else, will you?"

Rusty just grins at me with chocolate-covered teeth.

· · · · · ★ ★ ★ · · · · ·

THE MOMENT I walk into my mom's house, at least two people are shouting at me. One's my mom, telling me to close the door because she's not paying to heat the outside — never mind that I've been inside for less than ten seconds — and the other is my sister-in-law Violet, asking what I want on my name tag.

"Does it matter what I want?" I call back, still standing by the front door, basket in hand.

"It's a good starting place," she says, over the general din as I hang my coat on the rack and take my shoes off, then toss them on the pile. Somewhere under the pile there's a shoe bench, but I couldn't tell you where.

I pass through the living room, where Daniel and Levi both give my basket of scones a suspicious look, and head into the kitchen where Violet and June, Levi's fiancée, are sitting at the kitchen table with Sharpies and name tags.

"You haven't even done mine yet?" I ask, putting the basket down.

June glances at the basket, but doesn't say anything.

"You just got here," Violet says. "Everyone else got theirs when they arrived, too."

"You did theirs," I say, pointing at Caleb and Thalia's name tags.

"They're the guests of honor," Violet says, straightening them. "Well, Thalia is. And I guess Caleb gets to bask in her reflected glow."

"They're still coming, right?" June asks. "We didn't already scare them off somehow, did we?"

"This family? Never," I say. "Who could possibly get scared off?"

"Put *wiseass* on his," June tells Violet.

"I can't, Rusty's here," Violet says. "And then she's going to ask Daniel what *wiseass* means, and then I'm going to have to hear about it, and I don't want to hear about it."

"I'm nearly positive Rusty knows what *wiseass* means," I point out.

Violet just frowns at me, contemplative, and taps the Sharpie against the table. June joins her.

I watch them, wondering what it's like to have a normal family.

"Okay, got it," Violet finally says, and starts writing on the name tag, covering it with her other hand. A moment later, she tears it off the sheet and holds it out.

HELLO
My name is
SETH
• Older brother
• Stress bakes
• Co-owns the brewery

"You forgot *handsomest* and *best at ping-pong*," I say. I guess *older brother* is right if we're talking about Caleb, who's only got the one kind.

"No, we didn't," June says, grinning. "The name tag is perfect and correct. All hail the name tag."

I just sigh and stick it on the breast pocket of my flannel shirt, even though Thalia has already met me several times and even stayed at my house.

It's sweet of them, really. My family can be a lot some-times — just through sheer numbers — but they're almost always the good kind of *a lot*. They're the kind who'll hassle you and meddle nonstop, but out of love.

A few minutes later, Caleb and Thalia show up, and the pandemonium increases because Eli immediately tries to involve her in an argument he's having with Levi about wood, Rusty wants to show her something, and everyone else just sort of... *descends*.

Frankly, I'm glad for the distraction.

· · * * * ★ ★ ★ * * · ·

DINNER PASSES UNEVENTFULLY, if you can call a twelve-person dinner where at one point someone starts a chant of *free the tadpoles!* uneventful. Afterward, I volunteer to clean up. Caleb and Daniel volunteer to help me, and we fall easily into the old, familiar after-dinner pattern that we all shared until we moved out of the house.

"Thalia doing all right?" I ask Caleb, rinsing plates and handing them for dishwasher loading.

"I think so," he says, glancing over his shoulder toward the living room. "Last I checked, she was teaching Rusty to experiment on Thomas's brain."

Thomas is Rusty's four-month-old brother. He barely has a brain to be experimented on.

"So long as it's the careful kind of brain surgery," I say.

Behind me, Daniel snorts.

"When I left, Thalia was explaining object permanence and hiding a stuffed monkey behind a box," Caleb says. "Hopefully they haven't progressed to sharp objects just yet."

"There's no screaming," says Daniel, stacking silverware on the counter next to the sink. "I'll worry when the screaming starts."

"Not yet," Eli says from across the room, walking into the big farmhouse kitchen.

"The screaming?" I ask.

"The object permanence," he says, opening the fridge and grabbing a beer. It's one of ours, a Southern Lights IPA. "Every time the monkey comes back Thomas is surprised and delighted."

"Same. It's a cool monkey," Caleb says.

Eli grins, then leans against the counter right in front of the dirty dishes.

"You here to help?" I ask, reaching around him for silverware.

"Nope," he says, taking a drink. "I cooked, remember?"

"Then quit being in the way."

He moves about six inches along the counter, still drinking and giving me looks I studiously ignore.

"So," he finally says, when it becomes clear that I'm not volunteering anything. "Yesterday didn't go well?" he finally asks.

I rinse the hell out of a platter. It's the cleanest platter in the world.

"Yesterday went fine," I say, grabbing a dirty saucepan.

"You showed up hungover with scones," Eli says.

"I baked for my family."

"Which are good, by the way," he goes on. "Though the cardamom ones are still a little dry in the middle, you probably need a tad more liquid if you're not going to include fruit or chocolate."

"I'll make a note," I say, swishing water around.

"Why there are hangover scones?" Daniel finally asks.

"Because I love you all and want you to be happy," I say.

"Do you two know?" he asks, ignoring my answer.

I shut off the water and look at him over my shoulder.

"You're seriously asking them while I'm standing right here?"

"You've had your chance," he says, mildly.

Briefly, I wonder what it's like to have a family that doesn't consider your personal business to be up for public debate. Is it nice? Do people leave you alone every so often? Can you just make them scones without inviting them to form an investigative committee?

"One time, I want to keep my personal life personal," I say, balancing the pot atop the platter. It's a little precarious, but I'm feeling reckless. "Just once."

"Wow," Eli says.

"It's not an insane request," I point out.

"No, *wow* that you thought attending a four-hundred-person wedding with your ex was somehow going to stay a secret," Eli says.

"You went to a wedding with her?" Caleb asks.

He's now ignoring the open dishwasher and stack of dirty dishes to stare at me. I pick up a serving bowl and put it in the sink, pointedly ignoring him.

"Her younger sister got married, and Delilah's date had to cancel at the last minute," I tell them, calmly. "So I did her a favor."

"I'll say," Caleb pipes up.

I can practically feel the pointed stares shifting focus from me to him.

"He got home at six this morning," he explains. "Even tried to tell me he'd been on a run."

"Bless your heart, you tried it," Eli says to me, in a slow, sarcastic drawl.

I close my eyes, lean my head back, and count to ten before I do something stupid like throw silverware.

Normally, I don't mind the brotherly ribbing so much. It can be annoying, sure, but I've done my fair share in the past so I can't complain that much. Like when we told Eli that everyone knew he was having a *thing* with Violet, and I thought he might stab one of us with a carving knife.

Right now, however, I'm hungover as fuck, the coffee and aspirin is wearing off, and I feel like gum scraped off the bottom of someone's shoe. My eyes feel like sandpaper. My brain feels like sandpaper.

This morning, just as I was leaving the bedroom,

Delilah rolled over, still in bed, and for a moment I thought she was waking up. I thought that maybe she'd lift her head and open her eyes and see me standing there, dressed, ready to leave.

I thought maybe she'd tell me to stay.

She didn't. She didn't even wake up, so I got one last eyeful of her — on her stomach, face awash in wild orange curls, red and blue and orange of her tattoos bright against the white sheets, and I left just like I said I would.

For once I did the reasonable, sensible, *adult* thing, and it sucked.

"Why would I ever want to keep any of you from knowing my every waking thought and movement?" I ask, eyes still closed.

"Remember the time you dragged me into the attic and made me kiss Charlie while you watched?" Daniel says, sounding far happier than I'd like.

"Yeah, you really hated that," I deadpan, finally opening my eyes.

"Are you talking about me?" says Charlie's voice.

"Only nice things," Eli says.

"You better," she says, and walks into the kitchen. "Anyway, Thalia's entertaining both our children at once, so I think Caleb should marry her."

Caleb turns stop-sign red.

"Sorry," she says, coming over. "Just kidding! I mean, or not. Your call. I like her and all but there's no rush, I didn't mean to make it weird. Move at your own pace! Don't let society dictate how your relationship should proceed? Why are we all staring at Seth?"

Dammit.

"He went back to his ex again," Daniel says calmly. "Did you have a scone? They're good."

"They really are, I had a cardamom one and it was great," she tells me.

"You didn't think it was a little dry?" Eli asks, still leaning against the counter.

"I think I'm not gonna look a gift scone in the mouth," Charlie says. "Which ex, the bad one?"

"She's not bad," I tell the cabinets over the sink a little more forcefully than necessary.

"Oh, she holds you under her thrall to feed on your soul but she's not *bad*," Caleb says, shutting the dishwasher a little harder than necessary.

"What the *fuck*?" I ask, turning toward him.

"Name a time in the last ten years you've seen her and been happy afterward," Caleb says, crossing his arms over his chest. "Go on, I'll wait."

"Wait. Ten years?" Charlie asks.

"We've had a very on-again, off-again thing," I tell her, still glaring at my brother.

"Sure. He disappears for a weekend, she drains him of his life force, and then they don't see each other again for months," Caleb explains.

"Go fuck yourself," I suggest.

"Both of you stop it. This is Delilah, right?" Charlie asks, holding out her hands toward us, like we're children she can separate.

"Yes," we say in unison.

"Redhead with a lot of tattoos?"

"Right," I say, crossing my arms, leaning against the sink.

Despite myself, I think of her last night, in the mirror, wearing the robe. Letting me trace the lines of the clockwork heart tattoo on her warm, slightly damp skin. The way I could feel her chest rising and falling under my fingers.

And later, watching a trickle of sweat drip from the hollow of her throat and over it as she rode me slow and hard, her eyes half-closed, her lips parted.

"I took a yoga class with her last year," Charlie says. "She seemed cool. The squid tattoo is badass."

She seemed cool.

"It's a kraken," I tell her, and she grins.

"Actually, the main thing I remember is the time she farted in the middle of class and then laughed so hard at herself that she fell over," Charlie goes on, starting to laugh. "And I was the only other person who laughed, and you could tell the teacher was kind of mad but yoga teachers can't *get* mad so everyone just pretended it hadn't happened, which only made it funnier, and I thought the two of us might die. From laughing at a fart."

She clears her throat.

It's the first time in years anyone in my family has said something nice about Delilah. I stare at Charlie for a moment, lost for words.

"Anyway, don't tell her I told you that because it's not the most flattering story," Charlie finishes.

"Also, she once left Seth at a motel and he had to walk eight miles to get back to civilization," Caleb says, as if this is fun, new information.

"I didn't *have* to walk eight miles," I say, crossing my arms like it'll help keep my temper in. "I could've called any of you assholes—"

"A year before that after he saw her, he didn't answer his phone for a week and when Daniel finally went to his house, he was applying for jobs on Alaskan fishing boats," Caleb goes on, still talking to Charlie.

"You'd be awful at that," Eli points out.

"Before *that*, when he came back from his fuck weekend

he chopped so much firewood at Mom's house that there's still some left after four years," Caleb says.

"I didn't realize you two had been seeing each other," Charlie says, very politely.

I give Caleb a good, hard glare that doesn't cow him in the least.

"It's complicated," I admit, arms still crossed.

"That's a way of putting it," says Daniel.

"Seth just has a really delicious soul," Caleb says, and that's it.

I swear my vision crackles, and before it's fully out of his mouth I've turned toward him, unfurled my arms, taken a step so we're face-to-face.

"You're fucking your *twenty-two-year-old-student*," I say, managing to keep my voice low. "She got you *fired*."

Caleb doesn't move, but I can feel his whole body tense.

"I got myself fired," he says, voice matching my own. "And now *my girlfriend* is in the living room, playing with my niece and nephew. Where's Delilah?"

"At least I don't have to grade her papers."

A muscle tics in his jaw.

"I'd rather grade papers than get fucked and discar—"

"STOP IT!" hisses Charlie.

I turn, and she's standing two feet away, hands in fists at her sides. We both take a step back.

"Caleb, don't be a dick," Daniel says, calmly.

Caleb looks away, shoves a hand through his hair, the universal Loveless gesture of psychological distress.

"Sorry," he says, shooting me a glare.

He's not. I know he's not, but I'm glad he's being nice enough to pretend.

"Thanks," I say, then lean against the counter. "Sorry."

"Seth, you okay?" Daniel asks. "You seem rough."

"Fine," I say.

It's not true and everyone in this room knows it's not true because I showed up hungover with a giant basket of scones. Ever since I finally learned to bake a few years ago, it's been my go-to when I feel shitty about something.

Had to fire someone at the brewery for stealing beer? Bake some cookies.

Younger brother threw away his whole entire life for his student? Brownies can help.

Spent a day and a night with Delilah, only to leave before sunrise because without saying goodbye? It's scone time, baby.

Life is uncertain. Uneasy. Unpredictable.

A cake, however, is very straightforward.

I don't even like desserts that much — I give most of it away — but baking always makes me feel better. There are explicit instructions. Expectations are clear. If I fuck up a recipe the first time, it's easy to pinpoint where I went wrong and get it right on the second try.

And at the end, I've got a tangible, delicious foodstuff.

"I'm fine," I repeat, though my audience looks unconvinced. "It's what I do, right? One night, no strings, no big deal. Move on. I'm good at that."

I lean back against the sink and try for a charming smile, though the hangover gets in the way of that.

"I'm glad you're okay," Charlie finally says, though she clearly doesn't believe it. "Eli. Is there pie? We should put dessert out so we can get the kids home."

"Yes ma'am," Eli answers.

TWENTY-SIX

DELILAH

I glance up at the clock on the wall behind the counter. It's 4:07 on a cold, shitty afternoon, and that means my four o'clock appointment is *officially*, officially late, and I'm allowed to be a little annoyed.

Generally, I give people a five-minute grace period before I get annoyed with them for being late. Clocks are different, parking can be tricky, red lights exist, and God knows I'm not always precisely on time.

Ten minutes is pushing it. Sure, sometimes disaster strikes, but ninety-nine percent of the time people who are ten minutes late just need to get their shit together.

After fifteen, I consider someone a no-show and move on with my life and appointment book.

Deep down, I'm hoping this cover-up consultation is a no-show. It's been five days since Ava's wedding and I still don't feel up to my friendly-yet-bubbly-yet-professional persona. I mostly feel like sulkily making Sailor Jerry style knife-through-a-heart tattoos and telling nineteen-year-olds that the picture of an eagle ripping away their skin to reveal the American flag underneath is dumb, unoriginal, and won't look good in five years if the sun damage they've already got is any indication.

At 4:13, the front door to my shop opens and a woman with blond hair and an enormously puffy coat comes in, already talking.

"...and I completely forgot that they're fixing the light over on Harrison, and that intersection where it crosses Salem Church took me absolutely for*ever* to get through. And then of course I got stuck behind the school bus coming *all* the way down Smith Station, and you know they stop at every single house."

"I hate getting stuck behind the school bus," I agree, switching off my tablet and straightening up. "Welcome to Southern Star."

"Anyway, sorry I'm late," she says, and finally finishes shoving things into her purse. "I'm Mindy, I had an appointment?"

Then she looks around, taking everything in: brightly lit, big windows, incredibly clean. A lot of people seem surprised when they walk in, as if all tattoo shops are seedy dens of iniquity with dirty floors and walls hung with AC/DC posters from 1985.

Sure, some are. Plenty of people like that vibe in a tattoo parlor, but since mine's the first and only tattoo place in Sprucevale — small, Southern, socially conservative — mine's not.

Southern Star Tattoo Parlor is bright, cozy, and slightly kitschy. There's a waiting area with a mid-century modern-looking couch, a natural wood coffee table, and a tall cactus that's not doing spectacularly this winter. The floor in the front room is hardwood. There's a teal accent wall with my logo painted on it in bright pink.

"Of course," I say cheerfully, still leaning on the counter. "Cover-up consultation, right?"

Mindy comes right up to the counter where I'm standing. She looks over her shoulder at the door, as if she's nervous that someone else is going to come in, and she places her purse on the counter right between us. It's got about thirty keychains hanging off one side, and they all *clunk* into the glass top.

"Yes," she says. "You did one for my brother-in-law's brother's cousin's friend and it turned out good, so he referred me on back to you."

Excellent. I *love* a referral.

"What's his name?" I ask.

"Jim Faulks," Mindy says, and then leans in a little more, lowers her voice. "He just got out about six months ago? He heard about you from his parole officer."

Right. One of the many things I did during Dating Detox was start volunteering with INKredible Transformation, a questionably-named nonprofit that helps ex-cons get their prison tattoos covered at no cost to them.

I think Jim had an ugly, poorly-done spider on one forearm. Now it's a stylized motorcycle.

"Of course I remember Jim," I say. "How's he doing?"

"Back inside," Mindy says cheerfully. "You know how people are."

"Oh," I say.

There's a brief, awkward pause.

"Well, at least he's got a better tattoo now. What do you need covered up?"

At the question, Mindy's body language changes. She stiffens. She looks down.

"It's easier to just show you," she says. "In the back room, if that's all right?"

"Of course," I say, and double down on that prayer.

The back room of Southern Star is even more scrupulously clean than the front room, if that's even possible. I go through buckets of sanitizer every week, and every Tuesday and Thursday night a professional disinfecting crew comes through.

It's got mirrors, counters, two filing cabinets. A shelf of succulents along one wall, a colorful panoramic painting of the mountains, only they're pink and purple.

On one side of the room, there's a reclining chair that looks like a dentist's chair, and on the other side, I've got a massage table.

Mindy hangs her purse on a hook, then looks at me apologetically.

Mentally, I cross my fingers.

"It's on my…" She pauses.

Looks away for a split second.

"Booty," she admits.

I smile encouragingly. A booty tattoo I can handle.

"Not a problem in the least," I say, and snap on gloves. "I'm gonna have you sit in a minute, but it's best to get a look at it while you're standing first, if you don't mind pulling down — thanks."

She's already got her jeans over her butt, so I crouch down and study her ass. This position is always a little weird, but movement and gravity affect tattoos, so I like to get a look at them in all positions.

It's a script tattoo, the lines thin and wispy, so many flourishes and curlicues that it's total nonsense at first glance. Not a bad tattoo, but not a good one, either. Some of the ink is fading, a few of the lines are a little wobbly. A solid C+.

If she'd come to me, at the very least I'd have advised her away from that particular font. It's almost impossible to read.

"Well, the good news is that at first glance, I think a cover-up should work pretty nicely," I tell her, standing.

"It'll have to be a little bigger than the original tattoo, so it'll probably be visible in swimsuits and whatnot, but I think we could pretty easily work this design into something else entirely."

"What's the bad news?" Mindy asks, looking at me over her shoulder.

"I need you face-down and booty up on the table," I say.

"I get that all the time," she cracks.

She gets on the massage table, adjusts her clothes so I have full butt cheek access. I drape a towel across the other cheek because why be more naked than you have to with strangers?

"How long have you had it?" I ask, sitting on my stool and pulling over my billion-watt light so I can *really* get up close and personal.

"Five years, I think," she says. "Wait, no. Six? I already had it when I went on my sister's bachelorette weekend to Myrtle Beach because I remember drinking too many margaritas and talking to her friend Beth about it and I think her fifth anniversary was maybe last year, so…"

I move my head around some, adjust the light while she talks. I'm tempted to ask *who* put this unreadable tattoo on her, but that seems rude, so instead I let her start telling me about her sister's bachelorette party while I try to decipher it.

"She got this really amazing beach house," Mindy's saying. "It had an outdoor shower, and I guess it's for getting sand off of you but one night after a few tequila shots some of us went out there—"

Pv… Prapiv… Property
Good Lord.
Property of…
Yikes.

Ji... Le... Leth?

I tilt my head the other way.

Seth

My stomach knots. I read it again, slowly: *Seth*.

I can feel my heartbeat in every part of my body, most of all the gloved fingers still touching Mindy's butt. My lungs feel like they're filled with aquarium gravel, but I breathe in anyway.

The last word is easy to read, because I already know what it's going to be.

Property of Seth Loveless.

I want to cry. I also want to scream. I also want to gather everyone I know into this room, point at this butt, and shout, *This is why, this right fucking here is exactly fucking why*.

"—anyway they said they'd give me a hundred bucks if I'd take my top off and throw it out, and you know it wasn't even like anyone could even see into the shower because it had a wall around it, so I figured why not? And then—"

I think of him taking the bobby pins from my hair Saturday night, in front of the mirror. Slow, gentle. The shivers down my spine. Him getting all the concealer off my chest piece. The way he looked at it for the first time and didn't say anything.

I wonder if he was thinking of this tattoo. I wonder if he'd rather mine said, in ugly, unreadable script, *Seth Loveless fucked me up*.

"It's fixable, right?" she says, and I suddenly look up at her head to realize that she's watching me, her blue eyes staring down the length of her table.

I clear my throat. I clear it again. Arrange my face.

"You should get this removed," I tell her.

"I should?" she says, surprised.

Shit. I didn't mean to say that. I push a smile onto my

face, look at the tattoo again, as if I don't already have it memorized.

"You'd be a good candidate for it," I say. "Laser removal works best when you've got dark ink on light skin."

I want this tattoo gone. I know he's not mine. This tattoo is exactly why he's not, but jealousy already has its ugly dark tentacles wrapped around me.

"I thought that was real expensive," Mindy says. "Like a couple thousand dollars at least? And I'd have to go all the way into Roanoke for each session?"

"It's not for everyone," I say as lightly as I can stand. "Just wanted to let you know it's an option. You said you've had it about six years?"

"I think that's right," she says. "Does the exact number matter? I can go back through all the pictures in my phone and figure out when exactly I got it."

I have to bite my lip between my teeth to keep myself from saying *yes*, from asking me to show me the pictures of it when it was new and tell me who she sent pictures to and what they thought and if they liked it.

If he fucked her harder when he looked at it.

"I don't need the exact date," I say, jabbing at her butt cheek with my gloved fingers, just because I can. "It's just helpful to have a general idea."

"I think it's been about six years," she says, and then laughs, her voice muffled by the padded table. "We didn't even date for six weeks."

I stand. Breathe in, breathe out.

"Must have been short but intense," I say.

I walk over to a table, pull a bolt of tracing paper off a roll.

Mindy just sighs.

"Was it ever," she says.

I know I could say something. I could tell her that I,

too, had a short but intense affair with Seth Loveless. That he's also made me batshit insane sometimes. We could have camaraderie: two women, done wrong by the same man.

I don't want it.

"As far as coverups go, we've got a few options," I say. I sit again, tattoo practically staring at me. "If your main concern is rendering the text unreadable, we could use the other line work in a new design."

"Yeah, I mostly just want the name gone," she says. "My boyfriend won't do it doggie style unless I'm wearing crotchless panties to cover it up."

That's a lot of information from a woman who called it her *booty*.

"That gives us more options," I tell her.

"Marty wants me to put his name on there instead," she offers. "And I love him and all, but I'm already getting one name removed…"

"I generally advise against names in tattoos," I tell her, and start sticking the tracing paper to her butt, folding, carefully pressing. "For one thing, word tattoos don't tend to age well. They get faded or stretched, and next thing you know they're unreadable."

"And also you might not always be with the person?" Mindy says, dryly.

No shit.

"I like to lead with the technical reasons," I say. "For some reason, people don't love it when you suggest they're going to break up."

"I wish someone'd talked me out of this one," she says.

· · * * * ★ ★ ★ * * · ·

AFTER MINDY LEAVES, I clean.

I clean everything. I wipe down every surface. I practically wrench the tattoo chair apart. Scrub the floors, the walls. I autoclave everything I can find that can go into an autoclave, just for the hell of it.

As the smell of bleach rises through the air, so thick that I prop the back door despite the temperature, I think over and over again: *this is why*.

And I think: *I'm glad he left*.

This is what happens. It's never been a butt tattoo before, but it will always be something: a lipstick in his medicine cabinet. A joke from one of his brothers. A knowing look in the grocery store.

Some reminder that I'm a name on a list. One of fifty, or sixty, or a hundred. Another notch on a bedpost riddled with them.

When there's nothing left to clean in the back room, I move to the front and get to work: vacuum, mop, wipe. I pull the cushions off the couch. I grab the Windex and painstakingly clean every inch of the big plate-glass windows in the front, both arms aching by the end.

And when I'm finished, I look out through them, onto the quiet streets of Sprucevale at nine o'clock on a Thursday night, and I think: *Bird*.

He hasn't called me that in years, not since we were actually dating, not since before the hotels and the fuck fest weekends and the fights. Not since we were young and naïve and in the kind of wild, breathless, relentless, all-consuming love that's only for the young and naïve.

I don't know why he started again, and I refuse to think about it tonight. I'm just going to leave the shop, get takeout on the way home, and then watch the relentless pleasantness of *The Great British Bake Off* until I'm numb enough to go to sleep.

I shut off the lights, close the doors, lock them behind

myself. My breath fogs into the clear sky as I make the short walk to my car. Get in. Crank the heat.

Look through the windows, stars barely visible beyond the orange glow of a streetlight. I've got no idea where Scorpio is, or when it's visible, or what it looks like.

But I flip the sky off anyway, then drive home.

TWENTY-SEVEN
DELILAH

I watch the glossy wooden planks fly by under me, scuffed with years of sneaker marks. My *Nineties Girl Rock* playlist is blasting from a Bluetooth speaker, though given the way that Veruca Salt is getting lost in the vast space of the middle school auditorium, I'm not sure *blasting* is the right word.

"Try not to hit the pads this time!" Lainey shouts.

"Right!" I shout back, and shift my weight to my left foot, dragging my right behind me at what I hope is a ninety-degree angle.

My inner thighs scream. My outer thighs scream. My quads and glutes and calves and lower back all scream as I grit my teeth and keep my core as stable as I can to keep from spinning out like last time.

About a foot before the blue pads bolted to the gymnasium wall, I come to a stop.

"Yeah, baby!" Lainey shouts.

I put both skates back on the floor and take a deep breath. I'm tempted to lean against the wall, but I've got wheels on my feet right now and frankly, I don't trust any angles besides *straight up and down*.

"Woo!" I shout back at her.

"Great! Again," she calls, and I skate back to the other side of the gym, take a deep breath, and start the drill over.

There was a time in my life when I thought I knew how to roller skate just fine, and that time was a week ago when I impulse-bought several hundred dollars' worth of roller derby gear so I could join the Blue Ridge Bruisers, Lainey's team.

Yes, buying expensive shit because you feel bad is a total rich girl move. If I were a perfect person, I would've donated it to a children's hospital or something, but I didn't, because it turns out I'm deeply flawed.

Besides, if I were one of my sisters, I'd probably have bought a car or a pet tiger or something.

I stop before I hit the pads again, this time using my other foot. Lainey's now skating up and down the court in a giant figure eight, shouting encouragement as I stop over and over again, thighs shaking a little harder each time.

Finally, I give up and just smack into the pads. They don't smell great, but I stay there for a moment anyway, unsure if I can move backward without falling over.

"You need a break?" Lainey says, coming to a perfect stop right next to me.

"I'm not gonna be able to walk tomorrow," I tell her, and she laughs.

"You can make it to the bleachers," she says. "Need a hand?"

Gingerly, I push off the pads and skate backward about a foot without falling over. Somehow, I make it to the wooden bleachers, grab on to the bottom one, and land on them in an ungainly heap.

"After my first skating bootcamp session, I called in sick

to work the next day," Lainey admits, slowly skating backward across my field of vision. "Had to reschedule a ton of appointments, and I sure hated myself for it the next week, but I wasn't sure I could get up the stairs to my office."

I shift slightly and manage to put both feet on the bench in front of me, then sprawl backward onto the bench behind.

"My foot muscles hurt," I whine. "What the fuck?"

"Skating uses different muscles than walking, or running, or yoga," she says. "It's gonna hurt."

"How many more skills do I have to learn?" I ask, staring up at the caged lights on the ceiling.

The building that's now Sprucevale Middle was built in the 1940s as Sprucevale High and hasn't really been touched since, so it's retained all of its seventy-year-old high school glory.

Such as expanding wooden bleachers that have, according to legend, crushed at least one student to death. It's probably not true, but it's probably fun to whisper about when you're twelve.

"Let's not focus on that," Lainey says, gliding by again. "I think it's best to focus on the skills you've already acquired."

"There's so many left that you won't even tell me how many?"

"It's not like I know a number," she says, looping back. "Besides, some recent studies have shown that people are more likely to excel at a new task when asked to reflect on their accomplishments, rather than—"

I groan, cutting her off.

"Next is skating backward," she says, skating past me, backward. I finally muster enough energy to unclip my helmet, put it down next to me, and rest my sweaty head on the bleachers again.

"Is that hard?" I ask, still sprawled.

"Only at first," she says, gliding to a stop. "The first time you do anything is hard. It was hard the first time you did an inverse rainbow dolphin or whatever in yoga class, right?"

I lift my head up enough to just look at Lainey for a moment, trying to imagine what pose she thinks is called an *inverse rainbow dolphin.*

"Where you go over backward?" she says.

"A backbend?"

"Delilah, I *know* it's named after some animal and a state of mind," she says, hands on hips, trying not to laugh.

"I'm not saying I'm opposed to practicing hard things," I say, finally pushing myself up to sitting. "I just want to complain about how hard they are."

"Fair," she says, and starts spinning in a circle.

For a long moment, I watch her spin, arms out, locs held away from her face in a spiky ponytail. I'm head-to-toe in protective gear, but Lainey's just got her skates on, probably because she doesn't fall on her ass every time she turns around in these things.

She spins. I put my skates on the bench in front of me and look at them: bright teal with pink laces and pink wheels. If you're gonna buy roller skates on a whim, they may as well be visible from space.

"How many butt tattoos do you think there are?" I ask Lainey, who stops spinning to face me. For the first time, she wobbles slightly.

"Do you mean in the world, or with Seth's name on them?" she asks, rocking from skate to skate. "In the world? Millions, probably. You've got one."

"The other thing," I say, resignedly.

Unlike my sisters or my family, Lainey knows everything. We've been casual friends since high school, where she was a year behind me and also in Art Club, and best friends since I moved back to town two years ago.

She's an awesome badass weirdo who counsels troubled teens for a living, and I love her.

"Probably just the one, though you'd know better than me at estimating tattoo numbers," she says. "How many butt tattoos do you see?"

"Some?" I hazard.

They're actually not particularly common. Tattoos are expensive. Most people want to spend the money on something they can show off to the public.

"And of those, how many are names?"

I shift my feet on the bench, rolling my fun pink wheels back and forth.

"A higher percentage than tattoos in general, but not a lot," I admit.

"So, statistically speaking, there aren't likely to be a lot of butt tattoos in the Sprucevale region," she says. "And when you consider that the population of women who know Seth Loveless—"

I snort at *know*.

"—Is, in terms of statistics, very small, the number of butt tattoos with his name on them is likely to be vanishingly small," she finishes. "As in, I think you've probably seen the only one."

I sigh.

"What if there's a club?" I say, rolling my feet again. "Maybe there's a harem, Lainey. Maybe there's an entire secret society of women who have 'Property of Seth Loveless' tattooed on their butts, and he takes turns sleeping with them and admiring their butt tattoos, and how am I supposed to compete with a woman who'll put his name on her ass?!"

Lainey gives me a long, considering look as she floats

backward on her skates, then forward, all without lifting a foot off the ground. I recognize the look as her *a lot to unpack here* look.

"You should take up figure skating," I say.

"It's interesting that you're framing this issue as a competition with another woman, rather than a constantly-evolving series of choices with a complex history," she finally says.

"Wow, and which of those things do *you* think it is?" I deadpan.

She spins once, grinning.

"I'm neutral." She laughs.

"Liar."

"Fine. I think the butt tattoo is an unfortunately-timed and particularly visceral reminder of your issues with Seth," she says. "I mean, you came over last week you had two glasses of wine and stood on my couch gesturing wildly and shouting 'This is why, this is exactly why!'"

Past me is right, because this *is* exactly why Seth and I aren't together.

"It is," I say. "I fucking hate seeing someone at Walmart or the grocery store or downtown and knowing that we've done the exact same thing with the exact same person."

"Virtually everyone has former sexual partners," she points out.

"Okay, I hate seeing *everyone* at those places and thinking, *hey, all the women in the produce section right now have something in common!*"

I'm exaggerating, but Lainey knows it and does some more spinning instead of correcting me.

"And maybe one of them has a secret butt tattoo," I finish.

She swirls around one more time, then stops herself on the bottom bench of the bleachers, then carefully climbs in, stretching her legs in front of her and leaning back against the railing.

"All right," she says. "In my wildly unprofessional opinion, that's a fucked up tattoo to get, but I also think it says considerably more about Mindy than it does about anyone else, and it's particularly interesting—"

"There's that word," I say.

Lainey flips me off and keeps talking.

"—That she claims to only be getting it covered at the behest of another man, because God knows if I got that tattoo and then we broke up? I'd be scrubbing the shit out of it—"

"That won't work," I point out.

"—Okay, using one of those pore vacuum things for blackheads?"

"Do you know what a tattoo *is*?"

"Applying a belt sander to my ass—"

"Major infection, horrific scarring."

"Would you please engage with the spirit and not the letter of my statement?" she says, and I laugh.

"You'd figure out it," I say.

"Exactly. Though I also wouldn't get that tattoo in the first place. With anyone's name."

For a moment, she stares across the gym, suddenly distant.

"You okay?" I ask after a beat.

She sighs.

"I always wonder what leads women to do shit like that," she admits. "*Property of.* She has no idea."

Awkwardly, I pull my skates off the bench in front of me, and they land with a loud, echoing *thump* on the bleachers. Without standing — much, much too risky — I scoot over to where Lainey's sitting, get into the footwell next to her, and put my arms around her waist, my head somewhere around her boob.

"Thanks," she says.

"You're a lovely, magnificent jaguar," I say.

"You're a beautiful, stupendous manatee," she says back, putting her arm around my shoulders. "You still want to learn to skate backward, or should we call it a day?"

TWENTY-EIGHT

SETH

Then, one day, I see her.

I knew it would happen. It's happened plenty before. It's why we have the rules I hate.

It's a Thursday night, just after seven. I volunteered to take Rusty to her tap dance class to give Daniel and Charlie a break, and afterward she talked me into walking to the Mountain Grind for hot chocolate.

It didn't take much convincing. I'm a softie.

"She's kind of a know-it-all, but she's usually right," Rusty's saying. "And even though her parents were muggles, she's way better at magic than the boys. And she's *way* cooler."

Rusty sighs.

"You think Dad and Charlie would let me go to boarding school?" she asks, looking up at me.

"Not a chance," I say, grinning. "Wouldn't you miss them? And Thomas?"

"I'd be home for holidays and stuff," she says.

"I don't think boarding school is like the books," I say, gently.

Rusty gives me the most patronizing look I've ever seen on a child, and I have to fight not to laugh.

"I know Hogwarts isn't real, Seth," she says. "I mean a regular one."

I don't think Rusty actually wants to leave home and only see her family on holidays and weekends at the tender age of nine. The kid would be homesick like crazy.

I *do* think she's read a whole lot of novels about kids at boarding schools, both magical and ordinary, who get to have fun adventures, solve mysteries, and save the day, all without parental interference.

"Rusty," I say, and put a hand on her shoulder. "It's a ways away, but you're gonna *love* college."

She sighs again. Do most nine-year-olds sigh this much?

Fifty feet in front of us, a door opens.

Delilah walks out. The world tilts.

"Maybe sleep-away camp this summer," Rusty's saying.

Delilah waves to someone inside. Lets the door go.

Looks straight at us.

It's like a heat lamp. Always.

"Don't you think that would be educational?"

She stares at me for a moment, face unreadable. There's a yoga mat in a bag slung over one shoulder, her hair in a high bun, and she's got leggings and winter boots on. When she sees Rusty, she smiles.

"Hi," she says, shoving both hands in her coat pockets when we walk up to her. Her face is still slightly flushed, the edges of her hair damp. "Really nice night out, huh?"

No personal questions or comments. No inside jokes.

Just polite small talk.

"It's very nice," I say, my voice perfectly neutral. "Have you met my niece, Rusty, by the way?"

"It's been a while, I believe," Delilah says as Rusty holds out her right hand, *very* seriously.

"Charmed, I'm sure," Rusty says with a perfectly straight face.

Delilah grins so big I think her face might crack in half.

"Absolutely," she says, clearly trying not to laugh. "What a pleasure."

"Likewise," says Rusty, and lets Delilah go. She adjusts the strap on her shoulder again, looks me full in the face. The smile fades.

"Yoga?" I ask, nodding at the door she exited.

"Yep," she says. "And you?"

"Just finished dance class and going for hot chocolate at the Mountain Grind," I say.

I want to say *care to join us?* but I shut my mouth before I can.

"Well, I'll let you get to it," she says, turning on a bright smile again. The one that doesn't fully reach her eyes. "Nice seeing you. Rusty, I remain charmed."

"Later," I say, and try to catch her eye as she walks away, but I can't.

"Bye!" Rusty hollers, and that's it. That's all. Just *nice night* and *yoga class* and *hot chocolate.*

Not even *don't you think it smells like snow?* Or *they finally took the Christmas lights off the trees* or *how have you been?*

Rusty and I keep walking, and it's not until we reach the next crosswalk that I realize she's giving me a really funny look.

"What's up, kiddo?" I ask, already dreading the answer.

Rusty doesn't say anything. She just frowns up at me, like she's trying to add two and two on a calculator and the answer keeps coming up five.

"Nothing," she says, uncertainly.

· · · · · ★ ★ ★ ★ · · · ·

I STAND in the middle of the room, cross my arms, and look for the yellow dot.

I don't see it. The room is filled with kegs — on the floor, stacked two or three high, all jammed into this space — but I don't see the yellow marker I'm looking for.

I cross my arms a little harder and keep looking. Our inventory clearly states that we've got one more remaining keg of Deepwood Loch Scottish Ale, and the sports bar over in Grotonsville just asked if we had any left.

It's here somewhere. My inventory system doesn't lie. I just don't know *where*.

Footsteps enter, and I turn. Arms still crossed.

"You want to talk about it?" Daniel asks, standing just inside the doorway.

"About the fact that we have a clear, concise keg organizational system that our employees regularly flaunt by putting kegs wherever they're standing when they get bored with carrying them?" I ask. "Sure. They're all fired."

"I meant about the fact that you've been a miserable bastard for two weeks and especially for the last two days," he says, unruffled.

"I'd rather find the last Deepwood Loch and get back to work."

Daniel pushes the door closed, runs a hand over his face, and turns back to me.

"All right," he says. "Which color is it?"

"Yellow," I say. "Probably says DLSA on the side if you see that first."

For a few minutes, we look in silence, and I've got no choice but to either find the keg or wait for whatever Daniel's got to say.

He speaks up first.

"I don't hate her, you know," he says.

It's not the conversation starter I was expecting. I spent

several extra moments examining a keg of Irish Red Ale, just to make triple sure it's not what I'm looking for.

"Who?" I ask.

"In fact, I strongly suspect that you've been just as much of an asshole to her as she's been to you," he says, ignoring my question.

"So you didn't come in here to try and cheer me up."

"I came in here to see if I could do anything before our entire staff quits because one of their bosses is on the warpath for no apparent reason," he says, bending over a keg.

After a moment, he looks up and right at me.

And then he waits. And waits.

I'm the one who breaks eye contact.

"After Ava's wedding, I went back to her room," I admit. "Where I agreed to leave before we got into a fight, and I did."

Daniel grabs a keg by the top, pulls it away from the others, and sits on it. Leans his elbows on his knees.

"And?" he says.

I pull a keg against the wall, sit on it, lean back.

Then I give Daniel the rest of the truth. He knows most of it, but I tell him about the rules of interaction. About seeing her at the brewery. About saying no to Vera and then later, saying yes.

About proposing friendship only to kiss her in the dark a few hours later, though I keep it G-rated.

I tell him that she told me to leave, that she wanted to go back to those stupid fucking rules, that I agreed to both things because I know she's right.

"So I left," I say, lacing my hands together on top of my head. "And I saw her two nights ago, and we talked about the weather, and I hate it. This is what we do, over and over again, and I wish I could stop it and I can't. Every single time I think it's the last one and then I see her again and it's the right time and the right place, and I can't say no to her."

I tilt my head back and push the heels of my hands into my eyes.

"I've never turned her down," I confess. "God, not once. This is why I apply for jobs on Alaskan fishing boats and at breweries in Montana."

"What?" Daniel asks.

I take my hands from my eyes. He's blurry, but alarmed.

"I didn't seriously pursue it," I say.

"A brewery in Montana is miles more serious than a fishing boat," he says.

He's right. They called for an interview and I never called back, but I picked the phone up and thought about it a dozen times.

"Yeah," I admit, head still back against the wall.

"You're thinking of moving across the country instead of working it out?"

"It sounds ridiculous when you put it that way."

"Just a thought."

I take a deep breath, cross one ankle over the other knee.

"I thought the wedding might be different," I tell my brother.

This is the first time I've admitted it, even to myself. Daniel listens, silent.

"It was…" I trail off, clear my throat. "More complex than our other interactions."

Meaning, *we spent a long time together with our clothes on.*

"But now we're back to talking about the weather, and in six months or a year or something we'll just do it again."

"Then don't."

"That's the point of moving to Montana. I can't avoid her if I live here," I say.

"My next sentence is going to sound sarcastic," Daniel warns. "I swear it's not."

"I can't wait."

"Have you considered a clothed, sober conversation?"

He's right. He sounds like he's being a dick.

"We agreed not to—"

"If she'll fuck you nonstop for an entire weekend she'll probably agree to talk," Daniel says, his patience finally gone. He pushes a hand through his hair, which is getting floppy, and gives me an Older Brother Look. "I know you think she's made of sex pheromones walking around in a human suit or something—"

"Oh, my God," I mutter, face in hands.

"—sorry, Thomas is having a sleep regression and it's been *rough*," Daniel says.

He takes a moment, looking down at the floor.

"Listen," he finally says. "If you want me to hate her, and call her a witch and talk about how she boils frogs and eats souls and makes you dance like a puppet for fun or whatever, I will. But I really fucking hate seeing you hurt like this. So... try something else. Please?"

He stands, brushes his hands together, and heads for the door.

"And in the meantime, don't be such a dick to our employees," he says.

"You're not even gonna help me find the beer?" I ask, still seated.

In the doorway, he turns back. Then he points at a keg a few feet away from where he's standing.

It's the Scottish Ale.

"Good talk," he says, and then leaves.

In protest, I stay there for another five minutes.

265

TWENTY-NINE

DELILAH

I drive with my left hand and shake out my right, opening and closing my fist. Most of my day today was spent putting a huge, abstract piece on the thigh of a man with lots of patience and a high pain tolerance, and who told me he'd prefer to get it over with in as few sessions as possible.

Fine by me, though now my needle hand feels weird, not to mention the shoulder cramps. Even though afterward I grabbed dinner with Beau, who gave me the latest updates on Nana's Squirrel Adventure, I've still got knots.

Finally, my driveway comes into view. My house is a hundred feet back, a stand of forest between my driveway and the road, the house itself barely visible through the trees. I thought about buying a house in town, but this one had a sort of charm it's hard to describe — an odd, lofty, open-feeling farmhouse that seems equally suited to canning in the kitchen, vintage oddities in the living room, and naked dances around a bonfire in the back yard.

I haven't had a bonfire yet, nor danced naked in the back yard. Someday.

I pull in, turn my car off. Contemplate the darkness for a moment. Massage my right hand with my left, which helps, but not all that much. The cold is already starting to leach in from the window, and I take my scarf from my passenger seat, wind it around my neck even though it's a short walk to my front door.

I get out, shut the door, and a black shape unfolds from the steps to my front porch.

I scream and *bolt* back into the car, slamming the door shut. I hit the lock button about a dozen times in a row, my heart pounding and my mouth dry, suddenly freezing inside my coat.

Oh fuck there's a murdering Bigfoot on my front porch fuck fuck where are my keys I had them one second ago this is why Vera wanted me to live somewhere with a gate —

I finally pull the keys from my coat pocket, and with the cool metal in my hand, I finally take a deep breath.

It's not Bigfoot, I remind myself, and finally brave a look out my window.

The murdering Bigfoot... waves?

And the wave is *very* familiar?

I flop my head back against my seat and take another deep breath, my heart still pounding but now for an entirely different reason.

"What the hell?" I mutter to myself and open the door again.

"I thought you were Bigfoot!" I shout.

"Sorry to disappoint," he calls back.

"What are you *doing*?" I call, walking up the path through my front yard toward him, adrenaline still shivering through me. "Are you just sitting on my porch steps in the dark? The porch steps of a woman who lives alone?"

From the look on his face, he hadn't considered that part of the equation.

"I'm sorry," he says, and he actually sounds contrite.

I take a deep breath, still trying to settle my nerves, rub one hand over the back of my neck.

"I have a phone," I point out.

"I needed to talk in person," he says, and suddenly the rattle in my veins is replaced by an empty spot in my chest and I notice, for the first time, that there's something in his hand.

It's a basket. There's a cloth draped over it, and the empty spot blossoms into dread, dark and shiny, echoing the last time one of us showed up at the other's house with an offering.

It's working, isn't it? Our agreement?

"I don't know how to talk to you less," I say, just staring at this basket. "My life's here. My family's here. I have to go out in public—"

"I didn't wait on your porch steps in the cold for an hour to say we should never speak again," he says.

A cold breeze rustles through the leafless trees, tugs at the strands of hair not stuck in my bun and wafts one across my face.

"Then what did you bring a fruit basket to tell me?" I ask. "If you want to bribe me to leave town and let you be, that's not—"

He flips the cloth off and holds it out to me.

It's... scones?

"I like you," he says, simply, and it feels like my heart sticks to my ribcage, forgets for a moment that it should be beating.

I watch Seth, waiting. I don't take a scone. I wait for him to finish the sentence, to tell me the real reason he showed up at nine at night with baked goods. To deliver the blow we both know is coming.

"But?" I finally prompt.

"But nothing," he says softly. Still holding out the basket. I look down at the scones, back up at him. I dig my hands deeper into my pockets and will myself to stand up straighter.

"There's always a *but*," I say, and I make myself look right into his eyes. "I like you, *but* I also wish you didn't exist. I like you, *but* I love sleeping around. I like you, *but* we both know that liking isn't enough."

I breathe deep, look away again because the blank space in the pit of my stomach is still there, writhing, gnawing at me. I know that something ugly's about to happen. I can see it coming a mile off, like a train's head-light in the dark.

"Start over with me," he says.

I hold his gaze, swallow hard because that wasn't what I was expecting either. None of this is what I was expecting, and I've got no idea what to make of it.

"How?" I finally ask.

I also take a scone. They look really good.

"I hate pretending we're strangers," he says, voice low, quiet in the cold dark night. "I hate it. We aren't strangers. Even after all these years, you know me better than almost anyone and I'm tired of pretending you don't."

I want to protest, out of habit. I want to remind him of all the ways we've hurt each other, all the barbs we've thrown, the venom we've spat. I want to tell him that being strangers is better than being locked in a joust with each other, always aiming for the heart and running at a full gallop.

Instead, I take a bite of the scone. Mostly so I don't say any of those things.

"Blueberry-lemon," he says before I ask. I chew, swallow.

"Did you make them?"

"Yup."

I take another bite, the sweet-tart of a blueberry spreading across my tongue.

"You're wrong," I tell him.

"They're definitely blueberry."

"You're wrong that I know you. I didn't know you made scones. I didn't know you rode dirt bikes sometimes. I didn't know you sat on porches in the dark."

"I don't, as a rule," he says. "Ideally I won't be doing it again."

"I don't know you as well as you think," I whisper.

"I bet you know why I like baking," he says.

I take another bite, watch him in the faint moonlight.

Seth is beautiful. He always is, but right now the moon is behind the clouds, the pale white light diffused across the landscape. Everything in my front yard has a shadowless, unearthly glow, most of all Seth.

He looks like a charcoal drawing, all shades of the same color, his edges smudged and blurred by the dark. I wonder if any artist could ever do him justice.

"Because it's quantifiable," I say, after a moment. "It's predictable. If you do everything according to the instructions, you'll almost certainly succeed."

He smiles in shades of moonlight-blue.

"Told you so," he says. "Start over with me. We'll wipe the slate clean of all the bullshit we've said and done and we'll just be two people who like each other, going on dates and having movie nights and taking long romantic walks, and…"

He runs a hand through his hair, smiles at me.

"Whatever other cute shit couples do," he says. "Just say yes, Bird."

I breathe deep again, exhale in fog, look away from Seth and over at the driveway.

"So we just… pretend nothing has ever happened between us?" I ask.

Seth doesn't answer, just reaches his hand to my face. I try to stay still but I can feel myself tilting toward him anyway, like a flower toward the sun.

He brushes a crumb from my cheek. Looks at me. Lets his hand linger before lowering it.

"Exactly," he says.

"You really think we can?"

"I think it'll destroy me to keep fucking and fighting and being barely polite in public," he says, shifting his feet, the basket against his hip. "And I think that if I don't try this one last time, I'll never forgive myself."

My throat constricts, and I swallow against it, pressing my lips together. I've always been an easy crier and I've never liked it.

When I open my mouth, I mean to say *yes* or *okay* or even *I'd like that*, but what comes out is, "I miss you."

Seth's face changes, softens. Like he's just lowered a shield, and he steps forward, slides his free hand around the back of my neck and before I can tilt my face up toward his, he presses his lips into my hair.

"Come out with me Friday," he says, voice muffled, lips still against my hair. "Our very first date. If you're lucky, I'll kiss you goodnight."

"Just a kiss?" I tease, and he releases me.

"That's yes, then?"

I take a deep breath and close my eyes for a second, as if I have any wits left about me to gather.

"Of course it's yes," I tell him.

"There's one more thing," he says.

"You *are* Bigfoot."

"I want to wait to have sex."

Those words, in that order, take several moments for

my brain to process. I'd be less surprised if he unzipped his human suit to reveal an ape-man.

"What?" I finally say.

And then, still baffled: "Until... when?"

Sprucevale is small, southern, and has approximately four churches per capita, so when I hear *wait for sex* I automatically fill in *until marriage*, which was very much not Seth's attitude a few weeks back.

"A month?" he says.

I narrow my eyes and tilt my head.

"You can't do that," I say, simply.

"*I* can't?" he asks, grinning.

"What, you think you're God's gift to women?" I tease.

"Not women," he says, grin gone feral. "Just you."

I roll my eyes at him, but my heart beats a little faster, harder.

"You cocky asshole," I laugh. "Ever seen my tits in a push-up bra? You can't last a month."

"Only a month?" he says. "Come on, make it tough. A month and a half. I made you see God after Ava's wedding."

At least the dark hides my blush.

"I'm not the one who nearly passed out on the floor after we were done."

"That was the whiskey."

"Was it?" I ask, tilting my head slightly.

"The whiskey was a factor," he admits. "Two months. Bring it on, Bird."

"You'll never make it," I say.

"Only one way to find out. Deal?" he asks, and holds out his hand.

I slide mine into it, and we shake.

"Deal," I say, as he raises my hand to his lips.

"Friday," he says, still holding my hand. "Six. Don't be late."

"Do I even get a kiss?" I ask.

"Maybe at the end of our first date," Seth says. He grins at me again, all cockiness and rakish charm. "What kind of floozy do you take me for, Bird?"

"Drive safe," I tell him, laughing. He walks to my driveway, scones in hand.

I go into my house. Lock my door. Head to my bedroom.

And I fire up my vibrator, who will apparently remain my sole companion for the foreseeable future.

THIRTY

SETH

When I pull into Delilah's driveway Friday night, the first thing I see is eyes.

Glowing, beady eyes. Six of them.

Again. They were here the other night, too, and I'm starting to feel like they've got something against me.

"Scram," I tell them, getting out of my car. "Go on, *git.*"

The biggest raccoon sits down on the bottom step, like it's waiting for me to entertain it.

"Bastard," I mutter, and glance around for a stick or something.

Of all the varmints, I'm the most cautious of raccoons. Not only are they bigger than you'd think, I've heard Levi's *every single raccoon has rabies* talk more times than I care to remember.

I don't want rabies. I just want to take Delilah out on a date, so I grab a fallen branch and walk toward the porch, waving it.

"Get outta here," I tell them.

They glare, but when it becomes clear that I *will* poke them, they waddle off.

I toss the stick away, mount the steps, ring Delilah's doorbell before I can get nervous.

"Come in!" she shouts, barely audible through the door. "It's unlocked."

I obey, glancing back one more time to make sure the raccoons aren't following me. Sneaky, fearless bastards. My mom once came home to one lounging on her kitchen floor, surrounded by half-eaten bananas. She had to chase it out with a broom.

There's no Delilah.

"It's you, right?" she calls, her voice echoing through space, still invisible.

"Do you pay those critters to guard your house, or is this some Snow White setup where they volunteer because you're a magical forest princess?" I call back.

There are footsteps over my head, and a few moments later, she appears, leaning over the railing on the stairs to my left.

Purple leopard print robe. Wet hair. Holy fuck.

"You're early," she says, but she's smiling.

"I hope you're wearing that," I say, and Delilah looks down, as if she's forgotten what she's got on.

"Are we going to a pajama party hosted by Andy Warhol?" she asks. "I still don't know where we're going."

"I told you," I tease, forcing myself to make eye contact. "I'm taking you to a sock hop. I don't know how to be any more clear than that."

She puts her elbows on the railing, shifts her hips. The robe is made of something shiny and flowy — silk, do they make robes out of silk? — and it drapes against her in a way that makes my mouth go dry.

"Then I guess I have to go put on my poodle skirt and

put my hair in a ponytail with a bow," she says. "I'll be out in a few. Make yourself at home, there's a couch in the living room and drinks in the kitchen, I think?"

I don't want her to put on clothes. I want to walk up these stairs and pull open her leopard print robe and push my fingers through her damp hair and see what she tastes like right out of the shower, but that's the whole problem.

We've been in lust for years. Time to try something new.

"Reservations are at six-thirty," I tell her, taking off my coat and scarf and hanging them on the rack.

"I know, you keep reminding me." She laughs, pushing herself off the railing and disappearing, her voice getting dimmer. "You're the one who was early!"

"I'm not that early," I say, and glance at the clock on my phone.

Ten minutes barely counts as *early*, but I quit arguing and head into Delilah's house.

It's a surprise.

Maybe it shouldn't be. Maybe I, of all people, should know that a proper, staid exterior can hide a whimsical, airy interior, but I didn't even think about it.

The outside of her house is an old farmhouse, the same as every other old farmhouse around here: two stories, white siding, Adirondack chairs on the front porch. Windows. A door.

But inside it's open to the roof beams, the soaring ceiling clearly responsible for the odd acoustics. The entire ground floor is open, nothing but an island separating the kitchen from the living room. The back wall is glass almost floor-to-ceiling. One corner has a fireplace set in smooth black stones that go all the way up the wall.

The staircase leads to a second-floor landing that overlooks the living room, one of the doors slightly ajar. I can't really see inside from this angle, but despite myself, I sure do try.

Everything here is bright. It's *eclectic*. Hanging from the ceiling is a chandelier made of what looks like driftwood. The coffee table is glass and steel. The couch is deep brown leather, flanked on one side by a sleek, modern steel lamp, and on the other by a lamp shaped like a hula girl. The wall next to the fireplace is floor-to-ceiling with framed art: paintings and photographs and drawings. Prints. A vintage-looking poster for the Ringling Brothers.

I stand there for a moment, looking around, soaking it in. Even if I've never been in here before, it feels oddly familiar and comforting. Like it's a home I never knew I had.

Upstairs, a hairdryer starts, and I head into Delilah's kitchen. It matches her living room: a breakfast nook with benches upholstered in bright floral fabrics, wall above it covered in art, windows looking out onto her front porch. White cabinets, marble countertops.

After a few tries, I find her liquor cabinet. Delilah's selection is unusual, but I like a challenge, so I push up my sleeves and get to work.

I'm just pouring my concoction into the glasses I found when I hear footsteps on the stairs. Moments later, she walks into the living room.

I almost knock a glass over.

"I meant *grab a beer and sit on the couch*," she says, laughing. "You didn't have to play bartender."

I just shrug and glance at my hand so I can make sure I'm putting the cocktail shaker down squarely on the counter and not dropping it into empty space or something.

"I had to do something while I waited," I tease, still staring.

She's wearing a dress, the bright green of fancy olives.

It's high-necked, long-sleeved, knee-length. It's tied around the waist and moves with her and even though this dress is modest enough to wear to a meeting with the Pope, I feel like it was designed specifically to remind me of what's under it.

Her hair's down, her mane tumbling past her shoulders. Gray tights, brown boots. Freckles on her face, her neck, her forearms when she pushes up her sleeves and leans against the far side of the kitchen island.

I tear my eyes away long enough to crack open a can of seltzer that I found in her fridge.

"What are they?" she asks, raising one eyebrow. "I didn't know I had ingredients for... anything."

"A creation of my own devising," I tell her, pouring the seltzer. "Sweet vermouth, rum, a splash of lime, a little grenadine, and soda. Oh, and celery bitters."

"Fascinating," she says, putting her chin in one hand. "You think it's a good idea to make us drinks?"

I give each glass one quick stir and push one toward her.

"I've got no idea what you mean," I say, holding mine up. "I'm just a near-stranger who you let rummage through your kitchen. Besides, they're pretty weak."

She lifts her glass, clinks it gently against mine, and we both take sips. Delilah raises one eyebrow.

"Huh," she says thoughtfully, as we both lower our glasses.

"Well," I say. "It's not *bad*."

"I didn't know I had vermouth *or* celery bitters," she says. "Would you believe I don't actually drink that often?"

"Based on what I found, yes," I say. "For the record, you've also got Creme de Menthe and tequila, but I couldn't work those in."

"Thank God."

We both take another sip. The second one is better.

"Do I get a tour?" I ask.

Delilah scoops one hand under the glass, holds it from the bottom.

"You treat all your first dates like this?" she asks, smiling.

"Only the ones who give me free rein while they dry their hair."

"True. You could've stolen my TV, but look what you did instead," she says, sipping again. "You know, this really *could* be worse. I think I kind of like it now."

With her other hand, she picks up the cocktail shaker and swirls it once, like she's seeing if there's any left, and when it catches the light I realize there are letters on the side: DPN.

She sees me looking and puts it back on the counter, takes another sip of her drink.

"It was a gift," she says, as I puzzle at it for another moment. *DPN* aren't her initials.

"A wedding gift," she specifies, then looks at me, rolls her glass between her hands. "How clean is this clean slate, Seth?"

Delilah and Nolan Prescott. Of course.

"Whistle," I say.

"I used to be married," she says. "Got the cocktail shaker in the divorce."

"Don't tell me that's all," I say.

"There's an etched glass carafe here somewhere," she says, dryly. "And I'm pretty sure I wound up with the monogrammed napkins, too."

"You kept all those things?" I ask.

As if I'm a neutral party. As if these are interesting facts and nothing more.

"They come in useful sometimes," she says, shrugging.

279

I want to ask her what else she kept. I want to demand a detailed, itemized list: what she kept, why she kept it, whether she thinks of him whenever she uses it. What was so great about it.

And then, despite myself, I'd like to find everything on that list and break it.

"Are you going to tell me where we *are* going?" Delilah asks, draining her glass. "I can't believe I'm letting a near-stranger virtually kidnap me."

"Dinner and a sock hop," I say. "How many times do I have to tell you that?"

"So the answer is no, you're not going to tell me?"

I push the shaker and the carafe and the napkins from my mind.

"The answer is you'll know when you get there," I tell her.

"You sure are pushing it for a first date."

"You haven't kicked me out yet."

Delilah laughs, still fiddling with her empty glass, sliding it back and forth along the counter.

"That's your standard?" she teases. "If a lady doesn't kick you out, she must be having a good time?"

I put my empty glass down, grip the edge of the counter, lean in.

"Tell me, Delilah," I say. "Are you having a bad time?"

"Not at all," she says, her smile crinkling the corners of her eyes. "You still want that tour?"

"Of course," I tell her, and she nods me around the island and into the living room.

It's a brief tour. We don't even move from where we're standing, because when you're standing next to her couch you can see everything: the kitchen I've already acquainted myself with, the living room itself, the stairs, the second floor with a bedroom, a bathroom, and an office-slash-studio.

"Can I see the studio?" I ask her when the one-minute tour is over.

"Aren't we already late?" she asks.

"Then five more minutes won't matter."

Delilah sighs. She's wearing a long necklace with an amber pendant at the bottom, a scorpion trapped inside, and now she starts fiddling with it.

"I don't like showing people unfinished pieces," she says. "Or doodles, or anything that I've put down and I'm not sure I'm going to pick back up, or ideas I had that I abandoned, or just... anything not fit for public consumption."

I open my mouth to tell her that I'm not *people*, for God's sake, but I don't. The whole point of this is that I *am* people, so I just nod and say, "Fair."

I don't ask if I can see her bedroom.

As we're getting our coats, I notice the photographs on the wall by the front door. They're vivid, over-saturated, so bright I can't believe I missed them when I first came in. On the left is a photograph of a window, taken from across the room. Between the lens and the window is a couch with a girl sprawled on it, looking away. On the right is a photograph of an open door, a welcome mat in front of it, the greenest grass and bluest sky beyond the threshold.

"My mom's," she finally says. "When I moved back, I started going through all her stuff that's been in storage."

I think, briefly, of the things I'd say if this really were a first date. I'd say, *I'd love to meet your mom someday* or *why is her stuff in storage* or *she can't tell you where it is?*

But I'm not that much of an asshole, so I let the clean slate smudge because I know this part of the story: car accident, underage drunk driver. The teenager who was blitzed at eleven in the morning walked away, but Delilah's mom was pronounced dead on the scene. A month later, Delilah moved here and started her sophomore year at Sprucevale High.

"I like it," I tell her.

"Thanks," she says, and together, we consider the photographs for a long moment. "She mostly did weddings and babies and stuff, since that paid the bills, but the artsy, moody stuff was her favorite. Ready?"

I study the photograph for one more moment, then turn away, open the door for her.

"Ready," I confirm, and we leave.

THIRTY-ONE

DELILAH

"You *named* them?" Seth is saying, face lit by the blue light of his dashboard.

"I couldn't just call them *that one, that one,* and *that one,*" I say.

"You absolutely could've," Seth says.

"We have a relationship."

He just gives me a look.

"I bought them the fancy dog food!"

I get that look again, for an extra second this time.

"They eat garbage," he says, sounding baffled. "They're *varmints.*"

"You really are from around here," I tease.

"Because I said varmint?"

"Because you said it with *that* tone of voice."

"Tell me, Delilah," he says, a smile on his lips. "What tone of voice do fancy city folks use when they call critters *varmints?*"

"I'm pretty sure most fancy city folks think that *varmint* is a flavor of chewing gum," I say, laughing. "Anyway,

Larry, Jerry, and Terry are very happy to be my masked backyard friends."

Seth just shakes his head as he puts on his blinker, then turns off the main road and into a driveway.

Next to it, there's a big wooden sign that says FROG HOLLER in colorful letters, and suddenly, everything falls into place.

"We're going *square dancing*?" I ask, turning to face him.

Seth just grins.

"You nerd." I laugh.

"What's nerdy about square dancing?" he teases.

"Besides everything?"

"You've never even been before," he says, gravel crunching under his tires. "Square dancing is cool."

"We had to learn it in middle school gym, and it is *not* cool," I laugh. "I can't believe you're taking me on a date activity that I did in a gymnasium while the boys spent the week in health class learning about their dicks."

"I assure you none of the boys learned a single thing that week that they didn't already know," Seth says.

I lean my elbow on the window ledge, looking over at him. He's even hot when he drives, with one hand on the steering wheel and the other touching the gear shift with two fingers, relaxed and confident and in control.

"What?" He laughs when he sees me looking.

"I don't have a response that falls within the bounds of our agreement," I tell him as he pulls up next to a pickup truck and shifts into park.

"Which part?" he asks, narrowing his eyes at me. "The clean slate part?"

He shuts the car off, cuts the lights, pulls the keys from the ignition and suddenly it's near dark.

"The no sex part," I tell the dark as I unbuckle my seatbelt.

"We agreed not to do it, not to keep from talking about it," he says, and his voice is a lazy drawl, his features starting to come into view. "Unless you're telling me you were about to say something about middle school sex-ed so intensely erotic that I was going to throw the whole agreement out the window."

"Ew," I say, laughing.

"Good," Seth answers, and I can hear the smile in his voice, nearly see it in the dark. "Come on, let's go square dancing."

Outside the car, he takes my hand, and we walk toward the converted barn together.

"Unless," I say. "You brought me here to do corporate espionage."

Frog Holler is a cidery, so they make hard apple cider. Seth Loveless half-owns a brewery. Surely there must be some competition.

"Would that make it nerdier or less nerdy?" he asks.

"Depends on the espionage."

"Which is it if you flirt with the owner while I break into the backroom to discover their brewing secrets?" he teases, and I laugh.

"I think you're more Marcy's type," I say.

I wish I hadn't the moment it's out of my mouth. All I meant is that Marcy's straight and Seth is male, but the moment I say it and he doesn't respond that bright, ugly flower blooms in my chest.

"I doubt either would work," he says, after a moment. "How do you know Marcy?"

"We took a — uh, a dance class together," I tell him.
Did he fuck her? He can't have. She's married. He wouldn't. Right?

I take a deep breath and try not to show it.
Starting over, let it go. Clean slate.

"We hit it off and she ended up hiring me to paint the mural on the other side of the barn," I go on.

Seth stops in surprise, looking over at me.

"The big one?" he asks, pointing off into the dark. "With the frog and the apples?"

"Is there another mural?"

"I didn't know you did that."

We're almost to the barn, and from inside a voice calls: "All right, everyone, if you ain't got a place yet, find one!"

I study Seth's face for a moment.

"Is this a clean slate thing, or…"

"No," he says, and smiles, looking a little sheepish. "I've been it a hundred times and didn't know."

"I made the front page of the paper," I tell him as we walk through the door. "You didn't see that?"

I guess it was a slow news day. Seth just shrugs.

"No," he says. "Hand to God, I had no idea I'd been looking at your mural all this time."

"You two!" a man's voice calls from the stage. "You here to dance? Get your coats off and get up front!"

"Nerd," I whisper to Seth, shrugging out of layers.

He just winks at me.

"You like it," he whispers back.

· · · · ★ ★ ★ ★ ★ · · · ·

FINE, I like it.

Turns out square dancing is totally fun, which isn't something I ever thought I'd say.

As soon as we get our outer layers off, the man directing us from the stage informs us that we'll be joining the square nearest him.

His name is Bill, he's wearing a Texas tuxedo, and he

informs us that we'll be joining the square near the front of the dance floor so he can keep an eye on us.

After he says that, he winks. If he had a mustache, I think he'd be a dead ringer for Sam Elliott.

"You better watch out," I murmur to Seth as we walk onto the dance floor. "I bet Bill's got moves."

That gets a hand pressed to my lower back and a tingle up my spine.

"I didn't bring you here so you could do-si-do with someone else," Seth teases me.

"Did you bring me so you could steal cider secrets?" I ask, innocently.

"I brought you here because I've never tried square dancing and, to be excruciatingly honest, it sounds fun," he says. "There you have it. You're here for a fun date. That's all."

"Sorry," I say, laughing.

Turns out the *square* in square dancing is four couples who stand facing each other in — you guessed it — a square. Our square is us, one other first-time couple, and then two middle-aged couples who might the most pleasant and patient people I've met in my entire life.

"All right," Bill's voice announces a few minutes later. "Welcome to beginner square dancin' night! Now I know most of y'all haven't done this before, so we're gonna start you off real easy with a square through — curlicue — fan the top to a half tag — trade — scoot back — relay the deucey!"

Stunned silence reigns for a few seconds before about half the people there start laughing.

"I'm just pullin' yer leg," Bill says, and this time he waves to the still-chuckling musicians behind him, and they start playing a fiddle and a banjo.

Seth and I exchange an *I guess this is square dancing humor* look.

"Now," says Bill. "The person you brought is your partner, and the person to your other side is your corner. To start things off, you're gonna bow to your partner, bow to your corner, and then join hands and walk in a circle."

Right away, I step on Seth's foot.

· · * * * ★ ★ ★ * * · ·

THE SQUARE DANCING lasts for two hours. Bill gives us a thirty-minute break in the middle, so we get hard cider from the bar at the end of the barn and then sit on hay bales, drinking and laughing and talking with the other couples there.

Seth seems to know at least half the people in attendance. He even gets their names right and does things like ask how grandchildren and dogs are doing. How kitchen remodels are going. Whether they bought that new truck they were thinking about.

The whole time, I can't help but think: no *wonder* he's so popular with women. I knew he was charming, but until Ava's wedding it had been years since we were together in public, so I never really saw it in action.

The second round is harder than the first, because I guess easy mode is over. Afterward, I'm sticky and sweaty, holding my hair off my neck, pretending that I'm not breathing as hard as I am.

Seth, on the other hand, is grinning at me, both of his hands on his hips. He's also slightly sweaty — it's hot in here — the sleeves of his flannel shirt rolled right above the elbow, his hair slightly askew in that rumpled, unguarded way.

I keep looking at his forearms, because Seth has nice hands and *really* nice forearms: muscular and solid, distracting whenever he clenches his hands. I can see the veins, but they're not weird. Just… hot.

"So, you gonna be buying rhinestone cowboy boots and joining the circuit?" he asks.

"No to the second, but maybe to the first," I say, and look down at my shoes. "I think they'd look good on me. Maybe we can get matching pairs."

He gives me a quick up-and-down look. I hope the sweat between my boobs hasn't visibly soaked through my dress.

"Matching cowboy boots seem like a third date discussion, Bird," he teases. "I thought we were taking it slow?"

"Don't tell me you're afraid of commitment."

"I'm afraid of rhinestones."

"What did they ever do to you?" I ask, taking a deep breath and releasing my hair. It sticks to my neck again, but not as badly this time.

"To start with, they're damned liars," he says as we walk from the dance floor. His hand finds the small of my back as we move. I wonder if it's sweaty. If it is, it doesn't seem like Seth notices.

I step past a hay bale and give him a *what are you talking about* look.

"Pretending to be diamonds, but what are they, just bits of glass? Plastic?" he goes on. "It's all trickery and falsehoods."

"I had no idea you felt so strongly about rhinestones," I tell him.

"Neither did I," he admits.

It takes us another ten minutes to leave, because small town square dancing isn't the sort of event you can simply walk out of unless your house is on fire. Small talk is mandatory, and I think it might actually be a crime in these parts to leave an event without saying goodbye to everyone else in attendance.

Finally, we make it to the coat rack. Seth holds mine while I put it on, dons his own, takes my hand.

Pulls me in the opposite direction of the main door, toward the back of the barn.

"C'mon," he says, walking toward a door that says EMPLOYEES ONLY. "I want to see your mural."

"I thought you'd seen it."

"I didn't know you'd painted it."

"Does it matter now that you know?"

Seth nods to the bartender, then pushes open the EMPLOYEES ONLY DOOR and leads me through into a dark room, lit only by a bright green EXIT light.

"And *now* are we doing espionage?" I ask, blinking in the near dark.

"No, I've seen a storage room before," he says.

We go through the other door, and then we're out in the cold. I take a deep breath and enjoy it, my coat open and my scarf loose around my neck.

We walk over to the side of the barn, frozen dead grass snapping softly under our feet, cold breeze blowing through my hair, tugging at my skirt. Still casually holding hands even though we'd be warmer if they were in our pockets.

"What are you doing tomorrow night?" he asks, after a moment.

"I'm busy," I say.

"How busy?"

"Quite."

"With what?" he asks, looking over at me. He's frowning slightly, mock-offended.

"I have *plans*," I tease. "They don't concern you."

"All right, but are they better plans than going to Snowfest in Grotonsville?" he asks.

The last Saturday of every month, the next town over has a wintertime street fair. All the restaurants and shops stay open. There are hot chocolate stands, pie carts, soup vendors, and horse-drawn carriage rides.

"They're more inescapable," I tell him, still walking through the grass. "Olivia and Michael are having my whole family over for dinner so they can announce that she's pregnant."

"In that case, sounds like you can skip it," he says.

"But then she'll never make me the godmother," I say. "She might even bar me from the baby shower planning committee."

Seth stops, my hand still in his, and gives me a one-eyebrow-raised look.

"Just kidding, there's no way she'll let me off the hook for that," I say. "What, the four of you didn't throw an elaborate baby shower for Daniel?"

"We had a party and bought them baby stuff," he says. "Though Charlie made us promise not to have games or make her open presents in front of everyone."

I just sigh.

"I like her," I say.

"How about Sunday?" Seth asks.

"I could make Sunday work."

"And Monday?"

"You've never read a self-help book, have you?" I tease.

We're on a slight rise, off to the side of the barn, the mural of a frog jumping onto apples lit by floodlights.

"Are you implying that my self needs help?" Seth asks.

"I'm implying that all the books about dating tell you to

wait some number of days before asking for another date," I say. "You don't want to be too eager. Then your date might think you like them."

I read a handful of those books early in my detox. I didn't think much of them.

Seth just snorts.

"Fuck that," he says. "I like you and I'm eager to go on another date. Tell me about the mural."

I have absolutely no idea what to say, other than *it's a mural* and *Marcy commissioned it,* and I feel like I'm twenty again and trying my way through art school, feeling like everyone around me had a deep explanation for their abstract triangles that were *actually* representative of their struggles to come out to their family, and I was over there painting rainbow guinea pigs because I thought they looked nice.

I clear my throat.

"Well," I begin, pointing at the side of the barn. "That's a frog, and it's jumping into that basket of apples. Probably because it likes apples."

"Sure, but what do the apples *represent?*"

"They represent apples," I say. "I don't know, I failed out of art school twice."

"You went again?"

"And failed out again," I say, and look up at him. "Ta-da, double art school dropout, right here."

I give a small curtsey, and Seth rolls his eyes.

"They fucked up and this is great," he says.

"This mural took twice as long and cost twice as much as it was supposed to," I admit. "I had to paint over a week's worth of work because I had no idea what I was doing and when I actually looked at it, it was absolutely awful. I still have no idea why Marcy didn't fire me on the spot."

"Probably because you were willing to paint over the thing and start again," Seth says. "I think a lot of people would have just kept on with the ugly frog and acted like it was supposed to be that way."

The metaphor doesn't escape me.

"How *do* you paint something that big?" he asks, after a moment.

"I used a grid," I say, waving my other hand at the side of the barn. "First, I drew it on a piece of paper with the same dimensions, but a grid on that, and transposed it square by square to the side of the barn. It was very methodical. Sort of like a spreadsheet for art, you'd like it."

"I can appreciate art without spreadsheets, thanks," he says.

"But do you appreciate it more with them?"

"No comment."

We stand there for another moment: frog, apple, sunset, trees. I lean my head against his shoulder, the wool of his coat slightly rough against my cheek.

"What's it like to get things right on the first try?" I finally ask.

"What do you mean?"

I mean that his life seems charmed to me: he went to college and graduated, came back to his hometown, started a business with his brother. One, two, three, done.

"I mean, you didn't fail out of art school twice," I say.

"I probably would have if I'd attended art school."

"Come on."

He pauses a moment, adjusts his hand in mine.

"In college, I almost got a degree in literature, but talked myself out of it because what use is that?" he asks.

It's a rhetorical question. I don't answer it.

"I started an application to study abroad in London for a semester, but never sent it in," he says. "I graduated with a degree in economics, moved back to my hometown, took a job like I was supposed to overseeing the finances of a small mining company, and I hated every minute of it but they paid me well enough so I stayed. Because that's what happens, right? Hate your job and make a living?"

I nearly say *you never told me you wanted to study abroad*, but change it at the last second.

"I didn't know you wanted to go to London," I say.

Seth's quiet for a moment, his fingers flexing against mine.

"I decided I didn't want to be that far from my girl-friend," he says, after a long pause.

I think of all the things that I could say, but I don't say any of them. I want to tell him that I'd have wanted him to go, experience the world, then come back to me, but I know that's not what I'd have done.

At twenty, I'd have talked him out of it and into staying in Virginia. I'd have been afraid that he'd leave and find someone better than me, because I was insecure and selfish and felt like I was flailing my way through life.

I just watch his face from the side, but he doesn't look at me. As Seth talks, he's just looking at the mural, his eyes drifting over it like he's committing it to memory.

"And after college, Levi was off, in the woods, doing his mountain man thing," he goes on. "Eli moved away for ten years, and we'd get phone calls from Thailand and post-cards from Australia. Daniel found out one day that he had a ten-month-old daughter, and a month later he had full custody. Caleb followed his dream and went to grad school. And I was the stable one."

I don't know this man.

Standing there, in the cold, by the barn, the weight of that realization settles on me like snowfall: that all these years I've spent thinking I know Seth, I've been wrong. All

I've gotten since we broke up when we were twenty-two has been glimpses into him, skewed snapshots of his life at any given time, like taking a picture of a funhouse mirror.

To me he was wild, reckless, intense. He was the man who'd answer my calls at any time of night, who'd drive hours for a booty-call. He was the man who'd call me, voice rough, ask if I could be at some motel by sundown.

He talked dirty, fucked hard, broke my heart more than once, and I had no idea what the rest of his life was like.

"And the brewery came so damn close to failing," he says, sounding more amused than anything. "Actually, the first time I called y—"

He looks down at me, narrows his eyes.

"I called an ex when I thought it had failed," he says, circumspectly.

"She show you a good time?" I ask, feeling dangerous.

I remember that rendezvous. A year or so after our first. I'd just gotten to the end of my post-divorce *bad girl* phase, and the garter tattoos were pretty new. Seth liked them then, too.

We fucked. We fought. I cried all the way home, convinced I was an idiot for doing it again.

"Mostly," he says, and I laugh.

"I'd ask what the good parts were, but we've never even kissed," I say, leaning into his side a little more, trying to push the memory of that particular meeting from my mind.

"I don't want to start painting before I'm finished drawing the grid," he says, and grins.

"Are you trying to impress me with an art metaphor?" I ask.

"Are you impressed?"

I shift my stance so I'm now half-facing him, half-facing the mural, and I look over at it.

"There are plenty of muralists who just paint away with no guidance at all, and it looks fine," I point out, tilting my head. "They just barrel on straight ahead as the spirit moves them."

He turns toward me, lifts our joined hands, spins them so they're upright and palm-to-palm.

"Anything I've ever done right was with careful planning and strict adherence to regulations," he says, a teasing little half-smile on his face. "Sometimes the rules are there for a reason."

I step closer to him so that we're nearly touching. Carefully, without breaking eye contact, I kiss the closest knuckle of his index finger, his skin cool against my lips.

"Tell me the rules," I say.

"Don't you already know them?"

"I want to make sure I'm crystal clear."

Seth swallows. His fingers tighten in mine. His eyes go to my lips, linger, come back up.

"No past," he says.

I kiss another knuckle.

"No fucking," he says, and now he's smiling.

I put my lips to a third knuckle, hold my eyes on his.

"Is that it?" I ask, softly. "Only two rules?"

"Are you asking for more?" he teases, voice low and rough, trickling down my spine.

"Just surprised that's all," I say. "For your talk of careful planning and adherence to regulations."

"I can come up with more," he says, and one eyebrow twitches, and his smile deepens into one that opens a maelstrom in my chest. "No fuck-me looks. No wearing purple leopard print robes when I'm around. No dresses that make you look like a sweet society princess when I know you're covered in tattoos an inch below your neckline. No naming raccoons or laughing at my jokes. No telling me you're busy tomorrow night and can't see me until Sunday."

"Go on," I laugh.

"No enjoying yourself at square dancing," he says, and pulls me in. His other hand goes to my neck, his thumb on my cheek, his fingers in my hair. "No asking me for the rules. And don't you *dare* kiss me back."

Then his lips are on mine, warm as anything, and I forget the cold. I forget art school and London and I forget all the rules and I kiss him back as hard as I can.

He opens his mouth against mine, teases my lip with his tongue. Pulls back, his mouth millimeters from mine. Pauses. Kisses me again and this time it's urgent, needy, his other hand underneath my coat and pressing against my back and I find his tongue with mine and God, I want to drown in him.

This is why I keep coming back, again and again. This is what makes me cast everything else aside and throw judgment to the wolves, the reason I've never been able to stop myself.

Nothing else makes me feel like I'm a match, held to sandpaper. Like I'm a firework with a lit fuse, counting down the moments. With Seth, I always feel one second away from igniting.

It's a long time before we finally pull apart. We're both breathing hard, both wanted the other more than we needed air, and he rests his forehead against mine, thumb on my jaw.

"I missed you too, Bird," he finally says.

I don't answer. Just kiss him again, softly.

We kiss until the lights on the mural go out and we're plunged into moonlit darkness. We kiss as someone closes the barn door, gets into a pickup truck, leaves. We kiss until we can see perfectly in the dark, until we're both shivering, until we finally stop and I tuck myself against him, eyes closed, his chin atop my head.

Maybe this will work, I think, his arms around me.

Please.

Then we walk to his car and leave.

THIRTY-TWO

SETH

We go out again Sunday night: dinner and milkshakes at a cheesy diner, one of those ones with a jukebox at the table. I play her "I Want to Hold Your Hand" and she rolls her eyes at me, but she's smiling.

Then she plays me the Beach Boys song "Wouldn't It Be Nice," because she's making fun of me, so I play "Season of the Witch."

"Black Magic Woman." "I Put A Spell on You." Delilah runs out of quarters, so she has to borrow one to play me "Hound Dog."

Afterward, we walk along the river path hand in hand and talk about whether a boat could make it all the way here from the sea, and what kind of boat, whether anyone would want to. We walk for two hours without meaning to, down the river and back through town, until we're at the diner again and it's nearly ten o'clock at night.

Two nights later, we meet after work at the new gastropub downtown, and we drink beer and eat burgers and don't realize the time until the staff tells us they close in fifteen minutes. I kiss her by her car, out on the sidewalk, and I kiss her so long and hard that a pedestrian clears her throat at us.

We see movies together and share popcorn. We go wine tasting in the hills. Visit historical sites we've never heard of before and take audio tours. One beautiful Saturday we wake up early and hike to the top of Bareback Peak, have a picnic, and manage not to bring up the name until we're in the car, heading back to town.

We hold hands. I open doors for her and she rests her head on my shoulder when it gets late. We casually kiss hello and less-casually kiss goodbye. We text each other goodnight and good morning like total dipshits, but I smile every time.

And we make out like teenagers, sometimes in public: in movie theaters, in parks, in the front seat of my car or hers. I try to abide by the rules we set ourselves but it's impossible not to slip past them sometimes, like when she straddles me on her couch and I grind her hips against mine until I'm on the brink. When I reach for her waist and brush a nipple instead and before I know it I'm pinching them both as she moans into my mouth and God I want her right there, right then, up against the wall but somehow I stop.

We never spend the night.

After a few weeks, she brings me to dinner with Lainey and Beau. They're suspicious at first but by the end of the meal, I'm telling Beau about the time we had to throw out an entire batch of beer because a chipmunk somehow got in and drowned, and he's giving me a run-down of the top ten kinds of squirrel trap. We agree that they're all varmints.

Daniel and Charlie have us over for dinner, where Delilah agrees to design Rusty's first tattoo for her and then

Thomas has a blowout while she's holding him, but she washes the poop off her arm and laughs.

We tour a distillery with Eli and Violet. I can tell Eli is skeptical. I would be, too, but by the end of our double date Delilah and Violet have sampled the whiskey and Delilah is telling Violet that I once called stemmed wine glasses an 'inefficient use of space,' and Violet is laughing and telling Delilah that Eli has such an exacting system for his spice organization that she's not allowed to touch it.

"It *is* inefficient," I mutter to Eli.

"It once took me ten minutes to find the paprika," he mutters back. "I like her, though."

Levi and June take us on a hike one day, and Levi's harder to read — is it skepticism or just his quiet, steady personality? —but by the time we've hiked two miles he and Delilah are deep in discussion about how the sky isn't really blue, then about how red pigment comes from beetles, and by the time I hear her drop the bomb that the color magenta is a figment of our imaginations, I'm pretty sure she's won him over.

When we say goodbye that evening, he looks at her, then looks at me and nods.

Caleb is the holdout. Whenever I mention her, he changes the subject. If I invite him and Thalia somewhere with us, he's always got plans. He never comes out and says it, but I know what he's thinking.

I text Delilah all day, every day, about absolutely nothing. I send her pictures of bobcats that I think she'd like and she sends me back videos of turtles humping shoes. Before long, she knows all the gossip about the brewery employees, and I know what tattoos are popular this month.

It's working. Starting over and erasing the past is working. Keeping our clothes on is working, even though I feel like my skin might melt off in frustration.

It feels like a miracle.

I still hate that her cocktail shaker has another man's initials on it, or that a picture of the dog they briefly shared is hanging on her wall with a hundred other pictures, or that her copy of *Wuthering Heights* says *To Delilah, my wild-haired darling, Love Nolan* inside the front cover. I hate that she still sometimes wears a pair of earrings from him, and I've never once seen the necklace I gave her for her twenty-first birthday.

But those things don't matter. They're a cocktail shaker, a photograph, a book, earrings. Just objects from a time that's over and gone, and if I keep pretending they don't exist then sooner or later, I'll stop noticing them.

The past is gone. Right here, right now, is what matters, and it's all that matters.

· · * ★ ★ ★ ★ ★ * · ·

DELILAH AIMS her keys over her shoulder, and I hear her car lock behind us.

"Shut up," she says, when she sees me looking at her, and I laugh.

"You know you don't have to point—"

"Yes, you do," she says, putting her keys in her coat pocket, then taking my arm. "If the key isn't pointing at the car it won't lock, and that's all, end of discussion, aren't the hedges lovely this time of year?"

"I can't believe the butler hasn't shown up to give us piggyback rides into the house yet," I say. "Really slacking there."

Her hand slides down my arm until it's in mine, and even though we've done this a hundred times over the last few weeks, an electric thrill still races through me from fingertip to fingertip.

"Stop it," she says. "You know full well that they're nice, normal people who just happen to own a huge estate and spend tens of thousands of dollars every year on flower arrangements to *liven up the place*."

"I didn't know that," I say, walking across cobblestones.

In front of the Radcliffes' house — mansion, really — is a circular driveway with a fountain in the middle and a garage tucked off to one side, which is where we parked. The fountain is off since it's winter, but it's still impressive.

"You never noticed that the front hallway always looks like someone's either died or gotten married?" Delilah asks, lifting her eyebrows. "It's kind of Vera's *thing*."

"I've never been in here before, remember?"

"Right," she says. "Well, if these people act like they've met you before, just roll with it."

We climb the steps to the front door, where there's a lion-shaped knocker. Delilah lifts it and lets it fall, ignoring the doorbell button to the right.

"This is more fun," she explains. "I feel like a barbarian at the gates."

"And you enjoy that?" I tease.

"I like to play to my strengths," she says.

We wait. And wait. There's no noise inside the house, and no one answers the door. I study the pie in my hand.

"I should've put gold leaf on it," I tell her.

Delilah just sighs, reaches across me, and rings the doorbell.

"Gold leaf is kind of gross," she says. "It doesn't taste like much, but the texture would make the pie weird."

"That's precisely the sort of thing I would never have guessed," I say, and the door swings open.

"Ah, hello," says the man standing there. He's got on

khakis, blue polo shirt tucked in, and slippers. "Come on in."

"Dad, you remember Seth Loveless, don't you?" Delilah asks as we step inside. "From high school."

"Welcome," he says, and holds out his hand. There's a thick signet ring on one finger, and when he shakes my hand, he squeezes harder than strictly necessary.

I look him dead in the eye and squeeze back.

"Good to see you again, sir," I say, and Delilah's father grins.

"Please, son, it's Harold," he says, clapping my shoulder with his other hand. "*Sir* was my father. Come on, let's get that pie into the kitchen. I'll let the girls know you're here."

Harold turns and starts walking.

"*Sir?*" Delilah whispers, giving me a look.

"What? I was raised right," I tell her.

The entryway is big and open, and yes, there's an enormous bouquet of flowers on a side table, next to a gilded mirror. A chandelier hangs from the ceiling, and a staircase curves up and along one wall, leading to the second floor.

The decorations are different but the house is intensely, achingly familiar. I was here all the time while we were dating, partly because my own house always felt like there were too many people in it, and partly because this house was more than large enough to give us privacy.

Harold walks through the entryway, turns, leads us to the kitchen.

"Weather Channel says it's supposed to snow tonight. Real humdinger," he's saying as he walks. "Predicting six to ten inches, though the way the cold front is looking I'm expecting it'll turn to rain or sleet right around sunrise, like it's been doing all year."

"Typical," Delilah agrees.

"It's nice if you've gotta go somewhere but I do love the

look of fresh snow on the grounds," he keeps on. "And if you're talking skiing, there's just no comparison at all — hi, honey, Seth and Delilah are here," he says into the kitchen.

"Come in, come in," she calls from where she's standing on the other side of the massive kitchen. She wipes her hands on a towel, gives a final instruction to a woman standing over a cooking range that's at least double the size of mine, and comes over to give us both hugs.

"Darling, how are you, I haven't seen you in weeks," she says to Delilah, somehow enveloping her in a hug even though Delilah's several inches taller.

"Sorry, I've been busy," Delilah.

"I can tell, and I want to hear *all* about it," Vera says, glancing at me and then giving Delilah a huge wink. "Seth, welcome back! My goodness, that's a beautiful pie."

She takes it and also gives me a hug, and already I feel bad for making jokes about butlers and gold leaf. For all their faults and their enormous flower budget, the Radcliffes are warm, loving people.

"Can we help with anything?" I offer, once she's relinquished me, and Vera's eyebrows fly up.

"No, no, it's completely under control," she says, putting one hand on my arm. "But aren't you the sweetest thing for asking?"

"Huh, a 2015," Harold is saying, mostly to himself, as he examines the wine bottle that Delilah brought. "That was supposed to be an unusual year for Californians. Guess we'll find out tonight, won't we?"

"Dinner will be ready in about thirty minutes," Vera says tells him. "Why don't you go select some wine for tonight so we can open it and let it breathe before we eat?"

"Sure thing," he says, setting the bottle down on the table. "Seth, mind giving me a hand?"

"Of course," I say, the only possible answer to that question.

Delilah stands up straighter, looks slightly alarmed.

"Do you need any—"

"Bree was *just* looking for you," Vera cuts in smoothly, somehow making an interruption sound like the height of etiquette. "I do believe she's tired of playing pterodactyls by herself."

Delilah and I share a *so this is happening* look, and I give her a smile.

"We won't be a minute," Harold calls, and we leave the kitchen, wind back through the house until he opens a door under the main staircase, revealing the basement stairs.

"Seems as if the brewery's doing well," he says, flipping a switch and descending. "What's the market for small-batch beers like these days?"

"Booming," I say. "There's been a huge uptick in craft beer sales across the board the past fifteen years or so. People are more and more interested in drinking well-made and local, and once you've had a really great beer it can be hard to go back to Bud Light."

"Never could drink the stuff myself," he admits as he flips on another light, leads me through the basement. "Tell me, if I were to become interested in becoming a beer connoisseur, where would I start?"

The questions keep up as we walk through the basement, which has been finished into a lounge of sorts: a large television, leather furniture, wood-paneled walls. At the far end is another door that leads into the temperature-controlled room that stores several hundred bottles of wine.

It's strange, walking through here again: the room is the same, though the furniture is slightly different. The television is different, too, the pool table the same, the wood paneling the same.

We had sex on the pool table. We also had sex in the wine cellar, on the couch that used to be down here, and on an armchair.

And her bedroom, the library, the study, the upstairs bathroom that she shared with her sisters, the downstairs bathroom, the pool house, the tack room in the stable, and I'm certain there are several places I'm forgetting. We were reckless, stupid, and nearly got caught a dozen times because we were horny teenagers and had more hormones than common sense.

As Harold opens the door asks me another job-interview-type question, I glance over at the new couch. It looks comfortable.

I'd fuck Delilah on it, given half the chance, though this time I'd make sure the doors were locked first.

"I had no idea beers were collectible like that," Harold is saying, leading me into the cellar. "Perhaps I ought to dedicate a corner down here. Now, what did Vera say was for dinner? Pork?"

The door swings shut behind us. The wine cellar is almost exactly as I remember: four walls lined with bottles in specialized shelving, corks out, bottles backlit. A barrel in the center that's great for bending your girlfriend over.

"We'll probably need a few," Harold is saying to himself. "There's what, eight of us? No, ten, though obviously Olivia won't be drinking."

I wander to the wall, hands in my pockets, and start scanning the labels, pretending as if I might possibly have an opinion.

Harold pulls a bottle out, reads the label carefully, blowing dust from it.

"Son," he suddenly says without looking up. "I don't need to tell you to treat her right, do I? You seem as if you've become an adult."

There it is, the reason he wanted my help.

"Of course, sir," I say.

"Harold," he corrects me, finally looking up from the bottle for a moment. "That'll work just fine on my wife, but not on me."

"Sorry, Harold," I tell him. "And yes, I'll treat Delilah right."

He puts the bottle on the barrel and starts looking at shelves again.

"Figured as much," he admits. "I can't imagine her wasting time on you otherwise."

"Thanks, I think," I say, and that gets a smile from the man.

"Would you grab a Malbec from over there that looks good?" he says, gesturing at the shelves I'm standing by. "Freckles is a tough crowd. Her mom was the same way."

I grab a bottle from a shelf labeled *Catena Zapata 2018* and bring it down. I'd forgotten that Delilah's dad calls her Freckles, the only human on the planet allowed to do so.

"I never met her mom," I say.

"No, I guess not," Harold says, pulling out another bottle. "Don't tell Freckles this, but she could be a carbon copy of Meredith. The spitting image. I still miss her sometimes."

He frowns, puts the bottle back.

"What have you got over there?"

"Catena Zapata," I read, and Harold nods approvingly.

"I'm happy with Vera, of course," he goes on, pulling another bottle. "I wouldn't trade her for the world. God knows Meredith and I got along better as exes than we did for one moment while we were married. But you know how it is. People leave their mark."

"They do."

"I never did tell the girls that you asked for my permission all those years ago," he says, not looking up at me.

"No?" I finally ask.

I've spent so much time pushing the past away over these last few weeks that it's strange to have it bubble to the surface like this, to talk to someone who treats it as a fact and not a secret.

"At first I didn't want to ruin the surprise," he admits. "But after you high-tailed it out of here that night and I never saw you again, I figured it was best to keep my lips zipped."

"I appreciate it," I say, because I do.

"It wasn't for you, it was for Freckles," he says, perfectly matter-of-fact. "She never did tell Vera or her sisters the truth, and I can't say I blame her. Should we have the 2012 or the 2014 Plâce de Peche Cabernet?"

"The 2014," I say with far more authority than I feel. Harold puts another bottle on the barrel.

"Should the circumstance arise, don't ask again," he says, sliding the 2012 back into its slot. "Freckles doesn't need my permission."

"I wouldn't dare," I say, and can't help but laugh.

These days, I don't think it would cross my mind to ask him for permission, but ten years ago I was a college senior. Barely legal to drink. Determined to do everything just right, by the book. Dot every i and cross every t.

It still didn't work. I haven't let the possibility cross my mind again since.

"Should I bring up a port wine for a dessert tipple?" Harold asks. There are now seven bottles on the barrel, and he's turning them one by one, looking at the labels.

"Delilah's driving, so bring the whole cellar up," I say, and Harold finally laughs.

"I knew I liked you," he says, and claps me on the shoulder again. "Grab some of these and let's go."

We go back through the basement, climb the stairs, deposit the wine in the kitchen. Harold grabs a corkscrew, nods at me, and sets to work.

"They're probably in the family room," he says, dismissing me. "You remember where that is?"

"I think I hear them," I say, and walk back through the huge house, past the formal dining room, past the formal living room, past the stairs.

Before I reach the doorway, I can hear their voices, echoing through the hall.

"—invite Seth yet?" one says. Vera, I think.

"Not yet," Delilah says, and she sounds annoyed.

I stop, just out of sight. Invite me where?

"Delilah," a third voice admonishes. "You have to stop holding that poor man at arm's length like this. I can't believe you haven't invited him yet. You're thirty years old, how many chances do you think—"

"Could you not?" That's Delilah.

I'm still, silent. Eavesdropping, but too curious not to.

"I know you don't want to hear it, but I'm just pointing out—"

"Olivia. *Spare me.*"

"This is why—"

"Please?"

"Pterodactyls don't TALK!" shouts a small voice, and the adults laugh.

"All right, what do pterodactyls do?" Delilah asks.

All I hear is, "Like this!" the sound of small running feet, and Delilah's laugh.

I spent one more moment wondering where Delilah's not inviting me, and then I push it from my mind and walk into the room where she's standing at one end, arms out, gliding in a circle.

"We're pterodactyls," Delilah explains.

THIRTY-THREE

DELILAH

O livia carefully butters a single bite of dinner roll, then inspects it as if it might somehow transform into mercury-laced unpasteurized cheese. At last, she eats it.

"If it's a boy, sports, of course," her husband Michael is saying. "If it's a girl, I'm leaving that up to you, babe."

"Well, pink, obviously," she says, taking a sip of water. "But I don't want it to be Disney princess themed. I think that's been really overdone."

I slice the end off my asparagus and neatly take a bite, nodding along with Olivia for once at her decision not to Disney-princess-theme her unborn child's room.

"You could always do something gender-neutral," I point out.

All three of my sisters look at me with polite confusion and disdain, as if I've suggested having the baby sleep on the roof, or naming it Broccoli.

"I'd love a *real* princess-themed nursery," Olivia goes on, ignoring my perfectly valid suggestion. "She'll be the queen of our little castle, after all. If it's a girl."

She smiles and squeezes Michael's hand, and he nods.

I eat some more asparagus and try not to feel too much like an alien in my own family, because as hard as I've tried my whole life, I just don't *get* it.

I want to. Or, at least, I used to want to, before I gave up and just accepted that I'm a penguin among humming-birds. I tried my hardest to get as excited as the four of them over engagements and weddings and dress fittings and nursery decorations and all those things that women in this world are supposed to love and that I never did.

I like all those things. Love and weddings and babies are all great. I love the hell out of Bree and Callum, and even if Olivia's on my nerves right now, I'm excited for her kid, too.

I just cannot bring myself to care what its nursery looks like, and I'm pretty sure it's because I'm broken.

"...that senses when the baby moves, and rocks it back to sleep so you don't have to," Winona is saying. "They'd just come out when Callum was born, but my friend Jenn had one for her first and she absolutely raves about it."

Olivia's nodding along like she's trying to take notes, so I take the moment to find Seth's leg under the table and give his thigh a quick *you're doing great and it'll be over soon* squeeze.

He covers my hand with his, glances over, gives me a quick, secret smile.

"...concerned about the altitude, but my OB-GYN said it was all right. Still, I'll be keeping a close eye on things," Olivia says.

"Honey, Snowpeak's only at about five thousand feet," my dad interjects.

"Well, I'm just glad you're still coming," Vera says, indulgently. "Family weekends are so important. With *everyone.*"

Seth's leg tenses slightly under my hand, so I move it away and into my own lap, curling my fingers into a fist, fighting guilt.

In two weeks, we're going to Snowpeak, West Virginia on our annual skiing getaway, and I have yet to mention this fact to Seth. It's partly out of sheer thoughtlessness, because I honestly forgot it was coming up this soon, and partly because I want to invite him and also don't want to invite him.

Vera gives me a significant look. Then she darts her eyes to Seth before looking at me again and doubling down on the significance of said look, as if I didn't understand it the first time.

I hold my ground and look right back. We had a *talk* the week after Ava's wedding, once I'd stopped being the most hungover person on the planet, and it went better than I was expecting. I'm not sure I'm fully convinced that she's going to respect boundaries forever, but she at least seemed to acknowledge my point, so I'll take it.

"Yes, I can't wait," I say, practically daring Vera to say something to Seth.

Please let me deal with this myself, I think, trying to psychically beam my thoughts into her head. *I already fucked up, don't make this worse.*

She doesn't. Miracle of miracles, my stepmother looks away and takes another sip of wine. It feels like angels shine lights from above and sing the Hallelujah chorus.

Until Olivia slides right into that silence and pipes up.

"Seth, you're coming, aren't you?" Olivia pipes up. "We'd love to have you along. It's *so* much fun, such a nice, relaxing getaway, and the two of you could have some really romantic *alone* time."

I nearly throw my fork at her. Olivia knows damn well

that I haven't invited Seth, because she asked me an hour ago whether I'd invited him, and I said *no*.

"He's already made plans for that weekend," I say, smiling back at my sister, fork still gripped in my hand. "What was it you said you were doing?"

Seth and I look at each other. I've got a fake smile frozen on my face, and his eyes flash, even as the rest of his face stays neutral.

"I have to... help my brother find chairs for his wedding," Seth says, his eyes never leaving mine.

I kick myself for not supplying the lie.

"Oh!" exclaims Ava. "I love weddings! Which one is getting married? When's the wedding? Where's he having it? Has she picked out a dress yet? Are you a groomsman?"

Bless you, Ava, I think as Seth's eyes slide away from mine and he puts on his casual, easy smile.

"My oldest brother, Levi," he says. "It's in about four months, it's at a place called Treetop Lodge, which used to be an upscale hunting lodge in the 1920s, but now it's mostly an event space. I don't know about the dress, and yes."

"Treetop Lodge," she says, and turns to Thad, sitting next to her. "Babe, did we look at Treetop Lodge?"

"I don't think so," he says, though the man clearly has no idea.

"No," Vera says, authoritatively.

"Wasn't there some place we considered..."

And Ava's off, talking about weddings, half trying to plan Levi's, and Seth gives me another look.

I turn away, because I can't do this here, now, in front of my entire family. They all seem to think that I should be worshipping the ground he walks on for even considering me a viable dating partner, given my ancient, haggard status.

I'm being slightly unfair to them, but good *God* they can be a lot, and I don't trust them around him. I know we have long history that we're pretending doesn't exist, but we haven't even been dating for a full month. We haven't spent the night together yet, sort of. This time.

Olivia, who's in full monster mode tonight, has already insinuated that my thirty-year-old ovaries are shriveling as we speak. I think Ava's been dropping nonstop hints about ring shopping, and God only knows what my dad said to him in the wine cellar. They can't even behave for a few hours. I'm not forcing him to be around them for a whole weekend.

"What about helicopter skiing?" Michael asks. "I tried it when I went to Whistler in January, and it was a stunning experience. Really amazing."

"Babe, I don't think Snowpeak has helicopter skiing," Olivia says.

"They should," he says. "Maybe I'll talk to Evan about it, see if he'll consider offering it for VIPs or something."

Finally, I glance back over at Seth. This time, he avoids my eyes.

THIRTY-FOUR

SETH

"I didn't think he'd ever stop talking about heli-skiing," Delilah says, her breath puffing into the cold air. "What's it like to be so insanely self-confident that you think people are invested in what you're saying, even they're practically falling asleep in front of you?"

I just keep walking and don't respond right away. Not while we're this close to the house, where any one of her sisters could be listening at a window, just waiting for something interesting to happen.

"And it can't be good for the environment," she says, pulling her keys from her pocket, pointing them at her car and unlocking it. "Besides, what happens if you get hurt somewhere only accessible by helicopter? I guess the helicopter has to get you back out, but that seems pretty dicey."

Finally, next to her car, she stops. I shove one hand into my coat pocket, the other holding the now-clean pie dish.

"Were you going to tell me?" I ask, an edge sliding into my voice. "Or were you just going to disappear for the weekend?"

"I forgot," she says, and her eyes dart away. "It's this

annual thing, and it's been in my calendar but I didn't realize it was that soon—"

"Don't bullshit me."

"I'm not—"

"Not a single person in that room believed that I have to help Levi pick out wedding chairs," I say.

"That's because you came up with the worst lie I've ever heard."

"You made me lie!"

I'm loud, too loud, and we both look over at the house. Nothing moves. I shove a hand through my hair.

"I didn't mean to," she says, quiet but strained. "I didn't want my fucking sister to go and invite you in the first place, but I didn't want them thinking that we're on the rocks or something."

"And fuck what I think, right?"

"That's not what I'm saying."

"But you'll keep secrets and then have me lie to cover for you."

Delilah heaves a deep breath. Her cheeks are flaming, even in the dark, her eyes too shiny, her lips too red. Always an angry crier.

"We've been dating for a month and you're mad that I'm not bringing you on my family vacation?" she says, stepping closer to me, her breath frosting in the air. "Tell me. In your blank slate, start over scheme, would you bring a brand new girlfriend who you'd never even slept with on a vacation with your entire family?"

"I'd at least tell her I was going," I say. "If I brought her around my family, I'd at least give her some warning. And yeah, I might invite her if I thought she was worth keeping."

Delilah's eyes wobble, her whole face bright red, and all the muscles in her jaw twitch.

"God*damn*," she says, and a single tear spills out.

She turns away from me, hair flying, and walks away.

"Del—"

"Stay there!" she shouts over her shoulder.

At the edge of the driveway, by a tall, cylindrical tree, she stops.

Delilah stares at the tree. Or, at least, it looks like she's staring at the tree because her back is to me. She stares at the tree for a minute, then two.

Finally, she comes back, stands in front of me, clears her throat.

"I'm sorry," she says. "I should've at least told you I was going. It wasn't my intention to hurt your feelings."

I'm thunderstruck. Delilah and I have gotten in more fights than I can count, but I'm not sure I've ever heard her apologize before. I look at the tree — maybe it's possessed? — and then back at her.

"Thank you," I say.

"That was a breathing thing I learned in therapy," she explains, waving a hand at the tree. "It's to... I can be really... you know."

"I do know."

Delilah snorts. She takes another deep breath.

"They're crazy and you don't even ski," she says, her voice quiet. "I didn't want you to feel like you had to come and then listen to Michael talk incessantly about heli-skiing and polo, or discuss a nursery in great detail, or politely ignore ten hundred thousand million hints about finally making an honest woman out of me. Ava's been married for what, six weeks? and they're already after her about kids. They're a lot, and they stress me out, and I didn't want to make you have to deal with it yet."

I believe her. I just witnessed her family in action for a few hours, and she's right. But all the same there's the shadow of a whisper, deep in the back of my mind, saying *you're not a family vacation kind of boyfriend* and *if she were serious, none of that would matter*.

I push those away, stuff them back into a pit, and I reach out and brush my fingers along her cheek.

"Delilah," I say, softly. "Have you *met* my family? They're the definition of *a lot*."

She smiles, finally.

"It's completely different," she says. "I don't think my sisters know what a trebuchet even is. I didn't until Rusty showed me the diagrams. But your brothers don't act like your opinion doesn't count if you're not married."

It's true. My family is remarkably pressure-free, at least in that arena. Even when Daniel accidentally knocked someone up, no one wanted him to marry her.

"I really did forget it was in two weeks," she says. "I thought I still had a month or something. I've been distracted lately."

I wish it wasn't like this. I wish it were as simple as Delilah thinking *he's my boyfriend, he should come*.

But I let it go. I give her a kiss and we get into her car, and I remind myself about the blank slate, that nothing before this matters, and Delilah pulls around her parents' driveway, down the tree-lined lane, and away.

· · * * ★ ★ ★ * * · ·

THE FIRST SNOWFLAKE falls on Delilah's windshield when we're halfway back to my house, and she frowns at it.

"I thought Dad said it wasn't starting until after midnight," she says, anchoring both hands on the steering wheel.

"Could it be that the Weather Channel was wrong?" I say, and she laughs.

"I bet we'll hear about it," she says. "He loves to complain when people make wrong guesses about an inherently chaotic system."

More snowflakes fall. Delilah's hands tighten on the wheel. I fiddle with the windshield defroster so she doesn't have to look away from the road.

Within five minutes, it's pouring snow. Delilah's white-knuckling the steering wheel, going thirty miles an hour on the dark country roads, already gone gray with fallen snow.

"Should I turn around and go back?" she asks, voice tense.

I pull my phone out to check the map, just to be sure, but I'm right: we're closer to my house than to their estate.

"Do you want me to drive?" I offer.

"Are you any better at snow driving than me?" she asks.

"I doubt it."

"If someone's gonna drive my car into a ditch, it should probably be me," she says, and then we both fall silent again.

The snow keeps falling, thick and heavy, blanketing the road in what seems like minutes. There are no other tire tracks. We pass two other cars in the next twenty minutes, both of us tense and on high alert.

I have to remind myself to breathe. I have to remind myself that even if we go around a curve and hit something, we're not going fast enough to do ourselves much damage. That safety features in cars have come a long way in the past twenty years and at worst, one of us will break a bone.

I know if someone from, say, Michigan or Vermont saw us right now, they'd laugh their asses off, but this is the South. I can count the number of times I've driven in snow on one hand, because even when it does snow, it's gone in forty-eight hours, tops.

The roads aren't built for it. No one has snow chains. I think Burnley County has two snowplows for hundreds of miles of winding country roads.

The forty-five-minute drive from Delilah's parents' house to mine becomes an hour and a half, snow piling higher and higher the whole time. We both heave a sigh of relief when we turn from the country road onto a bigger one with streetlights, then into town.

And then, finally, into the parking lot of my townhouse. Delilah parks, pulls on the parking brake, then leans back against the headrest and exhales so hard it steams her windshield.

"Holy shit, I fucking hate driving in fucking snow," she says, clenching and unclenching her hands. "*Fuck.*"

She stops clenching her hands and starts shaking them out, and I do the same as her: lean back, try to let the tension go, but I can't. Not quite, no matter how many deep breaths I take.

"You okay?" I ask. Already the snow is sticking to the windshield, blocking some of the light from the street lamps in the parking area, mottling the shadows inside the car.

"I'm fine," she says. "Just... rattled."

Rattled. That's the word for it, that sense of darkness that keeps sliding away whenever I try to think of it too much.

I reach over and take Delilah's right hand.

She's trembling. It's slight but it's there, the faintest of tremors working their way down her arm and into her hand, so I start massaging. I work my thumb into the muscles in her palm, over the tendons and sinews, roll each finger between my own until finally, the shaking stops.

"Thanks," she says, softly.

"Stay over," I tell her.

Delilah takes a breath and opens her mouth, like she might protest, so I cut her off.

"*Please* stay over," I say, folding her hand into mine. "And go ahead and just say yes without making a fuss, because if you think I'm letting you drive any more tonight you've lost your damn mind, and you hate it when I tell you what to do."

She's laughing.

"You gonna threaten to go caveman again?" she asks lightly, her hand still in mine. "You never actually followed through the first time."

I grin back at her, the tension in my body starting to fade. The post-danger endorphins starting to kick in.

"I have no idea what you're talking about," I tell her.

"At Ava's wedding," she says. "When you went back to the chateau and I had to—"

She stops short. I shrug dramatically.

"Right," she says. "Sorry, I forgot about the slate for a minute."

"Don't make me take your keys."

"Yes, I'll stay, I don't have a death wish," she teases.

A brief flash of realization crosses her face.

"Or a stuck-in-a-ditch wish," she says, quickly.

"Thank you," I tell her, and finally unbuckle. "C'mon in, it's freezing out here."

THIRTY-FIVE

DELILAH

Seth pads into his kitchen in his sock feet, pushing a hand through his hair as he does. I'm still unwinding my scarf from around my neck, hoping it doesn't frizz my hair too much.

"I'll sleep on the couch," he says, his back to me. "Did I already say that? Do you want some tea?"

I hang my scarf and sit on the shoe bench in his entryway to pull my boots off, eyeing Seth's back as I do.

"It's your house, I'll sleep on the couch, and tea would be great," I say.

"Great," he echoes, looking up at his cabinets.

I don't want to sleep on the couch. I don't want Seth to sleep on the couch. I want us both to sleep in his bed, and furthermore, even though I'm still rattled and feeling all adrenaline-y from that drive, I'd also like to fuck his brains out while we both sleep together in his bed.

No, you had to make it two months, I remind myself, staring blankly at a spot on the wall. *Nice, Radcliffe.*

It's working, though, even if I think I might be the first person ever to die from horniness. Today was the closest we've gotten to a real fight, and by some miracle, I chilled out and apologized instead of doubling down on being an asshole.

"Do you have decaf?" I ask, padding sock-footed into the kitchen myself.

"Yeah," he says, still standing in the exact same place, looking at the exact same cabinets. "I've got, um."

He looks around, then opens a cabinet that doesn't contain tea. Closes it. Frowns.

"Hey," I say, and put my hand on his arm. He's tense as hell, even as he looks over at me and tries on that charming grin he's got.

"Where'd I put the tea?" he asks.

"Are you okay?"

"What? I'm fine," he says, reaching out to open another cabinet that also doesn't contain tea.

"Stop opening cabinets."

"I thought you wanted tea," he teases, but there's the slightest edge there, a wildness behind his eyes that's really weirding me out.

I close the cabinet, stand on my tiptoes, and put my hands around his face. He's still cold.

"I'm fine," he says, and he almost sounds convincing.

"Go sit down, I'll make tea," I tell him.

"Bird, it's—"

"Please don't make me throw you over my shoulder."

Finally, that gets a real smile, one with light behind his blue eyes.

"I'd kind of like to see that," he says, his hands on my wrists.

"I'd probably throw my back out, which is why you should go sit on your couch of your own volition," I say.

He leans forward, gives me a quick kiss on the lips.

"Fine," he says, and pads out of the kitchen.

I open the cabinet that *does* have tea and pull down a box of chamomile. It's pretty easy to find because Seth has one of the most ruthlessly organized kitchens I've ever seen, and I spent years living with Vera.

I've just put the kettle on the stove when I hear the soft creak of his stairs, and I stick my head out of the kitchen.

"That's not sitting," I tell him. He pauses, halfway up the stairs, and leans on the railing.

"I'm slipping into something more comfortable," he says. "Does that meet with your approval?"

Please be sweatpants. Please be sweatpants.

I think I blush, and I hope he doesn't know why.

"Fine," I tease. "But that ass better be on that sofa by the time this is done."

"Or what?" he calls, resuming his climb.

"Or you know what!" I shout.

Back in the kitchen, I look at the box of tea on the counter. I look at the kettle on the stove. I make a face.

Then I check Seth's fridge and pantry for ingredients, find what I'm looking for, and scrap the game plan. I've just put the new concoction on to heat up when he comes back down the stairs, and I poke my head out.

"Have I dressed quickly enough for your satisfaction?" he asks when he reaches the bottom. "I bet I've still got time for another costume change."

Seth's wearing a V-neck white undershirt and red-and-black plaid pajama pants, and I don't know whether I'm relieved or disappointed. They're still a thin, pliable fabric, and it doesn't take a whole lot of imagination to see his dick, but the pattern and the non-stretchy fabric hide it about thirty percent better than sweatpants.

"I approve," I say, making an effort to look him in the face.

"Thank God," he deadpans, and holds out a small stack

of clothes. "Here, I grabbed these for you. I think that's the smallest stuff I've got."

Right. I can't sleep in the dress and tights I wore to my parents' house, and they're not the comfiest for hanging out in, either.

"Thanks," I tell him, and he sits on his sofa, then gives me the thumbs-up.

I check on our still-warming drinks, then change in the bathroom. There's a moment of horror where I wonder if some other woman or women left these here and now I have to wear them, but as soon as I get them on I'm pretty sure they're his.

It's a black T-shirt with the old Loveless Brewing logo on the back and a pair of gray sweatpants that I have to roll the waistband on about ten times. As I do, I wonder if he's mocking me. He can't read my mind, right? My perverted thoughts are solely my own, right?

Just before I leave the bathroom, I hesitate for a moment and consider my outfit.

Then I take off my bra, because if I have to behave myself around Seth's dickprint, he can deal with my nipples.

When I head into the living room with the mugs, Seth is sitting on the sofa, one arm splayed across the back, mindlessly scrolling on his phone. His hair's messy and when he looks up at me, there's something in the way he looks, something in the way he tosses his phone onto his coffee table, that makes him look so... *young.*

Something vulnerable, sweet, innocent. Right now he looks exactly like the boy I fell for all those years ago.

"Thanks," he says, as I put the hot mugs down on the coffee table, then sit next to him.

Then, when he reaches out to grab a mug, he pauses, his hand around the handle. Stares into it like he can read a fortune in the fancy dash of cinnamon I sprinkled across the top, and then looks over at me with the strangest look on his face.

"What?" I ask, leaning over and staring into his mug of hot cocoa. "Are you allergic to something? You don't hate chocolate, do you?"

"No, no," he says, and finally picks it up. He doesn't stop giving me the weird look. "I just – did I ever... tell you this?"

I look from Seth's face to the mug and back again. Neither gives me any hint about what *this* is.

"Tell me what?" I ask.

"That my dad used to make us cocoa when the power would go out," he says. "I really never told you? Not even before?"

It might be the first time he's brought up *the before* intentionally since we agreed it doesn't exist.

I wrack my brain, slowly shake my head.

"He'd get out the camp stove and the canned milk and we'd all go on the front porch and drink cocoa and watch the storm," he says, and finally takes a sip. "In the summer, anyway. If the power went out in the winter we'd all pile onto the couches and have a fire, and if it stayed out overnight Caleb and I would push the beds together in Levi's room and sleep with him."

Seth laughs, then leans back into the sofa.

"He always seemed like the one who'd manage the best in primitive circumstances," he says.

Levi, the eldest Loveless brother, is now the Chief Arborist for the Cumberland National Forest and lives with his fiancée in a cabin that he built himself. I'd say he can manage.

I sit up straighter on the sofa, legs crossed, and pull Seth's head into my shoulder until he's leaning on me.

"What else?" I ask.

"When it would storm in the summer, Daniel and Caleb and I would go out on the front porch to watch it, and every time there was a lightning strike we'd all look over at the porch light to see if it was still on," he says. "I think Daniel would've run out and tried to catch the lightning if we'd let him. Caleb was always a little spooked by it, but liked being brave with us."

"And you?"

"I was always counting the seconds between the strikes and the thunder so I could know how far away the storm was and which way it was moving," he says, lifting his mug to his lips. "Someone's gotta compile the data."

"Want to turn out the lights and pretend the power's out now?" I ask. I run my fingers through his hair, tousling it, and I can feel him relaxing into me.

I don't touch Seth as much I'd like. I find myself shying away from these sweet, simple things because I know exactly where it can lead, and we made an agreement.

"Nah, it's bound to happen soon enough on its own," he says.

There's a long, silent moment where nothing moves, and there's no sound but the occasional creak of the building, settling into the cold, or his neighbors making the smallest of muffled *thumps* against their shared wall.

"Sorry about the drive," I finally say.

"Don't apologize. It wasn't your fault," he says, voice slow and lazy, his twang coming through.

"I can still be sorry."

He drinks the last of his cocoa, puts the mug on the table, then turns and arranges himself so his head's on my lap, his feet over the armrest of his couch.

"You sure you're okay?" I ask, settling one hand on his chest. He puts one of his own over it.

"I am now," he says.

I don't ask anything else because I know the story of how his father died: dark night, icy mountain road, single-car collision. Seth was eleven, almost twelve. It's no wonder that we bonded three and a half years later when I suddenly moved to Sprucevale.

I finish my cocoa and we talk, my hand on his chest. If I pay close attention, I can feel his heartbeat even through his ribcage, steady and true, and for once I don't wonder. I don't wonder who else has sat like this, talking about his family. Who else has made him drinks and worn his pajamas, who else has driven him home in a storm and stayed the night.

We talk about raccoons and squirrels and chipmunks and all the havoc they've wreaked. We talk about which grocery store in town — there are two — has better tomatoes, which has a better beer selection. I ask about the bookshelves lining the wall opposite us, his television in the middle, and he laughs and tells me how Caleb came and built them in a fit of heartbreak over his twenty-two-year-old student.

"Can you sow some more discord between them and get some side tables?" I ask, slumped on the couch, feet on his coffee table, his head still in my lap.

"This is why he thinks you're a witch," Seth points out.

"I thought it was because I have magical dick-raising powers."

"Decline to comment."

My hand is still on his chest, my thumb slowly stroking back and forth. Despite my comment, I don't look down at the dick in question. No good can come of that.

Well, no agreed-upon good.

"I still can't believe he banged his student," I say, looking at the bookshelves. They're very nice bookshelves.

"Is banging," Seth points out. "Present tense. It seems like a terrible idea, but they're happy."

"There's no accounting for taste."

"Says the woman with the octopus tattoo."

I glance down at where Seth is tracing along the bottom of my ocean tattoo: a sailing ship, pulled under the waves by tentacles. Above it, there's another, birds in its rigging, flying it away.

"It's a Kraken and it's very scary," I say.

"I like it."

"I broke up with someone over it once."

Seth's eyes meet mine, and for a moment I regret saying anything. I know the past officially doesn't exist but that's *our* past, not my past and his past.

"Sounds like his loss," he says. "He call it an octopus too many times?"

Just like that, I smile and relax and Seth closes his hand around my arm, covering a sailing ship.

"It was years ago, I didn't even have it yet," I say. "But when I was planning it and doing all the sketches and stuff, I was dating this guy who never *said* that he hated the tattoos I already had but who obviously did."

Seth doesn't ask why I was dating him, which is good, because I don't have an answer. I spent most of my twenties ensconced in serial monogamy, trading one mediocre boyfriend for another without ever asking whether I wanted a boyfriend at all.

"Long story short, he really hated that I was going to get this one, and after I made my first appointment for it, he told me that if I got this tattoo I wouldn't be attractive to him anymore, so I needed to call and cancel."

In my lap, Seth laughs. He *laughs* and I can't believe he's laughing over someone else I dated. I half-wonder if there were drugs in the cocoa powder.

"Anyway, now I've got even more tattoos and a different boyfriend," I say, dryly.

"Your different boyfriend likes them," he says, simply. "Always has."

The thought flickers across my mind: *Property of Seth Loveless*, but I push it away.

"Thanks. I like my different boyfriend," I tell him.

He's still tracing my seafaring sleeve: fingers on a red-orange tentacle, thumb brushing over the waving stained-glass waves. With his other hand, he pushes the wide sleeve of my borrowed T-shirt over my shoulder to where the waves fade but the Kraken goes on, no longer sea-bound, reaching out over the left half of my body.

Seth's fingers disappear under the sleeve of the shirt, onto my shoulder, and even though he can't see them, he's still tracing the tentacles to where they curve, just shy of my collarbone, where they bend onto my shoulder blades. If he's surprised not to find my bra strap, he doesn't show it, but then again I'm sure he knows.

Then his hand leaves my shoulder, the shirt falls back, and his other hand is sliding up my neck, into my hair, and he pulls me down for a kiss. He tastes like cocoa and a little like cinnamon as he opens his mouth and slides his tongue into mine, fingers tightening in my hair, my hand pressing against his chest.

I try to focus on the minutiae of this moment: his soft lips and the slight scratch of his day-old stubble, the strange angle of our mouths' meeting, his heartbeat under my palm counting away the moments. Anything to ignore the persistent ache, the gathering heat, the automatic flash-forward in my brain to a future where I'm riding him on this couch like I said I wouldn't.

Seth moves without breaking the kiss, pushing up on his other elbow. He lets my hair go and pushes me back and I laugh softly as our lips tangle and our noses bump, and he laughs too and bites my lower lip. Sits upright, sideways on the couch. Grabs my thigh and pulls me until my leg is draped over his and I'm leaning forward, mouths together, one arm around his shoulders and the other hand steadying myself on his hard thigh, the muscles tensing under my fingers.

We pull back a moment, as if we're considering, taking stock of this moment and how to proceed. I know he's already hard as fuck, his erection inches from my fingers, but I don't move away. I know the hows and whys of this agreement, the theory that if we restrain desire for long enough we can temper it so that when it comes screaming back, maybe it won't break us apart.

Instead he strokes my side, over my shirt, his thumb whispering past the curve of my breast, the material moving ever so slightly across my nipple and I close my eyes and lean in again, always hungry for more.

We're not touching, not really, I tell myself. *I'm still doing it right.*

His hand brushes down my ribcage one more time. Tongues on tongues, lips on teeth, and now his plaid pants are twisted between my fingers and there's a tug on my shirt, steady and insistent.

The material slides right over my nipple and this time, I make a noise.

"Fuck," Seth hisses.

Half a second later, I'm in his lap. Straddling him, his big hands locked around my upper thighs, pulling me in hard.

I've got both hands in his hair and I'm kissing him desperately, hungrily, like he's air and I've been underground for months. My hips roll against his, nothing but flannel between us as I swear I can feel every ridge and bump of his cock against my clit, his thick head pressing against my entrance.

It's torture. Pure, beautiful torture, and I hear Seth groan even as I think *technically we're not touching, there's clothing, technically this is okay* —

"I'm sorry," I gasp, even as I roll my hips again and press my clit against him, the ache in my core fuzzing out into pleasure.

"Me too," he growls into my mouth, kissing me again. He grabs my hips, lifts his against mine, grinding me down his entire length. Eyes closed, a noise coming from somewhere deep in his chest. "*God*, I'm sorry."

We don't stop. I don't know how to stop. Somewhere, buried deep in my brain is a sequence of events that goes *stand up, walk away, take the world's coldest shower* but those thoughts flit by like clouds on a sunny day: interesting but unreachable.

Instead we make out hard enough to bruise lips. Instead we dry-hump like teenagers seeking any kind of release at all even as I force my hands to stay outside his shirt, letting myself touch him but not all the way. Not quite.

He grabs my shirt again, the same way, pulls it so it whispers over my nipples. They're hard as diamonds, so sensitive it hurts, and he does it again until at last his hands are on my ribcage and Seth pushes me up, back, until I'm sitting upright and we're staring at each other, panting for breath.

I clear my throat, nod. His hands slide until his they're on my back, his thumbs on my sides, the black T-shirt stretched tight right across my tits, my nipples out and proud.

"Okay," I whisper, my voice still husky. "Okay. Well."

Seth's just staring at me, chest rising and falling, every curve and dip and ripple of every muscle on nearly-full display under his sorry excuse for a shirt. His eyes fall from my face to my tits, my belly, my hips, my thighs spread over his.

No one's ever looked at me the way Seth does. Not once. I was *married*, for fuck's sake, and my ex didn't look at me this way.

"Give me your hand," Seth says, and I hold one out.

He takes it in his, curls my fingers around his. Kisses me slowly on the knuckles, and when he does, his eyes meet mine.

In them is the most devilish look I've ever seen, almost like he's daring me to stop him.

Without saying a word, he presses my hand to my still-clothed breast, my nipple hard against my palm.

I laugh. I can't help it. I laugh and Seth grins at me, his hands back on my thighs as I slide both hands over my nipples, palms down, letting the Loveless Brewing shirt ride up.

"Like this?" I ask as innocently as I possibly can. It's not very innocent.

"Exactly like that," he says, his eyes never meeting mine.

I do it again, slowly. I pinch my nipples and grab my own tits and Seth watches me, that look on his face like this is the only thing he's ever seen worth watching. I drag the shirt up, over them. I gasp with the friction and flash Seth some underboob, and then he growls when I drop the shirt again, my hands under it this time, twisting my own nipples until I moan.

It feels good. It feels better with him watching me.

"Take it off," he says.

"This?" I ask, and flash him.

"You're a goddamn tease," he says, and pulls me in for

a quick, rough kiss. "*Yes*, take your shirt off and quit robbing me of watching you play with your tits."

I pinch them again and this time I moan into his mouth without even meaning to. Sparks of pleasure shoot down my back, and I pull away from him.

"You first," I say, my voice scratchy. "Take your shirt off, throw it over there, and put your hands behind your head."

He does. I slide my hands over my nipples again and watch him, muscles flexing and stretching in one fluid movement. He's more padded at thirty than he was at seventeen, or twenty-two, but he's still so fucking beautiful it takes my breath away.

"There," he says, lacing his hands together behind his head. "You gonna arrest me, Bird?"

"No," I say, and lean forward, take his wrists. I run my hands along his thick, muscled arms. Biceps.

God in heaven above, biceps.

"That's what you do when I'm sucking your cock and you're trying not to grab my hair," I explain.

Seth grins, more wolf than human, and his muscles flex under my fingers.

"Get that off and quit teasing me," he says, and I finally pull the shirt off. I touch myself again, let him watch. Lean in for a kiss.

"Tell me what you're thinking," I say.

"I think you should put your fingers in your pussy and tell me how wet you are," he answers.

I do it. I lean back, my other hand on his knee, and I push my hand below the rolled-over sweatpants and slide my fingers past my clit, between my slick lips, and plunge them inside me, my hips bucking as I do. The angle is a little awkward but I shift and push deeper and crook them inside myself, my palm flat against my clit, and I moan as I find that spot.

"Pretty wet," I whisper, my eyes half-closed. I do it again, press harder on my clit. I swear Seth's cock twitches as I make a noise.

"Show me," he says.

"And stop?" I say, moving my fingers again.

"No fair getting yourself off where I can't see," he says.

I pull my fingers out. The moment they clear my waistband, he grabs my wrist, brings my hand to his face, sucks my slick fingers into his mouth. Seth groans as he licks them clean, and when he's done, he pulls on my wrist until I spill forward and he captures my mouth with his.

He tastes like me, and it's sexy as hell. It's always sexy as hell, every single time he kisses me with my juices still on his lips.

"I miss the way you taste," he murmurs, lips still on mine.

"I miss the way you shiver when I get on my knees," I murmur back.

I can feel the animal grin more than I can see it.

"I miss the way you grab fistfuls of my hair when you're about to come," he says.

I'm rolling both nipples between my fingers. I don't know what I started, but now I'm breathing hard, trying not to moan.

"I miss the way you shout when I deep throat you," I say.

"I miss that too," he says, and his right hand moves under his waistband, wraps around his cock.

"Hey," I say, and pull his hand out.

Seth just lifts his eyebrows at me.

"Show it off first," I tell him, and press his palm to his cock through his pants. He groans and lifts his hips, pressing his hand against it, his other hand gripping my thigh.

"Like that, Bird?" he asks, his eyes at half-mast, voice rough and raspy and thick with need.

"Just like that," I breathe, watching him shamelessly. He does it again, groaning, and before I know it I'm pushing my own hand down, sliding my fingers over my clit, strumming myself softly.

The next stroke, the waistband of the plaid pants rides down and the head of his cock peeps out, nestled in the dark fur of his happy trail.

"Get your pants off," he murmurs. I obey, still watching, sliding the stretchy fabric over my hips, kicking them off.

"God, you're magnificent," he says, and now he's got his fist around his still-clothed cock, hips rising as he strokes himself.

"Off," I whisper, pointing at his pants, and he stops long enough to obey, his cock finally springing free.

If I were a poet, I would write sonnets about Seth's dick. It's long. It's thick. It's very pretty, as dicks go, and most importantly he puts it to very good use.

"Can I touch it now?" he asks, a teasing smile on his lips.

I don't answer. Instead I straddle him again. I take his hand. One by one, I wrap his fingers around his erection, and then wrap my hand around his. I kiss him hard as he strokes himself, the muscles in his arm knotting.

A moment later he grabs my other hand, pushes it between my legs. Even though it's my left hand, my clit's so swollen that it doesn't take any dexterity to stroke it between my clumsy fingers. I kiss him until his breathing goes ragged. I kiss him until I'm shaking, my clit so slippery that my fingers keep sliding off.

"Tell me what you're thinking," he says.

"How good it would feel if we fucked," I tell him.

He takes his hand off his dick. In a flash, I'm on my back on his couch and he's kneeling over me, then wraps his hand around his cock again.

"Fucked how?" he asks, leaning over me.

I drape one leg over the back of the sofa, curl the other around him.

"Slow at first," I say.

I put my hand between my legs again, the right one this time, stroke my clit. Seth's eyes follow.

"You want me to tease you?" he asks. "Find that spot that makes you come but make you wait?"

I just nod. My fingers move faster and harder. My back arches and my hips lift and Seth watches every inch of me, pumping himself into his fist.

"Then harder and faster," he says. He leans in, one knee between my legs, one hand next to my head. "Until you're saying my name and your pussy squeezes my cock so hard—"

I stroke harder, faster, my head turned to the side.

"—That there's nothing I can do except bury myself in you as hard as I can—"

I come, my fingers working my clit frantically, and my back arches and my hips lift and I think I whimper but I don't stop, not even when my leg shakes.

"—And then come inside you like you always beg me to—"

I'm trembling as I take my hand off my clit, slide it around the back of Seth's neck, look him right in his beautiful eyes.

"Come wherever you want," I murmur, and it's barely out of my mouth as he groans and strokes himself one last time.

It hits me in a hot line from my chest to my belly

button, spurt after spurt, and when he's finished, he drops his forehead to mine, breathing hard, gives me a long, deep kiss.

"Sorry," he says, and smiles.

I start laughing, my hand on his face.

"For?"

"Breaking the spirit of the rules, if not the letter."

"This doesn't count as you giving in?"

One more kiss, and then he pushes himself off me.

"If anything, it counts as you giving in," he says, grinning as he walks away.

"No, it doesn't," I call after him, still lying on the couch because if I move, I'm going to get cum everywhere and Seth's usually a gentleman. "I think we just did a great job of not having sex."

His downstairs bathroom door opens, and I hear the water running. A moment later he reappears, washcloth in hand, still stark naked.

See? Gentleman. Also, still an eyeful as he stands in front of his couch for a long moment, just looking at me.

"You gonna paint me like one of your French girls?" I tease. I've got one arm over my head, one leg on the couch, one foot on the floor. I'm sure my hair's doing something I wish it wouldn't.

Oh, and there's still jizz on me.

"Just memorizing what you look like right now," he says. "For future use."

"I'd pose, but I'm trying to avoid *getting jizz on your couch*," I say, pointedly.

"Like it would be the first time."

My brain sticks, suddenly, my thoughts running into each other. Did he just tell me that he's fucked other people on this couch? Where I'm currently lying, after not having sex but also not *not* having sex?

"Oh," I manage to say as he walks to me, then kneels.

"What? I live alone," he says, half defensive and half sheepish, wiping my torso off. "It happens."

The wet washcloth is warm. It's a nice touch.

After a moment, it hits me that he's talking about jerking off on the couch, not fucking someone else.

"Right," I say out loud.

"Right," he says, half-smiling. He drops a kiss on my shoulder, stands, pads away. I sit up and look around, wondering where my clothes went, but not wondering that hard.

When Seth comes back he's gotten a fuzzy blanket, and he puts an arm around my shoulder. I lean into him, curled on the couch, and we stay like that for a long time.

"Do you want to come on the ski trip?" I finally ask, half-surprising myself.

Seth laughs softly, turns his head. I think he kisses my hair, though there's so much of it that it's hard to tell.

"I didn't even ask you," I say, closing my eyes. "I just went ahead and over-thought the hell out of everything and decided I should spare you, but what's the point since you're—"

I stop short, because I almost said *you're going to have to deal with them sooner or later*, and... that feels like a lot to say, even right now.

"—invited," I finish.

"Do you actually want me to come, or do you just feel guilty now?" he says.

I twist my head against his shoulder to look up at him. Somewhere in the back of my mind I know that this is where we get into trouble, that there's something about sex that makes us too honest with each other, too brutal.

"I'll have a better time if you're there," I tell him.

"Then yes."

"You can get off work on short notice?"

"Please," Seth says, half-rolling his eyes. "Daniel's always taking off because of 'family stuff' or 'his kid is sick' or 'Charlie just had a baby,' I can go on a ski trip with my girlfriend."

"Do you ski?" I ask, off-handedly.

"I went once."

That pretty much means *no*.

"You wanna be my kept man who mixes drinks in the condo and hangs out in the hot tub?"

"There's a hot tub?"

I just snort.

"Of course there's a hot tub," I say. "There's a rooftop hot tub. I think there's three rooftop hot tubs. You think Vera Fucking Radcliffe is buying a condo in a ski resort that doesn't have a hot tub?"

"Not anymore, I don't."

"It'll be fine," I say, and snuggle into his shoulder again. "You'll be fine, just don't take anything personally and don't… listen to them."

"What if they give me directions?" he asks, teasing. "What if —"

"Don't be a dick," I tell him, yawning. "You know what I mean. You're not still gonna try to insist that you're sleeping on the couch, are you?"

THIRTY-SIX

SETH

I reach up and turn the exhaust fan on, not that it'll help a whole lot. My kitchen is still going to smell like breakfast until Tuesday morning at least.

"Do you always just have bacon in your fridge?" Delilah asks.

She's got a cantaloupe on a cutting board, and she's holding it with two hands, contemplating.

"No, you just got lucky," I tell her, opening the paper on the package. "Eli found some new artisanal butcher who he's in love with, and he got so excited that he got us all packages of bacon so we could, quote, 'see what it's supposed to taste like,' end quote. Except Levi, he got nothing."

She looks at me, cocks an eyebrow.

"Vegetarian," I explain.

"Not even tofu bacon?"

"He'd know it was a consolation prize."

"It's still a prize."

I flick water onto the cast iron pan, and it sizzles.

"Is it?" I ask, and drape a slice of bacon across it. Delilah just laughs.

"I've never actually had it," she admits.

We're standing in my kitchen the next morning, both still wearing pajamas from the night before. Delilah's hair is wound on top of her head, a takeout chopstick stabbed through it, and she's got a huge mug of Earl Grey next to her on the counter.

I never realized she was a morning tea drinker. It surprised me. Somehow I always figured that tattoos and caffeine overload went together, but there's no good reason for that.

I've got coffee. Strong. Black. Good.

"Are you supposed to cut cantaloupe lengthwise or... otherwise?" she asks, a knife in one hand. "Does it matter?"

"Lengthwise, usually," I say, and plop the last piece of bacon that'll fit in the pan.

I drink my coffee, watch the bacon, talk to Delilah about how to cut cantaloupe. It's normal, boring, the same thing that millions of couples around the country are probably doing right now.

But I like it. I really, really like it. I liked waking up next to her this morning. I liked that she snuggled into me for a few minutes before we got up. I liked the sound of her going down the stairs, turning on the kettle, yawning in the kitchen.

"You doing anything today?" I ask as she scoops seeds into the trash.

"Depends on the roads," she says. "You don't have a compost bin or something?"

"I live in a townhouse."

"It's got a back yard."

It's true. My townhouse has a perfectly nice, postage-stamp-sized back yard, complete with a deck and a few small trees. That said, I haven't spent a moment of my life gardening since I moved out of my mom's house.

"I think the roads are clearing up," I say, poking at the bacon with the tongs.

She looks over her shoulder, through the kitchen window, the light catching her right across the cheekbone.

"I might work on the storage unit," she says. "It's pretty close to finished, and at this point, I just want to get it done, you know?"

She puts the two halves of the cantaloupe on the cutting board. I grab paper towels, stack a few on a plate, take the dripping bacon out of the pan.

"Come to my mom's for dinner tonight," I say.

"Tonight?" she echoes, looking up at me in surprise.

"Yeah," I say, and drape more bacon onto the pan. "It's our usual Sunday thing, everyone will be there. You haven't come yet. You should."

"It's not — ow! *Shit.*"

Her knife clatters to the countertop. I look up in alarm.

"You okay?"

"You have sharp knives," she says, voice muffled by the thumb in her mouth. "Shit, that hurt."

I've already put the bacon down, and I'm scrubbing my hands of raw meat, drying them, grabbing her a paper towel.

"Here," I say. "Can I see?"

Delilah makes a face, then holds it up to me. Instantly, blood wells from the slice right across the pad of her thumb. I press the paper towel to her thumb, and she takes it from me, holding it tight.

"So, besides alphabetizing your silverware, I guess you sharpen your knives regularly?" she says, still making a face.

"Eli was over on Wednesday to talk about numbers and next steps for the brewpub," I tell her, picking up the knife and moving it away. "Number stress him out sometimes, so he sharpened all my knives while we talked."

"Ah," she says. "Well, give him my compliments, I guess? Is that burning?"

I turn again, and the bacon is definitely smoking.

"Shit," I say, and grab the tongs.

"You deal with that, I'm gonna go get a Band-Aid," Delilah says. "Bathroom?"

"Under the sink," I say, flipping the bacon and making a face. Half-burnt and half-raw is the worst kind of bacon. "Give me a sec, I'll come—"

"I stab people for a living, I can put a Band-Aid on my finger," she calls, her voice already echoing from the bathroom.

I hear the sounds of the cabinet opening, of things being pulled out.

And then: "Oh!" followed by silence.

A long silence. No sounds of cardboard boxes opening or Band-Aids being unwrapped. Just silence.

I frown and turn the burner off.

"You okay?" I ask, wiping my hands on a dish towel, walking for the bathroom.

When I turn the corner I can see her head over the top of the cabinet door and she looks at me, surprised.

"Oh! Yes, fine, I just found them," she says quickly, grabbing something off the floor. She clears her throat and opens the Band-Aid box. "I like the rainbows."

On the floor in front of her is the plastic shoebox where I keep my minor injury supplies: Band-Aids, gauze, Neosporin, hydrogen peroxide.

Next to it is a small pink zippered bag, a hairbrush, and a pair of black lace panties.

My heart falls clear through my chest.

"Oh, they're also unicorns," she says, examining the

Band-Aid as though it holds the secret to eternal life, her voice slightly strained. "Rainbow unicorns! Great."

"Sorry," I say, bend down, and grab those three things in one quick swipe and, without stopping, carry them to the trash can in the kitchen and throw them in.

Fuck. *Fuck.* I'd forgotten that those were in there, because apparently I haven't needed a Band-Aid in a couple of years.

Women used to leave things at my house sometimes, and I'd keep them until I could give them back or until I was sure I wasn't going to see that person again.

Except then Fall Fest with Delilah happened, two-and-a-half years ago, and I forgot to clean out my lost and found so those things have been back there for all that time.

In my defense, I did launder the underwear. I'm not disgusting.

I hear the sound of cabinets shutting, and a moment later, Delilah's back.

"Good as new," she says, holding up her thumb. It's got unicorns with rainbow manes on it now.

"I have those because of Rusty," I tell her, the pit of my stomach still swirling. "She got a skinned knee here once and was bummed that I only had boring Band-Aids, so I got cool ones. They're a couple years old."

"I shudder to think what she'd want now," Delilah says without looking at me. She picks up the knife again, considers the cantaloupe.

Underwear. It had to be black, lacy underwear. Fuck.

"Go sit down, I'll get that," I tell her, rescuing the last of the bacon from the pan. "Don't cut yourself again."

"Fine," she says, teasing and tense all at once. "You want orange juice?"

"Thanks," I say, and she pours.

We have breakfast and don't mention the brush, or the

bag, or the panties, and I tell myself: *clean slate. It doesn't matter.*

Those were just crumbs of the past, and they don't matter.

· · · · ★ ★ ★ ★ · · · ·

I HOLD my phone out in front of me, the flashlight shining into the narrow darkness, cobwebs sticking in my arm hairs. My nose tickles.

I *have* to clean under my bed more often.

Just as I've found a questionable pile of fabric on the far side, my phone rings in my hand. It's Caleb.

"Hey," I say.

"Why do you sound so weird?"

"Why do *you* sound so weird?"

He laughs.

"Seriously, though."

"I'm cleaning my house," I tell him, which is technically true. My phone flashlight is still one, illuminating the under-bed-space to my right and something that looks like a huge knot of computer cables.

"Are you cleaning your house from an iron lung?" he asks.

"Can I help you in some way, or did you just call to harass me?" I ask, scooting backward from under the bed.

"I called to see if you wanted me to pick you up on the way to Mom's," he says.

Right. I'm supposed to be there in an hour or so, but I've still got most of my house to scour.

"No thanks," I say, sitting on the floor and leaning against my bed. "I'm gonna be a little late."

There's a pause on the other end of the line.

"Because of cleaning?"

"Yes."

There's a longer pause.

"What are you cleaning?"

"My house."

My little brother sighs.

"You need help?"

* * * * ★ ★ ★ * * * *

WHEN I ANSWER THE DOOR, Caleb's standing there, alone.

"No Thalia?" I ask.

"She's visiting her brother," he says, coming inside, taking his coat off.

"Which one?"

"Rehab."

We walk into my townhouse, and I point at the fridge in case he wants anything.

"How's that going?"

Caleb just shrugs and looks around, like he's trying to figure out what I'm cleaning.

"Fine, I guess," he says. "He hasn't left it or anything, but Thalia was telling me how long it takes before an addict can really be considered *recovered*, so we won't actually know for a couple of years."

We. The way he says *we* about Thalia and her family, so casually. There's a longing inside me I didn't know I had.

"Shit," I say.

"Pretty much," he agrees. "What exactly are we cleaning?"

I rub my hands over my face and pull a cobweb from my hair.

"We're finding every single item that a woman has ever left in this house," I say.

Caleb just waits, his face very carefully neutral.

"Please," I add.

348

"Not what I was waiting for, though thank you for being polite," he says.

"Delilah found someone else's underwear this morning," I finally admit.

Caleb's face changes instantly, from neutral to alarm and horror and more than anything, concern.

"Oh, fuck," he says. "God, I'm sorry—"

"We didn't break up," I say, cutting him off.

Caleb blinks.

"Right," he says, though he's obviously surprised. "That's just…"

"Exactly the kind of thing we'd have gotten into a screaming match about before?"

"Something like that," he says, very carefully.

He's not wrong. Caleb is a lot of things — very smart, not a fan of Delilah, an outdoor enthusiast — but he's sure not wrong.

"We didn't," I say. "Everything is fine, I'd just like to find anything else that I've forgotten about and get it out of here."

"But you're fine and everything is fine," he says, still clearly not quite believing me.

"*Yes*," I say.

He looks around, like he's taking stock of the job ahead of us, surveying the living room.

"When they run search and rescue operations, the first thing they do is make a grid and then search each square meticulously," he says. "That seems like it might be a useful way to think about this mission."

I grin and ruffle his hair, which he hates.

"See? This is exactly why I called you," I say.

"What? I called *you* and somehow got suckered into a panty search," he says, already pacing the room. "I'll start over here. Do you have any rubber gloves?"

· · · ✦ ★ ✦ · · ·

DESPITE OUR THOROUGHNESS, we don't find that much: a tube of Chapstick in a side table, a mystery sock in a drawer, a powder compact hiding behind a can of shaving cream in the bathroom vanity.

We're in my bedroom — the last room to search — when Caleb grunts from the floor.

"Is that something?" he says, pointing. He's lying face-down on the carpet, his arm under my dresser, pointing. "It looks like fabric."

"Move, I'll get it," I say, and I don't have to tell him twice.

I cross my fingers that it's not underwear, reach under the dresser, and pull it out.

It's not underwear. It's too big to be underwear, the folds covered in dust and stuck together with cobwebs since I don't exactly clean the baseboards behind my dresser that often. When I shake it out, we both back up.

"Bingo," Caleb says, as we both look at the skirt.

It's short, pleated, plaid. A classic schoolgirl skirt, and just as soon as I've held it out to see what it is, I'm crumpling it in my hands, looking for the trash.

Caleb's just watching me and laughing.

"What?" I say, shoving it into the bin.

"Good thing she didn't find that," he says. "Looks like you had a good time, though."

I shoot him a glare, but it's not very effective. Possibly because I'm pretty sure I've also turned red at the fact that my little brother just found someone's sex costume under my dresser. Why did I ask him to help, again?

"It was a while ago," I tell him, as if that helps.

"Into that whole Catholic schoolgirl—"

"You really want to talk about who's into Catholic schoolgirls?" I ask.

Caleb shuts up instantly, then clears his throat.

"The outfit wasn't my idea," I tell him, and he wisely says nothing.

Each of the things we found today, I could tell you whose they were except for the Chapstick, which might even be mine. The panties belonged to a woman named Susan who was in town for a week and who I saw twice. Every so often, she still texts me to ask how I'm doing.

The hairbrush was Theresa's. The makeup bag was Lindsey's. The powder compact belonged to a woman named Gina, with whom I had an extremely casual relationship for several months.

And the skirt belonged to Gwen, a very enthusiastic woman who initially said she wanted the exact same things I did — no commitments, no strings, casual, physical — but who ended things when she wanted more than I could give her. She called once to ask if I knew where the skirt was, and I guess I could tell her now, but it's been so long that I'm sure she's gotten a new skirt.

I remember everyone I've been with. Names, faces, what we talked about afterward. If that's not enough I wrote everything down in a spreadsheet, afraid of being the soulless asshole who can't keep his lovers straight. It was never about notches on my bedpost. It was about doing something I was good at: making women like me.

The early women I wasn't kind to. Back then I didn't give a fuck beyond not knocking anyone up or getting a disease, so I fucked around and dated three or four girls at the same time, letting them each think they were the only one until I got caught. Someone spray-painted the word *MANWHORE* on my car, and I'm still not sure who.

I deserved it. I was the asshole who let them think I

might be in love with them, then took what I wanted until I was done. They'd call me their boyfriend. Occasionally they'd talk marriage or kids, or would want me to meet their families, and I'd string them along until I got bored.

Once I stood a girl up who I'd been seeing for a month because Delilah called and asked me to meet her, and in the feverish rush, I forgot to cancel my date.

I learned to be better. I learned to be honest, upfront, to find women who wanted the same thing I did: a sexual companion who could hold a conversation and who didn't want one whit more, who didn't care if I was doing the same thing with someone else. I learned to avoid women who wanted something I didn't have to give. Like Bernadette, the biologist who studies forest shrimp. Our relationship was pleasant, enjoyable, and when it was over, it was fine.

In short, I learned to be a waystation, a stopover for people looking for something better. A roadside attraction. An amusement park: a fun place to be for a while, but not a place anyone calls home.

That's all over now.

"Is that the whole grid?" I ask, glancing at a clock. We're an hour late to my mom's house, but it's not a big deal.

"Assuming that you didn't let women stash their underwear behind your pots and pans in the kitchen, yes," he says.

I lift the bag with the items in it, tie the handle in a knot, and swing it over my shoulder. Already I feel lighter, more buoyant, like my ballast has been lifted. It's done. They're erased, like they never existed.

The past is gone and the slate is clean again.

THIRTY-SEVEN

DELILAH

I lean over Mindy's butt, pulling my million-watt lamp to and fro, making sure I've been as thorough as possible spotting tattoo problems.

The only thing looking back at me is a tangle of wildflowers, purple and spiky. Even I can't find Seth's name anymore, and I'm the one who traced over it a few weeks ago.

I know it doesn't matter, but I feel lighter somehow, knowing it's gone.

"I think that's it, honestly," I say. "You did an amazing job of letting this heal."

"I really love lying around," Mindy jokes, and then laughs at her own joke. "Just kidding, I told my boss I had a back condition and had to stand for most of the day and he believed me. Didn't even ask for a doctor's note."

Unsurprisingly, sitting down is the biggest enemy of the butt tattoo.

"Well, it worked," I tell her, and stand. "I didn't even have to do much touching up. Let me wrap you up and you're officially on your way."

I have to fight the urge to smack her ass as I turn away. I always have to fight the urge to ass-smack when I see an unclothed one in my vicinity, which I know is weird, but asses are just so... smackable. It's not even a sex thing. It's just very satisfying.

Did Seth ever smack the tattoo? Seems like the kind of thing he'd be into. I bet he came on it.

NOPE. That is a rabbit hole that I, Delilah Radcliffe, am not going down right now because rabbit holes are stupid, pointless, and filled with rabbits. It doesn't matter where Seth came six years ago, it only matters that now, it's on me.

Then I take a deep breath and exhale, because this train of thought got a little weird and kind of sexual and I'm still at work.

"You okay?" Mindy asks from the table.

"Just got a little dizzy when I stood up," I tell her. "You remember the instructions, right?"

"Right," she says.

"You're gonna want loose-fitting clothes and no underwear for a few days," I remind her. "Long, flowing skirts can be your friend, if it's not too cold."

"Too bad I can't just be naked," she muses as I bandage her butt. "I bet my boss would require a doctor's note for that, though."

"Worth a shot," I say, and she laughs.

After she leaves, while I'm cleaning the back room before going home, Seth texts me.

Seth: Do I need to bring my tuxedo?
Me: Do you own a tuxedo?
Seth: Technically, no.
Me: I can't imagine you'll need anything better than business casual. A jacket, maybe.

I click my phone off, feeling guilty. I never told Mindy that I even know Seth, let alone that we're dating and I think it's serious. We weren't when she first came in, and even then it seemed pretty awkward to see someone's name tattooed on a butt and say, *hey, I also banged that guy!*

I mean, what's the etiquette there? Did I do it right? What would Emily Post say? If Vera and I had a very different relationship, I'd have asked her, but... no.

Seth: Still coming over?

Me: Of course.

Seth: Good, I need help deciding which cufflinks to bring.

Me: Just wear something besides t-shirts you got for free in high school and you'll be fine, I promise.

Seth: Don't insult my wardrobe like that.

Me: See you in thirty?

Seth: Perfect.

I put my phone back and finish cleaning up, locking all the doors, and leave through the back. It's been a week and a half since I slept over at Seth's house, a week and a half since I found the panties under his sink, and it's been fine except for every moment that I get some reminder of his *popularity*.

Mindy's tattoo. The fact that Stacey Hepp, who once sent him naked photos, is in my morning yoga class sometimes. The way women I don't even know look at him when we're together, like I'm invisible and they're remembering something nice.

It bothers me, and I hate that it bothers me. I hate that I can't do what I said I would and give us a clean slate, but I'm trying. I swear I'm trying.

THIRTY-EIGHT

SETH

"Is there anything else, Miss Radcliffe?"

The concierge smiles attentively at Delilah, who's pulling her purse back onto her shoulder.

"Can you remind me when the happy hour is?"

"From five until eight."

"Perfect, thank you so much!" she says and grabs her glass of champagne from the counter. "Ready?" she asks me, taking a sip.

I, too, am holding a glass of champagne, which was offered to me upon check-in at the Allegheny Crest Mountaintop Resort. It goes nicely with the massive stone fireplace, the leather sofas and armchairs, the carefully curated bowls of fruit, and the huge landscape paintings that adorn the walls.

"At your service, Miss Radcliffe," I say, following her down a plushly-carpeted hallway. Someone met us at the car and whisked away our luggage, and I presume that it's been taken to the condo and not stolen.

"Don't you dare start," she says, and takes my hand in hers as we walk.

"You did say *condo*, not *condos*. It's an important S."

"Slip of the tongue?" she says, making a face.

"I thought we were gonna be sleeping in a bedroom next door to Ava and Thad," I say, still drinking the champagne. "I packed for sleeping in a bedroom next door to Ava and Thad."

"Technically, they're still kind of next door," Delilah says.

We turn a corner, walk past a windowed nook with leather armchairs and a bowl of fruit. How much must this place spend on fruit that no one eats?

"In a separate condominium isn't next door," I say. "I thought I was sharing a bathroom with these people."

Delilah laughs out loud at that.

"Vera would never," she says, taking another drink. "Can you imagine if someone left an unused tampon where a man could see it? My *God*. Perish the thought."

Then she glances over at me.

"Sorry," she says. "I probably should've warned you. Though I also kind of forgot you didn't know."

I wonder, briefly, what else I don't know, and then I push the thought away.

I know Delilah's family is beyond rich and into the realm of *wealthy*, and I also know she feels weird about it even though it obviously benefits her. The vast majority of people can't drop out of college once and art school twice, then open their own business debt-free and she knows it.

Anyway, she owns a condo, as do all three of her sisters. Her parents own the penthouse upstairs. There's a whole Radcliffe wing of this place.

As someone whose family vacations almost always involved tents, I feel a little out of my element.

"You forgot I didn't know you owned a condo in a ski

resort?" I ask, still walking. This place is *huge*. "Tell me now if you've got a private island somewhere."

"I don't *think* so," she muses. Pauses. Then: "The condo was a gift, actually."

Hell of a gift.

"From your parents?"

Delilah drinks the last sip of her champagne, then stops at a door near the end of the hall.

"It was a wedding present," she says, pulling out the key. "It sort of became a tradition, because then Winona and Olivia and Ava also got condos when they got married and now there's a whole compound up here."

She pushes the door open, walks in, looks at me over her shoulder.

"Voila!"

This was *his*. This place belonged to him. He stayed here, he slept here. He sat on that couch. He ate in this kitchen and all this was *his* and now I'm here, in the place he's already possessed and left.

"I know it's kind of a lot," Delilah is saying as she tosses the keys on the counter, hangs her coat on a row of hooks near the door. "But I actually don't come here much and we mostly rent it out, and there's a certain *look* that people really want in their slope-side ski condo."

I finally unzip my coat, hang it next to hers.

"I guess you got it in the divorce?" I say, hoping I sound casual.

There's a stone fireplace, a huge flat-screen TV, leather couches. A kitchen with marble counters and a huge stainless steel fridge. It's all sleek and rustic at the same time, all perfectly matching. It doesn't look a thing like Delilah's house.

"Well, technically it's owned by the Radcliffe Family Trust, not me," she says, crossing her arms and surveying it.

"So it wasn't up for grabs in the divorce because it never became joint property. He kept his beach house in the Outer Banks, I kept this place."

"It's a hell of a place," I say, and she just laughs.

I'm not jealous of Nolan, her ex-husband. Not exactly. The truth is that I don't know the word for how I feel about the man who married the girl I was in love with, who got the huge wedding and the big house in the suburbs and even the cute dog. The man who apparently had a beach house of his own and God knows what else.

It's hard not to feel inadequate sometimes, like I'm unversed in all this rich people shit. It's hard not to see that I don't fit as neatly into her life as someone with his own beach house.

"I'm probably lucky that Vera and my dad didn't take it away again after I got divorced," she says, walking into the living room and looking at our suitcases, left there by some silent, helpful being. "Ava had a bedroom in their penthouse until a month and a half ago. I sound insane, don't I?"

"Should I really answer that?" I tease.

"I just mean that I wish it had been, I don't know, a graduation present or a birthday present or anything besides a wedding present," she says. "As if getting a man is the only thing that *really* matters and everything else is just fluff. Oh, good, there's an itinerary. I was afraid we might be left to our own devices for more than an hour here and there."

There's a sheet of paper on the table. Delilah grabs it, and I follow, reading over her shoulder and forcing myself to stop thinking about how many times her ex-husband ate at this table.

He's gone. I'm here. That's all that matters, right?

"We're expected at happy hour this evening, and that

one's labeled *casual attire*," she says. "Then after that is dinner in the Ridgeline Suite — that's Dad and Vera's penthouse — also *casual attire*, as is Family Game Night afterward—"

I pull the sheet of paper from her hands and spin her to face me.

"Delilah, it's okay," I tell her. "Whatever you think I think of you right now, I don't. I don't care if the toilet is made of gold and the fireplace is lined with diamonds."

She smiles, and I swear her shoulders relax an inch.

"I'm pretty sure they're not," she says. "But thank you."

"I can't believe I'm trying to make you feel better about being rich."

"That's why you're my favorite kept man," she teases, so I lean in and kiss her, and she's warm and soft and rises on her toes to meet me, and all that makes it easy to forget everything else about this and focus on her.

"Which one's our bedroom?" I ask when it's over.

"First left," she points. "It's the one with rubies and emeralds studding the walls."

I give her a look.

"Kidding," she grins. "Just a big-ass TV."

I pick up both of our suitcases and carry them to the bedroom. Sure, they've got wheels, but I prefer lifting them because I know she's watching and I know what Delilah likes.

The master bedroom does have a huge flat screen, along with another stone fireplace and a four-poster bed that's the biggest bed I've seen in my life. There's a sitting area and an en-suite bathroom with a soaking tub and a shower that's got an entire wall of buttons, one of which probably makes the New York Philharmonic show up to play you Vivaldi while you shower.

She's standing in the doorway, watching me, and

because of that, I take an extra moment before putting the suitcases down, one by one.

"Yes?" I finally ask.

"Just trying to think of more heavy things you could lift while I watch," she teases.

"Excuse me, miss, my eyes are up here."

"Mhm. Pick up the suitcases again?" she says, grinning.

"I can't believe you're objectifying me like this," I say, crossing the room toward her. "Keep it up and I'm sleeping in the other bedroom."

"Would that involve carrying the suitcase some more?"

"Don't tell me you'd pick that over getting to snuggle this hunk of burning love all night," I say.

She's still leaning against the door frame, and she reaches out, grabs the fabric of my T-shirt in one hand, tugs me closer as she looks up at me. My heart spins in my chest, dizzy.

"No, but I'd get to watch you pick up a heavy thing *now*, and we're not sleeping until later," she says, still tugging. "And waiting for what I want is so hard."

I don't answer her, just take her chin in my hand, run my thumb along the valley just below her bottom lip and as I do, Delilah tilts her head up, deep brown eyes looking right into mine.

"Worth it, but hard," she says.

Since the night she stayed over, we haven't done more than make out, even though all I want to do is throw out our no-sex agreement and lock us in the bedroom.

There's one week left. We both know there's another week. We talked about it on the four-hour drive up here and we agreed to honor it.

Because it's working. We haven't fought. I feel like I know Delilah in ways now that I never could have otherwise, this girl who prefers to draw with charcoal over pastels, who doesn't think much of Jane Austen but loves Emily Brontë, who feeds wild raccoons but has no mercy at all when it comes to spiders.

It's never been like this before. Not when I saw her once a year and we barely left the bed. Not when we were dating before, when we were both so young and so clueless and completely wild with lust.

It's taken us years, but apparently we've learned patience.

I lean in, kiss her slow. She slides her arm around my waist, straightens, and I feel like I'm sinking into her, the outside world dim and muffled.

We're still kissing when there's a knock on the door, and Delilah jumps, then laughs at herself.

"All right," she says softly, and straightens my shirt for me. "You ready for this?"

"Always," I tell her, dropping a quick kiss on her forehead.

· · · · ★ ★ ★ ★ · · · ·

"SETH??" a small voice whispers.

Bree's standing in the doorway to the room, backlit by the hall light as I peek out from behind a bed.

"SETH, ARE YOU IN HERE?"

I bite my lip so I don't laugh. Three-year-olds are the least subtle people on the planet.

"Yes," I whisper back.

"Oh!" she says. Small feet patter. Seconds later, she crashes into me, clearly unable to see in the dark.

"SORRY," she shout-whispers.

"You all right?" I ask, reaching one hand out to her small shoulder.

"I'M OKAY."

From the doorway, I can hear Harold's voice counting very, very slowly: "Teeeeeeen. Eeeeeleeeeeeveeeeen. Tweeeeeeeeeelve…"

"I think it would work better if we hid separately," I whisper to Bree.

Not that this is a great hiding spot. This guest room has two beds, and I'm between them, sort of hidden from the door. It's not exactly Sherlock Holmes's greatest challenge or anything.

It's closing in on ten o'clock, way, *way* past her bedtime, so she's a little punchy right now. Not to mention all the excitement of getting to drink lots of apple juice at the happy hour, running absolutely amok during dinner, and then getting ahold of the M&M's while the adults tried to play charades and she guessed *dinosaur* every single time.

"I WANT TO HIDE WITH YOU," Bree whispers.

"But if you hide somewhere else, it'll take your grandpa and Callum longer to find us both," I explain.

"SHHHHH."

All right, I guess that settles it: Bree and I are hiding together. Moments later, I hear "Ready or not, here we come!" from the direction of the hallway. Tiny feet run.

"Where should we look first?" Harold asks Callum, Bree's eighteen-month-old brother.

"That!" he shouts.

Bree claps both her hands over her mouth and stares at me, eyes the size of dinner plates. I know exactly what's about to happen, so I put one finger to my lips.

A giggle escapes her.

"No laughing," I whisper.

She giggles harder, unsurprisingly, both hands over her mouth as though that helps at all.

"Stop it," I whisper at her, mustering all the gravity I can. "Hide-and-seek is very serious, young lady."

Bree rolls onto her side, now hysterical with the giggles, and I grin, despite myself. That used to work on Rusty, too, though of course now she's far too sophisticated.

Moments later, small footsteps pound into the room, and a small, shadowy figure appears. The figure squeals with delight.

"Found us!" I tell Callum.

"Nice work, champ," says Harold's voice from the door. "Whose turn is it to count next?"

"MEEEEE!" shouts Bree, popping up.

"Oh! You were back there, too?" says Harold, feigning surprise.

"Yes!" she says with zero irony.

When I stand, one of my knees pops, and I shake it out.

"Any hiding spots with recliners?" I ask Harold, and he laughs.

"I'm counting," Bree announces. "One. Go hide! GO!"

I obey, and step into the hallway, blinking in the light. I've already hidden in all four of the penthouse's guest bedrooms, in one shower, and out on the balcony, which was the best hiding spot but way too cold.

I turn left for the living room to try my luck. It's massive, easily twice the size of Delilah's living room in her condo downstairs, so there's gotta be something.

As I head in, I can hear Delilah in the kitchen, still drinking wine and talking to her sisters and Vera. I wave at them as I head past, but I don't think any of them see me. Thad, Chris, and Michael — the husbands — are around here somewhere, probably talking about golf. Or polo. Or using polo horses to golf, I don't know.

In the living room, I stop and look around. From behind me, I hear Bree shout FIVE!! in what must be the slowest anyone has ever counted to twenty.

The curtains. Floor-length, heavy fabric. Perfect for a

hiding spot from a three-year-old and standing definitely beats kneeling on a hard floor again.

"SIX!" she shouts. I lean against the wall, figuring I may as well settle in. From the kitchen, there's a gale of laughter, and I smile to myself.

"You were completely certain you'd broken your femur," Delilah is saying.

"And then you scared the pants off her by telling her that if she had really broken her femur, she would've ruptured an artery and died," Vera says, her tone half-laughing, half-admonishing.

"I wasn't wrong," Delilah says.

"But you did convince me that I was going to die at any moment," Ava says, and Delilah laughs.

"Sorry," she says.

I wonder if I knew Delilah during the trip they're talking about, because I can absolutely imagine it: Ava, still a kid, hurt; Delilah, who got really into the macabre as a teenager, telling her all the ways she could be hurt worse.

"Was that the same trip when Nolan took you and me on the black diamond trails?" Olivia's voice asks.

The hairs on the back of my neck stand at the name. I wish they wouldn't, but they do.

"Goodness, no, that was years later," Vera says.

"I remember that day, though," Winona chimes in. "It was the first time I'd tried a double black diamond, and it was a terrible mistake."

Everyone laughs.

"You flew on down like it was no big deal, but I was way too scared, and of course at that point there was no way out but through," she says. "So he spent the next hour guiding me down as slowly as I wanted. Half the time I was sliding on my butt, and he was so sweet and patient the whole time."

There's a quick moment of silence. I close my eyes, tilt my head against the wall and hope it's awkward as fuck in there right now.

"I thought you'd died," Olivia said, and everyone laughs again. "I got to the bottom and you were *nowhere* to be seen."

"We found you drinking hot chocolate in the lodge," Winona teases.

"Anxiously," Olivia protests. "I was anxiously drinking it."

"Didn't he also somehow program the TV to come on at full volume at four in the morning and Mom called the Snowpeak cops?" Ava asks, to more laughter.

"Their response time was very impressive," Vera says.

"For the record, he felt really bad about that," offers Delilah.

It's not what I want her to say. I want her to say *what a moron* or *thank God I divorced him* or *how could I ever think I loved that man.* Not something as simple and neutral as *he felt bad.*

"I know, I got an enormous fruit basket with a very sweet apology note the next week," Vera says, sounding amused. "The papaya was delightful."

A fruit basket. Nolan gave fruit baskets.

"He had his moments," Delilah says. "Speaking of skiing, is there a plan for tomorrow?"

"Yeah, stop talking about Nolan, the new one might hear you."

"You mean—"

"Olivia, please," Vera says, cutting Delilah off.

"He has a name," Delilah says.

Now I feel like I'm eavesdropping.

"EIGHTEEN!" Bree shouts from down the hallway.

"Well, I can't go skiing, obviously," Olivia says, ignoring Delilah. "And I know the shopping in town is only so-so, but there's the *cutest* kids' boutique, so I was thinking I might get some things for the nursery there, it's too bad that we still don't know if it's a boy or a girl…"

"NINETEEN. TWENTY READY OR NOT HERE I COME!!"

Feet barrel down the hallway to the living room, and I put one hand out and wiggle the curtain back and forth, just to help her find me faster.

"You having fun, sweetie?" I hear Winona ask.

"Yes," Bree says, very seriously.

"All right," Winona says, just as Bree gasps.

"WHO'S THAT?" she says, and moments later, she's yanking on the curtains.

"Whoa! Careful," I tell her, parting them.

"I FOUND SETH!" she shouts, and then grabs my hand. "Come ON, now we have to find Grandpa."

"Yes, ma'am," I tell her, and we go look for Harold.

THIRTY-NINE

SETH

Eight and a Half Years Ago
(Two Years Before the Previous Flashback)

The bartender looks at Caleb's ID, her lips thinning. Her eyes flick to his face, and then back down.

"What's your name?" she asks.

"Daniel Loveless," Caleb says.

"Middle name?"

"Creed."

"Birthday?"

"October twenty-fourth."

"What year?" she asks, eyes narrowing.

Caleb pauses for a split second before answering, and my stomach drops.

"Nineteen ninety," he says.

At last, the bartender shrugs, tosses the three IDs back onto the bar.

"All right," she says. "What can I get you?"

We order beers, and as she's getting them, Levi glances over at Caleb.

"Told you," Caleb mutters.

"Don't involve me in your nonsense," Levi says, though I think he's smiling.

Is he smiling? He's smiling. Somehow, he's inscrutable, even though I've known him my whole life. He wasn't particularly enthused about Caleb borrowing Daniel's license to come out drinking with us, but he didn't protest that hard, either. Probably because Levi doesn't mind breaking the rules that he thinks are stupid.

When we get our beers, I hold mine up.

"To having a job," I say.

"Also to having a job," Levi says.

"To… declaring a major," Caleb says, somewhat less enthusiastically, and we all drink.

It's Friday night, the summer after college. Levi finished his master's degree in forestry the week before I graduated, and two months later, we've both managed to find gainful employment. He's even renting his own place, some tiny cabin out in the woods, though I'm still staying at my Mom's house, along with Caleb for the summer and Daniel and his kid Rusty indefinitely.

God, it's fucking weird that Daniel's got a kid.

We drink. After a bit, we head over to the pool tables. None of us is all that good at pool, but none of us is all that bad, either. Levi wins a game, then I do. Caleb's mildly annoyed but hiding it well.

He sees her first.

I'm trying to line up a shot, half-assedly calculating angles that will only work if I hit the cue ball flawlessly, when he whispers something to Levi. I ignore it, take the shot. The ball bounces off one side, then misses the pocket.

When I look up, they're still muttering to each and giving me weird looks.

"What?" I say, picking up my beer.

Levi just shakes his head and leans over the pool table, but Caleb's eyes flick over my shoulder.

"Nothing," he says too quickly.

I turn.

It takes a moment: The Whiskey Barrel is pretty popular, dive-y, fairly crowded on a Friday night. I think maybe it's nothing. I think maybe they're just being weird.

Then I see her. Standing there, at a cocktail table with one glass-enclosed candle burning in the middle, the bar's attempt at class. She's alone, leaning on her elbows, her shoulders up around her ears as she looks around like she's waiting for something.

It's the first time I've seen her since the night I fled her parents' house the week before Christmas.

Delilah looks different. Her hair's cut short, above her shoulders. She's wearing heels with jeans, a light-colored tank top, lipstick. I keep staring, dumbstruck, and then her gaze finally makes its way to me.

She's surprised. Somehow, I'm surprised I got caught, but I'm frozen in place, can't stop staring at her. Behind me, I hear the dull *clack* of balls knocking into pockets. Caleb says something, but I'm not paying attention.

At last, I nod. Once. I don't know what else to do. I spent the winter feeling like she'd kicked a hole through my chest. I got my first-ever C in a class. I felt a little better with spring, but not much. Every bit of progress felt like I was sewing myself together with a dull-tipped needle.

Delilah nods back, and the moment she does, a man materializes next to her. He sets a drink down on the table, and she looks up. Smiles at him.

It feels like a hole opens in the floor, and I fall through.

"Seth," Levi says, and there's a hand on my shoulder. "Your turn."

We finish the game. I lose catastrophically and couldn't care less as I drain my beer, wishing there were more.

"Next round's on me," I say. "Anyone else want something stronger? I could really use one."

"Sure," says Caleb, grinning because he's nineteen and not even supposed to be here.

"No thanks," Levi says, his face closed off, his beer only half-gone. "I drove you two, remember?"

At the bar, I order three well whiskeys, drink one on the spot, take the other two back to the pool table where I lose again, even more catastrophically. More whiskey. Another game. I'm not a big drinker, so it doesn't take long before I feel like I'm swimming through the bar, missing every shot, shouting at my brothers who are standing a foot away, slurring my words. Always keeping one eye on Delilah and *that man*, over at the table.

And then he gets up. Goes to the bar. I put my cue stick down on the table and then Levi's there, in front of me, sober and rational.

"Don't," he says, quietly.

I grab both his shoulders.

"It's *fine*," I say. I sway. He doesn't. "I just want to say hi. Make sure she's doing well. Wish her all the best in her new life now and all that shit."

"Seth," he says, but I'm already steering around him, aiming myself at her table.

She's got both hands around and almost-empty glass, mostly ice left. Even in the low light, I can see she's slightly pink, a little unsteady.

"You seem well," I say, nothing bothering with *hello* as I use the table for balance. "Good."

"Hi. I'm pretty well," she says. She looks at me like I'm a cobra, ready to strike. "I guess you graduated?"

"Yeah, I guess you didn't?" I say.

"Not yet," she says, her words edged.

She plays with her glass, staring at me, moving it from hand to hand. Something clinks, and I look down.

There's a diamond ring on her left ring finger, but I don't understand. I look at it, puzzled, trying to fit the pieces together but I can't. She's wearing a ring and it's got a diamond and it's on *that* finger and for the life of me, I can't figure out why.

Then at last, it clicks.

"What the fuck?" I ask.

She just clenches her hand into a fist.

"Are you fucking kidding me?" I go on. I can't look at her, only at that goddamn ring. God, it's big, and it catches the light, scatters it. Fucking sparkles. I feel like I'm falling into it. "Tell me that's some cubing zamboni fake jewelry bullshit."

Delilah scoffs.

"Of course not," she says.

"You got engaged?"

She doesn't answer, just rolls her eyes. Looks away.

"How could you get *engaged*?" I ask, and now I'm leaning across the table. Too loud. Don't care.

"It's a very simple process, honestly," she says. The words feel like a blade.

"You said," I start. Stop. "Seven, no eight months ago you said you loved me," I go on, and I might be shouting. "You said you were in love with me and we talked about how we'd be together and what we'd do after I graduated and—"

People are turning, staring.

"—Now it's *now* and you're getting married to someone else?"

"I guess I was wrong," she says, cheeks flaming under the freckles.

There's a presence at my side, big, wide, and it says, "Excuse me, you need to—"

"You're a monster," I tell her, my volume all the way up.

"Because I met someone I loved enough to marry?" Hers is too.

"Because you wouldn't know love if it punched you in the face!"

"All right, you need to leave," the presence says. "Both of you."

"Sorry," says Levi's voice. "I'm sorry, he's with us."

He grabs my arm, and I yank it away, finally look around: a pissed Levi, a tipsy Caleb, the bouncer like a stone wall.

"I can fucking walk," I tell them, and start for the door. Behind me, I hear the bouncer say *Miss,* and people are moving out of my way.

It's cooler outside. The parking lot is half-full, the lights harsh, and Delilah spills out of the door behind me, already shouting.

"—Because I didn't love *you* enough doesn't mean I can't—"

"Who the fuck is he?"

"None of your goddamn business!"

We've gone from shouting to screaming, standing three feet apart.

"Just tell me," I say. "Who. The *fuck*—"

The door opens and he comes out, looking like he's just finished a nice steak dinner, not like he's been ejected from a dive bar.

"What the hell is this?" he asks.

Polo shirt. Clean-shaven. Looks at me like I'm the pool boy.

"It's fine, babe," Delilah says. "It's nothing."

"You just got me kicked out of a bar," he says, jerking a thumb over his shoulder. "That's not nothing."

"Come on," says Levi's voice at my shoulder. "Let's get you—"

"You're heartless," I tell her.

"Fuck off."

"There's no heart in there," I say, pointing. Levi's got my other arm, his hand locked around my bicep. "Just a rock where it's supposed to be."

The man in the polo shirt puffs himself, stands an inch taller.

"Hey now," he says, and I turn back to Delilah.

"The world doesn't start and end with you, Seth," she says. Shouts. "I just didn't love *you*."

"Seth. We're going," Levi says, and now there's another hand on my other arm, and I stumble backward under their power.

"You know what?" I shout. "When you decide you don't love him either, give me a call because whether or not you love me, I sure know how to —"

She lunges forward and slaps me. Silence rings through the parking lot, nothing but background noise from the bar. Delilah looks astonished, still holding out the hand she used as a weapon like she's not sure what happened.

"Are you serious?" I say. I can feel the spot where she hit me but it doesn't even sting.

"*We're going*," Levi barks, and he actually raises his voice.

"No," I say, and struggle against them. "Tell me, Delilah. You fucking *tell me*—"

"Because I never loved you!" she shouts. "Is that what you want?"

I stop struggling, and Levi and Caleb half-haul, half-carry me back to Levi's pickup truck. They shove me into the back, perch me on a tiny jump seat, strap me in. I lean my head against the window and wonder if I'm going to throw up, and the last thing I see as Levi drives away is Delilah under the floodlights, her new man confused and impotent by her side.

"Fuck you," I mutter.

Levi can't take us back to our mom's house while Caleb's drunk and I'm trashed, so he takes us to the house he's renting. It's small, but it's off in the woods, so he likes it. He doesn't have a guest room, so he pushes aside his coffee table and gives us sleeping bags.

And he takes mercy on us. He gives me water, makes us toast. He sits both of us on the couch while he watches us eat. When we're done, he puts his arm around me, and I lean into my big brother's shoulder, Caleb on my other side.

"How could she be engaged?" I mumble over and over again. "How the hell can she get married?"

When I wake up, I'm on the couch, a sleeping bag draped over me, a trash can nearby. Caleb's on the floor inside the other. I'm twenty-two, so my hangover is gone with a cup of coffee and when Levi comes in, he's merciful enough not to say anything.

I never go back to the Whiskey Barrel, but that night, I go out alone to a different bar. I buy a woman a drink. Her name is Allison, and she smiles at me, laughs at my jokes, and at the end of the night she takes me home with her.

She's the second woman I've ever slept with, and I'm amazed at how easy it is. Later that week, I do it again: Natalie. Then again. Then again.

It doesn't fix what's wrong with me, but at least I'm good at it.

FORTY

SETH

Delilah comes to a hard, full stop, her skis scraping the snow beneath them.

Ten feet later, I finally halt, feet in full pizza position with my toes in and heels out.

"You doing okay?" she asks, pushing off her poles and gliding up to me, then stopping with no fuss at all.

"Great," I tell her, and try for a charming, winning smile. "You having a good time?"

"We can head back if you want," she says, pulling her goggle from her face, a smile around her eyes. "You seem like you might be done."

She's right. We've been skiing since the morning, and the sun's now hovering over the mountains, all of Snow-peak, West Virginia bathed in light that's still more gold than orange for now.

It's the second time I've been skiing in my life. Growing up, I had four brothers and there was no money tree in the back yard, so the one and only time I've been was for a friend's birthday in college.

Skiing is hard. I've fallen down more times than I can count, have a bruise blossoming across one knee, definitely did something funny to one elbow. I run and lift, so I'm usually prepared for physical activity, but muscles I didn't even know I had are begging me for mercy.

"How about I head back and you do a few more runs?" I offer. "You've been babysitting me all day, go have some fun."

"I wasn't babysitting!" she protests, laughing. "You made it down that intermediate slope all by yourself, you're doing great."

"I lost a ski halfway down, and after you got it back, it took me four tries to get back on my feet," I point out.

"That's because getting up is the hardest part," she admonishes, gently. "Aside from getting off the lift. I can't even tell you how many times I've had face-planted doing that."

Well, it was zero this trip. I, on the other hand, skied into a tree and fell over the first time I got off a lift while four-year-olds zipped past me like they were born to it.

"Go," I tell her, nodding back at the mountain. "I'm going to shower, grab a beer, and get in the hot tub. Come join me when you finish."

"Seth, are you incentivizing me to make it fast?" she laughs.

"Just saying I'll be slippery and wet when you find me," I say, lowering my voice. I am, after all, literally surrounded by families.

"And disappointingly off-limits," she teases.

"Says the woman who brought a white tank top to sleep in," I remind her.

Delilah's eyes crinkle, her goggles on her forehead.

Except for her eyes, her face is deathly pale with some sort of specialty sunscreen, and she looks a little like a strangely-colored raccoon.

Still fucking gorgeous, for the record.

"I didn't mean to," she says. "I *thought* I brought an appropriately black, oversized shirt, but I'm pretty sure it's still on my bed waiting to be packed."

No matter what she intended, she still wore a white wife-beater to bed last night, over rainbow pajama pants. Yes, it was practically see-through. No, she didn't wear a bra to bed, and yes, I think I deserve a gold medal for self-control.

"Ski a couple black diamonds and then come find me," I tell her.

"All right," she says, and offers herself for a kiss.

The moment our lips touch, I slide away.

"Fuck!" I mutter, trying to maneuver my feet into a triangle.

"Use your pole!" she says, and there she is, gliding alongside me.

I jab one into the ground and come to a stop. Then I give her a *look*, and she closes her eyes, laughs.

"Right here, with all these people around?" I say, low enough that no one but her can hear.

"Well, I'd rather keep it all for myself," she says, and puts one gloved hand on my chest. Kisses me, both my ski poles firmly jabbed into the ground.

"I can live with that," I murmur when she pulls back.

"You sure you're all right?"

"Just go enjoy yourself," I tell her, and wave her away.

I wait until she's turned and headed back for the lift before I make my way very, very carefully and slowly, toward the end of the slope.

· · · · ★ ★ ★ ★ ★ · · ·

Back in the condo, I toss my key onto the kitchen counter, leave my coat and ski pants in a heap, and collapse on the couch.

I don't move for at least half an hour, and secretly, I'm glad Delilah's not here. It was bad enough that she practically had to hold my hand for most of today while I fell down a mountain, everyone else zipping by; she doesn't need to see me collapse in an undignified pile.

Especially since I've got a sneaking suspicion that I'm the first boyfriend she's had to teach to ski.

I push the thought away and do some mindless scrolling on my phone. I play some dumb games. Check Facebook. Text my brothers' group chat about how much skiing hurts, and get back several sarcastic replies about my terrible free vacation.

Finally, I get off the couch. Walking doesn't feel wonderful, but at least I don't feel like my legs are rubber any more as I wander through Delilah's condo, turning lights on and off as I check the place out a little more thoroughly.

Two bedrooms, two bathrooms: one in the master suite, one off the living room. A stone fireplace and leather couches; a small but gourmet kitchen; a balcony; a dining area.

And tiny, tiny traces of *him*. A man's razor in a bathroom drawer. A single sock in a closet, neatly folded, on a shelf next to a pillow. A cigar, probably stale as hell, in a kitchen drawer next to some spatulas. They're all things that were obviously overlooked and left in corners, but those whispers of his presence tickle at my brain, like I've walked through a spiderweb and can't get the strands off completely.

Her life has whispers of him, but not of me. We were together for six years before she even met him, through high school and college. Big years. Important years, and yet I'm nowhere to be found. It's as if she's washed me away completely.

My phone dings, pulling me out of it.

Delilah: I'm gonna do one more run & then head in. You still in the hot tub?
Me: I will be.

She texts a bathtub emoji, and I put my phone back on the charger. Drink a glass of water. Rub my eyes, remember that I should shower before I get into the hot tub, and open a closet to find towels.

It's top-to-bottom white linen except for a single, solitary cardboard box on the floor. The corners are ripped. There's black marker on the side, text scribbled out so hard that it's unreadable. It looks worn, old, and it's so incongruous in this otherwise sparkling place that I can't help but bend down and open it.

I don't know what I'm expecting. Cleaning products, maybe. Old sweaters. A broken toaster, though none of those expectations account for the weight in my chest as I pull back the cardboard.

Haphazardly on top is a shining, pearlescent white book that says *Mr. & Mrs.* in delicate silver letters. The weight in my chest grows heavier, feels like it's pulling on my lungs, and I swallow hard.

I should put it back without looking, and I know it. I came to her and offered a blank slate. I'm the one who wanted to forget everything and start over. I owe her my ignorance.

I open it anyway, already hating myself.

The very first page proves me right. It's them, in front of the altar, deep in a kiss. He's wearing black and she's wearing a white strapless dress, hair piled atop her head, arms and shoulders blank.

I kneel on the floor. I stare, the weight of jealousy heavy in my chest, and I hate him. I hate him for swooping in and getting what I couldn't have. I hate him for whatever he did to make her divorce him. I hate him for haunting her life still, with this album and the sock in the closet and the cocktail shaker she still has.

I flip some pages. They're just wedding pictures, but they're *hers*, and I can't stop myself. She's happy, glowing, beautiful, and so, *so* young. I remember her this young. I remember her younger, the two of us just kids.

Under the photo book is more, and I put the book down, glance in. There's a jewelry box. Photo frames. Tchotchkes, a nameplate, a throw pillow, and I should stop. She'll be back soon, and I know – I *know* – I'm not meant to see this.

Just as I'm putting the book back, the photo on top of the pile catches my eye: her and Nolan, standing in front of the fireplace, posing together. His arm's around her shoulders and hers are around his waist, and she looks so perfectly happy and content that it shakes me to the bone.

I put the book in, shove the box back into the closet, take some towels. I shut the closet door and then walk back into the living room, stand there, and look at the fireplace.

Right there. They stood right there, so happy, posed for a picture. If I try hard enough, I think I can see their footprints still on the floor, no matter how much I don't want to.

Then I force myself to turn around, head into the bathroom, and take a shower.

· · · · ★ ★ ★ ★ ★ · · ·

"MIND IF I JOIN YOU?" I call across the rooftop patio, letting the door swish shut behind myself.

Jesus, the floor is cold, and I'm barefoot. I wish I'd known to bring sandals, but I didn't think to do so on a skiing vacation and Delilah forgot to warn me.

"Of course not!" says one of the women. "Come on in, the water's great!"

I set my beer down, pull off the fluffy white robe that I got from the condo, hang it up and get to the hot tub as fast as humanly possible. The sun's fully behind the mountains now and the temperature's dipped even further from today.

"We were just debating whether we should get a massage or go make margaritas," the other says as I ease myself into the water, beer once more in hand. "What would you do?"

I settle into a seat across from them, find myself smiling. They're both wearing bikinis, both probably in their forties, both reasonably attractive. Both watching me attentively in a way I recognize so I stretch one arm along the rim of the tub, take a sip of my beer, look from one to the other.

"What kind of massage and what kind of margarita?" I ask. They both laugh, even though it wasn't funny. The one on the right leans her head on one hand, stretching out her neck.

"Swedish, and on the rocks with a salt rim," she says.

"I'd probably go margarita, then," I admit.

"Told you," she says to the other woman, and they both laugh again. Then she leans forward, holds out one hand. "Hi, I'm Amy."

"Kate."

I introduce myself. We make small talk about all the bullshit you'd expect: ski conditions, the weather, what there is to do in a ski resort town at night. It's nothing, and it's going to stay nothing, but deep down I know sparked interest when I see it, and God help me, it makes me feel good.

I don't want it to. I want the fact that these women are flirting with me to make me feel nothing, but the box in the closet sticks in the back of my mind and each smile, each laugh at nothing, each flirty look gives me the tiniest boost.

"Four brothers?" Kate is saying. "My gosh, you must be tough as—"

The door opens, and we all look over.

Delilah walks out, hair piled on top of her head, wearing a fluffy white bathrobe. I feel my face nearly split in two.

"—nails," she finishes.

"Hey," Delilah says, sounding breathless. "Oh, my God, it's *freezing* out here."

"You gotta move fast," Amy advises. "Don't think about it, just go!"

Delilah laughs. Shrugs off her robe, hangs it, kicks off her flip-flops, rushes to the hot tub and my mouth goes dry.

She's wearing a black swimsuit. It's a one-piece, the straps crossing over her back, the neckline plunging further than anything I've seen her wear since we've been dating. Her tattoos are vivid even in the fading lights: ocean and mountains, Kraken and vines, sinking ships. The clockwork heart, the swell of her breasts around it. The lace garters on each thigh, a swirl of stars around one, the roots of a tree snaking through the other. The way the elastic digs into the soft flesh of her hip. I imagine it under my palm and shudder despite the hot water.

The muscles in one thigh flex as she steps down with a soft *oh*, her arms out as she balances, then sinks slowly into the water until it bobs over her chest.

I want her. It's that simple, one small fact at the center of a frenzied knot, so much looped and tightened around it that it seems complicated. Three words, eight letters, somehow enormous enough to blot out the sky.

I want her. I've always wanted her. I think I always will.

"Hey," I tell her, snake an arm around her waist, kiss her. And kiss her.

I meant it to be a simple *hello, darling* kiss but I can't seem to end it at the right spot. It's longer, deeper, and when I finally pull back, I'm breathless. I clear my throat.

"This is Kate and Amy," I tell her.

"Delilah," she says.

"My girlfriend," I offer, as if they didn't know. They shake hands across the hot tub. Delilah settles in next to me, her hair tickling my face, her hand settling on my leg.

"You know, Delilah, I have to tell you," Amy says. "I don't normally like tattoos, but yours are *beautiful*. Did they hurt?"

Delilah just laughs.

"Yes," she says. "Though not as much as you might think. Arms aren't too bad, but I've got one right here" — she pushes herself out of the water slightly, points at the spot where the raven is, across her ribs, pale cleavage shining as water sluices off— "and *that* hurt."

"Ooh, I bet," Kate says. "Is that the most painful spot?"

"I think feet are worse, or at least, that's what people seem to have the most trouble with. I'm also a tattoo artist," she explains.

Kate and Amy are *fascinated*, and I can't blame them. Delilah's fascinating. We talk tattoos, then piercings, then bad haircuts, and there's something wonderful about watching Delilah work her magic on these two strangers. No *wonder* the tattoo shop has taken off.

The whole time, her hand stays on my leg. Sometimes

her fingers move, and I can't tell whether it's with the water in the hot tub or whether she's teasing me as she talks. I just know that by the time Amy and Kate head off to margaritas — they finally decided — every hair on my body is standing on end, the whole of my mind dedicated to the path her fingers are taking.

"Have a great night!" Amy calls from the doorway, and then the two of them are gone and we're alone up here.

Delilah tilts her head back against my arm, her cheek against my shoulder. She presses her hand into my leg and all I can think about is four fingers and a thumb, the length of her thigh against mine. The way she looks at me and her neck curves away from her collarbone, the plunge of her neckline, the swell of her breasts.

"I have bad news," she says, raising one eyebrow.

"I'm the worst skier you've ever met."

Delilah scoffs.

"Shut up, you did great," she says. "You're sliding down a mountain on slippery sticks. It's hard."

"Every toddler I saw begs to differ," I point out.

"You're much farther off the ground than they are," she says. "A kid falls down face-first, they barely notice. An adult falls down face-first, it's an ER visit. I once watched Bree tumble down half a flight of stairs and then bounce up still asking for ice cream."

"What's the bad news, then?" I ask.

Her hand moves, or maybe it's the water. Half a centimeter up. I feel like my skin is glowing with heat.

"I can't leave this hot tub," she says. "It's too cold. It was cold before I got in, and getting out is gonna be even colder, so I live here now. Promise you'll write."

"You'll just get my letters all wet," I tease.

"Seth, I would be *so* careful with your letters," she says, laughing. "I would hold them super far away from the water while I read them."

"But then your arms would be cold."

"That's a sacrifice I'm willing to make to read your letters," she says, her head still on my arm. "A very small part of me can be cold."

Her hand on my leg moves, I think, or maybe it's the water. Another half-centimeter, the distance geometric, my desire logarithmic. I've been fighting myself since she walked out here in a bathing suit, but I'm losing.

"You do know there's an indoor hot tub, don't you?" I point out, just to tease her. "By the pool. First floor."

"But that one gets crowded, and this one's on the roof," she says. "A little privacy is probably worth never being able to leave."

My own fingers alight on her thigh, just below the garter. Her face flickers. Her chest rises, falls, breasts swelling above the water and then sinking beneath the surface again.

She's soft, slippery, flesh and muscle. Watching me with her lips parted as my hand pushes between her thighs, gripping her just hard enough for her soft skin to bulge between my fingers.

Nothing about her yields. She's soft the way the earth is soft: welcoming, giving, unconquerable. I'm falling toward her, parachute forgotten.

"And why would you want privacy?" I ask. I move my thumb along her skin, still gripping, and I feel her move her hips in response: microscopic, the angle of her leg changing by half a degree, but Delilah is a song I know by heart.

"Because my self-control is fraying at the seams," she says. Her fingers play with a fold on my swim trunks, and my whole leg shivers. My cock swells. There's nothing I can do. "Because you kissed me hello like you hadn't seen me for weeks."

I lean in, slowly. She straightens, her head lifting from my arm, her dark eyes locked on mine, and I brush my lips against hers.

Just a taste. Just a tease, just a test, just to see if I can do it and still pull away. I can, but not far. I can, but not for long.

It's slow as a first kiss, but nowhere near as tentative. I explore her mouth with mine. Gently, patiently, even as below the water my fingers sink further into her thigh and my thumb finds the edge of her swimsuit, the spot where fabric meets flesh, crosses the boundary.

She straightens, locks her other hand through my hair, traces her fingers over my neck. She parts her thighs and drapes one over my leg, her hand still between us, the side of my finger finding the edge of her bathing suit between her legs.

Delilah sighs, and it crashes over me like a wave. I pull her onto my lap and she bobs onto me, arms going around my neck, laughing as she leans in.

"See?" she says. "This would be *so* awkward with other people around. Can you imagine us making out in a hot tub while Bob and Jim discuss golf five feet away?"

"I'd rather not," I tell her, pulling her in. Her mouth is soft, open. "I hate golf."

She laughs, shifts on my lap, takes my shoulders in her hands. Squeezes until her fingernails dig in, then lets go. I'm hard as a rock underneath her, every tiny movement she makes echoing through my body.

"Nobody likes golf," she says. "They all just think everyone else does, so they pretend."

"I'm sure someone does," I say, and I wonder who *nobody* and *everyone* are. I wonder if they're in the box.

"Sure. One person, somewhere," she teases. "Everyone else just likes driving that cart around."

"You gonna make me do that next?" I ask. My hands are on her hips, pulling her in sideways.

"Are you saying I *made* you go skiing?" she says. An arm around my neck, a hand on my chest.

"Just that if it weren't for you, I'd probably be driving four-wheelers through the mud and shouting *yeehaw!* this weekend," I say. "You know, some lowborn redneck shit."

"That does sound fun," she says. Her mouth finds mine, pushes it open. Her body presses against me, and she pulls away, leans her forehead against mine.

Squirms on my lap until suddenly she's straddling me in the water, the heart tattoo right in front of my face, both sides bowed in by the swell of her breasts, shining even in the low light.

Her nipples are hard as pebbles in the cold air, and I close my hands around her ribcage. My thumbs on her sternum, breasts in the valley between finger and thumb as she rocks against me softly once, twice, a loose curl bouncing against my temple.

The tiniest movement, and I'll be across the line we've set. The line that's become the bond between us. The line that keeps us from falling off a cliff.

"So, you'd rather be out muddin' than here?" she teases, softly. "I'm not sure I believe you've ever even been."

"I went once," I say. I hook my thumbs beneath the fabric over her sternum, pull it down until I can see the very top of the raven's head, the fabric over her breasts denting into them. "It was enough. You get real dirty, turns out."

I pull harder on her swimsuit and this time she comes down, kisses me open-mouthed. Locks her hand around my neck, the other still on my chest, her hips grinding slowly against me.

I'm crumbling, fast. I don't want to think about the wedding album and the box, but I do. It's there, below the surface of my mind like a whale about to breach. The vast unknown of what he was to her, what she was to him. *Why*.

But I know what I've been, and I know how to make her forget everything else. I know how to possess her, at least in body, so I unhook my thumbs from her swimsuit and slide them across her cut-glass nipples.

Delilah *moans*. Her mouth is still on my mine and the sound vibrates through me, surprised and breathy. Loud enough to echo off another condo building and come back to us as she claps her hand over her mouth, faces still inches from mine.

I lean forward, take a knuckle between my teeth. Run my tongue across the ridges and wrinkles as I push my thumbs over her nipples again, this time flicking my thumb-nails over the flat.

She takes her hand off her mouth and kisses me, dragging her fingers across my face. She rolls her hips and makes a noise as she presses her clit against the thick ridge of my cock.

I groan. I'm not as loud as her but it's an accident, not intentional. I cup her breasts in my hands, pinch her nipples between my forefinger and thumb. I roll them, and she whimpers, works herself against me.

"Ever come in a rooftop hot tub before?" I ask, pinching even harder, the fabric skipping between my fingers. I'm afraid of hurting her, but she just sighs.

"Not yet," she whispers, and I push away the fabric of her swimsuit until her nipples are out, pink and puckered.

I stroke, roll, pinch. She rides me through two layers of

fabric so hard I'm afraid that I'll come first, and this is a communal hot tub.

"Tell me you miss this," I growl, low and breathless. "Tell me—"

"I miss this so fucking much," she whispers. "I miss *being* with you like—"

The rooftop door opens and she pulls back with a gasp, bolt upright. Tugs her suit back into place as I grab her hips, keep her steady.

"—And white is so cute, though, especially for a baby," Ava's voice says.

"You have to be fucking kidding me," Delilah mutters.

They come into view: two women and two men, though in the dark at this distance, I can't tell them apart.

"You don't think it's kind of girly?" Olivia asks, stepping out onto the patio. "Ooooh! That's so cold!"

"Told you to wear your-flip flops, babe," says Michael, her husband.

"It's not girly, it's white," Ava says, and then waves. "Hey, guys! Delilah, isn't white totally neutral? Like it's the absence of color?"

"Technically, it's the reflection of all colors," she says. Still straddling my lap, still breathing harder than normal. "Black is the absorption of color."

"I'm just saying, white is kind of feminine," Olivia says, carefully making her way toward us. "So I don't know if I should…"

"Go," I tell Delilah, voice low. "Now. *Go.*"

She pushes backward, stands. Hops up on the lip of the tub and swings her feet over.

"Bad timing," she says to her sisters, casual as you please. "We were just heading out, we've been in too long."

"Oh, boo," Ava pouts.

FORTY-ONE

DELILAH

"Sorry!" I say brightly, lunging for the robes and towels we brought out. "We've been here a while, and you know, you're not supposed to stay in a hot tub for too long…"

I grab a towel, wrap it around myself, glance back at Seth. He's giving me an urgent look that I'm pretty sure translates to *I don't want your family to see my dick*, and I grab the other towel, move back to the hot tub.

"Well, I'm not even supposed to be in the hot tub because of *the baby*," Olivia says. She's started emphasizing *the baby* whenever she says it, and it's not my favorite linguistic tic of hers. "I'm just going to dangle my feet in and keep an eye on Michael, haha!"

Seth glances their way, then in one smooth motion, he turns his back and spins over the side of the hot tub, feet hitting the ground at the exact same time he grabs the towel. It's around his waist in a flash, and no one but me notices that he's pitching a circus-sized tent.

Then his eyes meet mine, and he winks. I scrunch my

toes against the concrete floor as we grab our robes, pull them on.

"You don't even want to stay to hang out?" Ava says, holding something. "I brought the canned wine!"

"Ugh," Olivia says, not quietly enough.

I'm already putting on my flip-flops, belting my robe.

"What? It's good," Ava tells her sister.

"Nah, I gotta go get ready for dinner with Vera and Dad," I say, walking. "And, you know, my hair, it's—"

I just sort of wave my hands in the air and hope it's explanation enough.

"Seth could stay," she offers. "I feel like I've barely gotten to hang out with you."

That gets me, and I pause for a split second. Seth practically runs into me, his hand on my lower back.

Ava wants to hang out with Seth? Someone in my family wants to hang out with my Ford-driving, townhouse-owning, middle-class boyfriend?

"I gotta help her," Seth says, and makes the same hand motion I did.

"Have fun, guys," Thad says, his arm around Ava, guiding her to the hot tub. "C'mon, babe."

Then I'm inside and the door shuts behind us and as soon as we're out of sight Seth spins me. Grabs the lapels of my fluffy white robe, pulls me in with a force that takes my breath away, crushes my mouth with his.

It can be easy to forget how powerful he is. I know he's tall, broad, and has muscles I want to lick, but I rarely see how well he can use it. Yesterday, with the suitcases, maybe. A few weeks ago when he pulled himself up onto a tree branch to retrieve a projectile for Rusty.

Or now, when I'm the object of his power unleashed. He walks me backward, guiding my feet with his, not letting me go for a second.

Finally, I pull away. Grab his hand. He laces his fingers through mine and power walks through the halls of the building.

When we get to the condo, he's already got his key out and doesn't let me go as he unlocks it, shoulders the door open, pulls me through. Pushes me up against the wall as it clicks shut, pulling the belt from my robe so hard I'm afraid he might rip it.

"I still haven't come in a hot tub," I murmur as he covers my mouth with his.

I grab his robe, pull him into me. Push it from his shoulders and let it fall.

"That's your sisters' fault, not mine," he says, nips at my bottom lip. "Or was getting off while people talk about golf a fantasy and not a disaster scenario?"

His hands are inside the robe, hot on my cold skin, and I shiver. He pulls at my swimsuit again, roughly this time, the muscles in his forearms cording as both breasts pop out.

I laugh, raspy, his lips already on my throat, his fingers rolling my nipples again so hard it almost hurts. Almost.

"Disaster," I say, and the robe falls off, pools around my feet. "I'd much rather come along with you."

He chuckles, breath hot against my neck. Teeth scrape skin. A tiny, brief flash of pain, and his mouth.

"Seth," I murmur. "Don't leave—"

He doesn't stop as he covers my mouth with a hand.

"You think I don't know my way around you by now, Bird?"

I lick his palm in response, salt and chlorine. He twists his hand, brushes a thumb across my lips. Straightens, kisses the spot beneath my ear, sucks the lobe into his mouth.

"If I leave a mark, it's because I mean to," he says, guttural as dirt.

I find his cock through his swim trunks, press my hand against it and the cold, wet fabric warm in seconds with his heat.

"And why would you mean that?" I ask.

Seth drives his hips into me, and I squeeze. Grab his shoulder from behind with my other hand, the muscle thick and hard, and I sink my teeth in.

Not hard enough to hurt, but hard enough to get a gasp and a growl and an extra twist of the nipple he's still pinching.

"Because I like finding them later," he says. His voice is a harsh whisper, and I let his cock go, tug at the laces holding his swim trunks on. "And I like thinking about you finding them and remembering what a good time you had."

I tug. The laces come free, Velcro tears apart, the shorts fall off, his cock springs out.

He kisses me fiercely, my hand circling him again, stroking. His length is hard and hot against my thigh, and Seth groans so loudly that I hope no one's walking by outside.

"Off," he says, and pulls at my bathing suit, tugging the straps over my shoulders and down, mouth never relenting. I untangle my arms, pull them free, push at the wet fabric still covering my hips.

"Fucking wet spandex," I hiss, wriggling. "I swear, it's—"

I wriggle and it's finally over my thighs, my knees, and then I stomp and kick and half-turn and nearly fall over because there's never been anything less sexy than getting out of a swimsuit, and Seth grabs my arm, catches me.

"There," I gasp, just as he pushes me against the wall again, only this time I'm facing it and I gasp at the contact, my skin already puckered from being wet and cold, my fists clenched over my head.

He pulls at my hips, fingers sinking into flesh, mouth on the back of my neck, cock pressed against my lower back. His hands roam, feeling me like we've never touched before.

Then he pauses. He stills his hands against my ribs, and they feel white-hot.

"You're freezing," he says.

"I'm fine," I say, even though he's right, every inch of my flesh goose bumped.

He doesn't move his hands again.

"Um, there's a thermostat," I say, very much not thinking about the thermostat.

His lips move slowly against my neck, like he's thinking.

Then he smacks my ass, steps away, grabs my hand.

"C'mon," he says, and pulls me to the bathroom.

He pushes me against the sink. Tweaks a nipple.

"Don't move," he says, and steps to the glass-walled shower, reaches in, starts the water.

"You can't tell me what to do," I tease.

He frowns, flips a knob.

"I just did."

I lean back into the counter. I prop a foot against the cabinet, my eyes glued to Seth, slide my hand down my belly, over my thigh. He turns at my sharp inhale and looks back at me, rubbing my clit with one hand.

"I've never been good at following directions," I say, the words exhaled in a rush. I'm even wetter than I realized, so sensitive that I'm already on edge.

If Seth wasn't feral before, he is now. He glances into the shower one more time, steam already pouring from the stall, crosses the small bathroom toward me. Takes my hand by the wrist and anchors both of them onto the counter, pressing my palms into the cool stone.

"Congratulations," he growls, leaning into me, pushing me backward over the counter. "You found the one time that I don't want to watch you get yourself off."

He crushes his mouth against mine, invades me with his tongue. His teeth slide against my lip, send shivers down my spine even as the steam from the shower is billowing against the ceiling, floating down, winding around us.

"You don't?" I ask, still teasing.

"I'd much rather do it myself."

His lips drop: my neck, collarbone. He doesn't let my hands go, keeps his locked tightly around my wrists. I struggle against them for half a second, but it's just for show, and he laughs with his lips around one nipple.

Seth bites, sucks. I moan. The bathroom heats, the water in the shower pounding down, steam curling through the air until my skin is warm and damp. Lips against my raven tattoo, dragging over my stomach, the slight hill of my lower belly.

I part my thighs without being told, Seth on his knees in front of me. He looks up at me as his tongue finds my clit, gently, *gently* teases it, and I whimper.

His hands tighten around my wrists and he teases, teases, the lightest touch on the single most sensitive point of my body until I'm fully bent backward, panting for breath, head resting against the mirror over the sink.

"It feels better when you do it," I say.

Suddenly he drags his tongue over my clit, hard and slow.

I shout, gasp, arch my back. I pull my hands against his and this time he lets me go, flicks my clit one more time, and plants my foot on his shoulder, hand gripping my ankle. I use him as leverage and push up until I'm sitting on the counter and he drags me forward, thighs spread.

Then he grabs my hands, puts them back where they were. Holds them with his own and teases me again: flick, flick, flick, *drag*.

"So much better," I gasp out. He rewards me with another hard, slow drag of his tongue, and I roll my hips forward, seeking more, but he doesn't give it.

Seth teases me with quick, deliberate flicks, swirls. Twice I'm on the brink, and twice he leaves my clit and slides his tongue between my lips, teasing at my entrance until my breathing evens back out.

The third time I nearly come, he pulls away entirely, his lips finding my inner thigh. My eyes fly open.

"Wait, no," I say, voice ragged. "Go back."

He doesn't. Instead he lets my hands go and stands, leans over me, swipes one thumb along my wet slit as he does. I groan quietly, and then his mouth is on mine and I lick my juices from his lips.

"I missed *that*," he says, curling his hands over my body again: belly, hips, breasts. "Who knew heaven was listening to you moan with my tongue on your clit?"

I'm surprised to discover that I've got one foot in the sink, the other on a towel rack, and I move them both, sit forward. Pull him toward me, my legs on either side of his torso, looking straight into his eyes for once.

The shower's still going, the bathroom so filled with steam that I can barely see the opposite wall. We're both slick with it, tiny droplets gathering and merging on skin, and I mean to answer but instead I kiss him again and slide my hands over the muscles in his shoulders, his arms, his chest. I bend my head and lick droplets from his neck, the hollow of his throat as his hands skim down my back.

Seth pulls me off the counter so I'm standing in front

of him and he's towering over me again. My hand goes to his cock, circles it. Squeezes, and he groans. Grabs my ass, holds me against him. Ravishes my mouth with his.

I wriggle, stroke his cock again. He doesn't relent, still backing me against the counter.

"Move back," I murmur.

"Why?"

"I can't get on my knees if I can't move," I tell him.

"I don't want you on your knees," he says.

The deepest kiss, my thumb stroking over the thick head of his cock. A growl erupting from his chest as I rub the slick drops into delicate skin. Bodies pressed together so tightly it's hard to tell where he ends and I begin, skin slick, steam swirling with every movement.

"I want you standing," he says. Pulls back, takes my hips to spin me, but I understand exactly what he wants and I'm already turning, my palms flat on the counter in front of me.

Seth fits himself to my back, wraps an arm over my torso from waist to shoulder, and I kiss his hand. He lifts a finger and I lick it, suck it into my mouth, drag my tongue over his fingerprint.

"I want you just like this," he whispers. "Tattooed and wicked. Enthusiastic as fuck. The girl who haunts all my wet dreams."

His hand between my legs, and I move them apart, pitch forward slightly.

"Only the wet dreams?" I murmur.

His fingers find my entrance, slide inside me knuckle-deep with no hesitation. As if he knows my body as well as he knows his own.

"You're in other dreams, too," he says into my ear, working his fingers inside me, his cock steel against my back. "But I figured you'd rather hear about the ones where

I make you shout my name than the ones where we have breakfast together every morning."

I turn my head, wrap my hand around the back of his neck. Drops slide down my body, and I suck them from his neck, salty and sweet.

"No marks," he teases, and I laugh. Do it again.

"I know my way around you, Seth," I tell him. "You think I don't have every last inch memorized?"

He pulls his fingers out, takes my hips. I arch and bend forward, on my toes. The thick tip of his cock draws a line over my back, between my buttocks, glides between my lips, slippery and swollen.

"Delilah," he says, a rough whisper. "Still?"

"Still," I whisper back, and then he's inside me and pushing deep, deeper, my hipbones crushing against the sink with force. It's not gentle but I don't need gentle. I don't want gentle. I want the full force of *him*, a wave crashing over me, a howling thunderstorm after months of drought.

I push back, bracing myself against the mirror with one forearm, the other behind me, seeking him out even now. I want more, more, I want skin and muscle and bone, to be taken so thoroughly I have handprint-shaped bruises tomorrow.

I hear myself whisper his name, as if in gratitude: *Seth, yes*, and like he can read my mind he wraps an arm like a steel band around me again. Fucks me hard, slow, deep.

"Delilah." His voice in my ear, lips against the shell, and even though he's bare inside me it sprinkles a shiver down my neck.

"Tell me you're mine."

I curl my fingers through his, over my shoulder. Swipe my forearm along the fogged mirror so it clears and I'm looking into those eyes: the sky, the sea, maybe both.

"I'm yours," I manage. "I'm yours, of course I'm yours. I'm always yours."

Harder, again. I gasp and he pinches a nipple, nudges my leg with his. Changes the angle and thrusts again, and this time I swear I see stars.

"There it is," he says in my ear. "I live for the moment when I fuck you just right and you go from sex kitten to boneless and wild with my name on your lips."

"Seth," I say. "Tell me."

"I'm yours, Delilah," he says instantly, his eyes on mine through the re-fogging mirror. "Of course I'm yours. I've always been yours."

I'm melting, burning, glowing with heat. I brace against the mirror and push myself back into him, the rhythm furious, frantic. He holds on to me, our skin slippery with the steam, fucks me like we can meld. There's nothing careful, nothing tentative. Nothing but total certainty.

I come in a wave, the orgasm swelling inside me, cresting, teasing. I gasp. I moan. I might beg, because I also come babbling nonsense: *yes yes oh god oh fuck Seth yes Seth please Seth.*

I come and it crashes over me, washes everything away, and I don't stop. I don't slow, even when I'm trembling, not until Seth digs his fingers into my shoulder and pulls me back down, and I clench as he jerks inside me, his shout echoing off the bathroom walls.

I sag, forearms propped against the mirror, forehead against the cool glass. My whole body is shaking, the combined exertion of sex and skiing, and I'm breathing like I just came up for air from minutes underwater.

He leans against me, forearms against the mirror around mine, face against my hair. Chest against my back. Breathing just as fast and hard as me. I feel like I should say something, but every time I try to think of words, my mind turns to clouds floating across a blue sky.

After a moment, Seth flattens his hands over mine, still on the mirror. Clears his throat against the steam.

"Every single time," he says, slowly. "I think, that's it. That's the best one. It's all downhill from here."

I start laughing, still pressed against the mirror, trembling and punchy and lightheaded.

"And somehow, I have yet to be right," he says. Kisses the back of my neck. "Jesus Christ, Bird."

I flex my fingers on the mirror so his fall between them, then close my hands, push back from the mirror and wrap our arms around myself. Seth shifts, comes out of me, a slight warm trickle down one thigh.

"Jesus Christ, Seth," I agree, in his arms, tucked under his chin. The right place. Always the right place.

We stand there for a moment. Several moments. Then Seth kisses the side of my head and pulls his arms away.

"I'm gonna turn the shower off," he says.

FORTY-TWO

SETH

We're half an hour late to dinner with her family. It's at the fancy steakhouse next door, and when we get there, they're already well into their appetizers.

"Delilah! I was starting to think you weren't coming," Vera calls, waving us over. "Here, let me call the waiter back. Do you want something besides wine? Here, let's get another bottle, and we'll also…"

Delilah gives my hand a squeeze before we sit.

"I'm *so* sorry," Delilah says when Vera takes a breath, smoothing the napkin onto her lap. "I got the time wrong, I thought this was at seven-thirty, not seven."

Winona, seated across from us, gives Delilah a look. Then she gives me a look. Then she gives Delilah another look, very clearly trying not to laugh.

My hair's wet. Delilah's hair is still slightly damp. She's got one sleeve pushed slightly above her elbow, the bottom of a lake barely visible, and when she catches Winona's eye she pulls it down.

"Didn't you get the itinerary?" Vera asks, eyebrows raised.

"I specifically asked the front desk to make sure they left it somewhere plainly visible, since I still remember the year they put it on the couch and Winona nearly missed our luncheon."

"I did. It was my mistake," Delilah says. "I should have consulted it more frequently."

"Well, thank goodness you two are here," Vera says, and smiles. "It's hardly a family dinner without you! Seth, how's your stay so far?"

Under the white tablecloth, I put my hand on Delilah's thigh, just above her knee, and give her a slight squeeze. She puts her hand on mine and squeezes back.

"Wonderful," I say, silently thanking the powers that be that Delilah did the lying. "This place is beautiful."

Vera smiles, her face lighting up as she leans in.

"We were so happy you could make it after all," she says, and Delilah squeezes my hand again.

There are appetizers, wine, fancy bread. Winona and I laugh about Bree's hide-and-seek skills and her love of a television show called *Dinosaur Train*, which as far as Winona can tell, is pretty much about dinosaurs who ride a train. I tell her how much Bree reminds me of Rusty, and reassure her that Rusty's the greatest.

Olivia's moved off of nursery colors and onto baby names. Vera is regaling Delilah with a dramatic story about a fundraiser with an unclear charity policy, and how horribly it went off the rails. Her brothers-in-law are having a detailed discussion about cars I'll never own. Salads arrive, and I triple-check that I'm using the right fork.

"Seth," calls Ava, seated next to Winona, leaning in. "How was your first time skiing?"

"Second," corrects Delilah, pulling herself from the fundraising conversation.

"It may as well have been my first," I point out, and Ava laughs. "Hard, but fun."

"Skiing is hard," Ava agrees. "I can't imagine having to learn as an adult."

"The whole pizza, french fries thing did feel a little juvenile," I tease Delilah, who smiles and rolls her eyes.

"Sure, but you remembered, didn't you?" she says.

"It didn't save me."

"I learned as a kid and last year I fell butt-over-teakettle on a run that wasn't even hard," Ava offers. "One of my skis came off and a ten-year-old returned it for me."

"They should have an area that's just for adults trying to learn," I say. "So no one has to watch us disgrace ourselves."

Ava laughs again.

"Sure, but at a certain point you really just have to go do it," she says. "Like, I was totally terrified of the black diamonds runs until finally Nolan just took Delilah and I down the—"

She stops mid-sentence, her blue eyes wide as she glances at Delilah.

"Down Crunch Street?" Delilah asks, taking a bite of salad.

"Right," Ava resumes. "He pretty much had to talk me through every single turn, but he was so sweet about it. Anyway, it's just practice! Muscle memory and stuff. Besides, you're kind of tall so you've got further to fall and that makes it harder. Do you guys want more wine?"

Ava tops our glasses off. We keep talking about skiing, and even though Nolan doesn't come up again, I can't quite shake the feeling that he's standing right behind me. That he could talk to Vera about her fundraiser and the brothers-in-law about cars, take Ava down the hard ski runs, know which wine to pick.

That maybe it's no wonder he's the one she married.

But then Delilah leans in toward me, her hair brushing my shoulder, and she points her fork at an olive on my salad plate.

"You gonna eat that?" she asks.

"You know I'm not," I tell her and she stabs it, pops it into her mouth, smiles at me.

"Thanks," she says. "You want a crouton in exchange?"

· · * * ★ ★ ★ * * · ·

I CAN'T SLEEP.

I don't know why. Between the skiing, the sex, and the wine, I should have been out before my head hit the pillow, but instead every time I finally doze off, I wake up again half an hour later with the strange, unsettling feeling that I've left something undone, some problem unsolved.

I lie awake, tick through all the possibilities. There aren't many, because I'm on vacation, and nothing needs my attention in the middle of the night in West Virginia.

I fall back asleep, barely. I wake up in a huge, comfortable bed, Delilah warm and naked next to me. I still feel like there's something moving just underneath my skin.

Finally, around four in the morning, I give up. I get out of bed, pull on a shirt, a sweater, my plaid pajama pants. I walk into the living room, rub my eyes, wish I'd brought slippers with me, pad to the fireplace and turn it up.

I'm standing exactly where Nolan was in the photo I found, the one hidden in the closet underneath towels and sheet and her wedding album. I look down at my feet. I walk quietly to the bedroom door, close it silently.

The box is exactly where I left it, of course, under a stack of sheets and towels, all bleached perfectly white and folded neatly. I take them out, put them on the floor.

The cardboard sags in my hands, and for a moment I think it's going to give way and send everything crashing to the floor, waking Delilah up. I brace it with a hand underneath. Look at the bedroom door again.

I know better than to think I'm acting right as I place the box gently on the dining table, push the flaps aside. I know that the clean slate and starting over were my idea. I know she's long-divorced and the past isn't supposed to exist, let alone matter, but none of that stops me.

The album is still on top. Hardbound, leather cover, glossy pages inside. I flip through it and try not to linger on any one page: the kiss, the first dance, the posed photo under a lit archway. Her family is there. Her sisters are teenagers; Vera looks remarkably the same.

The photos I found before. The two of them, standing *right there*, looking happy. Her hair shorter, her face rounder, his arms circling her middle like he's caught her and is pulling her back.

There's more. A birthday card, the greeting that came with flowers. A few more photos, one with them on skis. A cutesy, fake-rustic sign that says "Mr. and Mrs. Prescott." Tchotchkes. Their wedding guestbook.

And then, at the bottom: a small jewelry box that rattles when I pick it up. I'm pretty sure I know what I'm going to find, but when I pop it open, I'm still surprised.

There are two rings. One's expected, the glittering monster I saw on her finger at the Whiskey Barrel. The other I've never seen before: a matching wedding band, tiny diamonds embedded in delicate gold.

I don't think about the fact that tens of thousands of dollars of jewelry are sitting in a cardboard box in a closet. I don't even wonder what they're doing here.

I just try to imagine them on her finger, and I can't.

I'm still staring at them when the bedroom door opens and she leans out, naked except panties, blinking.

"Hey," Delilah says, voice foggy. "You okay?"

"I couldn't sleep," I tell her, folding my fingers around the rings as if I can hide what I'm doing.

"Yeah, that bed is a little weird," she says. Yawns. Stretches. The Kraken and the vines move like they're alive. "It just takes a little…"

She trails off, arms crossed over her chest, leaning in the door frame.

"What are you doing?" Delilah asks, suddenly sounding more awake.

I tighten my hand, the diamond digging into my palm.

"I was looking for a towel."

She walks over. Stands at the table, her hair coming loose from a braid over her shoulder. Looks at the cards and the book and the photos and the sign. Grabs the box, peeks inside.

Finally, she looks over at me, her cheeks going pink and her expression unreadable.

"Is this why we fucked?" she asks, voice low as the calm before the storm.

She knows me. Isn't that what I told her the night I brought scones? She knows me, and it's going to be my undoing.

"No."

Her cheeks flush even redder.

"It wasn't because you found this while I was out skiing and you wanted to mark your territory?" she asks. "And now you're going through my shit at four thirty in the morning, making sure you marked everything there was to mark?"

"We fucked in the bathroom because that's what we—"

"After we specifically talked about it in the car yesterday? After not fucking was your idea in the first place, because fucking was all we did and you wanted to try something new?"

I unclench my fist and toss the rings on the table. Delilah watches them, arms crossed again, like she's protecting herself despite wearing nothing but her panties.

"How do we start something new when you've got your wedding ring kicking around in the bottom of a closet?" I snap. "How do I start something new when the man you left me for is everywhere? When your family can't stop talking about him?"

"God forbid someone mention my ex-husband," she says, sarcastic and sharp. "I was married. It happened. I can't undo it. I could throw all of this away and it wouldn't undo shit."

"Then where am I?"

She pauses, frowns.

"Is this a trick question?"

"He's still here," I say, pointing feverishly: the rings and the photos and the book and everything spread on the table. "He's in the cocktail shaker in your house, he's in that photo of the dog, he's in those earrings you like. I was with you for six years, and all you've got is the man you left me for."

"I didn't leave you for him."

"Really? That was a hell of a turn—"

She's turning away, stalking toward the bedroom.

"I broke up with you and *then* started seeing him," she shouts. The lights go on, but the door doesn't close. "He had nothing to do with it."

"Sure," I say.

She reappears in the doorway, dragging a sweater over her head.

"I broke up with you because I didn't want to date you

anymore," she shouts. Her head pops through, her hair wild, and she pulls it out. "That's it. That's all. I broke up with you and I wiped you out of my life and *then* I met Nolan. Whatever you think of me, don't you dare think I cheated on you."

She turns back into the bedroom. I realize I'm pacing back and forth. One by one, I crack all my knuckles, turn, pace, try not to feel as if she's just thrown a knife and nicked a vein. I'd always thought our breakup with because of him, somehow. Not because she just didn't want me.

"You could rid your life of me but not him?" I shout back at her, somewhere in the bedroom.

"Oh, don't worry, you popped up," she says, and she's back in the doorway, angrily pulling on the rainbow pajama pants. "On Mindy Drake's ass, for example."

I stop like I've been hit by a cartoon hammer.

"Now that we're talking about it, are there any others?" she says, arms crossed, head tilted. Her voice is faux-sweet, laced with venom. "Am I gonna see *Property of Seth Loveless* on any other butts in the future, or do I get to be done with that now?"

I swallow hard. Fuck. *Fuck.* I haven't thought about Mindy or her tattoo in years.

"That's the only one I know of," I tell her. Quietly.

"And how about the panties and the makeup and the hairbrush under your sink?" she says. "I can't keep my wedding album, but you've got souvenirs of all these other women?"

"Not souvenirs," I say. I'm pacing again, a sensation under my skin like something's boiling. "I never kept souvenirs, they didn't *matter*—"

"OF COURSE THEY MATTERED!"

I stop dead in my tracks. Hold my breath at the sudden volume, violence.

In the silence that follows, you could hear a pin drop.

"I never dated them," I say, my own volume rising. "It was just fun, a release, I never felt anything —"

"Besides getting your dick wet?" she says, and now her voice is shaky. Eyes glassy. "Do you know how it sounds when we finally have sex after waiting that long and then hours later you tell me sex doesn't matter? It sounds shitty! It feels shitty! It feels like I'm a name on a list with a check mark next to it!"

"If I could go back in time and undo *everyone* else right now, I would," I say, jabbing a finger at the floor. "But I can't."

There's a pause. A long pause. I realize what I'm waiting for, and I realize she's not going to say it.

"I wouldn't," she says, voice flat. "And if you and I had gotten married, you and I would have gotten divorced."

I walk away from her, back to the table. It's so still that it feels like time has stopped, and I stand there. Look down at the photo album.

"How long?" I ask her.

"How long what?"

"How long do I have before you get bored and leave me for some rich prick with a nice watch and boring golf stories?" I ask. I don't turn around.

She exhales like the wind's been knocked out of her.

"Before I get bored?" she says. "Me? You spent years plowing through Sprucevale dick-first and you think *I'm* going to get bored of *you*? I will *never* be enough for you. Not after that."

Before I can answer, there's a loud knock on the door.

"Is everything okay?" Thad shouts.

I turn and look at Delilah. There's a single streak down her face, her eyes brimming with fury.

"Delilah?" calls Ava.

Delilah looks away, takes a deep breath. Shoves her hands into her eyes.

"I'm going to answer the door and tell them you had an emergency," she says, voice wavering with forced calm. She puts her hands down, looks at me. "And then you're going to take my car, and you're going to leave. I don't give a shit where you go, I just want you gone."

"Del—"

"I don't want you here!" she says, voice rising. "You don't belong here. Is that what you want me to say? You don't belong here. Get out."

She walks past me to the door, an angry blur. Stops in front of it, takes a deep breath, and before she opens it I walk away from her, into the bedroom. Throw my suitcase on the bed.

"Hey, sorry," I hear her saying. "Seth had some kind of beer emergency, so he has to go back right now..."

Less than five minutes later, I'm gone.

FORTY-THREE

DELILAH

I fold my legs onto the chair, watching the mountain. There's a mug of coffee cradled in my hands, though it's already ice-cold. The mountain's blue, then silver, then pale yellow as the sun comes up behind me, washes it with light.

I take a sip of the disgusting coffee and make myself the colors change, committing myself to it even though I don't like sunrises.

I'm not a morning person. I'm not getting up early to rejoice in the promise of a new day while breathing in hope and light or whatever shit morning people do. If I'm seeing a sunrise, it's probably because something's gone wrong and I never went to bed.

For instance, right now.

I take another sip — ugh — pull my feet up further, onto the cushion covering the metal chair. It doesn't help the cold but it gives me something to think about it, at least.

I couldn't sleep after Seth left. I didn't bother trying. I put all the shit back in my box. I put the box back. I stormed around the condo for a little while before remembering that the lobby has free coffee starting at five in the morning, so I threw a robe on over my sweater and came down here.

And now I'm sitting on the balcony, overlooking the town, watching the sun come up in the freezing cold because it feels like what I want right now.

I want to sit here until I can't stand it, then go roast myself by a fire. I want to get drunk and just off a ski lift, just to see what happens. Get a full-face tattoo. Run naked through town. I want to do something reckless and destructive and transformative, because right now I'm so fucking tired of myself I can't stand it.

Behind me, the balcony door opens, and I sigh into the coffee mug.

"Hey, Freckles," my dad says.

I turn, surprised.

"You're not cold?"

"Hey," I say.

"Well, here's a blanket," he says, and hands me one, thick and woolen with a geometric pattern. I recognize it from the penthouse.

"Thanks," I say.

He settles in the chair next to me, fully dressed in slacks and sneakers, a puffy parka, coffee in a travel mug. I'm still in pajamas, a giant sweater, a robe, and slippers. We must make a hell of a pair right now.

"Your mom and I got into a fight up here once," he says, leaning back, sneakered feet crossing at the ankle. "We were here for our first wedding anniversary. I think you were about six months old."

I was born about six months after my parents' wedding, and yes, that's why they got married.

"What about?" I ask, eyes still on the mountain.

He sighs, laces his fingers together around the mug he's holding.

"I don't even remember," he says, thoughtfully. "That might have been the one over the eggbeater."

They divorced before I was two, so it's not exactly a secret that they didn't get along.

"Sounds travels, huh?" I say, looking into the mug. I don't want to have this conversation, but at least it's with my dad, who'll relay it to Vera, not with Vera herself.

"A bit," he says.

"Sorry," I say, and tilt my head back against the glass wall behind me. "I know it's… I know I'm me. Sorry you had to hear that."

He reaches out, over the arms of our chairs, and puts an arm around me.

"It's great that you're you," he says, punctuating it with a shoulder squeeze.

"It doesn't feel like it," I say, too tired and spent to do anything but tell the truth. "It mostly feels like…"

I trail off, my mind blank as the morning sky.

"… I do everything a little bit wrong, and that spirals into me doing everything a lot wrong," I finish.

There's a long, considered silence.

"I wish your mom was still around," he finally says. "I miss her sometimes, even now."

I exhale, my breath blurring the sky.

"Me too," I say.

"You're so much like her," he says. "I think by now, you'd be great friends."

I can't help but laugh, my head still back against the wall. When she died I was fifteen, and I was an asshole in all the ways fifteen-year-olds can be assholes, so we were going through a rough patch.

"Well, we had a lot in common," I say.

"I mean it," my dad says.

"Thanks," I say, then take another sip of cold coffee. Grimace. "I just feel like such a fuck-up."

"Freckles, everyone sitting on this balcony right now has gotten into a shouting match with a partner in the dead of night," he says, sounding very stoic. "It's just the way of things. Besides, you can't fuck up badly enough that I won't still love you."

I shift positions so I can lean my head against his shoulder and close my eyes.

"I love you too," I say.

We stay there like that for a few minutes. The sun keeps rising. I wonder if Seth's back in Sprucevale yet, or still on the road, or even going back to Sprucevale, or maybe he's already in a cheap motel —

"Can we go back inside?" I ask, cutting off my own train of thought. "It's kind of cold out here."

"Thank God, I thought you'd never ask," my dad says, already standing, offering me his hand. "How about I take you to breakfast? There's a great hole in the wall that Vera never wants to go to."

I wrap the blanket around myself and shuffle toward the door.

"Sounds perfect," I say.

FORTY-FOUR

SETH

By seven-thirty that morning, I'm on the outskirts of Sprucevale. The drive should have been longer by an hour, but I did ninety the whole way back and only stopped once.

I want Snowpeak, West Virginia and skiing and Delilah and her family in the rearview mirror. I want to stop hearing her say *I just want you gone.* I want to stop seeing the look on her face when she mentioned Mindy's tattoo.

Even her car smells like her. It feels like her. There's a hula girl on the dashboard and her sunglasses in the glove box along with three half-empty bottles of sunscreen and it all reminds me that it happened again.

After everything, it happened again. We fucked and we fought and now I'm driving away from her, furious and heartbroken, like I'm stuck in some nightmare time loop. I can't believe I'm not used to it by now. I can't believe that I don't have a system for dealing with my post-Delilah weeks; a Gantt chart or something that says *sleep for eighteen hours* and then *bake three cakes, play video games, take up CrossFit. Find someone new for a night.*

Only this time is worse, because this time wasn't two nights in some motel. This time was nearly two months. This time was square dancing and ice skating and hiking and cooking, movie nights on the couch and driving to the mountains just to see the sunset.

This time hurts in a new, astonishing way.

I'm a few miles from my house when I realize my problem: I'm still in Delilah's car, not my own. I could park it at my place, but I don't want to text her about it. I don't want to look out the window and see her getting into it. I don't want to think about this car ever again, so instead of going home I pick up my phone, think for a moment, and then call Levi.

"Yes?" he answers.

"I need a favor."

"All right."

"I need a ride from Delilah's house to mine," I tell him.

Levi waits, as if for an explanation. I don't offer one. His silences might work on other people, but I've known him for thirty years.

"I'll be there in about fifteen minutes," I go on.

"Send me the address," he says.

When I pull into her driveway, he's already there: standing next to his truck, wearing jeans and boots and his winter coat, watching something in her yard.

I park, get out, walk over. He notices my face, my pajama pants, the car I showed up in, but he has mercy and just nods at Delilah's yard.

"She feed them?" he asks.

I follow his gaze to a raccoon, sitting on its back legs, watching us expectantly.

"Yeah," I say, and my voice sounds like dirt. I clear my throat. "That's either Terry, Larry, or Jerry."

"You really shouldn't feed wildlife," he says, with the air of someone who's said it a thousand times before.

"You've got birdfeeders," I point out.

He shrugs.

"They're birds."

"They're life and they're wild," I say, my voice sharpening. "Is that not wildlife?"

Something flickers on his face that might be the tiniest smile.

"True," he admits. "Got a suitcase or anything?"

I grab my stuff from her trunk, put her key under her mat, and climb into Levi's truck. It's a relief to drive away with my brother at the wheel, in this vehicle that smells like sawdust and dirt and not her shampoo. I close my eyes and drift halfway off, glad that I called the brother who knows how to be quiet for a minute.

When we get to my house, he comes inside with me, then takes off his coat and shoes like he'll be here a while. I just watch, tired and drained.

"You should probably get some sleep," he says. "You look like you've had a night."

I'm sure I do. My eyes feel like someone's held a match to them. My throat hurts like it's sore from being tight for so long.

"I'm not really tired," I say, because I can't imagine sleeping.

"Do you want to change your clothes?"

Right. Pajamas, still.

"Good idea," I tell him, and turn to go upstairs. When I glance down, he's rolling up his sleeves, phone between his shoulder and his ear.

"Hey, June," he says softly as I head into my bedroom. "I might not be back for a couple of hours…"

FORTY-FIVE

DELILAH

Nine Years Ago
(Eight Months Before the Previous Flashback)

Winona pops her head around the corner and gives me a very serious thumbs-up.

"Coast is clear," she says.

I swallow, trying to vanquish the tightness in my throat or the lump in my chest.

"Thanks," I say, my voice about an octave higher than it should be.

"Ava and Olivia are out shopping," she says. "Mom's wrapping presents and on the phone with her sister, and Dad is... somewhere, I guess. You sure you're okay? Do you want some water or something?"

I wave in the direction of the glass already sitting on a side table. Winona nods, still clearly worried.

Then she comes into the den and takes my shoulders in her hands. Even though she's my younger sister, not even out of high school yet, somehow she's always the one comforting and advising me, not the other way around.

"You'll be fine," she says, soothingly. "People break up all the time."

"Thanks," I say, nodding.

I almost tell her *not like this, they don't, not when they've been dating since high school and they're supposed to be perfect together and live happily ever after* but I know, somewhere deep down, that she's right. It's just a breakup. Thousands of them happen every day.

"I'll keep running interference," she says. "Let me know when it's over?"

I just nod again, because I don't trust my voice. Winona pats me one more time, then turns and walks out of the den.

I start pacing. Christmas is in a week, so the room is done up to the nines: garlands on the walls, bows over the fireplace, perfectly-appointed tree in one corner. It gives a weird, jolly vibe to the whole ordeal and makes me feel even crazier than I already do.

As I walk, I plan what I'm going to say, heart in my throat.

I think we should take a break for a while.

That's it. Just a break, not a *breakup*. After a month or two I'm sure we'll both have realized how much we really love each other and we'll get back together, and this time it'll be great and perfect and we won't fight nearly every day because we'll have seen the other side.

Then, this spring, he'll graduate and get a job back here, and we'll get engaged and married and that's it, that's the happy ending. It's a story I've told myself again and again over the past month or two, even as I'm not sure I believe it myself anymore.

I love Seth. I've always loved Seth. I always will. Right?

A new wave of panic rolls its spikes over me. *Right?*

And then I can't panic anymore, because there's a

knock on the door. I force myself to walk over. Take a deep breath. Pull it open, and there he is.

"Hey," he says, grinning. He steps into the house, leans in for a kiss. His hand is cold on my face, and I can't bring myself to give him more than a peck on the lips, because more than that feels like lying.

"Thanks for coming over," I say, and my voice sounds strange, oddly formal even to myself.

Seth just laughs.

"Of course, Bird," he says. "I wanted to see you."

"Come on," I tell him, and walk back to the den. I feel like I'm a robot giving a tour: *here's the foyer and here are the stairs and that's a bathroom and...*

"Your family around?" he asks, eyes following the big staircase to the second floor.

"They're here somewhere," I say. "You know."

Once we're in the den, Seth takes my hand. Leads me over to the tree, glowing with twinkling lights. Takes my other hand, holds them both in his. Looks deep into my eyes, his own that a shade of blue I've searched for but never found.

Slowly, a smile cracks across his face, and my heart hammers so hard I'm sure he can hear it. My stomach twists. I think I might throw up.

"Delilah," he says, softly.

Say it, I tell myself. *Say it. Say it.*

Sayitsayitsayitsayitsayitsayit.

Seth reaches into his pocket. Keeps my left hand in his.

Gets down on one knee, and this cannot be happening.

It can't. It *can't*. I'm vaguely aware that I'm supposed to be happy about this, but instead I'm horrified, frozen. Powerless to make this stop.

"Seth," I say, the word brittle.

He opens a box, the ring inside. Looks up at me with those eyes, the most perfect shade of blue.

"Delilah," he says, solemnly. "Will you marry me?"

There's a moment, then, where all the sound drops from the world. There's a silence beyond silence, still and heavy.

When it ends I'm already shaking my head, pulling my hand out of his. Stepping backward like he's just offered me a tarantula.

"No," I'm saying. "*No*. I can't."

He's frozen. Shocked. I keep shaking my head.

"What?" he says, without moving, that single word full of pain and betrayal. "Why?"

"I think we should take a break," I blurt out. "Just some time apart so we can think about things and not talk and not see each other, because things have been so bad between us lately and I think if we just took that time apart it would really help. So a break. Just for a while."

The box snaps shut. He stands.

"A *break*?"

I nod like a puppet on a string. He shoves his hands into the pockets of the coat he never even took off, looks away. Swallows hard, his Adam's apple bobbing.

"We can't take a break," he says. "I know it's been rough lately, but that's temporary, Bird, I'm gonna graduate in May and then I'm coming back and we'll be together, and we'll get—"

"Please don't."

His knuckles are white around the ring box, and the guilt is huge, overwhelming. A shadow trying to eat me alive.

"I'm sorry," I tell him. I step forward, stop, because Seth is hurt and my urge is to hold him, comfort him, but

422

what do I do when I'm the source of the pain? What do I do when this is my fault for not loving him enough?

He shakes his head. Shoves the box back into his pocket, steps away from me.

"I don't want to take a break," he says. "I want our plan, the way it was supposed to be—"

"This wasn't our plan!" I say desperately, but Seth keeps shaking his head.

"I can't take a break," he says, his face falling.

I swallow hard, and a tear spills down my cheek. I didn't even realize I was crying.

I want to say a thousand things right now — that I'm sorry, that I didn't want to hurt him, that I love him but not enough, that I want to keep him but I don't — but I can't get any of them through my lips.

"That's it," he whispers.

"I'm sorry," I say again, and he shakes his head like he can shake me off.

"It's okay," he says, his voice sounding strange, strangled.

Then he steps forward. Puts his hand to my face. Bends down.

Kisses me for the last time, and then it's over.

"Goodbye, Bird," Seth says, and then he turns and leaves the house.

I don't know how long I stand there, crying. Winona finds me, makes me sit down. I never tell her what really happened.

Then next time I see Seth, it's eight months later at a dive bar.

FORTY-SIX

DELILAH

PRESENT DAY

The car ride back feels like the longest car ride in the history of car rides. Thankfully it's with Ava and Thad, not someone else, and Ava keeps up a bubbly, cheerful running commentary for most of the time, as if she can cover over the unpleasantness of the night before.

She can't. I feel like hell in the back seat of Thad's BMW, wishing that we didn't have to stop at every single vista point and Starbucks along the drive, but somewhere in the back of my mind I know that Ava is, in her way, being extraordinarily kind to me.

I also know that Ava at twenty-two is probably a better person than I was. For all my misgivings, she and Thad seem really good together: she listens, rapturously, to his stories. He laughs at her jokes in a way that suggests he's besotted. She's not me, thank God.

When we get to my house, my car's there. I wave goodbye to Ava and Thad, look through the windows, in the trunk, but there's nothing to suggest anyone else's pres-

424

ence. The key is under my welcome mat, and when I step inside, I hold my breath against the tiny spark of hope, buried in my chest.

My house is empty. The spark flares, flickers, dies. No one's there. Not even a note.

Not that I thought that there would be. Not that I thought I deserved anything but this silent emptiness, because I'm the one who shouted *I want you gone* and I'm not allowed to get upset that he did what I asked.

That night, I go over to Lainey's place. She lives in a stately brick house near downtown, on a fancy street where her neighbors routinely report her to the homeowner's association for her Black Lives Matter flag.

We watch *The Bachelor* and I tell her about the fight. Then I tell her again. We get tacos delivered from Gloria's, Sprucevale's best and only Mexican restaurant, and then I cry into my carnitas and I tell her one more time, now with angry editorializing.

She says all the right things, like *that must have really hurt your feelings* and *absolutely, it's a betrayal*. She holds me while I ask her what's wrong with me that I've done this again and again, and she gently reminds me that humans are nothing but flesh and bone running on less electricity than it takes to power a lightbulb.

It does make me feel better, which is why we're friends.

We share a churro. We judge the romantic choices of everyone on *The Bachelor*, and that night, I sleep in her guest room because I don't want to leave her warm, wonderful house.

· · · · ★ ★ ★ ★ ★ · · · ·

AVA CALLS. Winona calls. Vera calls. Even Olivia calls, and I ignore them all. The only call I answer is from my dad, and I swear him to secrecy.

They call again. I know I'm being an asshole and making them worry more, but their concern feels like a burden that I can't carry right now.

My cousin Georgia calls. Wyatt, her brother, texts, then calls, then texts, then calls. I don't answer any of them, because answering them feels like climbing out of a hole I've dug myself into and I don't even have a ladder.

Life goes on. Work goes on. I do touch-ups, line work, color work. I have a consultation about a full-back tattoo of a stylized wolf, and it's badass as hell. I cover up an ex-con's grinning frog tattoo. It's a busy week, and I wonder again if I should hire a second artist. Move to a bigger studio. Develop my business plan beyond *make this work so I don't have to ask my dad for money*, because I'm somewhat startled to realize I've already done that.

Whenever I look in the mirror, I fantasize about tattooing something on my face, just to do it. A star. A teardrop. A tiny broken heart. It doesn't really matter what, though if my volunteer work has taught me anything, it's to be careful with face tattoos because apparently they all mean you've murdered someone.

I keep avoiding calls from my nice, well-meaning family.

Then, one night nearly a week after our fight, I do it.

Not on the face. That's too much. It's on the inside of my left wrist: a small, black star, about half an inch across. It's been a couple of years since I tattooed myself — that's how most tattoo artists learn at first; we almost universally have some very bad thigh tattoos — and I have to lash my forearm to the chair with gauze to hold still, but I manage.

I turn off the gun. Wipe the blood. Sit back in the chair,

hold it up, examine it for flaws. It's not much, but it's there, and it's plain as day, out in the open. Hard to hide, not that I'm going to.

People will know. Everyone will know, and Vera will be upset, and my sisters will be politely baffled, and it's fine. People can think what they like. I'm the kind of person who has a fully visible wrist tattoo, and as Lainey has advised me: their thoughts are not my concern.

FORTY-SEVEN

SETH

The day I get back from West Virginia, I skip dinner at my mom's house without telling anyone. I know all my brothers will be there, most with their wives and fiancées and girlfriends, and I'm going to have to see them be happy, functional couples, and I don't think I can.

Instead, I buy fifty pounds of flour and five pounds of butter and at least that much sugar, not to mention chocolate chips and vanilla extract and sprinkles and cinnamon and whatever else strikes my fancy in the baking aisle at Kroger.

I make croissants, something I've never done. While they're rising, I make chocolate chip cookies. When they're out of the oven, I find a recipe for hazelnut biscotti that looks satisfyingly rigorous, and I get to work on that.

That's in the oven when there's a brief knock on my door, and then Caleb walks in without waiting for an invitation.

"Hey," he says, and he eyes the cookies cooling on the table, the stand mixer, my shirt caked with flour and sugar and butter. "You weren't at Mom's."

"No," I say, leaning against the counter. "You talked to Levi, I guess?"

Caleb nods, walks to the table, and grabs a cookie.

"She break up with you again?" he asks, mouth full.

There's a moment where all I can hear is the blood, rushing through my ears.

"Get the fuck out," I tell him.

He swallows.

"I—"

"Yeah, we broke up again and I don't need you to come rub it in my face that you were right," I say, voice building. "I know this happens. I know this always happens, and I know the next thing out of your mouth is going to be *Delilah's an evil soul-sucking witch,* so how about you just leave before that, okay?"

"That's not why I'm here," he says calmly, holding out his hands, half a cookie still in one.

"She's not," I say, louder still. I push the top of the stand mixer down, toss a spatula into the sink so hard it bounces back out. "She's — she paints murals and she does yoga and she feeds raccoons and she's a little weird and pretty funny and her hair smells nice and she's not a bad person. She's just a person."

"Seth," Caleb starts.

"So you can fucking leave," I say, both hands on the kitchen island, leaning in. "Don't you dare come to my house and be shitty about Delilah."

Caleb takes a deep breath.

"I didn't come to be shitty about Delilah," he says. "I'm sorry. I've been an asshole."

I crack the knuckles on one hand, anger already dissolving.

"I came because you're my brother and I knew you'd need me," he says, shrugging.

I take a deep breath, bend over the counter, rest my head on my hands for a moment.

"Sorry," I say, eyes closed.

I hear him come over to the island, pull out a stool, sit down. A plate clatters onto the countertop, and then he puts a hand on my head and pets my hair.

It's nice.

"I don't hate her," he says, slowly. "I just hate how much she hurts you."

"It's not her fault," I say, voice echoing off the counter.

He keeps petting, his hand slow, thoughtful.

"I hate how miserable you always are after you see her and things go badly," he says. "I hate that you've gotten your heart broken over and over again, and blaming it on her was easy."

Finally, I look up. Caleb cracks his knuckles, considers my face for a moment.

"You look like shit," he says, gently.

"I did it again," I say. I sound hollow, even to myself. "I fucking did it again, Caleb. I didn't learn. I'll never learn. I tried something different and I thought it was working but then I went and did it again."

"Well, I think both of you did it again," he points out. I tense, instantly.

"What did I just—"

"I'm not making a judgment. I'm stating a fact," he says, taking a cookie off the plate and putting it in front of me. "You've never gotten into a one-sided fight with her before and I'm guessing you didn't this time, either."

I shove half the cookie into my mouth, come around the island, grab a stool, carry it back to where I was standing. I eat the other half of the cookie.

"I found a box of stuff from when she was with her ex," I admit.

I tell my little brother everything. *Everything* everything, starting with Ava's wedding and going through to last night and me driving back here in my pajamas, watching the sunrise through the mountains. Halfway through he gets up and makes us tea, so when I finish I'm staring into a mug of chamomile.

"Shit," he says.

"And that's just this year," I say.

There's a brief silence. Caleb glances at the cookies, then watches me.

"What if this is it?" I ask, chin in hand, elbow on counter. "What if this is just how it is, forever? The two of us back and forth and up and down, over and over, like that graph that does the——"

I wave my finger in the air, demonstrating.

"A sine wave?" Caleb asks. Of course he'd know.

"Yeah, that."

"You need to get some sleep."

My eyes feel like someone's been walking on them.

"I know."

He mirrors my position, thinks for a moment.

"You missed it, but at dinner, Levi spent a good five minutes complaining to me about how June never remembers to clear the hair out of their shower drain, so inevitably it backs up, and when it does, it becomes *his* problem. And he's annoyed about it, because no one likes backed up shower drains, especially when it's someone else's hair."

"Wedding still on?" I ask, sipping tea.

Caleb laughs.

"Of course," he says. "He still lights up every time she looks at him, even when he's annoyed about the drain."

"I wish my problems were about hair in the shower."

Caleb goes quiet, tapping his tea mug with a few fingers.

"That's your thinking noise," I say.

"Do your problems have to be worse?" he finally asks.

"Our problems *are* worse," I point out.

"But do they have to be?"

Something about the question makes me uneasy, so I stand, take our empty mugs, put them in the dishwasher. I check that the light in the oven is off, that the croissants are still looking alright.

"They're old wounds," Caleb finally says, after a long time. "You could stop pouring salt into them."

Could I?

My impulse is to tell my brother to fuck off, that he doesn't know what he's talking about. That he can't possibly understand, but I swallow the words and don't say anything.

"Do you want any more cookies?" I ask, pointing. "I'm gonna pack those up to take to the brewery tomorrow."

Caleb grabs two more, one with each hand.

"Those croissants ready yet?" he asks.

"Still rising."

"Any chocolate ones?"

"The fuck do I look like, a bakery?" I ask, and he laughs.

"Figured I'd try," he says.

FORTY-EIGHT

DELILAH

The text said the party was in the back yard, so I park on the street and walk around Lainey's house, six-pack in one hand. It's quieter than I expected, but maybe this is the quiet kind of roller derby party.

But when I get there, it's nearly empty. Just the fire pit and two people, casually talking.

Then I stop in my tracks.

"Wyatt?"

"You're right, she *is* alive," he says to Lainey.

He grins, leaning back in his wooden chair, a beer bottle to his lips.

"I had no choice," Lainey says, straight-faced and solemn. "He arrived shortly before you did. I'm sorry."

Wyatt laughs, his head back, one ankle crossed over the opposite knee, and Lainey glances over at his reaction, the tiniest smile on her lips.

"What?" I ask, baffled from two directions at once: that Wyatt is here, and by that weird thing Lainey just said.

"She just called me Darth Vader," Wyatt says.

"Lainey, be nice to Wyatt," I tell her.

"He liked it," she says.

"No, I didn't," Wyatt says. He's grinning.

"What are you even doing here?" I say, putting the beers I'm carrying down on a table, then sit next to Lainey, leaning in toward the fire.

"I volunteered to make sure you were alive and all right," he says. "Since you're ignoring me, my sister, *your* sisters, and Aunt Vera. Do you know how many women you've worried?"

I grab a beer. Lainey hands over the opener, and I pop the top off, take a drink, lean back in the wooden chair.

"Sorry," I say, and I mean it. "I just… I needed a minute."

Wyatt sighs.

"Why?" he asks, sarcastically, and I snort.

"I love them, but they're a lot," I admit. "Have you ever had to tell them you broke up with someone? They act like you've chopped off your own foot."

Wyatt just makes a grunt of disapproval.

"Anyway, we colluded to get you over here," Lainey says. "It seemed better than taking your picture with today's newspaper."

"They're not *that* worried," I say.

Silence.

"Right?"

"Olivia swears that last weekend she was awakened at four in the morning by a crash and a scream," Wyatt says.

Next to me, Lainey's lips thin by a hair as she looks into the fire.

"She wasn't," I tell him, rolling my eyes. "She was on the warpath all weekend, though, and I've got no idea why. Hormones? Altitude? Too many hormones for the altitude?"

"Not how any of that works," Lainey says.

434

"But you *are* okay, right?" Wyatt asks, leaning forward slightly.

"We just got in a fight," I say, waving the beer bottle. "A word fight, I mean. Verbal? Whatever means we screamed at each other a bunch without any physical violence."

Wyatt nods. Lainey's still looking into the fire, stone-faced, but then she glances at Wyatt, then at me, then seems to snap out of it and take another sip of her beer.

"I'll call Vera tomorrow," I promise, then sigh. "I'm sorry, I just — it's been the shittiest week..."

My phone chirps, and I jump. There's a split second when my heart leaps, but then I pull it from my pocket and see Ava's name.

"Shit," I mutter.

Wyatt's craning his head around to see the screen.

"Did you somehow just summon her?" he asks.

"No, it's Ava," I explain. "I'll call her back—"

"Answer it," Wyatt demands.

The phone chirps again.

"Answer it. Delilah. *Answer it.*"

"It's the sweet baby angel, just answer it," Lainey says.

I stick my tongue out at both of them, then answer it.

"Hey," I say, squeezing my eyes shut. "I'm really sorry I haven't—"

"Delilah?"

Ava sounds weird, like she's out of breath or something. I sit up straighter, give Lainey and Wyatt an alarmed glance.

"What's wrong?"

"Can I come over?" she asks, her voice wobbly.

"To where?" I ask, stupidly. "Are you okay?"

There's a long, long pause.

"Thad and I had a fight," she says, miserably, then sniffs. "We were out of pasta, and tonight was supposed to

435

be spaghetti night and so I said I'd get some on the way home from work, but then I had to stay a little bit late and I forgot—"

She takes a breath, and I interrupt, gently.

"I'm at Lainey's house," I say, raising my eyebrows at Lainey. She nods. "Do you want to come over here?"

"Okay," she says. "Thanks, Delilah."

"Is *she* okay?" Wyatt asks, frowning, when I hang up.

"I think she and Thad got into their first fight," I say, putting my phone away again. "And I guess now I'm the sister who's good at fighting with partners? Fuck."

"You're the least likely to blow smoke up her ass and she knows it," Lainey counsels.

"Agreed," Wyatt says.

Fifteen minutes later, we hear someone shouting *Hello?* Around the front of the house, so the three of us call Ava back. She's wearing jeans with knee-high boots over them and a black wool winter coat, somehow looking perfectly put together even though she's obviously been crying.

I, on the other hand, am wearing jeans for the first time all week. I've worn leggings to work for the past three days, because the idea of putting on anything less comfortable than that just sounded like torture.

"Hey, y'all," she says softly, then frowns. "Wyatt?"

"He's making sure I'm not dead," I say, pop the top off a beer, and hand it over as she sits. "What happened?"

Ava takes a deep breath. She stares into the fire. Then, she comes to some kind of decision, guzzles half her beer, and looks determinedly at the three of us.

"Tonight was supposed to be spaghetti night," she begins.

The gist of the fight is more or less that Ava forgot to get pasta on the way home from work, Thad snapped at her about it, she snapped back that it's *always* her job to get

436

pasta, and things devolved from there until she was shouting about dirty socks and he was detailing all the times he'd turned her curling iron off for her before the whole house burned down, not that she ever bothered noticing.

In other words, just a fight, but I think it's their first one and Ava is distraught.

"Could you get a curling iron that turns off automatically after thirty minutes?" I ask.

"Probably," Ava says.

"It sounds as if you both might be feeling under-appreciated and taken for granted right now," Lainey says. "I think that's not uncommon with recently married couples."

Okay, she's way better at this than me.

Ava's nodding.

"And, I don't know," she says, looking down at the beer. "It also feels like we just got married and we're already in this routine? And spaghetti night is part of that routine? And sometimes I don't want that, I want him to be exciting and sexy again and surprise me—"

Her face goes bright red, and she glances at Wyatt. He pretends he heard nothing.

"Have you told Thad that?" I ask.

"No," she admits. "I don't want him to think... I don't know. That I'm needy?"

"Sweetheart, you're allowed to have emotional needs and express them," Lainey says.

"Just tell him," I say. "You're married. He knows he has to take your feelings into account, but you have to tell him your feelings. And if you do that and he doesn't, divorce his ass."

Ava stares into the fire. She drinks her beer. She drinks some more beer, still staring.

"Is that what happened to you and Nolan?" she finally asks.

"Sort of," I admit. "I mean, not really. It was…"

I drink the last of my beer.

"I fucked up," I tell her. "Promise me you won't tell your sisters or your mom."

Ava leans forward, wide-eyed.

"I shouldn't have gotten married," I start. "I should have spent a year backpacking the world and *finding myself* or something, but instead I married someone eight years older than me because I wanted to be someone else and I thought I could force myself into some other mold."

Wyatt's also leaning forward, frowning. He doesn't know this story, either. Lainey's one of the few people who do.

"Anyway, he had this life plan all laid out, and part of the plan was that six months after we got married we started trying for a baby. And I agreed to this, for the record. I was not at all sure that I wanted to have a baby that soon with him, but instead of saying that out loud, I just went along with this plan."

I grab another beer, pull one foot onto my chair, and point at Ava.

"Definitely don't do that," I tell her. "After the first month, when my period showed up, I was so relieved I cried. Then I felt guilty for being relieved that I cried about that, and then I think I just cried for the hell of it, but I wanted so badly to be the right kind of person that I didn't say anything and we kept trying."

I pause, drink some more beer. Even though this story is years old and water long under the bridge, it still sparks deep guilt and the creeping, unsteady feeling that I'm not a good or brave person.

"Then next month, my period was a week late," I go

on. "I've had two panic attacks in my entire life, and they were both during that week. I didn't tell Nolan."

I take another drink.

"But I did go to my gynecologist and get an IUD," I say. "Which I didn't tell Nolan about until we'd been 'trying' for another four months and he was starting to think we had fertility issues."

Ava is *agog*. She's full-on staring at me, wide-eyed, open-mouthed. Wyatt's giving the fire a *dude, did you hear that?* look.

In some fairness to me, we were a bad match and shouldn't have gotten married. It wasn't until a few years later that I finally recognized some of his manipulative, controlling tendencies, and I think he sometimes saw me as more of a prop than a person, but I was definitely still an asshole.

"And then, we got divorced, and then I ran off and fucked Seth in a hotel in Harrisonburg and we've been stuck in this stupid fuck-and-fight cycle ever since," I say quickly.

I think Ava's eyes might fall out of her head.

"I thought you hadn't seen him since you broke up?" she gasps.

I grimace.

"You guys have been together this whole time?"

"*Not* together," I say. "Extremely not together."

We drink the rest of the beer while I slowly and excruciatingly tell Ava and Wyatt everything. I'm not sure I like it, and it's sure not how I thought today would go when I woke up this morning, but they're both cooler about it than I expected.

"Oh, *yeah*," Ava scoffs when I get to the very end. More drinks have appeared, and she's now had three. "We knew there wasn't a brewery emergency. We're not total idiots, we could hear you two screaming at each other like you'd found him in bed with a farmyard animal."

"Damn, Ava," says Wyatt.

"Sorry," she says, but she's grinning.

"Do you at least feel better about Thad?" I ask.

She sighs.

"Yes," she says. "It's just so hard! Why can't things just always be great? I don't want to have to ask him to appreciate that I always buy the pasta, you know? Can't he just do that?"

"Ava," I say. "My sweet baby angel. Listen. You like Thad more than you like being angry at him about spaghetti, right?"

Her face scrunches.

"Being angry is *fun*," she says. "But, I guess."

"Then talk it out and let it go," I tell her. "It's not rocket science."

In my peripheral vision, I can see Lainey turn her head and give me a *look*. I ignore it.

"All right," Ava says, standing. "I'm gonna — oh *noo*."

She wobbles on her feet, arms out for balance.

"You're more than welcome to stay in my guest bedroom," Lainey says, then looks at me. "You too."

"Thanks," I say. I've only had two beers, but Lainey's house is nice and warm and cozy and comfy, and mine is far away and feels like all the times Seth's been in it.

"I should call him, though," Ava says. "Do you think he's worried? I hope he's worried."

"He's worried," I confirm.

Wyatt walks over to me and offers his hand, pulls me out of my chair.

"Do you need a place to crash?" Lainey asks him as Ava wanders away on the phone.

Wyatt looks down at her, and I *swear* he almost says yes.

"Nah, I only had one," he says, holding up the beer bottle. "But thanks for the offer."

· · * * ★ ★ ★ * * · ·

LAINEY'S GUEST room has a bed and a couch. Ava insists that I take the bed, and she also insists that it's not because I'm old and decrepit.

Even so, I have a hard time falling asleep. The new tattoo on my wrist itches under the bandages. I can't believe I actually told my sweet baby sister — who, at twenty-two, is not all that sweet, nor all that baby — the whole sordid truth of my relationship with Seth, and I also kind of can't believe she wasn't fully scandalized.

And worst of all, I can't stop thinking about the very good advice that I heard coming out of my mouth: do you like him more, or do you like being angry more?

I finally fall asleep, only to jerk awake, my mind still spinning like it's a flywheel set in motion. Fall asleep, jerk awake.

I wonder if I actually learned anything from my shit-show of a marriage and divorce. Asleep. Awake. I wonder if I'm mad at Seth for any reason except that he's mad at me because I'm mad at him because he's mad at me, and maybe we've been digging this hole deeper for years and there's nothing at the bottom of it.

Asleep, awake. How *dare* he think I want a boyfriend who talks about golf. Asleep, awake. I'm not enough. I can't be enough. Statistics and probability and mathematics all say that I won't ever be enough.

Asleep, awake. But the past mattered. It always mattered. There's no erasing it, no sweeping it under the rug, no acting as if everything came before didn't decide today.

Asleep.

Awake, and it's morning. We didn't close the curtains last night and sunlight is streaming into the bedroom. Over on the couch I hear Ava make an awake noise.

I had an idea during one of my asleep / awake cycles last night, and it's come back to me.

"Hey," I say, still facing the ceiling. "Are you any good at crafting?"

Ava sighs a long-suffering sigh. Rolls over. Waits for me to look at her.

"Bitch, I was in a sorority," she says.

I burst out laughing.

FORTY-NINE

SETH

I'm lying on my couch, nearly to level 1,568 in Candy Crush, when there's a knock on my door.

"No," I mutter to myself, and swap some more jelly beans.

The knock sounds again, louder this time. That means it's almost certainly a sibling.

Not that there was any doubt. Most other people in my life have the decency to call or text first.

"I'm the first one here?" Eli asks when I open the door.

I stand in the doorway, not inviting him in.

"What does *that* mean?"

"It means I'm the first one here," he says, giving me a taunting, delighted grin I don't really like. "You should probably get dressed."

I'm in an old Loveless Brewing T-shirt and plaid pajama pants, because five minutes ago, I was playing phone games on my couch, but I step back and let him in anyway.

"I'm fine," I tell him.

"Of course you are," he says, taking off his coat and

hanging it up. "That's why you texted me at one o'clock this morning asking if there's a meaningful difference between heavy cream and whipping cream."

"It's an important question."

He walks into my kitchen and leans against the island, eyeing a plateful of cookies.

"You're going to be the leading cause of obesity among Loveless Brewing employees," he says.

"Those are tahini," I say, nodding at the plate.

"Ooh," he says, grabs one, takes a bite. Considers. "Odd, but pretty good."

Next is Daniel, who knocks but doesn't wait for a response before trying the door and finding it unlocked. It occurs to me that all four of them have keys to my place, so I should probably be grateful that Eli didn't just waltz in.

He joins us at the island. Eli points out a small white spot on the back of one shoulder, so Daniel gets a wash cloth and dabs at it.

"You sure you don't want kids?" he asks Eli sarcastically. "Once they stop spitting up, they start teething."

"I'm the world's happiest uncle," Eli says, taking another cookie.

"I don't need an intervention," I say, knowing full well that resistance is futile. "This has happened before. It happens all the time, I just need—"

"You scheduled a phone interview with a brewery in Kansas," Daniel interrupts, putting down the washcloth and taking a cookie. "Weird. What are these?"

"Tahini," Eli says. "It's the same stuff that makes hummus taste like hummus."

"I like it."

"Were you going through my emails?" I ask, leaning on the island and pinching the bridge of my nose between my fingers. "Do I have to start locking my—"

"You added it to your work calendar, dipshit," Daniel says, genially. "The one you shared with me at least five years ago?"

"You look at that?"

Daniel doesn't dignify that question with a response, just gives me a look.

When Caleb arrives, he's got a duffel bag with him and doesn't even knock.

"Hey," he says, walking over. "Mind if I put this upstairs?"

"Yes," I tell him.

He grabs a cookie and eats it as he walks away, toward the stairs.

"These are good," he calls as he climbs. "What's in them?"

"Hummus," answers Daniel.

"Tahini, which is also used to flavor hummus," corrects Eli.

When Levi gets there, he knocks. Eli shouts for him to come in.

"You all ready?" he asks, coming over to the table. He's got on a black wool coat, not his usual Carhartt work coat, which means something is *really* up.

"Let's go," says Daniel, brushing his hands off.

"Should we drive together?" Levi asks.

"Drive *where*?" I ask.

"You shouldn't wear that," Caleb says, apparently noticing my pajamas for the first time.

"Why?"

"Different pants, at least," opines Levi. "Can I have one of these? They look good."

I give up. I'm not going to win a battle of wills with all four of them, and besides, lying on my couch and playing dumb phone games while trying not to think about my ex isn't that great of a night either.

"Go for it," I say, and walk for the stairs.

"Weird but good, right?" Daniel confirms.

"What's in them?"

"Tahini," I call, climbing. "Which is the thing that makes hummus taste like hummus, they're not hummus cookies."

"I know what tahini is," Levi calls back.

· · * * ★ ★ ★ ★ * * · ·

APPARENTLY, being the sad-sack guest of honor means I get to ride shotgun. Eli drives, since it's his car, which leaves Levi, Caleb, and Daniel in the backseat. None of them look thrilled about it, but it seemed easier to take one car.

When we park, I sit there for a moment, just looking at the sign. Last time I was here, it was cracked, peeling, and in an ugly faux-western font. These days it's surprisingly classy: WHISKEY BARREL in a nice serif, lit from below.

"You know I'm banned for life from this place, right?" I ask.

Everyone but me opens their car door.

"That was eight years ago," Levi says, extracting himself. "And they never did strike me as the sort of establishment that kept careful records."

He's right, of course. The inside of the Whiskey Barrel is also new, and now it's the trendy kind of divey, instead of the divey kind of divey. The neon beer signs are gone, the carpet replaced with wood, the barstools faux-industrial instead of from the 1980s. There's a craft beer selection, including our very own Southern Lights IPA on tap. I get something else.

I keep waiting for the familiarity to strike me, but it doesn't. I've thought about that night a hundred times, maybe a thousand, but right now I'm back in the place where it happened and it just seems far away.

"It's different in here," I tell Levi, looking around as we walk to the pool tables in the back.

"Interesting," he says. "I guess things change."

It's busy, but not crazy. We get a pool table with no problem. Eli immediately organizes some sort of tournament, the structure of which I don't bother to follow, and informs Daniel and Levi that they'll be playing each other while he, Caleb, and I drink beers and watch.

"How's Thalia?" I ask, since I haven't yet today.

"Good," he says, and smiles like he can't help it. "I mean, she's going a little crazy, finishing her thesis and waiting to hear back from graduate programs, but she's good."

I still find it strange that he's dating someone still in college, but I keep my mouth shut.

"And you?"

"I'm actually okay," he says, taking a sip of beer, then putting it down on the table. "I'm getting a couple of recruiting calls a day from people who want to pay me way more than academia ever did."

"Cyber security stuff?" Eli asks.

"Some of it," Caleb says. "Apparently there's more demand for mathematicians than just teaching other people how to be mathematicians."

"So you're really okay?" I ask, and he laughs.

"I really am," he says. "I mean, I don't have a job *yet*, and it won't be the same, but my life didn't implode the way I was afraid it might."

"You sound surprised."

"I jumped and didn't know where I would land," he admits, watching Daniel miss a shot by about six inches. "There were times when I was afraid I gave up too much, but now that I'm on the other side it feels kind of good. Whatever happens, it was the right thing."

We all drink. Levi lines up a shot, takes it. Balls click together, but from his frown, I suspect that whatever he was hoping for didn't happen.

"Relationships always have an element of diving into the unknown and praying for the best," Caleb says, and gives me a look. It's pretty similar to the look Levi gave me ten minutes ago. Almost as if they're related or something.

I'm tempted to tell him that I know what happens. The same thing always happens and I wind up here, drinking with my brothers, wishing it hadn't.

Except the bar's changed. My brothers have changed. Daniel's got two kids. Eli's happily married to his old nemesis, Levi's engaged to his best friend's sister, and even Caleb has a girlfriend. It's me who's still stuck, holding onto old hurts like they're a lifeline.

I'm not going to look over and see her with another man, his ring on her finger. That was a different bar, a different Delilah, a different time.

It's a strange, slow shock when I realize the last thing: that was a different *me*.

Pool balls click. Daniel whoops and Levi laughs. Eli makes some sort of notation, then grabs my shoulder.

"You," he says, and points at the pool table.

We play. I don't excel and I don't embarrass myself, but I'm glad to have something to do with my hands, something to think about besides how time moves and we bend to it. Besides how the past echoes through everything but doesn't have to shape it.

"Seth," Eli says. I'm bending over the table, trying to line up a complicated shot that's almost certainly going to fail.

"Eli," I say back. I wonder if I need more of that blue chalk stuff. It always helps, right?

"She your soulmate?"

I take a deep breath, ignore his attempt at a psych-out, and take the shot. It doesn't work the way it did in my head.

"What kind of question is that?" I ask. I gesture at the table, waiting for him to take his turn.

He doesn't. He leans against it, the end of his pool cue on the floor, and spins it between his fingers.

"A yes-or-no one," he says.

"Fine. Yes," I say, mimicking his stance.

Eli grins.

"I lied. It was a trick question," he says. "There's no such thing as soulmates."

"Then why—"

"I wanted to see what you'd say," he says. "Because if you said *no*, then fuck it, have another beer and forget the whole thing. But you've got a whole different problem."

I just wait. Eli's clearly winding himself up to something, and it can be best not to get in his way.

"There's no such thing as soulmates," he repeats. "And that means nothing is going to save you. Not fate, not true love, not your destiny being written in the stars or some nebulous concept of *she's the one*. The only thing that matters is whether you want to be with her enough to work for it."

He grabs his beer from a side table and drinks, watching me.

"So romantic," I finally say.

"Effort is romantic," he says. "Putting in the work is romantic. Talking through it is fucking romantic, Seth."

"Take your turn," I say.

Eli shrugs, puts his beer down, and plays pool.

449

· · · · ★ ★ ★ ★ · · · ·

He kicks my ass. I have another beer and keep looking over at the spot where she was sitting all those years ago.

Only I can't remember where, exactly, she was. I can't remember what it looked like when I first saw her, whether she was standing or sitting. The tables have changed, the layout has changed, the decor has changed.

I want to be angry, but I can't even remember how. All I can do is wish she were here.

"Okay," I say, coming up to Levi and Caleb at a table.

They halt their conversation — probably about trees or tents or advanced degrees, I don't know — and look at me.

"I need your help," I tell them.

"Sure," Caleb says.

"Building something."

"What do you need built?" Levi asks.

I tell them.

They look at each other. Levi frowns. Caleb shrugs.

"It's not a good idea," Levi says. "It's pretty irresponsible."

"You agreed to build a nine-year-old a trebuchet," I point out.

"I'll do it," Caleb says. "It'll be fun."

Levi sighs. He takes another drink of his beer.

"All right, I'm in," he says.

FIFTY

DELILAH

"This feels kind of cutesy," I say, examining a sticker pack that says *Way to go!* In big pink letters.

"Then don't use that sticker," Ava explains, patiently.

"You never know, he might like it," Lainey points out.

I look down at what I've got in my cart: an overpriced, flat-bound journal with a classy black cover, glue, corner stickers, watercolor pens, washi tape, decorative paper, and a multipack of glitter.

The glitter was Ava's doing. She seems to think I'm going to need it at some point, and frankly, I don't know that she's wrong. Glitter's a pain in the ass, but I like it.

She looks into my cart skeptically.

"This doesn't feel like enough stuff," she says, matter-of-factly. "You're sure you don't also want to decorate some water bottles? Or make some t-shirts? Ooh, or friendship bracelets? I haven't tried those for years but I remember them being really fun."

"This isn't for spirit night at the sorority," I say. "This is..."

I stop, because I still haven't fully explained to myself

what I'm doing. It's a craft? An apology? A *you were right about some things*? A *you mattered all along*?

"It's a gift," Lainey says, simply. "And the recipient isn't really into friendship bracelets."

"I mean, I've never asked," I point out.

"I feel okay making that assumption," she says.

"Okay, but at least get puffy paint," Ava says. "Just a little? How can you come here and not get puffy paint?"

I make a face, and Ava just laughs.

"Joke," she says, rolling her eyes. "I'm not ten. C'mon, let's go make this *dignified* scrapbook for your man."

· · * * ★ ★ ★ ★ * * · ·

WHEN I BRING the box out, Lainey and Ava are sitting at my kitchen table, waiting. All the crafting supplies are there, neatly organized on one side. Lainey laughs at something that Ava said, and Ava gives a wicked little grin.

"All right," she says, standing up when I put the box down on the table. "Do you want to give me a run-down of what I'm looking for, or should we just dive in and see what we can find? How are we grouping things? Chronologically, or thematically, or do you want to do some sort of chromatic organization? I know you're an artist."

Apparently my little sister has turned from *Ava, sweet baby angel* to *Ava, sorority social chair*. I'm starting to see how she climbed as high as she did.

"I don't know," I say. "I'm not even totally sure what's in here, I never really went through it, I just put more stuff in sometimes and then shoved it into the back of my closet."

"We could see what's in here and then decide," Lainey suggests.

Ava nods, once. It's very official. I have the urge to offer her rubber gloves, just to watch her snap them on and get to work.

The first thing out is a Loveless Brewing cardboard coaster, pilfered from Fall Fest two years ago. Then hotel key cards. A bottle of hotel shampoo. ("You definitely can't scrapbook that," offers Ava.) Notepads. Printed directions. A receipt, the various odds and ends of our non-relationship that punctuated my regular life. The bright spots I kept going back to, even when I thought I shouldn't.

There's a cocktail napkin from the Harrisonburg Marriott, and underneath that, the photos. Down here it's all jumbled together, a whole slew of stuff that I threw in this box all at once. Us in a formal prom photo, my fluffy purple dress so big it's almost out of frame. Candids of us at my house, at his house, doing cute young couple stuff. Selfies from when I visited him at college.

Gifts: cards, a necklace, a bracelet. One of those bobbing-head drinking birds that he gave me once. Ticket stubs from movies we saw together, the ink barely legible. Letters he wrote me while we were apart, tchotchkes, all the flotsam and jetsam of a relationship.

There's so, so much. There's more than I remembered, but somehow, I know every single thing. I remember the necklace with the star on it, the eighteenth birthday card signed *Love, Seth*, the ticket stubs from when we went to see *Avatar* together and the 3D glasses gave him a headache.

And I remember the things that aren't here: the first time we kissed, standing outside Sprucevale High, the football field in the distance. When I got my driver's license before him and a new car from my dad, and we'd drive to empty parking lots and make out.

Holding hands in the hallway. Getting told at a school dance that we weren't allowed to dance like *that*. The way it felt to see him from across the cafeteria for the first time each day, an explosion in my chest every time.

The confusion and elation and startling pleasure of the first time we took our clothes off. The terror of buying condoms from Walmart, afraid that I'd see someone I know, or that the cashier would announce it over the loudspeaker, or just the enormity of having to admit that I was probably going to have sex with someone.

When we finally did it, on the bed in my parents' guesthouse.

All of it in this one box. It's overwhelming. It's exhausting. More than anything, it's strange to realize that a decade and a half after we met, he still makes my heart leap.

Thank God for Ava and Lainey, who make it bearable. Ava attacks the ocean of objects with a curator's methodical eye, placing things in context, deciding which decorative tape goes best with the key card from the Marriott. She doesn't bat an eye at all the stuff from motels, nor does she even blink at the discovery of a single (still factory-sealed but very expired) condom.

I'm beginning to wonder if I've underestimated my youngest sister.

Finally, she climbs onto my couch and stands there, looking down at the timeline we've made. Lainey and I are both drinking canned wine and sitting on the floor, but Ava nods a few times, surveying what's spread in front of us.

"I think that's right," she says. "I like the narrative this presents. It'll get the job done. Though, you know, if you really wanted to impress, him I know where I could get a confetti cannon —"

"No," I interrupt her.

"Come on," says Lainey. "Live a little."

An hour later, they've both left. Ava kisses me and tells

me that I'm a sparkling unicorn, and Lainey gives me a big hug and says she's proud of me.

I walk back into the living room. I stand on the couch myself, frown down at everything we've put together: coordinated and well-thought-out, neatly put together. Properly in a timeline, each phase of our relationship coordinated by a different color of the rainbow.

As if it was neat. As if anything about this were orderly or planned, as if it was a smooth transition instead of starts and stops and ups and downs. I stand there, on the couch, for a long time. Thinking. Remembering. Letting myself be alone with all this for the first time in years and years.

Admitting the enormity of what I'm looking at.

Finally, I get off the couch. I get another can of wine from the fridge — Ava recommended it and she's right, it's totally good — and then I sit on my floor and get to work.

FIFTY-ONE

SETH

I'm staring at the forest in my mom's back yard when Caleb comes out of the backdoor and crosses to me, holding out a mug of coffee.

"Mom says hi," he tells me. "She also didn't even ask me why we were building this, just told me that anything in the shed is fair game to use."

"I didn't always like having three older brothers," I say, still contemplatively looking into the trees. "But being fourth-born has its benefits."

"You don't even know," Caleb says, grinning. "I think I got in trouble twice. They were *way* too tired."

I hold up my coffee mug, and we clink them together, then both take sips. It's hot, strong, and black, which is exactly what I need since the sun isn't far over the horizon.

"Trees are nice," Caleb says, after a moment. "I'm sure that's why you're staring at them. Just thinking about how nice trees are."

"They do provide us with oxygen," I say. "That's nice."

It's true: trees are nice. But Caleb is also fully correct in his suspicion that I'm not staring into the trees because they're nice. I'm staring because I think something I want might be in there.

Possibly. Maybe. If I'm lucky. The trick'll be finding it, though.

"You gonna share with the class, or...?"

"Not yet," I tell him. From the other side of the house, I can hear tires on gravel, meaning that Levi's probably just arrived. "First things first."

· · · · · ★ ★ ★ · · · · ·

THE PROJECT IS DONE before noon. When I suggested it, I imagined it taking all day. Several days. Turns out, when you know what you're doing, simple structures don't take that long.

"I still think it's a bad idea," Levi says, looking at the finished product.

"Again," I say, "you've been helping an elementary school student build medieval—"

"And yet, that feels more responsible than this," he says.

I snort and glance past the structure, into the forest again.

It's there, somewhere. I've got time.

"Excuse me," I tell my brothers, pull out my phone, and step away.

"He was staring at trees a bunch before you got here," Caleb says to Levi, shrugging.

"I'm sure it was because he thinks trees are nice," Levi says, and Caleb snorts.

I find the name I'm looking for and call. It rings three times, and then he finally picks up.

"Hey," I say. "I've got a strange favor to ask."

"And you're calling me?" Silas says, a little fuzzy on the

other end of the line. My mom's house doesn't have the best reception.

"Let me know if it's something you can't do."

Levi, who was quietly surveying my mom's back yard, turns and gives me a look.

"How about you tell me what it is first?" Silas says.

"Is there any chance you can get me a metal detector?"

On the other end of the line, there's a long pause.

"A metal detector?" he says, sounding stumped. "Why?"

"I need to detect metal and thought you might know someone," I say. Another look from Levi. "Listen, if I'm asking the impossible of you—"

Silas laughs.

"Asking me to break into the Library of Congress and steal a first edition of *The Federalist Papers* is impossible," he says. "Metal detectors? Nah."

I almost ask, but decide to hold off until he's here.

"You sure?" I say. "I could always call someone else if it's too hard."

Silas snorts.

"Don't you dare," he says. "Tell me where you are, I'll get you a metal detector in two hours."

When I hang up, Levi's still giving me that look, and I start to feel slightly guilty.

"I'm not sure that was nice of you," he says. "You know how he is."

"Do you know a better way to get a metal detector in a couple hours?" I ask.

Levi is trying very, very hard not to smile.

"Probably not," he admits.

"Stone cold, Seth," says Caleb, but he's grinning.

"I'll apologize when he gets here," I promise. "Should we go eat lunch while we wait?"

· · * * ★ ★ ★ ★ * · ·

ONE HOUR and forty-five minutes later, Silas shows up with three metal detectors, a huge roll of bright yellow police tape, and a detailed search plan involving a grid. I've already spent the past half-hour reconstructing the search parameters as best as I can, so we get to work.

It's fun at first. There's tons of stuff on the forest floor, especially close to the back yard: bottle caps, crushed aluminum cans, the aluminum spirals from notebooks. Silas finds an entire three-ring binder buried under years and years' worth of leaves, worksheets and homework mostly rotted away.

Still visible is a very large C- on one of the papers, so we decide it was Daniel's.

There's more. Nails, bike chains, old barbed wire. Old shotgun shell casings. A small, heavy sphere that might be a Civil War-era bullet. A metal ring that I think is from a stove and Silas thinks is from an old-timey headlight.

News spreads, and by afternoon, we've got more help. Silas takes a break, and Rusty steps in, enthusiastically excavating a door hinge from the forest floor. Daniel reminds her a thousand times about tetanus and makes her wear gloves.

Caleb takes a turn. My mom takes a turn. Levi takes a turn and gets grumpy about all the trash we find in nature. June and Violet show up at various points to help out.

When the sun sets, we still haven't found it and the grid is almost done. Everyone else heads back but I keep look-ing, knowing that with every sweep of the detector I'm less and less likely to find what I'm looking for. Sure, I could come back tomorrow and search a wider area, but I don't know how useful that would be because my memory is crystal clear.

I know where I stood. I know I squeezed it in my bare palm and stared into the woods, the trees naked of leaves, the cold wind blowing. I remember thinking that this was stupid, that I should just return it, that throwing it into the woods where I'd never find it wasn't going to accomplish a single thing.

And then I remember winding up and hurling the thing as hard as I could into the trees. It flashed once in the low, cloudy light, and then it was gone. I remember how savagely victorious I felt in that moment, how triumphant. How it felt like I'd gotten some kind of revenge and that made me freer, lighter.

It didn't. It took me years to finally learn it, but lashing out at someone who hurt you doesn't do shit except cinch the noose a little tighter around your own neck.

BEEP.

It startles me out of my thoughts, and I sweep the detector over the area again, slowly this time.

BEEP. BEEP. BEEEEE—

I sigh, pushing away the leaves with my foot. Swing again. Still beeping, so I crouch, put down the detector, and start brushing away the soft, dark soil of the forest floor in the fading light.

I don't find anything, so I dig a little harder. My fingers tear through tiny, hair-like roots, unearth tiny chunks of rotted wood, and I brush them all off, hope I don't touch anything too disgusting in my search for what's probably an old bolt or, if I'm lucky, a quarter.

I see the sparkle before I touch it. I hold my breath. I lean in, digging around it, reminding myself that it's probably a stainless steel ball bearing or some ancient refrigerator piece, and I pull it out.

It's an engagement ring. It's *the* engagement ring. It's caked with dirt. One of the prongs that holds the diamond is missing, and the ring itself is slightly bent, but the gold still shines and the diamond still catches the light.

God, I was dumb. I was dumb to throw it in here, and I was dumb to propose in the first place. Our relationship had been crumbling for months. I thought that this was the way to make her stay with me, and I was heartbroken and furious when it didn't work.

When I head into the house, my mom's in the kitchen, drinking a glass of wine and using her laptop on the kitchen table, papers scattered around her.

"Any luck?" she asks.

In response, I just hold it up. She holds out her hand, and I walk over, put the ring into it.

"It's pretty," she says, turning it over, then handing it back. "Though I could have sworn I taught you boys not to throw diamond rings into the woods."

I just laugh and walk over to the kitchen sink to wash it off.

"I'm sure we'd all be better off if we'd just listened to you," I say.

"You're teasing me, but you're right," she says.

We're both quiet for a moment, and I can feel her watching me.

"Yes?" I ask.

"Just wondering what you're planning on using it for now," she says, an incredible casualness in her voice.

I shut off the water, dry my hands, dry the ring. Stick it in my pocket.

"Well, it's an engagement ring," I tease.

My mom sighs. She stands, comes over to me, takes my face in her hands.

"Seth," she begins. "My favorite fourth-born child."

"You say that to all your fourth-born children."

"Don't be a smartass," she says, very calmly. "And

Delilah is a lovely, vibrant, delightful person who I would be proud to have as a daughter-in-law *someday*, but that's only going to happen if you do right by her now."

I put one hand on my chest, over my heart.

"Mom, I promise not to fuck this up," I tell her.

She nods once, then pulls me in for a big hug.

"Good luck," she tells me.

FIFTY-TWO

DELILAH

I knock again, just to be sure.

Still nothing, the inside of the townhouse perfectly quiet. He's not here. I knew he wasn't here the moment I drove up — no car, no lights — but I spent the last hour doing color touch-ups on Tinker Bell and practicing what I was going to say when he answered.

Except he's not answering, because he's not here, and this scrapbook feels like dead weight in my hands. Maybe this was a dumb idea. Maybe he's out at a bar charming the panties off someone named Riley, and any minute now they're going to pull up and want to know what I'm doing here. Yes, it's six o'clock on a Monday night, but I don't know Riley's life.

I lean my forehead against his front door, cool in the early evening of almost-spring, and take a couple of breaths. To be honest, I didn't plan for this: I thought I'd waltz up to his door, present this scrapbook, say my piece, and he'd stop being mad at me and we could work things out. At least, that's what I was hoping for.

There's an alternative, of course, where I pour my

heart out and show him this book I made and he stands there in the doorway, shadowed like a Caravaggio painting, and tells me it's still over. That some wounds won't ever heal, some pasts can't be mended, and could I please just leave him alone.

I could stick around and wait, but the thought of sitting on his front steps and getting more anxious by the minute is wildly unappealing.

It's fine. I'll come back tomorrow.

Maybe I'll even call first. What an idea.

I drive home too fast, reckless with unspent energy. I blast Neko Case and sing along as loudly as I can with the windows cracked, the scrapbook riding shotgun.

A quarter mile from my house, I pass a big green truck going in the opposite direction. At the last moment, the driver lifts his fingers from the wheel in the universal small-town sign of *I see we're on the same road, how y'all doing?*

"Wait," I say, out loud, to myself. I glance in the rearview mirror, but it's no help.

That was Levi.

Was that Levi?

I think that was Levi.

I turn down the music, look in my rearview mirror again, and pull into my driveway.

The tail lights of Seth's Mustang glow in my high beams. My heartbeat doubles. Every nervous, terrified thought I've had today comes racing back and each one brings a friend.

And then he appears. In the fading daylight he steps around the corner of my house, coming into the driveway from the back yard, and he stands there in my headlights: the angles of his face blown out and shadowless in the blinding light, hair askew. He raises one hand, shades his eyes, head turned slightly away. Like he's ready to brace against whatever comes next.

I take a breath. I can hear the beating of my heart, fast but steady, and I can feel it thumping through every limb.

Then I grab the scrapbook, turn off the headlights, and get out of the car.

I don't know why he's here. He could tell me he never wants to see me again. He could tell me he just wants to fuck it out and that's all. He could tell me something brand new that would break my heart all over again.

I'm giving him the chance to wreck me one more time, and I know it. I'll survive. Sooner or later I might even get over it, but I'm not letting this end without finally putting my heart on the table and showing him where his name's carved into it.

"Hey," he says, as I walk up to him.

I swallow, hard. My palms are sweaty.

"Hey," I answer. Then: "No scones?"

"Sorry," he says, and smiles. He pushes one hand through his hair, a gesture I know so well I see it in my sleep. "But I did try to be less terrifying this time."

If he were a bear, I'd be considerably less nervous right now.

"Thanks," I say. The scrapbook is sweaty in my hands, and I look down at it, blood rushing through my ears. Courage. *Courage.*

I clear my throat. I try to remember the words I practiced.

"Seth," I start. *Thump. Thump.* "Listen, I know we've fought a lot—"

That's not it.

"There's," I start, not sure where that sentence is going. "This has been weird and hard…"

"Bird, I'm sorry," he says, after I trail off.

Bird. My heart swells.

"Me too," I say, palms still sweaty against the book I'm holding. "I'm so tired of getting in fights and trying out these stupid workarounds and—"

Behind him, the floodlights in my back yard flick on. It's probably a squirrel, but I lean around Seth just to make sure it's not —

There's something back there.

I pause, frowning. It's… a box? A wooden box?

A big, colorful wooden box?

"Is that yours?" I ask, all my nerves suddenly forgotten.

Seth sighs, smiles.

"Well, it's yours now," he says. "And I hope you like it, because I can't imagine how I'm going to bribe Levi to bring his truck back so we can move it again."

Seth holds out one elbow, and I loop my hand through it, mystified. He guides me through my back yard, and it doesn't take long for it to reveal itself.

It's a doghouse-sized castle, complete with turrets and a ramp that looks like a drawbridge. It's painted in bright technicolor: the walls cerulean, the towers kelly green, the door magenta, the turrets a bright violet.

Over the door, in neatly stenciled white letters, it reads *VARMINT PALACE.*

I'm rendered fully speechless.

"I thought Terry, Larry, and Jerry would like it," Seth finally says.

I clear my throat. I clear it again. I've completely forgotten everything that I was going to say to him.

"I can't say I know their taste in architecture, honestly," I tell him.

I'm still staring.

"You built a raccoon castle?" I say. "That's what I'm looking at, right?"

"Yep," he confirms. "You like it?"

"I do," I say, and that breaks the spell. I step forward, touch a turret, look into it. I crouch and look through the doorway. It looks big enough for all three of them to fit in at once, though I've got no idea if raccoons snuggle.

Then I straighten, face Seth. He's watching me, his eyes still cerulean in the faded light.

"I like you," he says, and a smile tugs at one corner of his mouth. "That's all, really. I like you. I like that you're funny. I like that you're stubborn. I like that you're always up for adventure and I like that you only have really weird liquor in your house and I like that you have a million beautiful tattoos and I even like that you feed disease-ridden varmints because you're soft-hearted."

This time, I know better than to ask about the *but*.

"I like you too," I say. "Even when I wish I didn't."

"I can't be without you anymore," he goes on, softly. "I thought I could, but I was wrong every single time."

He steps forward, puts a hand on my cheek. The flood-lights behind us flick off, and suddenly we're in the slate-blue of near darkness.

"I'm the man who'll answer every time you call," he says, simply. "Whatever you ask, I'll say yes. Like it or not, Bird, I'll be yours until the day I die."

I take a deep breath and put my hand over his, slot our fingers together.

"I'm not gonna leave you for someone who likes golf," I say, softly. I don't trust my voice because I'm afraid I'm about to start crying. "That's not what I want. I want *you*. If I wanted someone else, I'd be with someone else."

I swallow hard, close my eyes.

"I know it took a long time to get here, but it's you, Seth."

He kisses me, then. His other hand cups my other cheek

and he kisses me, softly. Carefully, but not gently, like he knows exactly the pressure I can bear.

"You're enough," he murmurs, my face still in his hands. "You were always enough. You always will be."

Now it's my turn to kiss him, my hand on his face, my fingers curled in his hair, suddenly possessive. The still-healing star on my wrist winks at me in the darkness, and after a long kiss, I pull away.

"You were right," I tell him. He raises one eyebrow. "Back at the condo, when you found the box of stuff from my ex—"

"I'm sorry," he murmurs.

I put my fingers over his mouth. He raises the other eyebrow, too.

"I tried to erase you and I couldn't," I tell him. "You were always there, Seth, even when I tried so hard to forget you. I tried to replace you and wound up calling you the moment I filed for divorce."

I slide my fingers from his lips, and he takes my hand.

"You never told me that part," he says.

"It was an hour after Nolan got the papers," I say. "Sixty minutes to work up my nerve, just in case I had to beg."

I take half a step back, hand him the scrapbook. The first page is us at Ava's wedding, one of the professional shots. We're dancing in each other's arms. He's grinning and I'm laughing, the people behind us a blur. Instead of all the stuff we bought for the scrapbook, the page under the photograph is a drawing, all in pink and gold: the wedding fading into bubbles, drifting away; a bird winging its way across the top.

Seth holds it up to the nearly-gone light, brings it in. Turns so his shadow isn't over the book.

The next page: the program from a production of *Guys*

& Dolls our high school put on. A piece of torn notebook paper that says *Delilah Loveless* in my big, loopy teenage handwriting. On the page underneath, the view of the football field from the nook where we first kissed. I can tell from his face that he recognizes it, even in the low light.

Seth holds out his hand, and I take it. We walk back to my house, past the cars, go inside. We sit on the couch, his arm around me, and I look at what I was up most of the night making.

In the end, I didn't lay it out the way Ava thought I should. The book doesn't tell a story because we both know the story already, by heart, inside and outside and upside down.

It's more abstract: organized by mood, feeling, sense. The first time I met his family is grouped with when he gave me a key to his college apartment: times when his home was mine. A prom photo and a hotel key, together. The coaster from Fall Fest backed by a two-page almost-pornographic drawing of us, horizontal on a couch. All that's visible is one nipple, but it's clear what's going on.

Seth understands. He knows, intuitively, laughs at some of the pages, runs his fingers over others like he wants to touch what's inside them. He teases me sometimes and kisses me sometimes and when he reaches the last page, I'm curled into him, still on my couch, my head in the curve of his neck.

It's the label from a bottle of Frog Holler Cider, pulled off and stuck to the page. On it there's a picture of the barn and an apple tree, and on the page underneath I drew the rest of the scene: hills behind, stars above. In the distance, two tiny figures holding hands.

"That's the night I knew it could work," I say, softly. I don't know if it's the most romantic thing, but it's the truest thing.

"I knew before that," Seth says, pulling me in closer.

I nuzzle against his neck.

"No, you didn't," I say.

"I did. I knew in the car."

I'm laughing. So is he.

"No, you *didn't*," I say again.

"I had a vision," Seth says. "Of us in twenty years, my hair going gray, and you in the passenger seat with a giant map arguing with me about directions. And I knew."

"What, that we could argue?"

"That I loved you," he says, the rumble of his voice reverberating through me. "And that whatever happened, I'd fight for it."

Tears prick at my eyes, and I bite my lips together. Take a deep breath.

"I love you too," I say, and we kiss again.

FIFTY-THREE

SETH

The sliding glass door in the living room opens and closes again, and a few seconds later, Delilah comes back into the kitchen with the plastic container of kibble.

"Nothing just yet, but I think I tempted them," she says. "Once they're in front of their new digs, they'll be curious and check it out, right?"

I rinse the dish soap from a pan, then stack it on her dish rack.

"Maybe they need better treats to tempt them," she muses, leaning back against the counter next to the sink. "Do raccoons like filet mignon?"

I give her a look, trying not to smile, and wash a spatula.

"What about chocolate truffles?" she goes on, pure mischief in her voice.

I take a deep breath, shut the water off, and reach for the towel, determined not to be baited.

"Oh! Lobster!" she exclaims. "Everyone likes lobster, right?"

"They're varmints!" I finally say, despite myself.

Delilah laughs, and I toss the towel onto the counter opposite her.

"They eat trash," I tell her, though I'm grinning. "And they're a damn nuisance."

She leans forward, grabs the front of the button-down flannel shirt I'm wearing, and pulls me toward her.

"You're a nuisance," she says.

"I'm a nuisance who just did the dishes while you frolicked with the local fauna," I tell her, anchoring my hands on the edge of the counter.

"Well, the dream is to go full Snow White and have the animals do the dishes while we lounge around eating ice cream," she teases. "Besides, do I even need to remind you who built the raccoon castle in the first place?"

"I'm starting to regret not just getting you a necklace," I tease back.

"Sure you are," she says, then lets my shirt go.

She slides her hands down my torso, hooks two fingers under the waistband of my jeans, tugs lightly, the backs of her fingers cool against warm skin.

My whole body shivers.

"Stay over?" she says.

I lean in and kiss her. She's soft and warm and opens her mouth under mine, her hands going under my shirt, cool against my skin. I get goosebumps that have nothing to do with temperature.

"But I didn't even bring a toothbrush," I tell her, and I can feel her smile.

"Don't tell me that you didn't think beyond the varmint palace to the makeup sex," Delilah says. "What, you didn't use a flow chart?"

I hook my fingers through the belt loops on her pants, tug at her slightly, press myself against her, cock already stirring.

"One, flow charts are for decision making, not planning," I say. "And two, I just wanted you to say yes. I didn't even think about what came after."

"How could I resist a home befitting Terry, Larry, and Jerry?" she asks, laughing.

And then, softer: "How could I resist you?"

"I'm sure there's a thousand ways."

"And yet, none of them interest me."

Her hand on the back of my neck, pulling me down, my mouth onto hers. They way it feels when we kiss, like something inside me locking into place.

This is it. This has always been it.

"Seth," she says, voice still soft, holding my forehead against hers. "Promise me something."

"Anything."

"Can I tell you first?"

I stroke my thumbs across her sides, bare skin right above her hips. Her body shifts, the slightest movement, but it sends a rush through me anyway.

"Fine," I tease.

"That next time we fight, it's not over," she says. "Promise me that next time we fight about something, we'll go for a walk or do some gardening or bake bread, but then we'll work it out and stay together."

I want to refuse. I want to say *no, we'll never fight again, everything from here on out is happily ever after*, but that's the worst kind of promise because it's one I can't keep.

I can't swear to perfection or permanent bliss, but I can swear to stay by her side.

"I promise," I tell her. "But I need you to promise me something."

She swallows.

"What?"

"To always believe me when I say you're everything I

473

need," I say. "Take me at my word when I say I love you, and only you."

She smiles, laughs softly, and I can feel her relax.

"I promise," she says.

We kiss: softly, tenderly, like a couple at the end of a movie. It's a sweet, chaste kiss, the kind that comes with flower petals and love sonnets, the kind that whispers *I love you* to a sleeping princess at sunrise.

It ends. I pull away, dizzy, and Delilah looks up at me, all freckles and brown eyes.

Her hand drifts along the back of my neck, over my collar, flattens along my shoulder. She runs her thumb quickly over my dirt biking scar, tilts her head slightly, cups my shoulder in her hand.

I flex, and she laughs, suddenly.

Then she *blushes*.

I do it again, of course, and her cheeks turn even pinker.

"You're blushing," I tell her.

"No, I'm not," she says, her eyes still on my arm.

I press myself against her, grip the edge of the counter, lift. Delilah bites her lips and tries not to laugh and the flush goes down her neck, but she also wraps her hands around my biceps and squeezes.

"The fuck are you blushing for, Bird?" I tease.

"Shut up," she suggests, cocking her head to one side.

"You having a good time?"

"What did I *just* say?"

"That I should be seen and not heard, apparently."

"Not what I said," she says, still trying not to laugh, hands gripping my shoulders. "I'm a very sophisticated woman and I love you for your beautiful mind and exceptional wit."

"But you want to fuck me because you like my muscles."

Now she's grinning, her hips shifting against mine. I wonder how wet she is already, and it's tantalizing.

"And your personality, I guess," she says, and hooks one finger under the top button of my shirt. "That's not bad."

She undoes the button, slides her hand down, undoes the next and the next until my shirt is open, her hands all over me. I kiss her again and she stands on her toes, her hips bucking against mine, the soft rhythm of her going straight to my aching cock.

I'm tempted in a thousand directions: to spin her around, bend her over, take her over the counter still mostly-clothed. I'm tempted to spread her right here and bury my face between her thighs. I'm tempted to let her get on her knees and watch her lips close around my cock.

But then she pushes my shirt over my shoulders and bites my lower lip, and before I've even gotten my shirt off her hands are tugging at the waistband of my pants, pulling me harder against her.

I grab her ass, lift her onto the counter, and she lands with a soft "Oh!" of surprise and a grin before I crush her mouth with mine, pinning her against the cabinets.

She wraps her legs around me, back arching. I lift her sweater and she pulls it off over her head, static electricity crackling and alighting in her hair, her skin bold and bright as ever. There's a black tank top, too, and she pulls that off like she's impatient.

Under the tank top is a black lace bra, her breasts swelling up and out of it, practically smashing the clock-work heart. With every breath she takes her skin presses against the fabric, straining against it.

Delilah goes to kiss me again but I grab her by a shoulder, hold her against the cabinet because I'm busy staring.

"I didn't even tell you," she says, breathless and amused all at once.

I run my other hand over a breath, slide my thumb along the seam between skin and lace.

"Tell me?" I echo, letting my other hand join it.

Fuck. *Fuck.* She leans back against the cabinet, toys with one finger under a black bra strap.

"I went to your house today," she says. "I took the scrapbook over to see if you'd take me back."

My brain is currently lacking for blood, so that takes me a minute to figure out.

"Wearing this," I say.

"In case the scrapbook didn't work," he says, softly.

I put my hand over hers, twist a finger around the same strap.

"There's no possible world where I don't take you back," I tell her, pulling it over her shoulder. "And God help me, there's no possible world where wearing this doesn't also work."

I tug the strap under her nipple pops out.

"Good to know," she murmurs, and then I lick it, swirl my tongue around it, listen to Delilah's moan above me as it hardens in my mouth and I can tease it with my teeth. I do the same to the other nipple and she tightens her hand in my hair, her bare heels against my back.

Finally, she brings her mouth to mine again, pressing forward. Her skin is warm and electric against mine and I grab her hips, pull her against me. She makes a noise into my mouth and I can feel her smile. I pull her even closer, my fingers digging into denim, and then she's off the counter.

Unbuttoning her jeans, pushing them over her hips, finally kicking them off.

The panties match: black and small, the same lace as

her bra. When I slide my hand between her legs, she makes a noise and rolls her hips, the fabric already damp. She palms my cock, hard, and I push my fingers under the fabric, play with her clit until her breathing goes erratic and she moans, one foot propped against the lower cabinets.

When I stop, she sighs in disappointment as I pull her away from the counter.

"Upstairs," I tell her. "Now."

I add in a hard ass-smack for good measure, and it's *very* satisfying.

"Or what?" she teases. Her fingers find my zipper.

"Or I have to fuck you on the counter, and I *just* did that last weekend," I tease.

"I liked it last weekend," she teases back. The zipper is down and she undoes the button and grabs my cock and I stop breathing for a moment.

"I know," I manage to get out. "Most of Snowpeak, West Virginia knows."

She squeezes me again, and I grab her ass with both hands because I can.

"I like your outfit and I'd *really* like to watch you walk up the stairs in front of me, how's that?" I say. "Soft, flat surfaces are nice to fuck on sometimes. Do you want more reasons to go get on your bed, or will those suffice?"

She kisses me, lets my erection go, fixes her bra so her nipples are hidden again.

"I guess those are good enough," she teases, and walks away.

Walk isn't the right word. She knows I'm watching her and Delilah *sashays* up the stairs, hips swinging from side to side, and I feel like I'm being hypnotized. Before she gets to the second floor I've already grabbed one garter, the bright red bow winking between my fingers, my thumb in the crease between her thigh and her ass.

At the top of the stairs, I hook a thumb under the lace panties, pull them off, leave them there. Her bra stays in the doorway to her bedroom and before I toss her onto the bed I pull her to me again, her back to my chest, run my hands over her body as she sighs. Melts.

I push my fingers between her legs again and they slide through wetness as she leans her head back against my shoulder, eyes closed, lips parted. Hips rolling back against me, the pressure both delicious and exquisite torture.

Then I spin her, kiss her, and toss her onto the bed, and she laughs in surprise.

"Don't tell me you weren't expecting that," I say.

She sits up, forward, grabs the waistband of my undone pants, pulls me toward her.

"I didn't know you wanted a bed so I could be a projectile," she says, and then I'm on my knees, between her legs. My cock springs free and I kick my jeans off.

"Projectile?" I say, voice going low as I grab her again, shove her further onto the bed, the bottoms of her thighs resting on the tops of mine. "I just like tossing you around sometimes."

I kiss her deep, pinch a nipple.

"You're bouncy and you make good noises," I tease as she wraps a hand around my cock again.

Then, I groan. She squeezes, strokes me from root to tip. The head of my cock bumps against the soft, smooth skin of her inner thigh and I move my hands between her legs again. Toy with her clit even as I thrust into her hand, helpless.

Finally slide my fingers inside her tight, slick entrance and circle her clit with my thumb and Delilah moans. She lifts her hips, one leg around my back now, strokes me and pushes my fingers deeper inside her all at once.

I add another finger and move them against the front

wall of her channel, in time my thumb on her clit. She moans again, her head to the side, fist still around my cock. I push deeper, burying my fingers in her up to my knuckle and I know I've got the right spot when her back arches so hard her whole body comes off the bed.

I stop before she comes, take my fingers out of her. Move over her and give her a long, deep kiss as she strokes me one more time and then guides me to her entrance.

"I love you," I murmur.

"I love you too," she says, eyes wide, her other hand stroking my cheek.

Then, suddenly, her eyes light up and she grins. Delilah twists under me and before I know it I'm on my back.

I let out a surprised "*Oh*," and then she's holding me down, throwing her leg over me, straddling my hips, cock crushed between us.

She's laughing, pressing her body against mine. She grabs my wrists and holds them over my head as I push back against her in a token struggle.

"Good noise," she says. Kisses me, biting my lip. Rolls her hips against my cock until I groan into her mouth and she laces our fingers together, pushes me back harder.

"Ride my cock and I'll make more," I tell her.

"For such a nice mouth, it sure is dirty," she teases, and she lets my hands go. Pushes herself upright, and I grab her thighs by the garters, push them apart, squeeze until my fingers sink in.

"Dirty?" I ask, grinning. Squeezing, pushing as she reaches behind her and grabs me again. "Dirty is telling you that I want you to ride my big fat cock with your wet pussy until you come so hard your eyes rolls and your legs shake."

She lifts on her knees, one hand on my chest, her whole

glorious body stretched above me. I grab the base of my cock, hold it steady, and she sinks onto it.

This is when she yields to me. Her body yields, slowly, her tightness inviting, enveloping. She yields skin-to-skin with nothing between us, her eyes sliding shut, a sigh escaping her lips as she gives herself over to me.

And this is how I know she's enough because this is what I crave, what I dream about at night: Delilah soft and vulnerable like this, stripped down to her core. Delilah with her freckles and her inked skin and her untameable hair. Delilah who burns so bright it blinds me sometimes.

I bottom out in her and she groans. Leans forward, both hands anchored on my chest, pushes her hips back. My fingers are digging into her thighs so hard she might have bruises later, but I don't think either of us minds.

"Tell me how much you like this," I growl.

She clenches around me, and I groan.

"I love this," Delilah says. Hands on my chest. Hips move again, roll, flex. *Fuck.*

I pull her down again, hard, and she makes a noise.

"I love your cock inside me," she says, breathing hard. "I love your dirty mouth. I love how good you feel and I love how hard you are to resist, and —"

She rocks back again, gasps.

"And I love you," she finishes.

"I love you too," I whisper, and she smiles at me.

"Good," she murmurs.

She finds a rhythm, her hands on my chest. It's slow and it's deep and it makes her say my name as she rises, falls, grinds her hips into me and clenches her hands on my chest. I'll have half-moon marks there tomorrow but right it feels too good to do anything about it, the pricks of pain blending with the whole-body pleasure of her, bringing everything into sharp relief.

I love this about her, too: her honesty when we fuck, the way she lets me give her what she needs. The way she's never been coy about how good it feels or how much she likes it.

The way she breathes, *I'm gonna come* when she gets close. She leans into me, slides down my cock, moans with her head thrown back. I pull her hips down as far as I can and she grinds herself against me and she moans *make me come Seth, makes me come, make me —*

The words stop when she clenches around me, become nothing but sound. She rocks against me and I pull her down, onto me, going as deep as I can until she jerks with every stroke and she kisses me fiercely.

"*Fuck*, that felt good," she says, our lips still touching.

"Sure looked like it," I tease her, and she laughs softly, dipping her head next to mine.

I hold onto her hips and slide into her again. She groans into my ear.

"Still feels good," she says. I do it again and she gasps. Bites my ear. I fuck her harder and this time she grunts and then she pushes back, sits up.

Delilah anchors her hands on my thighs. She lifts up and arches back until the only part of me inside her is the very tip of my cock, and then I watch her take me in one hard stroke.

It might be the best thing I've ever seen. It's even better because she moans when she does it. It's better because of the white-hot pleasure that shoots through me, because her tits bounce, because there's some absolute, primal satisfaction in watching the woman you love ride your cock and like it so much she can't stop.

She does it again, harder, and this time when I meet her she gasps with pleasure. I move my thumb to her clit and stroke her in the same rhythm that we set, trying to memo-

481

rize everything about this: the way she looks, breathes, sounds.

The way she suddenly slows down when she's about to come, taking me in hard and deep, muscles fluttering around me. I stroke her clit harder and faster and she whispers *fuck yes, Seth*, and she comes even harder than the first time.

I follow her by seconds while she rides me, pussy clenching me like a vise as I come inside her. I feel like I'm capsizing into the sea, overturned and wrecked, like she's destroyed me and now I need her to put the pieces back together.

When we finally stop moving, I sit up, still inside her, put my arms around her waist as she wraps her legs around me.

There's a long, slow kiss. There are her hands in my hair, on my back, my shoulders, my arms. There's Delilah everywhere, which is right where I want her to be.

"Bird," I murmur. "I love you."

She kisses me deeply. Slowly. Mouths open, tongues together.

"I love you too," she says. "You know."

"I do," I tell her.

FIFTY-FOUR

DELILAH

I tilt my head against Seth's shoulder, warm and slightly damp against my cheek. We've moved, but not much: sitting up against the green velvet of my headboard, pillows and blankets scattered around us.

"Shit, I didn't even ask if you were okay to bareback," I say, too lazy to be properly concerned. "Sorry."

His head is back against the headboard, and he smiles, laughs softly.

"Bird, I promise I'd have said something," he tells me.

"I mean, I'd hope so," I say.

For the record, I didn't really think that he went out, got some unprotected strange, and then built me a raccoon castle and said he'd always love me. It's just a courtesy I should have remembered.

"I'm mildly insulted that you asked," he teases, eyes still closed. "I haven't fucked anyone else since you moved back, you think I'm gonna start now?"

I frown at him, mentally play his sentence back. Then I do it again.

"What?" I finally say.

He opens his eyes, looks at me.

"I'm kidding," he says. "Asking is responsible, I'm not insulted."

"The other part."

"Well, it's hard to get an STD from your hand."

"You haven't slept with anyone else since I moved back?" I ask. "Since Fall Fest and the weekend in the motel?"

"No," he says, as if confirming the obvious.

I just look at him. I look at him for a good, long time.

"I told you that," he says, his face suddenly uncertain.

"You definitely didn't."

"I must have."

I just tilt my head at him, and he clears his throat.

"Hey, Bird, guess what?" he says. "I haven't been with anyone else in the two and a half years since you moved back to Sprucevale, isn't that cool?"

"You're impossible," I say, but I'm smiling.

"I'm sorry, I thought I'd told you," he says, then leads back again, laughs. "Fuck, I felt like it was written on my skin."

"It's kind of a lot of text, but I could definitely do that for you," I say.

His hand drifts to mine, takes it, turns it over. It's my left, a Band-Aid still over the new tattoo.

"What happened?"

As an answer, I take the Band-Aid off. Underneath, the star is black and shiny, still slightly pink around the edges since it's still healing.

"Got another one," I say. "Well, technically, I gave it to myself. Luckily I've gotten better at them."

Seth cups my hand from below and looks at the tiny tattoo for a long time, thinking.

"That one's gonna be hard to hide," he finally says.

"I know," I tell him. "Fuck it."

He leans in and kisses me on the temple.

"Vera and my dad are gonna hate it," I say, still looking at the star. "Winona's going to quietly disapprove but not say anything, Olivia's going to make a face, and her husband is going to express some sort of terrible *concern* about me ever having a job interview, as if I don't have a job."

"I like it," Seth says.

"Thanks," I tell him. "I like it too. And I'm done letting their opinions override my own."

He gives me another kiss on the temple, and this time his lips linger a moment longer, his hand still under mine.

"Stay there a second," he says when he releases me, and gets out of the bed.

He looks around. Stretches. Runs a hand through his hair, which fixes nothing, and finally grabs his pants and reaches into the pocket.

When he gets back on my bed, there's something in his fist. Seth wraps an arm around my shoulders and I lean into him, his other hand still hiding something.

My stomach tightens, and I swallow. I try to push away the sudden dread creeping through me.

"This is just a gift," he finally says. "I swear that's all. It's not a question or a contract or some kind of obligation. It's just something I wanted you to have, and that's all it is."

I look over at him, because I have no idea what to make of that speech. His blue eyes meet mine.

"Okay," I say.

He holds his fist in front of me, exhales, and opens it.

"Here," he says.

It's the engagement ring.

Sitting in his palm, it's smaller and simpler than I remember. Everything that happened after imbued it with so much meaning and significance that it looms large in my memory, but it's just a gold ring with a diamond.

I hold out my hand, and he pours it in.

It's the first time I've ever touched it. The day he proposed I only even saw it for a few seconds, still in the box, and that's all. Amazing how something that takes up so little space seemed to fill the room.

"You kept it?" I finally ask.

"Well, sort of," he says.

I take it in my fingers, look closer at it. One of the prongs is missing, and there's grime in the setting.

"Did you feed it to a tiger?" I ask.

"Technically, I threw it into the woods behind my mom's house after you broke up with me," he admits.

I don't ask why. I know why. Seth takes a deep breath.

"And then yesterday, I called in the cavalry with metal detectors and we ran a search-and-rescue operation for it," he goes on. "It's probably some sort of miracle that it didn't get taken off by some critter."

I sit up straighter, the ring still in my hand, Seth's arm still slung over my shoulders.

"Why?" I finally ask. "Why not leave it?"

"Because I threw it in there to hurt you," he says, slowly, looking down at it. "I know that doesn't make any sense at all, but it's what I wanted to happen. For a long time I thought that if I hurt you back like you hurt me, I'd finally get over it, but I never did. I tried every single time we fought, but seeing you cry never made me feel one lick better."

He shifts against me, strokes my arm with his thumb.

"So it's time to let go," he says.

Carefully, I turn my left hand and slide it onto my ring finger.

It fits perfectly. I flatten my hand and look at it, the small diamond winking in the low light.

"I'm not proposing," he says, a smile in his voice.

"Good, I'm not accepting," I tease back. "Just curious."

"It's not bad," he says.

I think it's a quarter the size of the ring Nolan gave me, maybe less. That was a huge, honking thing that he liked to see on me but *loved* to see other men look at. I fell for it, though, the idea that the size of a diamond had anything to do with my value as a person or someone's love for me.

"I got married because I thought doing that would fix me," I finally say, still looking down at the ring.

"You don't have to explain yourself, Bird," he says.

"I want to."

"Then I'm listening."

I take a deep breath, close my fist, try to quickly arrange everything that I've worked through in therapy or talked about with Lainey or even meditated on in yoga class.

"I felt awful when I broke up with you," I say. "I'd just failed out of school again, my mom was dead, I didn't know where my life was going, all my old friends were about to graduate college and my new friends were getting high and then going to their jobs at Subway, but somehow it felt like breaking up with you was the thing that made me feel so truly awful. So when I met someone else, I thought... maybe that was the answer. Maybe I just needed to be with someone and I'd feel better."

I take the ring off my finger, fiddle with it.

"And it felt like everyone I knew was pushing me in that *you need a man* direction, and I knew so many people who got married right after graduation, so when I met Nolan and he proposed a couple of months later, I said yes even though deep down I think I always knew it was a bad idea to get married."

Finally, I look over at Seth. After a moment he leans in, plants a kiss on my bare shoulder.

"If you and I had gotten married, we would've gotten divorced," I tell him, quietly. "Someone else wasn't going to fix what was wrong with me. I had to do that. I destroyed everything I touched back then."

"Bird, you still destroy me," he murmurs. "But the pieces are yours."

I close the ring in my fist, lean in, and kiss him softly.

FIFTY-FIVE

SETH

FIFTEEN YEARS AGO

I t's the first day of sophomore year, and there's a new girl at Sprucevale High. We don't get a lot of new students, especially not in high school, and no one will talk about anything else.

There are whispers that her dad is really rich. There are whispers that she moved here because something really bad happened, though no one is quite sure what.

I don't see her until second period, when she's in my English class.

The whispers didn't tell me she was pretty. They didn't say anything about her being so pretty that it makes breathing feel weird, like there's something hitching in my chest.

Pretty in a way that's startling: wild red hair and freckles, wide cheekbones, full lips. Brown eyes.

Delilah.

Sometimes, I glance at her and she glances at me, across English class, and it feels like a hole's been opened in my chest and I'm falling through. It's brand new, a little terrifying. Nothing like any crush I've had before. Nothing like the thrill of looking at naked women on the internet. It's a pull like I've been run through and hooked.

By third period, I've got a crush.

By fourth, I'm full-on infatuated, even though we've still never spoken.

Then, at lunchtime, it happens. I see her sitting by herself, at a table in a corner, and I have an idea that *terrifies* me. I stop in my tracks, backpack hanging from my shoulders. My friends wave at me, and I wave back.

I almost go sit with them, but there she is. By herself. Drawing something I can't see, sitting by herself, this girl who makes me feel like my insides are sliding out.

The whole walk over I don't think I breathe. I nearly chicken out at least five times, but then, I'm standing next to her table. The drawing in her notebook looks like a raven, its head turned over its shoulder.

She looks up at me, and I smile.

"Hi," she says, and smiles back. It feels like being wrapped in warm golden thread.

"Hi, I'm Seth," I manage to say. "Can I sit here?"

FIFTY-SIX

DELILAH

PRESENT DAY

Thalia half-turns in her chair, facing me, tapping the program against one leg.

"And then at the end, they *both* propose to her? Even though she's the one choosing?"

"It's weird," I agree. "Though the nice Bachelorettes usually don't let the guy they're rejecting get that far. The dude makes some speech, and sort of goes to kneel, and she's like, 'Noooo, don't do that!'"

"But God forbid she propose."

"Exactly."

"Do any of them actually get married and stay together?"

Around us, people are drifting through the rows of seats, greeting one another, sitting down. The trees above us sway in the breeze, shade moving and shifting.

It's a beautiful day for a wedding.

"I think a couple have," I say. "I don't watch it religiously, I mostly drink wine with my best friend and marvel at the life choices being made."

Thalia laughs, throwing her head back, and I grin.

When Seth told me Caleb's girlfriend was a year younger than Ava, I worried. I remember myself at twenty-two all too well, and I was absolutely not the kind of person anyone should have switched careers for.

But Thalia's nothing like I was. She's got her shit together in a way that took me years. I think she's probably more mature than I am now.

They'll be fine.

"That actually sounds really fun," she says.

"Let me know next time you're in town, we'll make it happen," I offer. "You'd love Lainey, too."

"I think I already do," Thalia says, just as a small, chubby hand enters my field of vision.

I turn my head to see Thomas grinning at me, mouth open, drool on his chin, reaching for my hair.

"Can I help you?" I ask.

He just reaches harder against Charlie's arm until he finally makes contact, and I start laughing. Charlie looks over from her conversation with Violet and sighs.

"Dude, you can't just grab hair," she says, putting her finger into his outstretched hand and wiggling it. "It's impolite."

Thomas, who has no use for her finger, shoves it away and reaches for me again.

"I can take him," I offer. "This'll keep him entertained for a while."

"Sure, if you don't mind," Charlie says.

Thomas doesn't mind, and a moment later, he's on my lap, patting at my hair with wide eyes.

"Hey, cutie," Thalia says, leaning in. "I like your outfit."

Thomas, who's currently nine months old, is wearing a

very small and adorable suit, along with a bandana to catch the drool. It's a lot of look.

He grins at Thalia and makes some noises, showing off all five teeth.

"The bib with the suit *is* a strong choice, but you're making it work," she agrees. "Though I can't help but notice that —"

She stops as music fills the air, the opening strains of something bluegrassy, and everyone in the audience turns, goes silent.

The aisle between the two sets of chairs leads to a path that cuts between two trees and then disappears. It's only about fifty feet until it comes out the other side, by the old hunting lodge-turned-wedding venue, but it makes the clearing where the ceremony's taking place feel magical, like it's in the middle of nowhere.

After a few moments, June's brother Silas emerges, a leather-bound folder in his hand, and walks very officially down the aisle, taking his place behind a microphone at the front.

Thomas giggles at nothing, and Charlie looks over.

"You like Uncle Silas?" she whispers.

Next are Rusty and Hedwig, Levi and June's dog. Originally, Rusty was supposed to be the flower girl, but when it came time to get the outfit, she decided that *flower girl* wasn't really her thing.

She then decided that her thing was *beastmaster*, and now she's wearing a three-piece gray suit, her curly hair piled on her head, and walking Ringbearer Hedwig. When they walk past our row, she glances over at Charlie like she's a little nervous.

Charlie grins and gives her a giant thumbs-up. Thomas squeals, because he's obsessed with his big sister. They sit in front of us, and Charlie leans over and gives Rusty a kiss on the back of the head.

Finally, the wedding parties walk in. One by one, each Loveless brother glances at our row as they escort a brides-maid down the aisle. Daniel grins at Charlie, Thomas, and Rusty. Caleb winks at Thalia. Eli gives Violet a serious, smoldering *look*.

"He must've found the note I put in his pocket," Violet whispers to us.

Seth is last. His hair's behaving for once, his suit fits perfectly, and honestly, he's just hot as fuck. When he walks by, he gives me a look like he's laughing at some private joke we have, and then Thomas pulls my hair.

The music changes, and everyone looks to the back again. A moment later, Levi and Clara step out from the path. She says something to him, and he laughs, then smiles the whole way down the aisle. At the end she gives him a huge, long hug, then sits next to Rusty.

"How'd I do?" she whispers.

Rusty gives her the a-ok sign.

Then we all stand. I heave Thomas into my arms, Charlie gives me a *you good?* Look, and I nod.

June and her parents emerge and walk down the aisle. Her dress isn't quite traditional: it falls to just past her knees, and it's mostly white with blue flowers embroidered on it.

Thomas grabs at my hair, and I remove his hand. He tries the other one. I block that too and look up to see June hugging her parents, and then turning to Levi.

He lights *all* the way up, like he's giddy to see her. They join hands, she takes her place, and then he leans in and whispers something in her ear.

June laughs, and I swear Levi lights up even brighter. He kisses her hands, grinning.

Silas clears his throat into the microphone, and they both look up.

"Excuse me," he says, and the whole audience laughs. "Not yet."

June says something we can't hear, but Silas just shrugs.

"Listen, you're the one who thought it was a good idea to give me a microphone," he says, and everyone laughs again.

He flips open the folder in a very official manner.

"Please be seated," he begins. "Dearly beloved, we are gathered here today to celebrate the union…"

I check out Seth again. Still hot. It's the same suit he wore to Ava's wedding, since Levi thought the idea of making his brothers buy new suits was ridiculous, and I take a few moments to fondly remember the way it looked on the floor that night.

"…at this gathering," Silas is saying. "If anyone has any ___"

He frowns.

"No one's objecting, I thought I took that part out. Sorry," he says, and then grins. It's a *very* charming grin. "If you've got an objection, take it up with me later."

More laughter, and the wedding proceeds as weddings do. They wrote their own vows. June cries. Her maid of honor cries. Violet cries. I cry. Levi wipes away a tear, and when I look at Seth, he's clenching his jaw pretty hard.

Then, finally, Silas declares them husband and wife, and they kiss. The whole audience erupts into cheering, and when they walk back down the aisle, Levi is grinning and laughing like I've never seen before.

Now Charlie's crying. Violet hands her a tissue.

"Right?" she says, and Charlie nods.

· · * * * ★ ★ ★ * * · ·

VIOLET and I walk down a brick walkway, between some flowers, and into a small clearing with a single statue of a cherub in it.

"I don't think this is the Eagle's Nest Garden," she says suspiciously. "Shit."

"No eagles *and* no nests," I agree, and we both pull out our phones to look at the itinerary June sent us.

"Is this the north side of the lodge or the south side?" she asks, flipping her phone around.

I just look at her, and she starts laughing.

"I have no idea," I say, also laughing. "Do you have a compass? Where does the sun set?"

"Of course Levi would have us orienteering to get to the photo session," she says.

The garden finds us before we find it, in the form of Eli leaning past a tangle of trees and shouting Violet's name.

"Did you get lost?" he asks.

"No," she says, laughing.

"You got lost."

"I chose to find you in a different way," she says, stands on her tiptoes, and gives him a kiss.

"*Did* you get lost?" Seth asks, and I turn.

He's still shined up like a penny, so I spend a moment checking him out as is my right.

"Not technically," I say, and adjust his corsage by a fraction of an inch.

He catches my hand and pulls me in for a kiss. It's chaste, family-appropriate, but longer than just a *hello* kiss.

"You did great," I tell him.

"I did nothing," he points out.

"You looked good doing it?"

He grins.

"Go on."

There are shouts, and we turn to see several people waving at us.

"Groomsmen again!" Caleb shouts, and Seth sighs.

"At least we haven't had to jump yet," he says.

I wander over to Thalia and watch it unfold. Being a wedding photographer looks like herding cats who don't know how to smile properly.

Then they want a shot of the whole family, so Violet and Charlie head into the chaos, along with the kids. Over in girlfriends' corner, Thalia and I look at each other but don't move.

"You two!" Clara shouts. "Come on!"

I'm happy to plunge myself into the chaos.

· · * * ★ ★ ★ * * · ·

I SHUT the glass door behind me and walk out onto the patio overlooking the forest. It's dark, and Seth turns as I walk up to him, a whiskey glass in one hand. I lean on the railing next to him.

"Cooling off for a minute," he says. "I didn't expect Levi to have this much of a *party*."

"Well, June's also involved," I point out.

"True," he says, and then he turns around, his back to the railing. He grabs my hand and pulls me over to him. "You having a good time, Bird?"

"I'm having a great time," I tell him.

"Good," he says, and kisses me.

It's the long, slow kiss I didn't get earlier, the one I wanted right after the ceremony was over. The one I couldn't give him in front of his entire family and half the Forest Service.

When it ends, he's still got a hand on my waist, my arms around his neck, and he sips from his glass over one.

"You want to know something?" he asks, giving me that slightly off-kilter smile I love.

"Sure," I say.

"You looked hot with a baby," he says, fingers stroking my back.

"Seth, that's the weirdest thing you've ever said to me," I say, laughing.

"It's not that weird," he says. "Also, I'm kind of drunk, and you were hot with a baby. I'm not saying the baby was hot. The baby was cute. *You* were hot. I think you'd also be a hot pregnant lady. And a hot bride. Really, you're just hot."

I'm still laughing, leaning against him, and I'm glad it's dark because now I'm blushing. It's been three months since the Varmint Palace, and while on the one hand it seems like that's too soon to be telling me I'd be hot while pregnant, it's... not.

It's Seth. For us, time is a little blurred: has it been fifteen years, or since Ava's wedding?

"I hear babies are bad for your sex life," I tease, and he laughs.

"I'm not saying *now*," he says. "One, you're still babyproofed," — that's what he calls my IUD — "and two, I am not done enjoying our two-of-us time."

He finishes off his drink, sets the glass down, puts his hands back on my waist. The dancing is in full swing inside, and he's got his jacket off, his sleeves rolled up, his tie loosened.

Have I mentioned how fuckable he is like this?

Fuck. A. Ble.

"I think they're doing the cake soon," I say, sliding my arms around him.

"Good, I like cake," he says, and slides his arms down my back.

Then he grabs my ass. He squeezes. He cups, caresses.

"You're grabbing my ass in public," I point out.

"Yeah. It's great, right?" he asks, and I laugh.

He's slightly drunker than I thought, and he leans down, cups my face in his hand, suddenly serious as he looks into my eyes, thumb on my cheekbone.

"I want this for us," he finally says. "All of this. I want the wedding and the babies and the cake and all that stuff, but I want... *this*. I want love and joy and family and celebrations like this and I want it with you."

"Seth, you have it," I tell him. "This is yours, too. You get to share it. It's your family, your celebration, your joy."

"And the love of my life."

I stand on my toes, bring his forehead down to mine.

"And the love of my life," I whisper.

We kiss. It feels like the stars wheel through the sky overhead, like trees sway and sigh, like the clouds part and the moon shines through. It feels like birds fly and fairies get their wings.

Then, the door opens. Small feet thump out, and we turn to see Rusty, now in a vest and shirtsleeves, run up to us.

"Uncle Seth! Delilah!" she says. "CAKE!"

Then she's gone, and we're both laughing.

"All right, you heard her," Seth says, and stands up straight, takes my hand.

Then he looks over at me, his face naked, vulnerable.

"I love you," he says.

I kiss his hand, held in mine.

"I love you too," I tell him.

Together, we go back to the celebration.

EPILOGUE

DELILAH

Two Years Later

"There's no way it hurt this much the first time," he says, still staring at a spot on the ceiling.

"Probably because you talked less," I say, dabbing at his skin again.

"You have no idea how much I talked," he says.

"It's an educated guess," I tell him, the gun still in my hand. "Everyone knows that the more you complain about it, the more it hurts."

He turns his head and looks at me, though he's very careful not to move anything else.

"Did Lainey get that from some study?" he teases. "What are your sources?"

"That one's folk wisdom, but folk wisdom is usually right," I admit, sitting back. I grab the light and move it around a little, press my fingers into his arm, double-check the lines and the dots and the brand new star that matches the one on my wrist.

"I'd flex for you, but my arm kinda hurts," he teases.

I roll my eyes at him, still smiling.

"That tattoo must have *really* hurt," I say in faux-sympathy.

"Okay, okay," Seth says. "Point taken."

I switch the gun off, put it back on the tray, and hold up a mirror so he can check it out a little better.

"Perfect," he says, and touches his arm with his other hand.

I grab his wrist, still wearing gloves.

"No touching," I tell him.

"You this handsy with all your clients?" he asks, grinning.

I put the mirror back but don't let go of Seth's wrist.

"Most of them know better than to poke a brand new tattoo," I say.

Seth just grins and pulls his arm away, bringing my hand with it. He's still in my dentist-style tattoo chair, and when I try to let him go he just grabs my hand himself and keeps pulling.

"Hey," I protest, but I don't protest too hard. "We're not done."

"You look like you need a break," he says, very seriously.

"That would be wildly unprofessional of me," I say, leaning on the arm of the chair.

"I promise not to tell the... Board of Tattoos?" he says, raising one eyebrow.

"Yes, our very real central governing body is notoriously strict," I deadpan.

I pull my hand free of his, then take my gloves off and toss them on the tray, too, as Seth reaches over and grabs the belt loop of my denim shorts and tugs me toward him. He took his shirt off while I touched up his constellation tattoo, so now he's reclining half-naked in my chair and giving me a lazy *hey there* look.

"I don't usually do this with customers," I tease, not budging.

That gets a double eyebrow raise.

"Usually?" he says, voice going low, and I grin.

"Hardly ever," I say.

"C'mere," he says, and grabs the waistband of my shorts, tugs gently.

I stand, swing my leg over the chair, and straddle him.

"And definitely not with customers who complain as much as you did," I say, leaning forward.

"I thought maybe I could get some sympathy kisses," he says, and I laugh. "What?"

"From me?" I tease. "Of all people? Harden the fuck up, Seth."

"Damn," he says. "Guess whose Yelp review just got lowered to three stars."

"Three?" I protest. "You took off two stars for that?"

"Just one," he says.

I sit back, still on his lap, and put my hands on his knees. My shorts are riding up, garters visible, and I can see him sneaking looks. Apparently, they *still* haven't gotten old.

"You would four-star me for a great, free tattoo?" I ask, mock-offended.

"I was gonna offer you the option of earning the fifth star."

"Let me guess," I say, tapping a finger against his knee. "By being a great conversationalist? Ooh, or for giving you really clear aftercare instructions?"

"Close," he says, and grabs the bottom of my tank top, winds the fabric around his fingers.

"For opening the shop on a Sunday, then," I tease, leaning forward.

"Almost," he says, sliding his hands over my butt.

I rest my forearms on his chest, lower my face to his.

"Then I don't know what could *possibly* earn me that extra star," I say. "Enlighten me."

He kisses me, obviously. He cups my ass in his hands and I roll my hips against him and kiss him back, long, slow, lazy kisses. We make out with no ulterior motive, just to make out, because we've had the *no sex in the tattoo shop* discussion before.

Also a *no sex in the brewery* discussion. Health code, et cetera.

After a few minutes, he runs his hand down my arm to my wrist, circles it lightly with his fingers until his thumb is right on my star tattoo. He looks at it, then lifts his arm, looks at his.

"You like it?" I ask.

"I do," he says, rubbing his thumb over my wrist. "Thanks."

"I should bandage it," I point out.

He pulls me in, gives me one more long kiss.

"Love you," he says.

"Love you too," I say, then give him a quick kiss on the forehead and stand.

* * * * * ★ ★ * * * * *

"Last week, someone brought in a beautiful, solid oak hundred-year-old table that had been plastered over with superhero stickers in the seventies," Charlie says. "And not even real superheroes. Knockoff ones I've never heard of, like The Bulk, who's purple and wears green shorts."

I laugh, beer in hand, feet up on the deck railing.

"I've never heard of The Bulk," I say.

"I'm sure there's a reason."

"Who thought that was a good idea?" asks Caleb, sitting on my other side.

"The table, or The Bulk?"

"Either. Both," he says.

"Maybe the table was owned by whoever created The Bulk," I say. "Otherwise, why would they have all those stickers?"

Charlie just sighs.

"I had to do things to that table," she says, taking a sip of her beer and gazing over the back yard. "Things I'm not proud of."

I sigh sympathetically.

"It's all right," I tell her. "We've all had to fuck the furniture now and then."

To my right, Caleb makes a surprised noise, then starts coughing.

"Dammit, Delilah," he manages to get out. "I was *drinking.*"

"Sorry," I say, as Charlie laughs.

"I was just surprised," he says, still clearing his throat.

"That she said *fuck?*" Charlie asks.

"No, I was not surprised that Delilah said *fuck,*" Caleb says, as if that's the most ludicrous thing he's ever heard. "It was the whole thing. It's over now. Carry on."

"I think we should keep talking about fucking the furniture," Charlie says. "Which piece of your dining room set do you find most erotic, Caleb?"

"I hate this conversation," he says, but he's grinning.

"Tables do have those nice… legs," I say, trying to think of something slightly sexy about tables.

"Sure, that's a word," Caleb teases.

"That's why tablecloths exist," says June's voice behind me.

I tilt my head back and there she is, holding a glass of water.

"Because table legs are erotic?" Charlie asks. "This is really making me look at my job from a new angle."

"It's from Victorian times, and you know how they were," June says, pulling up a chair.

"Secret perverts?" I say.

June points a finger-gun at me as she sits.

"Bingo," she says. "I read once that tablecloths were to cover up scandalous table legs because men simply couldn't control themselves otherwise. Dunno if it's actually true."

The three of us all happen to glance at Caleb at the same time.

"Okay, I hate that you all just looked at me," he says. "I'm not even the one who started this conversation about fucking furniture."

Now June starts laughing.

"It's a long story and I don't think I can trace it back," Caleb tells her.

"I don't think I want you to," she says, still laughing. "I think this is perfect and delightful just like it is."

We all go quiet for a moment, facing out into the yard where Seth and Thomas are playing kickball.

Or, rather, Seth is slowly and carefully rolling a big rubber ball toward Thomas, who is watching it with all the seriousness and intensity an almost-three-year-old can muster, and then wildly swinging one leg several moments too late.

Then, he chases the ball and throws it vigorously, with both hands, sort of in Seth's direction.

I'll just say it: Seth is hot with a toddler.

"Someone's gonna sleep well tonight," Charlie says.

"Yeah, kickball really tuckers Seth out," I say, and she laughs.

"I have to admit, now I understand why some people choose to have their kids when they're twenty-two," she says. "He just runs. All day. His two modes are *sleeping* and *sprinting*. I'm tired."

Suddenly, Thomas is sprinting toward us, something in his hand. He stomps up the deck stairs, then runs over to us.

"It's a pinecone!" he shouts.

Charlie sits forward and holds out her hand.

"Ooh, how exciting," she says. "What's it—"

"It's for Caleb," he informs her, and goes straight for his uncle.

"Wow, thank you," Caleb says, as Thomas deposits his prize. "You know what kind of tree this comes from?"

"He just runs," Seth says, coming up the stairs behind Thomas.

"Yup," says Charlie.

"Did Rusty just *run?*"

"I think she did a little more sitting still," Charlie says, fondly watching Caleb and Thomas discuss the pine cone. "It's hard to compare, though."

Behind us, the sliding glass door opens, and Levi walks over to June, puts his hands on her shoulders.

"You need anything?" he asks.

"I'm fine," she says. "Thanks."

He leans down and plants a kiss on the top of her head.

"I need that," I hear Thomas say, and then a second later he's full-bore toddler sprinting to Levi.

"This is a pinecone!" he shouts.

"Hm, let's see," Levi says, crouching next to June. "You know what? You're precisely right."

"It's got seeds," Thomas informs him.

"I feel like my thunder's been stolen," Caleb says, and Charlie laughs.

"I gave him life and he didn't even look at me," she says. "Savage."

· · * * ★ ★ ★ * * · ·

DINNER IS MACARONI AND CHEESE, prepared by Chef Rusty under Eli's guidance, along with salad and collard greens and succotash. It's all very Southern, and Rusty is positively delighted when everyone says they love it.

After dinner, she and I sit on the front porch, watch the stars come out, and I get a full rundown of what's going on in sixth grade at Sprucevale Middle. In brief: the science teacher, Mr. Albertson is the worst, her friend Kimmy has really been on her nerves lately, her new friend Megan is just the *coolest*, and *eeeeveryone* in her grade has a crush on this boy named Dale, but Rusty doesn't see the appeal.

I strongly suspect she's got a crush on someone, but she's not naming names and I'm not that nosy.

We talk for a while about the robotics camp she's starting next week, and then it's time for dessert. Everyone eats pie and does some more shouting and laughing, and through it all, I keep catching Seth staring at me.

We head out a little while later, and when we get into the car, Seth casually looks over at me, then clears his throat.

"Mind if I run a quick errand on the way home?" he asks.

"Sure, where to?" I ask, leaning back in the passenger seat.

"Frog Holler," he says, and flips on his turn signal. "You know how we're doing that hopped cider collaboration? There's something I have to go pick up over there. For that. It won't take too long."

I give Seth a searching look as he checks the road and

then pulls out of the driveway, picking up speed. After a moment, he glances over at me.

"What?" he asks, a strand of hair coming loose over his forehead.

He's going to propose.

I don't know how I know, but I do. I'm instantly and completely certain, and I try not to laugh.

"Nothing," I say. "It's a nice night for a drive over there."

We talk as we drive: about the fact that June is probably pregnant, about whether Rusty has an adolescent crush on Silas, about whether Victorian really wanted to fuck tables or if that's a weird myth.

There's a part of me that wants to tell him to pull off to the side of the road so I can lean over, kiss him, and tell him *yes*. As different as things are now than ten years ago, I can tell he's still nervous.

He doesn't need to be. We live together. We've talked about getting married and having kids, because we're adults and partners who talk about major life events. He already knows what the answer is.

But when he turns into the Frog Holler driveway, he shifts into neutral instead of second and then curses when the engine roars.

"Sorry," he says, and then shoots me that charming grin.

"Need me to drive?"

"I need you to keep your commentary to yourself," he says, and this time I do laugh. We've got the windows down, and the warm breeze comes through and tosses my hair around. It'll be a nightmare to untangle later, but right now, it feels free and wonderful and I don't care.

The barn comes into view, all the lights off. No cars in the parking lot, but the floodlights on the mural are all lit.

Seth pulls up carefully, parking his car as precisely as if he were in a tight spot between two minivans.

Before we get out, I do lean over and kiss him. He pauses a moment, then sinks his fingers into my hair, kisses me full force.

"What was that for?" he asks, thumb still on my jaw.

"I can't just kiss you?" I ask.

"You can kiss me, and I can be suspicious," he says, pressing his lips to mine again.

"Come on, you've gotta get the… whatever you said," I tease, and we get out of the car.

It's dark, the moon nothing but a sliver in the sky, the stars out in full force n the warm summer night. We link hands as Seth leads me away from the front door and toward the rise overlooking the barn.

I know exactly where we're going. We stop at the same spot where we kissed after our last first date, and Seth turns, looks at me.

His face cracks into a wide smile, and he starts laughing.

"Did I fool you for a second?" he asks, and I bite my lips together, trying not to laugh myself.

"With your story about having to get cider on a Sunday night?" I ask, tilting my head to one side.

"Come on, it wasn't that bad."

"Seth," I say, and take his face in my hands. "You're not a good liar. I love you so much, but you can't lie."

He's still smiling, and he leans in until our foreheads and noses are touching, his fingers in my hair again.

"Marry me anyway?" he asks, softly.

I feel like I'm soaring. Even though I knew what was coming, I'm instantly giddy, lighter than air.

"Yes," I say. "Yes, of course."

I kiss him fervently, feeling like I might bubble over. I

wrap my arms around his shoulders and he lifts me up, and we laugh and kiss and he swings me around and I yelp, then laugh some more.

Finally, he puts me down and reaches into his pocket. I'm expecting a box but the ring is just in his fingers, glinting in the light.

It doesn't look anything like my other rings. Not the one that he threw into the woods; not the one that Nolan gave me that I donated to an auction for a women's shelter last year.

This one looks vintage and art deco, the stone set deeply into the metal.

I look closer, and realize there's something in the stone. Seth clears his throat.

"Maybe a year ago, I came across this jewelry maker who makes jewelry with carvings in the backs of the stones, so that when you look at it from the front, it looks like there's something inside," he says.

I look closer and realize it's a bird, wings spread.

"I thought you'd like it," he says, takes my hand, and slides it onto my finger.

"I love it," I say. "I love you."

"I love you more."

We kiss. On the barn, the mural glows, and the stars shine above, and the breeze whispers through the lush foliage of the forest, through the grass below our feet.

"I want to take back something I said once," he tells me when we break the kiss.

"About how I must have been raised by wolves if I think I can put a plastic bowl in the dishwasher?" I ask, gently.

"Absolutely not," he says, grinning. "I'll stand by that until my dying day."

"It was on the top rack," I point out.

"About how I'd take anything back," he says. "I told you once that if I could undo the past, I would."

He winds a curl around one finger, watches my face.

"But that's what it took to get here," he says, simply. "And this makes everything else worth it. If changed that I'd change this, and I would never change this."

I swallow hard, because there's a lump in my throat.

"Me either," I say. "You're worth the fight, Seth."

He kisses me again: gentle and slow, full of promise, longing just below the surface.

"I would do anything for this," he murmurs. "Fight any fight. Climb any mountain. Sacrifice every valuable thing in my life. This is worth it. You're worth it."

We stand there for a long time, on the grass, under the stars. We talk about love and we talk about raccoons and we talk about the past and we talk about whether we should rearrange the living room, all the lofty and banal things that make up a life together.

I know it's anything but easy, but standing here with him, I do know this: it's simple. Love is simple. Everything surrounding it can be hard and messy and complicated, but at the center of it all, love is sweet, clear, and true.

Finally, we walk back to his car, hand in hand. We drive home. We sleep in the same bed, wake up next to one another that morning and the next and the next, and it's not perfection, but it's always him, and it makes my heart leap.

For Seth, my heart always leaps.

THE END

ABOUT ROXIE

Roxie is a romance author by day, and also a romance author by night. She lives in Los Angeles with one husband, two cats, far too many books, and a truly alarming pile of used notebooks that she refuses to throw away.

Join her mailing list for release updates, free bonus scenes, and tons more!

www.roxienoir.com
roxie@roxienoir.com

9 781735 216058